RACHEL L. SCHADE

EMPIRE OF MONSTERS

CURSED EMPIRE 3

RACHEL L. SCHADE

EMPIRE OF MONSTERS

CURSED EMPIRE 3

DRAGON SHADOW PUBLISHING

OTHER BOOKS BY RACHEL L. SCHADE

Silent Kingdom Series

Silent Kingdom (Book 1)

Forsaken Kingdom (Book 2)

Broken Kingdom (Book 3)

Cursed Empire Series

Empire of Dragons (Book 1)

Empire of Traitors (Book 2)

*For those who grieve the ones they've lost:
Love may be the cause of your pain today, but it will be the source of your strength tomorrow.*

PRONUNCIATION GUIDE

People

Lo'laeni (LO-lane-ee)
Nolanhou (No-LAWN-hu)
Jaliana (JAY-lee-ahn-uh)
Kovi (KOH-vee)
Ettonou (ETT-uh-new)
Caesiem (KAY-see-um)
Xalenos (Zuh-LEE-nos)
Adtriatus (AY-dree-at-us)
Revaed (Ruh-VAYD)
Pauni'a (PAWN-ee-uh)
O'emia (OH-em-ee-uh)
Mio'e (MEE-oh-ay)
Naina (NAYN-uh)
Karye (KAR-yay)
Eloiyah (Ell-oh-EE-uh)
Marukio (Muh-ROO-kee-oh)
Ilowhe (IL-oh-way)
Rhi'il (REE-uhl)
Huvoki (HOO-voh-kee)
Meli (Muh-LEE)
A'elli (AY-ell-ee)

Locations

Alrenor (Al-REN-or),
Alrenian (Al-REN-ee-uhn)
Forwyth (For-WITH),
Forwyn (For-WIN)
Teramyl (TARE-uh-mill),
Teramese (TARE-uh-meez)
Inalgoth (I-NEEL-goth)

Other

Ryke (RY-kee)
Karos (Kair-OHS)
Elhani (Ell-HAN-ee)
Nesrelle (NEZ-rell)
Vylae (Vill-AY)
Kowra (KOW-ruh)
Hilvoku (Hill-VOH-ku)
Elha'tonu (Ell-AH-toh-new)
Nestrae (NESS-tray)

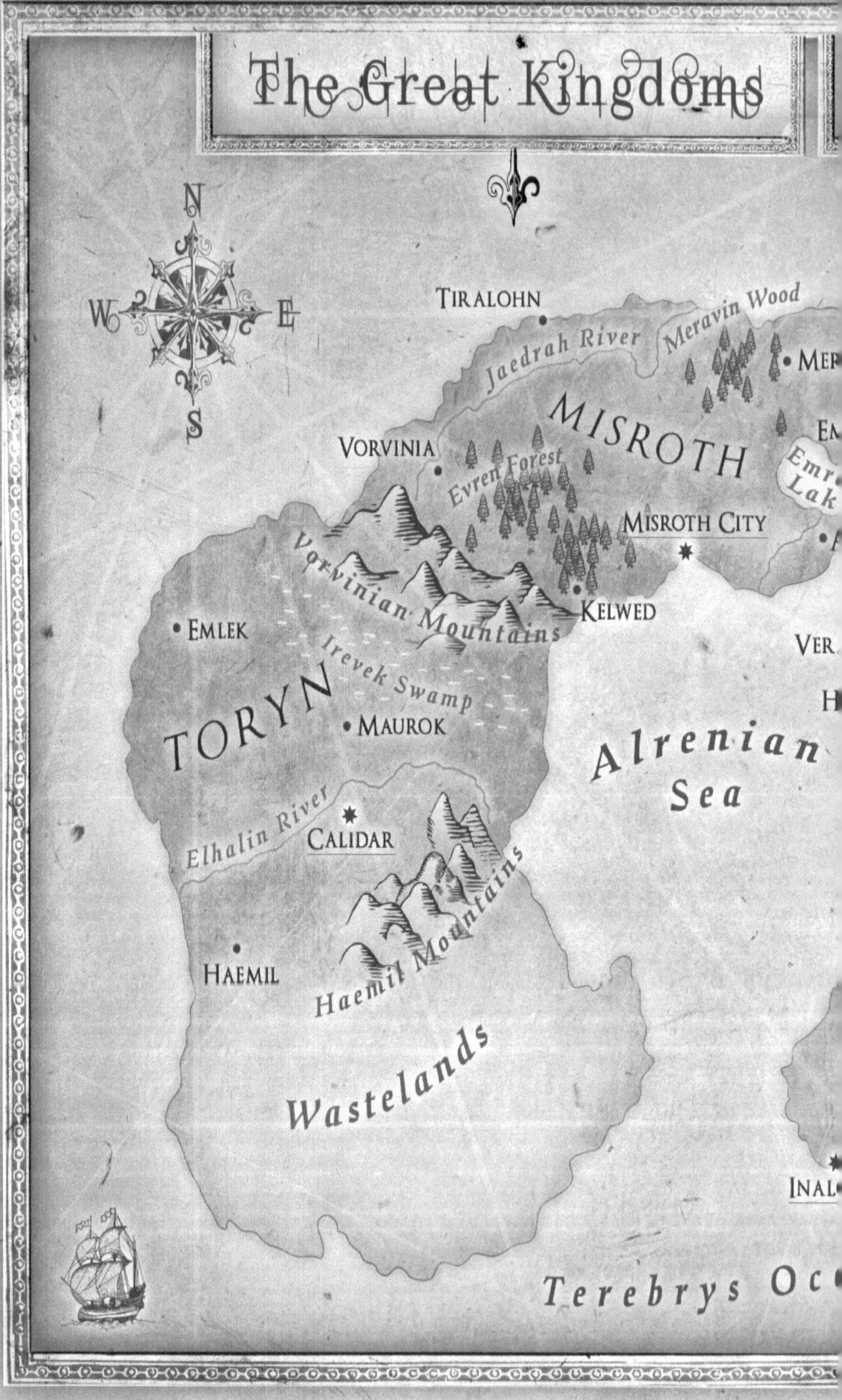

The Great Kingdoms
N
W
E
S
TIRALOHN
Jaedrah River
Meravin Wood
MER
MISROTH
EM
Emr
Lak
VORVINIA
Evren Forest
MISROTH CITY
Vorvinian Mountains
KELWED
EMLEK
VER
Irevek Swamp
H
TORYN
MAUROK
Alrenian
Sea
Elhalin River
CALIDAR
Haemil Mountains
HAEMIL
Wastelands
INAL
Terebrys Oc

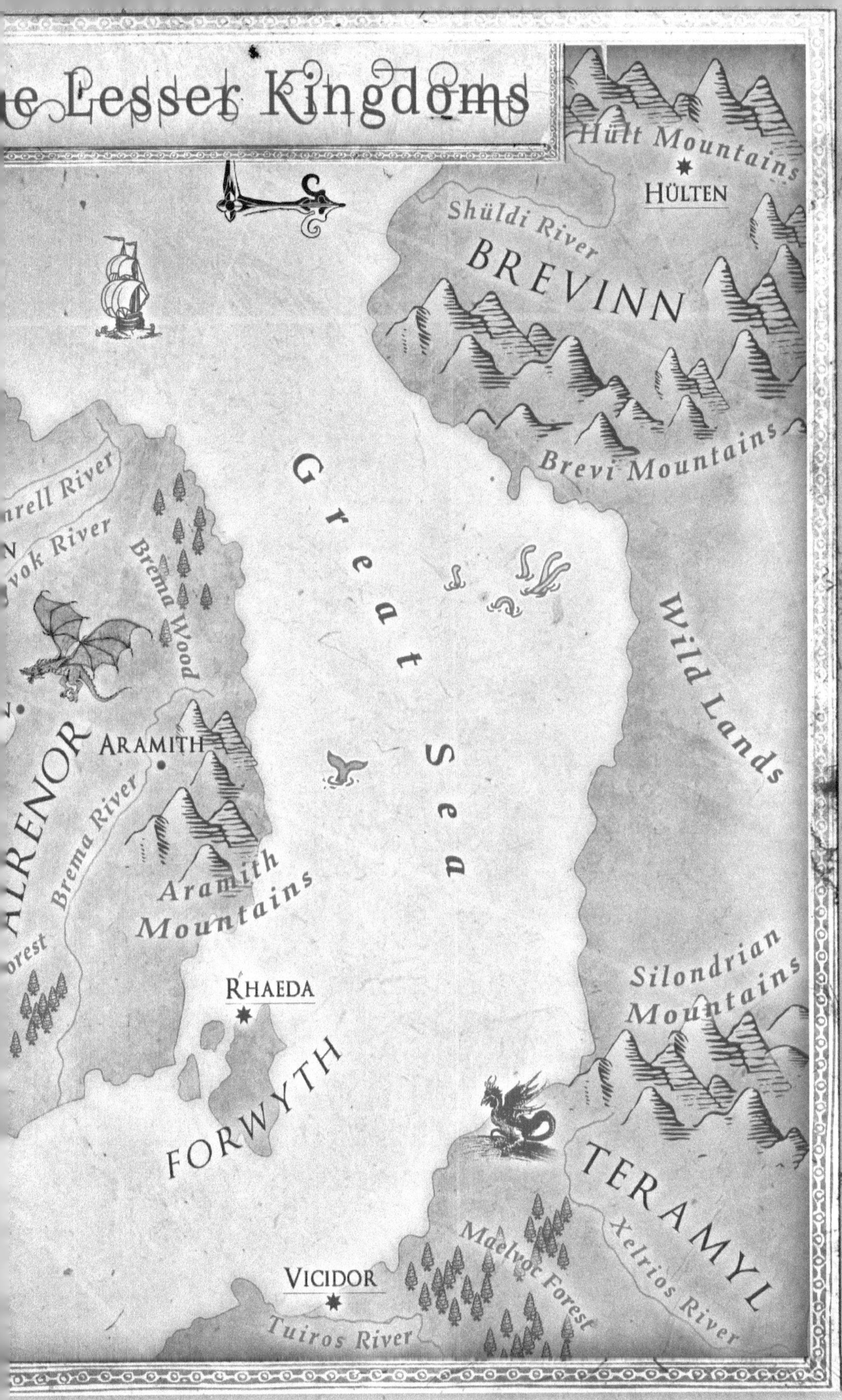

The Lesser Kingdoms
Hült Mountains
HÜLTEN
Shüldi River
BREVINN
Brevi Mountains
Wild Lands
Great Sea
anrell River
vok River
Brema Wood
ALRENOR
ARAMITH
Brema River
orest
Aramith
Mountains
RHAEDA
FORWYTH
Silondrian
Mountains
TERAMYL
Xelrios River
Maelvoc Forest
VICIDOR
Tuiros River

CHAPTER ONE

Lo'laeni Nolhanhou

It was the night Karye had slaughtered us all over again. This time, there was a new enemy, a new location, but the blood drenching the earth, the thuds of bodies piling up around me, the cries of pain and horror—they were all the same. Even the downpour and the restless, stormy clouds overhead reminded me of that terrible night.

As I dodged swinging swords and fists in the Aerekni Academy courtyard, I tried to choke back the urge to gag. The stenches of sweat and fear and death all mingled together, mixing with the briny scent of the sea as a stormy wind sent the rain sideways. The drops hit hard, stinging my cheeks. I felt half-blind and crippled as I skidded and slipped along the cobblestones, my boots finding the slick patches weren't only from rain and mud, but also from pools of blood.

Emperor Revaed, the conniving *boeri*, had saved my sisters from Alrenian rioters at the abbey only to force me to choose between the lives of the nuns or of the soldiers at Aerekni Academy.

I'd let my enemy entrap me. The thought filled me with rage and horror, blocking out my ability to hear Elhani's voice, to access my magic. I had no weapon, nothing but my lithe muscles that allowed me to be swift and light on my feet. To survive.

But my blood was roaring in my ears, crying out for revenge. I scoured the ground for an abandoned weapon and wondered if I could earn myself the title of emperor-slayer as well as empress-slayer. If I could find the arrogant, pitiless Revaed and seize back my empire from his greedy hands. Just like I'd seized my freedom from Karye three years ago.

There was no room for fear in my heart. Only hatred, dark and deep, and anger that increased my focus, sharpened my courage. Fueled my strength. I wouldn't let him harm another one of my people. I'd fight back.

Finding a sword near one of the Forwyn bodies, I lifted the blade, trying to ignore the blood dripping off its surface, trying not to wonder if it belonged to a Forwyn soldier. With a fierce cry, I rounded toward my enemies, fending off attacks. I joined the cruel dance of battle, my skin growing slick with rain and sweat and blood.

I plunged my sword into a body, not waiting before I raced onward to fend off the next enemy. One. Two. My brain was numb, refusing to process the brutality and ugliness around me, but I kept a running tally of every soldier I was forced to kill.

To help my people, I wouldn't hesitate. I couldn't.

Everywhere, Teramese soldiers in their dark uniforms surrounded Forwyn soldiers, their sheer numbers and advantage of surprise helping them cut down my people ruthlessly. The wide courtyard was full of the dead and injured. And far too many of those casualties were from my side.

I ducked beneath another swinging sword, my eyes seeking out General Ilowhe—my father. It would be a cruel, brutal trick if I'd just found my father only to lose him so soon afterward. My eyes snagged on a tall figure fighting fiercely near the center of the fray, and my heart eased, if only a little. He was still alive. For now.

A soldier seized me by the hair, yanking me back so roughly I swallowed a cry of pain. He snarled and pressed his blade against my exposed neck, giving me a chance to stare up into his face.

I froze, the fight draining out of me. He was a Forwyn soldier, a young man from Aerekni Academy. Someone who should have been my ally. Someone I'd fought to free, to help, until I'd been forced to bring the enemy to his door.

"Forwyn traitor," he sneered, but there was more hurt than anger in the lines etched across his brow. His eyes narrowed with pain. "The *amara'rekni* was supposed to be a leader, a symbol of hope, something greater for us all."

I swallowed, careful not to move too much and let the slick blade slice my throat. I set my jaw, defiance coursing through my veins.

Elhani, I thought, stretching out my senses past the screams around me, past the drumming rain beating against my cheeks, past the screeching of steel against steel. I blocked out the stink of battle and the unusual chill and darkness consuming Inalgoth in the growing storm. Instead of the feeling of sodden clothes and cold metal against my skin, I focused on the warmth of magic that I knew flowed around me, inside me.

It took an instant, an instant I didn't have. The man's gaze darkened and he tensed, lifting the blade as if to swing and sever my head from my body. I growled and threw myself at him, taking him by surprise. He grunted as I slammed into him, knocking us both down, splashing in puddles of mud and gore. Before he could recover, I dropped my blade and slammed my fist in his face, bloodying his nose, and leapt up, stomping on his sword arm.

Rage and pain twisted his expression as he cried out. His face said one thing, clear as day: *I will kill you.*

He tried to seize my ankle, and I knew that once he grabbed hold of me, his greater strength and training would spell my ending. But I was faster, and trained in the art of survival. Even without the use of a weapon, I knew how to dodge and evade and strike back, thanks to Naina's years of training and exercises.

Before he was on his feet, I'd recovered my sword and disappeared once more into the press of fighting bodies, diving and leaping and sidestepping to avoid killing blows. I was as swift and unobtrusive as a wraith, as the men's own shadows—there and gone in the blink of an eye. Even the bodies I had to dodge couldn't throw off my lightness of foot.

We were severely outnumbered, and we needed reinforcements. I knew where to look—if they would listen. Maybe they'd hate me, maybe they'd refuse to fight. Maybe they'd insist they'd taken vows of peace.

But they were full of the same fire as me. They had the same drive to protect our people.

It took me only a matter of moments to reach the gate, still wide open. I charged down the path and raced toward the towering buildings of Inalgoth. They were all but blotted out by the grey sheets of rain.

I had to find my sisters and tell them our time to fight had come.

I longed to make myself invisible as my feet pounded against the rain-slick cobblestones of Inalgoth, tracing a path at a gradual incline toward the abbey. But my blood raged like churning waves beating against the shore, as wild and restless as the lightning flashing over the Great Sea.

Inalgoth had been immersed in chaos. On my way to the abbey earlier, I hadn't encountered any of the rioting Alrenians, but now my path ran straight into their midst. They must have scattered further throughout the city as the evening drew on. I turned a corner and there they were, gold-tinted skin shimmering even beneath the dark, churning sky. Their eyes flashed with each strike of lightning overhead, adding to the hungry, almost rabid expressions on their faces. Clothed in leather armor and adorned with traditional Alrenian weapons, they appeared wilder than the warriors I'd grown up fearing. Those had worn glistening dragon scale armor and had carried themselves with pride.

These people appeared feral and desperate, like warriors who had hidden in the wild for years or crawled out of holes in the earth. Their leathers were blood-splattered and their rain-soaked hair clung to their faces.

Rather than stalling them, the storm seemed only to be feeding their frenzy. They fought fiercely, just like the old tales of Alrenian conquests said they could, cutting down row after row of defending Teramese. Their victims were strewn in piles across the street, staining the puddles red.

Worry bit me as I scanned the corpses' faces, wondering if I'd recognize Caesiem among them. But I shook it away when I realized these Teramese were guards on foot, not the regiment of soldiers on horseback Caesiem had ordered to be assembled before he left.

One of the Alrenian women lifted her eyes and stared straight at me, a wicked grin curling her mouth. She slammed her sword into the gut of the Teramese man she'd been fighting, letting him collapse unceremoniously to the ground. As she wrenched her blade free, I lifted my own sword and fell into a fighting stance.

"A little Forwyn rat," the woman sneered.

I didn't have time for this. I needed to find my sisters and get back to the academy.

Snarling, I stepped forward. Water dripped down my face and ran into my eyes. I blinked and breathed deeply, trying to block out everything but the song that I knew was there, softer than everything around me, yet stronger than anything else I knew. Elhani's magic could end this fight before it began—if I could only focus.

The Alrenian paused several yards away, tilting her head and studying me. "You think you're better than us," she said. "Your people claim to be chosen, with your strange magic and odd customs. But your power isn't greater than ours." She twirled her sword through the air, so quickly it was just a silver streak in the rain. "Our gifts have returned, and I do not fear you."

She lunged, as reckless as an angry bull. Before she could swipe her blade at me, I dodged. She spun, but I was already moving again, kicking at her shin and leaping toward her, plunging my blade toward her exposed side. With a hiss of surprise, she parried at the last moment and lashed back at me. I sidestepped, darting away and putting space between us once more.

The move bought me time: a moment to breathe, a moment to quiet the adrenaline pumping through me and focus on Elhani's voice. His song roared in my ears, louder than my pulse or the rain or the thunder. Its warmth tumbled through me like an irrepressible wave, powerful and beautiful and deadly.

While I blocked the woman's next strike, I unleashed the magic inside me.

"Leave! Turn back!" I exclaimed. My voice rang out unnaturally loud, echoing over the pounding rain. "Do not kill another Forwyn."

The Alrenian staggered back as if struck, her face contorted. More lightning tore apart the sky, and this time, terror rather than bloodlust gleamed in my enemy's eyes.

"Leave," I repeated, my voice as low as a growl, as loud as a war drum.

With a pitiful whimper of fear, the woman threw her sword with a clatter and fled, vanishing down the road.

It took a moment for me to catch my breath, to shake away the buzzing power that tingled in my blood. Strapping the sword to my belt, I stalked toward the nearest corpse and seized the dagger at its side. It felt comfortable and natural in my hand—more natural than the sword. Hastily, I added it to my belt and resumed my run, this time clinging more closely to the shadowy edges of the streets and tracing a path that mainly followed side roads and alleys. There, the city felt abandoned, most of its citizens having long since sought refuge from the rioting and the weather.

The storm rose in its fury, rain continuing to lash at my cheeks and thunder roaring so loudly I knew the lighting was striking close—far too close. I could practically taste the electricity on my tongue, mingling with the tang of the sea and the sharp scent of mud. I wasn't even sure if it was late enough for the sun to have set—I'd lost all concept of time—but the roiling clouds overhead had built to the point that they'd submerged Inalgoth in darkness as thick as midnight's embrace. Worse still, the rain made it even harder to see, draping the city in a silver haze that repeatedly dripped into my eyes.

And so, despite my wariness, the ambush came as a surprise. I didn't see the shadow hovering on the rooftop, didn't hear the pursuing footsteps until it was too late. Slowing beside a closed storefront, I spun around to face my latest enemy, my hand reaching for the dagger at my hip.

Too late. The shadow flung something dark and swift, and blinding pain shot through my hand and up my entire arm. I turned my head to find my hand pinned to the wall behind me by a dagger, blood streaming freely from the wound. My opponent's aim had either been perfect, slicing into the mortar between the bricks to lodge my hand just right, or it had been an atrocious strike of good fortune for him or her.

Over the thundering in my ears came a ragged scream—*my* scream—as white-hot agony shuddered through me. I was trapped, too overcome by pain to think straight. Sheer panic clutched me as my eyes watered and I shivered, shock already taking hold.

Gritting my teeth, I forced myself to clear my mind, to blink away the gathering spots threatening my vision. I would *not* lose consciousness. I concentrated on my advantage: it was my left hand that was pinned, not my right. I could still draw the dagger at my hip, still fight back.

"Pathetic," an all-too familiar voice snapped, close enough now to be heard over the storm.

My pulse was a horse desperate to gallop free, but my rage was as consuming as dragon fire as I studied the approaching figure.

Mio'e.

CHAPTER TWO

Kovi Ettonou

Marukio was bleeding out in my arms. Not long after he'd arrived at the academy, we'd realized that our mothers had been sisters. Ever since, I'd looked out for him, one of the only family members I had left. I'd assisted him with studying and training at the academy, and I'd helped him gain experience as a guard at the palace. And now, I couldn't help him.

I'd seen death enough times to know there was nothing I could do, even as I shouted for a healer, for anyone to help us.

Reaching up, choking on his own blood, Marukio grasped my shoulder. A scarlet stream trickled from his mouth when he opened it, as if to speak. But they were words he never had the chance to say. His eyes froze on some distant point, like he was staring into the Golden After…

And he was gone.

Arms trembling, I laid him down, staggering to my feet when I sensed someone charging for us. Fingers slick with my cousin's blood, I lifted my sword and drew myself into a fighting stance. Anger honed my senses and sharpened my determination. I wouldn't flinch away from killing every last one of these Teramese invaders if it meant saving my brothers and sisters. Saving the young men and women I'd studied with and trained alongside, eaten meals beside and jested with.

But when I lifted my eyes, the face I met was not Teramese, but Forwyn. My father, Elder Ettonou, dressed in overly garish attire for this bloody battle. In his fist, he clenched a dripping blade.

My gut seized with revulsion.

"You are the lowest of traitors," I spat. "Marukio is *dead* because of you."

The weapon trembled in his hand, but his jaw was set, his dark eyes alight with a fevered gleam. "Then I hope he chose the correct side, and died serving his people and his new allies, as I am."

"Of course he didn't. He was loyal to his people and our freedom, unto death. He would never betray us like you have."

"No," he said solemnly, "I'm not betraying the Forwyn cause. You and the rest of the Aerekni soldiers are. You vowed to serve your people's best interests. This is not about pride. The Teramese offered to give us *everything*, a comfortable life where we could finally ally with an army who could give us power over the Alrenians, and you refused?"

I blinked, momentarily too shocked for words. "You—how can you *think* like that?" I demanded.

Hurt and anger warred within me, but anger won out. After all, who was this man before me? Even though he was my birth father, and a part of me had longed to get to know him and make him proud, it was clear now that he was little more than a stranger. He hadn't lived up to the stories my mother had told me about him as a child—either he'd greatly fooled her, or he'd changed after her death, lost in his lust for vengeance. He was blinded by his anger. His need to harm the Alrenians was greater than his need to protect his own people. To protect *me*.

"Anyone who gets in the way of letting us finally make the Alrenians pay is our *enemy*." He stepped nearer, face contorted with rage. "And you—you're the worst of them all. Standing against our allies, the Teramese, after you consorted with Jaliana when all you were meant to do was defend us against her wicked, violent ways. Not grow attached to the whore!"

Rage rippled through me, but I forced myself to swallow it back and inject calm into my voice. I listened for Elhani's song, strong and soothing as it always was. "What are you going to do then?" I asked softly. "Kill me?"

Something flickered across his face. Regret? Grief? Fear? It was gone too soon for me to be sure.

"Of course not," he said through gritted teeth. "But you'll be under closer watch after this. I'll make sure you are never close enough to associate with Jaliana again. I know she's poisoned your mind—"

My laughter was harsh, ringing out over the clashing battle, the pounding rain, and the rolling thunder. "No, but revenge has poisoned yours." I swallowed against the pain still threatening to rise up and consume me, blotting out the anger that made me feel clearly. See clearly. I drew on my magic and commanded my father. "Stop. Leave this place. Never show your face in the palace or Aerekni Academy again."

Slack-jawed, Father dropped his blade. It clattered into a bloody puddle at his feet, and just like that, he turned and weaved his way through the battle. No one touched him, as if they saw he was unarmed and his gaze was distant. As if they knew he no longer posed a threat.

Grief washed over me, even if I was convinced it was a wasted emotion on that pathetic husk of a man, whatever was left of who my father might have once been. Forcing him away from the battle was the greatest mercy I could offer him, even if he wasn't deserving of it.

I wasn't sure how the connection between us would work after this. I knew the sensation of his emotions would linger—rage and pain, sharper and hotter than anything I'd ever felt before—just as my ability to sense Jalie's emotions remained. I'd never given a lasting command, though, and I didn't know if the power would remain intact once Father was out of my presence. Perhaps as soon as he left the academy, the power of my command would snap, and he'd come right back.

Maybe then, one of my brothers or sisters would kill him, and I'd have to feel his final emotions.

But right now, that wasn't my concern. I'd done what I could for the snake. Beyond that, I was finished with him. Finished with his hatred, his abuse of Jalie, his quest for power and vengeance that ignored the welfare of the very people he claimed to care about.

Scanning the courtyard, I sought out General Ilowhe or my best friend Rhi'il, heart pounding in my chest when I noticed how few Forwyn soldiers were left fighting. Relief poured through me like a balm when I spotted my friends Huvoki and Mhel still standing and fighting alongside one another. But there were many more others who were not. There were too many bodies clothed in Aerekni Academy uniforms, too many of my fellow soldiers lying wounded or dead, trying to defend this fortress, their people. Nausea crawled through me as I stepped over those bodies, trying not to let my gaze linger on their empty eyes, staring up into the drenching rain and flashing sky.

We hadn't been prepared for this, that was painfully clear. Aerekni Academy had once produced elite soldiers, Dragon Keepers, and guards when the Alrenians had controlled it, and for the past three years of Forwyn control, we'd also prided ourselves on our rigorous training. We believed our own warriors were just as skilled as the Alrenians had been. But even if we were, there weren't enough of us. Three years had only produced one class of graduates. Too many of the bodies littering the cobblestones were of boys and girls who hadn't even finished their training, or who had only just begun.

A Teramese woman swung her sword at me, aiming to slice my head from my neck. I spun and lodged my blade in her gut, dropping her effortlessly to the ground.

I'd just stepped forward, trying to press into the thick of battle to join my fellow soldiers, when the emotions I'd been trying to mute flooded through me. Jalie's emotions.

This time, they were too powerful to ignore, so strong they squelched out my connection to Father's feelings. Surprise, horror, anger, grief, and pain swirled through me in an all-too familiar whirlwind. They reminded me of the tangled emotions of the dying.

Panic crushed my chest. *Jalie, hold on,* I thought, my mind racing. She was fierce and strong, a survivor if I'd ever met one. And she carried a curse, along with Nesrelle's powers, making her all but invincible. *She can't be dying. She can't be hurt.*

I shook my head, as if I could block out the feelings that easily and erase their implications.

Elhani, I prayed. I squeezed my sword hilt in my bloody fist and stalked toward the nearest Teramese, blind rage coursing through me. *I know we don't deserve your protection, I know we've both made mistakes. I know she made a deal with the wrong Immortal. But please, please, don't let her die. She could be the key to uniting the Alrenians and Forwyn. And I…I can't lose her. Please.*

I plunged my blade deep into my target's chest. Beheaded another. I was barely aware of the blood coating my hands, splattering against my face, or the rain pouring into my eyes and lashing at my cheeks. Of the screams of the dying, muffled by the raging thunder. Of the flashes of lightning that illuminated grisly, gut-churning images.

Once, I would have counted every kill. Memorized every face. Now, I was consumed with emotions too large to make room for regret.

All I knew was rage and desperation.

I'll do anything, pay any price, I vowed.

I kicked back another Teramese soldier, letting his body fall to the ground, and I brought down my blade to end him.

Spare her.

I whirled and sliced off a Teramese hand, immune to the horrified screams of the soldier crumpling in pain, until I cut them off with another swipe of my sword.

Spare my people.

CHAPTER THREE

Nesrelle, Queen of Death

There was something musical about the screams of death in battle, in the way countless voices and timbres rose up, their notes blending together to form one thunderous final cry. It made my eyes burn, not with tears of regret, but with power, with euphoria. It was a rush I'd never stop wanting, those moments when I witnessed a mortal soul leave this world.

Despite the fact that humans knew their lives were finite, they never stopped striving against death. It was pathetic, really. Choking for air during their last, strangled gasps. Stretching for help while their lifeblood flowed from their wounds. The chill of death, that final darkness, would descend and still they would cry out in rage and defiance.

It was fascinating how they thought they could fight and win against something so strong, so inevitable.

Smoke and ash rained from the sky, caught in the currents of the chill wind. It layered the wide cobblestone streets of the city of Aramith, once a proud city filled with wealth from the lucrative mines burrowing within the Aramith Mountains. Now it was burning, relentless tongues of flame consuming carefully carved woodwork and sending buildings and homes tumbling to fiery deaths.

My Alrenian army, the men and women who had pledged themselves to me for a taste of my power, had come to destroy the Teramese and save their people. But they'd succumbed to my bloodlust, and now no one was safe. Not the arrogant Alrenians. Not the scheming Teramese. And not the pathetic Forwyn.

The city was burning and my army was tearing through it, destroying anyone and anything that stood in their way without regard to who or what they were.

I sucked in a heady breath of air, relishing the taste of destruction on my tongue.

Scanning the soldiers and citizens strewn together throughout the street, I assessed them, watching their blood and breath and souls leave their bodies, one by one. A few still lived, but not for long.

Distant cries erupted from further within the city, where the fighting was still intense and survivors were still defending Aramith. All in vain.

Kneeling beside one of the men still wheezing for his last breaths of air, I smiled. Maybe he'd see me as a benevolent angel, here to lead him to the afterlife.

He was Alrenian, his golden skin shimmering in the dying light from the ash-darkened sky. Wide, gold-flecked eyes, already appearing glazed and unfocused, turned up to me. His blood was gushing from a wound in his stomach, and it was clear he didn't have much more time.

I welcomed the warmth of his blood as I brushed my fingers over the wound, savoring the way it felt against my fingertips.

"Please, help me," he choked, his voice strangled, desperate.

How many pleas and bargains had I heard over my endless lifetime? Thousands? Hundreds of thousands? They, too, had a musical note to them, a cadence I couldn't help but smile and blink back tears for.

He probably mistook my glistening eyes as a sign of compassion.

Reaching out, he seized my arm. "Please," he whispered, tone hoarse.

Zakren, I remembered. *His name is Zakren, and he was an officer in little Jaliana's army. Once as a child he had a fever that nearly killed him—to this day he has recurring nightmares of seeing me watching him, waiting for him. He's proud and stubborn, with a wife and child somewhere in this very city. He thought he could fight and protect them here. He's terrified of the dark, of things he doesn't know or see or understand, and to him, death is the greatest looming darkness of them all.*

He recoiled slightly as my smile fell and I let the coldness I felt show through in my expression. "Tiresome, how you mortals always expect something from me," I muttered.

Lifting my eyes to the heavens, I unleashed a growl. Let the Life-Giver restrain me now, when my power was tumbling through me, hot and unstoppable.

"This one's time has come," I cried out, knowing he had no choice but to hear me. "All I can do is hurry the seconds along, and surely you will not stop me."

I slammed a palm against Zakren's face, leeching the remaining threads of life clinging to him. His scream was raw and agonized and beautiful, more entrancing than the distant chorus of death, because this one was near and flooding my veins with that much more power.

It ended sharply and abruptly. His soul tore from his body, melting away like a vapor until it was gone, into the afterlife.

Rising, I licked the blood off my fingers and strode deeper into the city, finishing off the dying as I went. Drawing strength and joy from the heavy clouds of despair permeating the air. Wading through the destruction and flames.

The cries for mercy were endless, but I heard only their music, ringing through my ears, coursing through my veins, and feeding a hunger that would never die.

CHAPTER FOUR

Jaliana of Alrenor

In the darkness, Mother's voice rose, soft and sweet, like the notes to the lullaby she'd once sung to me as a child. But the words were all wrong, not sweet at all, but taunting. Vicious.

Pathetic, she sneered, and I could see her face, but not as it was in my memory. Instead it appeared the way it had when she'd materialized in my tent at the Alrenian army encampment, with dark, empty eyes and a terrible slit marring her throat. There was no gentleness or love in her expression. *You were supposed to be great, to be chosen, to be empress. But here you are, tucked underneath your dragon's wings and bleeding out. Slain at your own soldier's hand. Stabbed with your dragon's claw in a battle you lost. Aramith has fallen—not to the Teramese again, but to your twisted army. What sort of leader are you?*

I tried to open my mouth to protest, though I wasn't sure what I meant to say. It didn't matter, because my mouth was as dry as sand, coarse and full of the bitter taste of old blood.

Maybe I was already dead. I tried to search the darkness, but Mother had vanished as suddenly as she'd appeared, and there was nothing. Only emptiness, and numbness, and cold.

And then—blinding pain.

My eyes shot open as I found I could open my mouth and make a sound after all. I screamed, raw and primal as a dying animal. It tore at my throat, but I couldn't stop, because the agony tearing through me was worse. A vice-like hand clasped me by the arm, yanking me upward, but I was too consumed by my agony to make sense of my surroundings.

Darkness. Nothing.

Until I met a pair of cold blue eyes, endless as the deepest part of the sea, unsettling as staring into the face of death.

Because that was exactly what I was doing.

The pain abated, though the Queen of Death's hold of me didn't loosen. She dragged me into a sitting position, leaning me back against something hard and warm. I blinked and noticed Ryke's emerald wing extended above me, blocking most of the steel-grey sky. Out over the sea, storm clouds were brewing, but we were far enough inland it would be milder here, or perhaps even pass us by. I couldn't tell if there were battle sounds around us, or even if there were any left living. Other than corpses, I couldn't see anyone. Other than Nesrelle, the world seemed eerily still. I couldn't even hear my own pulse in my ears.

Maybe I wasn't dying, with Nesrelle here to take me to the afterlife—maybe I was already dead. Maybe my soul would be hers forever, even after death, and this was the beginning of endless torment.

"Nesrelle," I croaked. My parched tongue struggled to move. I still felt cold—far too cold.

"I chose you," she snarled, anger twisting her beautiful features. Her red locks tumbled wildly about her face, reminding me of flames dancing on a pyre. "You carry the curse and the will to wield it. You begged me for power, and I gave it to you." She seized me by the neck and slammed me back against Ryke, eliciting another cry of pain from my aching throat. Behind me, I heard my dragon shudder, enraged, but Nesrelle lifted her chilling gaze upward and spoke in a voice that wouldn't be disobeyed. "Be still."

Blinking against the dancing spots across my vision, choking for breath, I stared back up at Nesrelle, trying to understand. Still clutching me by the neck, she stared at me, gaze piercing as if she could see straight through to my soul. "Each year I have the power to claim a life, just *one* time when *I* can decide the moment someone dies, when I lead their soul away. But this year, my claim is different. I am using my power to *spare* you. Even though here you lie, weak and dying." She growled, animalistic and terrifying. "Pathetic. But you don't have a right to be. You're *mine*. My weapon, my plague, my executioner."

She loosened her grip, but more pain wracked through my body. I didn't think my weak muscles could force myself to move again, and yet at her touch, they spasmed, twisting my body. As if I could manage to pull away and evade her torment.

I lost myself in another scream, eyes closed against my torment. Finally, finally, it subsided again, her cold touch vanishing. I reopened my eyes to find myself no longer on the battlefield in Aramith.

Cool mist brushed my cheeks, matching the chill I felt inside my own veins. Everything lay still and quiet, a perpetual grey blanket of clouds hovering overhead. It thrust the world into a gloomy half-light that wasn't quite full darkness. Shadows lingered on the edges of my vision, but all I could see around Nesrelle and me was a wasteland of rocks and long-dead plants. Even the dirt looked like ash, colorless.

"The Wastelands of my people," Nesrelle murmured, her red lips curled into a smile. "The first ones to pledge themselves to me, the ones who became the nestrae, my dedicated worshipers."

If my body didn't feel empty and paralyzed and cold, like I was carved from ice itself, I might have shuddered. I remembered the stories I'd heard of the nestrae, Nesrelle's demons who lived within the

Wastelands south of Toryn, but the tales seemed more like rumors. Growing up, Alrenor had been cut off from the outside world, so I'd never had reason to fear the nestrae, even in brief moments when my imagination had wondered if they *were* real.

On the wind, somewhere beyond the clinging mist and the patches of shadow, hissing whispers filled the air in a language I didn't know. *"Iyg kurick Nesrelle."* The sound raised the hairs along my arms, even as the strange voices continued to chant and hiss all around me, like creeping wraiths closing in.

"Am I dead?" I demanded, staring Nesrelle in the face. If this was to be my end, I wouldn't be afraid. I'd honor my mother's memory by facing my fear of death with courage, unflinching. I wouldn't beg Nesrelle for life again, like I had in my fevered state after I'd been poisoned in the palace. She may have said she would spare me, but what did that mean to her?

Nesrelle laughed breathily. Once again, she was a beautiful woman in appearance, her features no longer twisted in a fearsome snarl, though something dark and ominous gleamed in the depths of her blue eyes. "I refuse to let you die," she said with a wicked smirk. "I told you, you are mine. But you don't seem to have fully learned that lesson," she added, an edge creeping into her dream-like voice.

I scowled, even as I realized my heart was beating steadily in my ribcage once again. Strength returned to my body, enough that I was able to glance down, to see that though a hole remained in my dragon scale armor, there was no wound. Only dried blood coating my skin and armor. I drew a deep breath, but something told me to stay seated, to not rise in Nesrelle's presence. She looked like a queen bent on vengeance, and for the first time, I felt real terror. In that moment, I realized every other time I'd feared her had only been like an echo of the true emotion, like a child's fear when she had no idea of the depths of darkness and despair that lurked within the world.

Now, I had a taste of Nesrelle's power, and I had no doubt she could make me suffer. As much as I despised it, I was at her mercy.

Clenching my jaw, I spoke through my teeth. "What do you mean?"

Mist coiled about Nesrelle like a snake, slithering around her shoulders. It hung about her head like a silvery crown. All around us, her demons—her *worshipers*—kept up their eerie chanting. "Your goal is the crown and the destruction of the Forwyn," she reminded me sharply, "not swooning like a little girl over one of their soldiers. Not making covert deals and stealing kisses. The only deal that matters is the one you made with *me*."

Fury lanced through me, hot and sharp, and this time, I forgot my terror. I stood, staring Nesrelle down. "My goal to take back my throne remains unchanged."

"But not your goal for revenge," Nesrelle hissed, leaning so close I could feel her cold breath on my face. It smelled like winter's chill…and rotting dead things. Her teeth were sharp points, glistening pearly white against her blood-red lips. "You'd throw it all away for a handsome face. For a few stolen moments of pleasure? For some flimsy little feeling?" She seized my chin, lifting my face roughly. "I told you what comes of falling in love with a human."

"I *am* human," I protested.

"No, you're a plague." Nesrelle's eyes gleamed. "You said so yourself."

I swallowed against the dryness in my throat, pulling back to free myself of Nesrelle's icy grasp.

"And have you forgotten so quickly of your mother? Of the fact that it was the Forwyn who took her from you?"

Tears burned my eyes. "But not Kovi."

Nesrelle's laughter was a harsh bark, ringing out over her murmuring nestrae. "You know as well as I that if he had the opportunity, he would have done the deed himself."

"And maybe he had a right to that revenge, same as any of us," I said, finally voicing the feeling that had been building within me for far too long. My body shook. What was I saying? That my mother had deserved to die? I couldn't deny that it seemed she had been as cruel and wicked as the Forwyn had claimed, that she had caused even more suffering for them than the Council of Elders had brought to my people and me.

"Fine, so your mother was a monster," Nesrelle said, waving her hand airily. "But so are you." She stepped closer. "And I know you've dreamt of the day you could face her killer, the one who robbed you of the person dearest in the world to you. I know how many hours you've spent trying to puzzle out who it was." She slammed her palm on my shoulder, startling me. "I can show you."

I blinked, staring dazedly up at her. The shadows around us seemed to be closing in, growing larger as they crept forward through the mist. But as they grew larger still, I realized they weren't shadows at all—they were huge, hulking forms. The demons approaching, surrounding us, speaking in clicks and hisses that made my blood run cold.

"But first," Nesrelle went on, as pain shot through my body again, sharp agony that dropped me to the ground even as she continued to clutch me, "my nestrae will remind you of who you are and where your true allegiance lies."

CHAPTER FIVE

Caesiem Xalenos

Darkness lay like a heavy blanket over Vicidor, thick clouds blotting out the stars. The night was humid, the heat oppressive, but that was normal in Teramyl, something that I only noticed now because it felt more intense than even the air in Alrenor. It made a tendril of hair cling to my forehead and beads of sweat collect on the back of my neck.

A breeze tasting of damp rainforest and briny ocean rustled through some of the palms towering over the ramshackle buildings, whispering in the stillness. No one walked on this little side street I stood upon, where the homes were nothing extraordinary, but not all completely dilapidated and abandoned, either.

I sucked in a deep breath, both hating and relishing the sights and smells and feel of home. The home where I'd suffered, found salvation, and somehow begun to lose myself, all over again.

It was strange to feel like I truly was present in Teramyl, when I knew that this was only a vision, one pulling me in so vividly, it felt like it was real. Like I'd traveled across the Great Sea and cut through the Terebrys Ocean to stand in the Teramese capital again. But I knew my body was truly in Inalgoth, on a bloodied street riddled with the corpses of fallen Alrenians…and far too many of my own soldiers.

This was a vision Meli, the strange, truth-gifted Alrenian with Forwyn blood, had plunged me into. One that she'd claimed would tell me who I really was. I imagined that in the present, my body was still sprawled out on the cobblestoned street as the Alrenian rioters attacked my soldiers. In the vision, I didn't notice any pain, but I knew my arm was still wounded from the arrow that had pierced my shoulder.

But here, consumed within Meli's gift, I had a chance to discover the truth about my past.

My heart thundered in my chest at the thought. Did this mean I'd finally discover who my parents had been? Why they'd left me alone in the world?

Scanning the street eagerly, I sought out any clue. I didn't quite recognize this part of the city right away, until I studied it a bit longer and realized it was a modest section I'd thieved in a few times. By the time I'd haunted this street, many of the homes had been abandoned, some painted in red markings to warn others that it was condemned because someone had contracted the plague within. Those were homes where either the occupants had been taken away to die in a plague center, where there was little more the healers could do than make them comfortable. Or where the family had died inside together, their home becoming their tomb.

Despite the hot night, I repressed a shiver at the memories. As a youth, I'd stumbled into a few of those homes on excursions to find provisions, coins, or goods I could sell or trade. The scent of death had always been oppressive. The corpses, in various states of decay, had been lying in bed or sitting in chairs, a grisly final moment frozen in time.

Now I stepped forward, confused by the vision. My understanding of the Alrenian gift was that it could be shared in mere moments, imparting images and knowledge to the recipient quickly. This felt like a truth I'd have to search for. Did I have to haunt this street again, in a moment in the past? Scour through some of these same homes, back when those corpses I'd once found were still alive and healthy? I ground my teeth at that terrible thought.

Turning, my footsteps took me, as if by habit, in a route that led me to the Teramese palace. It towered high over the city, built on a tall foundation of rock like a pedestal to keep out the threat of floods. It gave the impression that it was always watching the citizens below, which, given the fierce Xalenos royal family's reputation, was perfect for instilling fear and obedience. To this day, it made a sense of foreboding settle in my gut when I remembered the stern glances the High Imperator had always given me, but his son Revaed's warmth had countered that. Made me feel at home in spite of my fear.

The guards manning the gate didn't notice me, instead keeping their eyes trained ahead, their postures perfectly stiff and still. I slipped past them like a ghost, pushing open the heavy doors and walking the extravagant halls from memory. Unlike the cold marble, grand columns, and open pavilions of the Alrenian palace, the Teramese one was adorned in thick carpets, colorful mosaics, bright furniture, and heavy tapestries. It all leant a warmth to the space, dulling the echo of footsteps and making everything feel as homey as it was grand.

Or perhaps that was just my impression, because it had been *my* home for so long.

I found the High Imperator and Revaed within a cozy study, the hearth unlit due to the balmy air. A few windows were open to the night, though the breeze did little to cool the space. Together, the Xalenoses were leaning over documents resting on a long desk in the middle of the room. I took a moment to scan the books lining the shelves, to sink my shoes into the carpet. To draw another deep breath, this one filled with the scents of the flowers outside and the coffee in the two mugs resting at the pair's elbows.

The High Imperator was a younger version of the grey-haired, silver-eyed man I'd known, but the difference was slight. His hair was mostly black in this moment and the wrinkles on his face were fewer. The stern expression and piercing light in his eyes were the same. When he lifted a calloused hand and pointed, I was reminded that this was a cruel ruler who was unafraid of carrying out punishments, rather than leaving all the dirty work to his guards and soldiers.

Revaed, however, looked very different from the man I knew. He was only a teen here, his face still full of boyish charm. When he glanced up at his father, I saw a deep desire to please burning in his violet eyes, to win approval and pride. He wasn't the same confident, easygoing leader I knew today, the one who could spurn his father's wishes and choose his own path.

The High Imperator leaned back in his seat, something almost close to a smile crossing his lips as he studied the sheet of paper between them. "There's another to add, the most exciting of all. The Adriatus family just welcomed their firstborn into the world, only a month ago. A son who is already showing promising signs of power the likes of which I've never seen in my lifetime."

Revaed's eyes widened. "An infant with magic already manifesting?" He cocked his head to the side. "What kind?"

The High Imperator's smile was wolfish. "Water." He tapped a pen against the paper, close to the family name he'd just mentioned and jotted down. Nothing more than a ghost in this scene, this memory, I dared to step closer and lean over the desk. The paper was full of family names, along with notes for different types of magic beside each one. Water. Earth. Air. Fire.

My heart thudded against my ribcage when I realized that the final family name was the only one to have *water* written beside it. And there was a reason the vision had taken me to this night. Could this name be…?

I hadn't finished the thought before the High Imperator was speaking again. "We will set him aside, of course. Train him especially closely, spare no expense on him. And we will need our most elite soldiers and mages working with him daily. Naturally, though his magic is already strong, we will gift him a powerful pendant to match it. He could make a true difference—become a symbol of hope for our people." He paused. "Do you understand? I want you to check in on him yourself, often." He sniffed. "Make yourself *useful* somehow."

Revaed nodded along, his face tight. The meek expression he wore was unfamiliar to me, as if he hadn't yet found the courage to stand up to his father. "Yes, sir."

A quiet dread simmered inside me.

"However," the High Imperator went on, "they refused to surrender him to us."

Revaed blinked in surprise.

"They want to oversee his training themselves," his father went on, sneering. "And they outright refused to send him to the palace to live. They're breaking one of our most sacred laws."

Revaed sat back, concern bunching his forehead.

"It's not often I've witnessed such disloyalty, which is why I brought you here. To learn." The High Imperator's gaze was piercing. "Tell me what to do with them."

Revaed spoke in a deadpan voice. "We'll do what we always do when anyone dares disobey us: refuse to tolerate it. We'll send men to procure the child and…" He swallowed. "We will *remind* everyone what happens to anyone who refuses the Xalenoses."

The High Imperator dipped his head, a contented smile on his lips. "Defective but not entirely useless, I see." He waved a careless hand. "Fetch our best guards and give them their orders. Don't fail in this, or there will be consequences. The Adriatus boy must be brought back, and I want his parents' heads. You're dismissed."

My head spun, fury and revulsion whirling inside me like a hurricane. A wild, strangled sort of sound erupted from my throat, and almost instinctively, I tried to call upon my magic and hurl it toward the two sitting obliviously in their seats.

But this was only a glimpse into the past, and I could not stop it. I couldn't change what had already happened. Couldn't erase the shock of betrayal and hurt tangling inside me when I saw Revaed do *nothing*. And this had been my fate, my parents' fate, they'd so casually been discussing. I was sure of it now.

I blinked, and the scene fell away, replaced with a new one as vivid as the last. Now, I stood inside a modest bedroom, a man and woman throwing clothes and other belongings frantically into bags as they spoke in hushed tones. A lantern rested on a dresser, casting long, flickering shadows on the plain white walls. Despite the heat, the windows were closed tightly against the night, the curtains drawn.

It was too easy to note the familiar features on the man and woman. Her hair curled in gentle waves down her back, the same stubborn way my own short locks liked to curl around my ears. His eyes were bright and clear, the same piercing blue as mine. Her body was constantly in motion, each step graceful and light on her feet, the way I could move; his features were cut like mine, from the straight nose to the square jaw. When she spoke, there was a melody to her voice that made me sure she'd had a lovely singing voice, and her mouth moved in a way that made me wonder if our dimpled smiles would have been mirror images.

My parents.

The ache in my chest was more intense than I'd thought it could be, considering I'd never known these two, not truly. How could I grieve people I'd never met? That I hadn't ever even seen until now, in nothing more than a vision?

Tears blurred my eyes all the same.

"Mother, Father," I murmured, as if they could hear me.

But in this moment, I was the crying baby in the crib near the dresser. I was nothing more than a chubby thing with a small patch of dark hair, already curled slightly in a stubborn wave, like one of the restless waves of the ocean I would one day draw so much power from. There was a cup of water resting on a nightstand not too far away, and I could sense the power this infant version of myself was using to pull little droplets into the air. They glistened, like frozen silver raindrops, in the air above the child—above me—as I cried fitfully.

The woman cast an anxious glance in the infant's direction. "We need to go *now*," she whispered, as if she feared the pull of the magic would be felt from outside the house, drawing others to them.

And then, as if Meli herself were forcing the vision along, everything rushed at a rapid pace. I was present and not present—inhaling the familiar, damp scent of Vicidor as images whirled past. My parents were running, my mother holding me closely, as shadows I couldn't quite make out chased them through the night. It seemed as if I watched days go by for them, leaving me a silent witness to their struggle: their life in hiding, clinging to the quiet, dark places of the city as the High Imperator's forces locked it down, cutting off their exits. Trapping them.

Until the images slowed to show my mother, shaking and weeping, her face sweat-drenched and her eyes bloodshot with an all-too-familiar look. The plague.

I felt ill when I noticed that my father appeared just as terrible as my mother did. They wept as they stood outside the run-down home I'd grown up within, laying down a crying infant and carefully pinning something to his front: a crumpled piece of paper bearing the only information they'd dared to share. *Caesiem.*

"No," I whispered, as if I could change the past. As if I could bring my doomed parents back to life. As if I could stop my mother from stepping away from her bundled child, tears streaming down her face, and slinking off with her husband into the deepening shadows as another night fell over Vicidor.

Answering tears swam in my own eyes, and hurt I'd thought I'd moved past ached in my chest. Longing to know these parents who were nothing but strangers swept through me, but it was an impossible wish. I'd always thought so, but now I knew for certain. Whether they'd ultimately died from illness or at the hands of the High Imperator's men, it didn't matter.

They were gone.

They'd fought for me. Hid and lived on the streets to try to save me from a life I was now living. A life in service to our empire.

As a hundred twisted emotions rushed over me, I opened my eyes and found myself in a dim room. The walls were plain sandstone, windowless and cool, giving me the sensation that I was somewhere underground. Even the air smelled damp, of earth and distant sea. I couldn't hear the cries of battle or even the tumult of the storm anymore, only quiet whispers from some other room.

Strapped to a cot, I blinked as Meli withdrew her hand from me and sat back in a nearby chair. As if all this time she'd been touching me, to consume me in a vision as she brought me here.

Pain lingered in my shoulder, but a quick glance showed me the wound had been tended and wrapped in bandages. How long had I been lost in that vision? How long had Meli been clinging to me as whatever healers she was allied with worked around her?

"Why capture us and bring us here? Why not just kill us?" a familiar voice ground out.

I turned my head to find Valentra strapped to a chair nearby, her dark hair falling from her braid in wild waves about her face. Sometimes, her eyes appeared gold, and other times, they were silver like her brother's. I'd never understood if they were a mixture of the two colors, or if it had to do with a trick of the light. Now, her eyes were molten silver and blazing with hatred as she studied Meli.

Turning away, I drew a deep, settling breath, trying to concentrate on the distant pulse I could sense, even here: the ceaseless waves of the sea beating against the shore. The familiar weight of my pendant hanging from its leather cord was gone, gifted to Lo, but the difference in my power was insignificant. Unlike other mages, my magic was strong even without the help of a pendant to keep the power of the water close to me and help me channel it.

Just because Meli had shown me a glimpse into the truth of my past, just because she'd said she wasn't planning on killing me, didn't mean she wasn't an enemy.

When I lifted my eyes to meet her dark ones, I found her gaze piercing yet steady. "I think as a seemingly important officer in the Teramese army, you understand the use of living prisoners," she said, without meeting Valentra's eyes. "But…you do not have to be prisoners." As if to drive home her point, she stood and drew a knife from her belt. She sliced through my binds and offered me the weapon with a single nod toward Valentra, signaling that I could be the one to free the woman.

Anger boiled inside me. "What do you want from us?" I demanded. Was it not enough she had me questioning my entire *life*, my whole purpose, with the visions she'd shown?

Meli strode across the empty room toward the door, a gentle smile playing about her lips. "I will give you time to process. But, soon, I want you to tell me who you really are, young prince. And then," she added, swinging open the door and offering me the barest glimpse of a dim stone hallway, "I want you to tell me what you will do next."

She slammed the door shut behind her, and the sound of a heavy bolt sliding into place echoed in the ensuing stillness.

CHAPTER SIX

Lo

The pain was a screaming, throbbing sensation that made it difficult to focus. I blinked away the dots consuming my vision.

But I refused to be trapped here, cornered in an alley where a girl who should have been an ally and friend, not an enemy, could slay me. I was sure she'd dump my body off somewhere unceremoniously. The harbor. A dumpster. Pauni'a and my other sisters would never know what had become of me.

Maybe it's what you deserve for leading the Teramese straight to the Forwyn soldiers. Right for the kill.

I shook off the dark thought and gritted my teeth, extending my free hand until I gripped the hilt of the dagger piercing my left palm.

Queasiness pummeled my stomach and scraped up my throat as I tugged, ignoring the pain. The roar that escaped my mouth sounded pure animal: rage and agony.

Mio'e froze a few feet away, her eyes widening at the sight. Maybe I looked crazed as I pulled the dagger free, blood gushing from my wound. I lifted the blade, slick with my own gore, though the rain quickly washed it to the cobblestones at my feet.

"You deserve to die," she spat. "You deserve every ounce of pain I'm about to inflict upon you." She pounced, another blade shimmering in the silver downpour as she slashed.

It was a deadly dance, but I was quick on my feet, too. She'd been a slave until only recently, whereas I'd been exercising and training with the nuns for years. I held my bleeding hand close to my chest and dodged, answering her attack with one of my own. My dagger struck flesh, earning a startled yelp from Mio'e as she scrabbled back. Blood trickled from a slash along her arm.

She stared at me with pure hatred.

"I don't want to kill you," I rasped, forcing myself to concentrate on the adrenaline rushing through me, the instinct to fight. That was all that blocked out my pain, that kept me conscious.

Mio'e scoffed. "You didn't want to kill the Alrenian empress either, you self-righteous *traitor*. But you had no qualms about murdering Wilvhe. Or Renni."

I shook my head, the guilt long dispelled by what I now knew. I'd only ever fought back to survive, to defend myself and the ones I loved. And Elhani forgave me. I could still see the love shining in his eyes from when he'd met me on the beach, still hear his voice promising me I could serve my people. That I wasn't damned and lost. I was found, with a brand-new purpose burning in my veins.

"All I did was defend myself."

Mio'e rolled her eyes. "Like I believe you," she snarled, and swung her weapon again. "You want mercy for the vile Alrenians, but you can't even offer it to your own people."

I staggered back, avoiding the strike from her blade, but not quite evading the wound her words dealt.

With my failure to protect the Forwyn at Aerekni Academy, *those* words stung.

"I'm *trying* to help our people now! There's a battle happening at the academy, and I'm trying to get help!" I snapped in frustration, lunging at Mio'e. "So lower your weapon and get out of my way, or I'll do what I have to."

"Yes, you'll kill me too," Mio'e sneered, rage contorting her features as she kicked—and missed. I swept up with my own leg and sent her reeling to the ground, splashing in a pink puddle of our mingling blood.

Catching my breath, I stared at her. Pain still throbbed through my hand, and I feared if I lost much more blood, my strength would fade, and I'd lose the advantage. Maybe instead I could run and leave Mio'e here, leave this ridiculous fight for the one I needed to join.

But I was sluggish in my pain, and Mio'e lashed out too quickly, seizing my legs and tugging. I slammed into the street beside her, the impact jarring my bones. The taste of iron coated my tongue as water splashed into my mouth. She reached for my dagger, and I grappled with her, my injured hand slick with blood. My muscles shook with my pain as I struggled to wrench the blade away from her.

At last, I rolled, slamming my knees into her chest and forcing all my weight on top of her. She grunted and lost her hold on my dagger. I pressed the blade to her neck. "Surrender and live," I panted. "Or remain a slave to your cause of vengeance, and die, a *failed* avenger of blood."

Mio'e shuddered, struggling to breathe evenly. The anger in her eyes seemed to give way to something else. It was a brief flicker of another emotion, one that I thought might have been fear. And then it was gone as she lifted her chin.

"You disgust me," she spat. "I'll die before I quit fighting."

Sadness rippled through me. I didn't want to kill her. But if she lived, she would never stop fighting me. Never stop being an obstacle in the way of my hope to save my people. And time was running out. I had to find help and return to the academy before Father and his soldiers were all slain.

I clenched my teeth and tensed my arm, preparing to slam the hilt into her temple and knock her unconscious. Threatening to kill her had all been a bluff—I wouldn't, not unless I had no other choice. But she needed to think I would.

Pounding footsteps interrupted my thoughts, drawing both Mio'e's and my attention down the street. The rain had eased just enough for us to make out the silhouettes of leather-clad Alrenians, armed to the teeth and scanning the street for bodies, living and dead, with vicious intent. We were far enough away, crouched in the gathering dark and rain, that they hadn't seen us yet. But they would.

I cursed and turned back to Mio'e. "See? We don't have time for foolishness," I hissed. "We have real enemies coming this way. Fight *with* me and help save Forwyn lives." I swallowed. "And we can finish this fight between us later."

Lightning flashed overhead, reflecting in Mio'e's eyes as she glared at me. "My vow to Elhani is sacred."

I dug my knee harder into her ribs, eliciting a groan. "I thought you were dedicated to saving lives! What's more important to you?" I demanded. "Revenge, or saving our people? Killing me, or stopping those Alrenians?"

Mio'e drew a strangled breath. "Fine! But I will only stand beside you as long as there are other enemies to fight."

"Good," I said, yanking back my blade and jumping to my feet. I didn't offer a hand to her, letting her stagger to a stand and retrieve a bloodied sword lying discarded in the street all on her own. She wasn't a friend, was barely an ally. But at least, for now, she wasn't trying to kill me.

We both whirled toward the Alrenians just in time. The lightning drew their eyes to us as surely as if we had targets painted upon our backs. With gleeful, predatory grins, they stalked forward, lifting weapons dripping with rain and blood.

Unlike the first Alrenian I'd encountered, these wasted no time with taunting words. Three men and two women charged for us without delay, wielding their axes and swords with deadly grace.

Mio'e unleashed an enraged battle cry. I gritted my teeth, trying desperately to stave off the waves of dizziness washing over me as my blood dripped onto the cobblestones. My left arm hung limply at my side.

Elhani.

I dodged the first swing of an axe, ducking low and rolling, slamming my dagger into the man's knee. He screamed and swung again, this time with his fist. The impact against my temple made sparks dance across my sight, but Mio'e had already shoved her sword into his gut. With a grunt, she pulled it free, leaving him to stumble back as the other Alrenians fell upon us.

Rising again was far too difficult than it should have been. I struggled to draw my sword, and another Alrenian slammed it easily from my loosening grip. It clanged uselessly to the street, while I swayed like a drunk. The world tilted and spun, and I wasn't sure I'd be able to defend myself much longer. I could feel unconsciousness threatening to pull me under.

I dropped to the street, blinking through hazy vision as a woman stormed toward me, her grin bloodthirsty and cruel.

I was going to die, wounded and defenseless, with my sword lying mere feet away from me.

Elhani, I thought again, unable to form any other coherent thoughts, other than my wild drive to fight. To live. To help my father and his soldiers. By now, they might have already been lying dead in the academy courtyard.

There was an answering hum of music, low and sweet, yet still stronger than the endless rain, the rolling thunder, and the Alrenians' fearsome, almost animalistic cries.

In an instant, a form stood beside me, extending a hand to help me up. She was impossibly beautiful, with flawless brown skin and curls that tumbled past her shoulders. She was cloaked and hooded against the night, but the rain didn't seem to touch her, didn't seem to extend beyond the glowing aura surrounding her.

A guidespirit.

Heart pounding, I took her hand with my uninjured one, and all my pain, weakness, and dizziness vanished. She yanked me to my feet as a jolt of strength and energy shot through me, swift and bright as the lightning tearing the sky apart.

When I blinked, she was gone.

I dove for the first Alrenian's axe, lying useless on the street beside him as he bled out. Ignoring the gruesome sight, I lifted the weapon and met the next attacker, strike for strike. Duck, swing, sidestep—my movements came in a natural rhythm, like my nights running through the streets, or my mornings sparring with Pauni'a. I didn't let myself hold back or flinch away when I struck the killing blow. These Alrenians had filled the streets with corpses, and wouldn't hesitate to add me and other innocent Forwyn to the piles.

Later, I would let myself feel the horror, the ugliness of battle. Later, I would let myself mourn the evils of a world that forced me to resort to violence to save lives. Later, I'd let myself wonder if any of the Alrenians truly did deserve mercy, if there ever was a chance we could find common ground.

Now, I committed everything to Elhani. *Stop them. Save my people. Save the Forwyn. Don't let it be their blood filling the streets when this night ends.*

Elhani's words from our meeting on the beach burned through my soul, my love for my people driving me forward. *World changer.*

"Lo!" the familiar cry jolted me from the fury of battle. A rush of relief flooded me.

I glanced over my shoulder to see new forms emerging from the waning downpour. Their silhouettes looked like they were edged in silver in the dimness. Pauni'a. O'emia. My sisters.

Faces set in determined lines, the colorful ribbons in their braids soaked and partially unraveled, they charged for the Alrenians without a beat of hesitation. Their weapons were things they'd clearly taken off the streets: bloody swords and axes. Two had bows with a handful of arrows left in the quivers strapped to their backs.

My sisters swarmed forward, quickly overwhelming the final Alrenians with their sheer numbers. Two arrows downed a woman and a man. A swift slice of Pauni'a's sword stopped the other woman before she could lift her blade against me. And the final man—as soon as he saw his downed comrades and found himself surrounded by Forwyn women bristling with weapons and glowing with fury…he dropped his sword and ran.

Mio'e snarled and raised her sword, moving as if to give chase.

"Don't bother," O'emia said. "Likely a Teramese guard will catch and finish him off."

I turned to her. "You chose to fight," I said, voice full of awe.

"Of course," Pauni'a said fiercely, stepping forward to envelope me in a crushing hug. "After what those Alrenians and Teramese did to our numbers…we realized this was a battle we couldn't shy away from. We are a part of it, whether we want to be or not. Joining to defend our people is what Naina would have wanted us to do."

"And *none* of the blood we've shed tonight was innocent." Eyes blazing with indignation, O'emia stared at the bodies strewn on the cobblestones before us. The rain had slowed considerably, turning to a steady drizzle around us, and the churning sky had settled. Only a few dull, occasional flashes of lightning lit the capital streets now, and everything seemed unnaturally quiet and still. The aftermath of battle.

"I came to find you," I said, my voice hoarse. "Our soldiers are outnumbered. We need all the help we can find." It felt like ages had passed since I'd fled the academy courtyard, and I feared we'd be far too late. But we had to try.

I could feel Mio'e staring at me, could practically sense her shock vibrating through the air.

Pauni'a grinned. "Lead the way."

The other women nodded, their grips tight on their weapons. There was no doubt or judgment in their gaze when they assessed me, only fierce pride. And love.

I shook my head, fighting the ache in my throat. "Thank you," I managed. *Thank you for still loving me. For still fighting with and for me.*

Though her eyes were still red-rimmed from her grief, O'emia flashed me a bright smile. "Nun or not, you'll always be our sister. I know Naina would have said the same."

Spinning toward Mio'e, I settled my sword hilt in my damp hands, studying her. Shockingly, she looked weary, but not angry. "Either you're with us or against us," I said. "But there's a battle happening right now, and our people are dying."

There was a moment in which she stared, as if trying to read the expression in my eyes. Something flickered in her dark gaze, something that could have been lingering hatred, or maybe the dying embers of an anger she'd directed at the wrong person for far too long. And then it vanished. She set her jaw, raindrops still dripping from her shorn hair and down her temples.

When she spoke, her voice was unwavering and strong. "*For now,*" she said, "I'm with you."

CHAPTER SEVEN

Kovi

I was breathless, taken aback by the sheer impact the pain and fear had over me. Wherever Jalie was, whatever was happening, she was in the worst kind of torment, and there was nothing I could do.

In my helplessness, in my desperation to stop her suffering, pure fury consumed me. There was nothing but blood and sweat, mud and an Elhani-cursed downpour that made it nearly impossible to see…or to move quickly. Only the flashes of lightning helped illuminate the courtyard in garish instants that revealed how devastating the carnage had become. Even the thunder and driving rain worked against the last of us Forwyn, concealing the sounds of enemies approaching from behind till the last moment.

Worse still, doubt and defeat were nearly driving me mad as I watched hordes of leather-clad Alrenians pour forth, leaving the streets of the capital to take advantage of the havoc here. They sliced down Teramese and Forwyn without mercy. They fought like people possessed, moving with a swiftness and fury I didn't think was possible.

"Praise the Life-Giver!" an Alrenian shouted, and others took up the cry. "Our gifts have returned!"

Horror snaked through me. Their legendary gifts of war and courage, the ones that let them conquer and brutalize kingdoms, were manifesting in their citizens again?

Elhani help us all.

Screaming hair-raising battle cries, the Alrenians moved through our numbers ruthlessly, causing even the Teramese to stumble and regroup. To shout out desperate commands to one another over the storm. A vengeful part of me hoped Revaed was somewhere in the midst, staring his approaching death in the face of one of these heartless Alrenians.

And I'd tried to believe in a dream where Jalie and I could convince the Alrenians to no longer be enemies to the Forwyn. I'd been a fool.

"It's a massacre," Rhi'il choked out, staggering to my side while General Ilowhe fended off attackers on the other. Rhi'il was bleeding, or maybe he was covered in a considerable amount of enemy blood. It was difficult to tell when we were all smeared in gore and rainwater, mud and sweat.

General Ilowhe said nothing, his form a rigid line as he fought, unyielding. Unbending. Refusing to let the devastating losses piling up around us break him. I knew as well as he did that there was no retreating from this, no chance we could try to save a handful of surviving soldiers and students to fight another day. We were trapped, completely outnumbered and hemmed in within the very sanctuary we'd once relied upon.

This would be our last stand.

Lo

As my sisters, Mio'e, and I ran back through the city, back toward the academy, I took in the carnage around us. Far too many of the districts had been sites of rioting and death. Bodies littered the streets and bloody puddles flowed over cobblestones. Some corpses even floated in the canals, staining the beautiful sight of the starlight reflected in their waters.

Teramese soldiers searched through the dead or tended to wounded, carrying them off the streets. Others had returned to their patrols, scouring a city that now lay eerily quiet, the streets empty of both rioting Alrenians and other citizens. Lost in their grim tasks, they ignored us just as we ignored them. I supposed this meant that the Teramese had won, in the end. Had the Alrenians given up and crawled back into whatever holes they'd been using to hide their weapons and plot their rebellion?

Gritting my teeth, I tore my eyes away and focused on the dark silhouette of the academy, rising beyond the city walls. From this distance, I couldn't tell what was happening. It was only a dark smear on the horizon. The battle could still be raging, or it could already be over, with nothing but Forwyn corpses and victorious Teramese reigning over our once-mighty fortress.

Please don't let it be so, Elhani, I begged as we left the capital and approached the academy.

When I led my sisters through the open gates, I steeled myself for whatever awaited me.

The number of Forwyn surivors was horrifyingly low, most gathered in a few tight knots of fierce defenders trying to hold back the onslaught of both Alrenians and Teramese. The Alrenian rioters must have joined the battle.

Unleashing a scream of fury, I hefted the axe I'd taken off the streets and charged. There was no room for fear in my body, not when I saw the horrors Revaed had unleashed upon our soldiers. Upon men and women who should have faced enemies in a fair fight, on a real battlefield, never like this.

I hurled every ounce of my indignation at the foes before me, leaping over bodies and pools of blood. I didn't falter, didn't hesitate. Behind me, my sisters echoed my wordless shout.

We were Elhani's aching heart for our suffering people. We were Elhani's justice. We were his rage.

Teramese and Alrenians alike gaped, caught off guard by the sight of nuns rushing into battle. The air around me crackled as my sisters called upon Elhani's magic. It coursed with such a powerful rush through the air that I was overcome with warmth, with a strange sense of peace in the midst of this chaos.

O'emia and Pauni'a caught up to me, but in an instant they'd vanished. Their enemies had no way to defend themselves as the women sprinted ahead of me and attacked unseen.

An Alrenian's startled cry cut short as a sword appeared only when it pierced his gut. He collapsed just as a Teramese woman fell to her invisible attacker.

Hate-filled eyes met mine, shimmering with Alrenian gold flecks or bright Teramese colors. I slowed, waiting for them to come to me. But I didn't call upon invisibility as they sprinted forward, shouting curses in their own languages. I hoped they recognized me from the Teramese coronation ceremony, when Revaed had revealed my identity. I wanted them to know the *amara'rekni* fought for her people again.

Kovi

An overwhelming sadness gripped me, as fierce as my anger.

I didn't want to live to see the fall of my people, I thought. And though I knew there were countless other Forwyn scattered throughout Alrenor, I also knew that if we lost here today, if no Aerekni soldiers survived, there would be no recovering from this. We were a beacon of hope, the most elite fighters and the citizens most rigorously trained in magic. No one else would manage to build an army that could match the strength we'd risen to. The Teramese would hopelessly outnumber the remaining Forwyn, and the Alrenians would overpower them with their returning gifts and their generations of warrior training. Once we were gone, the Forwyn would lose their freedom again.

But when I lifted my eyes to scan the courtyard once more, seeking out our survivors, I saw her. General Ilowhe's daughter Lo, surrounded by other Forwyn women, most clothed in grey clothes marking them as nuns, and all armed with weapons already dripping blood.

They made startlingly fierce figures, their mouths set in determined lines. With earth-shattering battle cries, they flung themselves headlong toward the battle. Enemies faltered in shock, giving me an opening to drive my sword into a nearby Teramese man.

And then—warmth and power flooded the air, a wave so powerful it nearly rocked me off my feet.

Magic.

There was nothing else to do. It was my duty to survive, and to ensure the rest of the soldiers around me survived too.

Spinning toward an onslaught of several Alrenian soldiers, I hurled every ounce of my concentration into my magic and the authority it possessed. "Throw down your weapons! Surrender!"

Wild-eyed and furious, the soldiers obeyed, screaming in frustration to find their hands moving of their own accord. Their weapons clanged against the cobblestones, splashing more mud and ichor on the general, Rhi'il, and me. Spines rigid, eyes burning with hatred, they dropped to their knees in the filth before us.

I could feel their hatred swirling through me, as strong as if it were my own emotion.

Scanning the carnage, I saw clumps of Forwyn soldiers still trying to fend off the Teramese and Alrenians, but I knew simply disarming this small group wasn't enough. Nausea swept through me at the knowledge of what I'd have to do.

I couldn't control every single enemy soldier at once—I'd learned through trial and error that six was the most I could ever command at a time. As soon as my power drifted to try to capture others, these ones would pull free of their false surrender. My only choice was to kill them while they were incapacitated, or watch them return to slaying the rest of my fellow soldiers.

Grim-faced, Rhi'il and General Ilowhe moved forward in the same breath that I did, seeming to understand exactly what had to be done.

Elhani forgive me, I thought as I sliced my sword clean through the neck of the first Alrenian soldier. His rage was mine as he died. *Jalie, forgive me.* I killed the next, his despair nearly stealing my breath away. *I told you I had to choose my people first.*

My victims' horror, rage, fear, desperation—each emotion coursed through me ruthlessly, until I wasn't sure there was anything left but an empty hole in my chest. Until it was impossible to tell which feelings were mine, and which had belonged to the dead.

Maybe we're all monsters.

I gritted my teeth and wiped at the blood soaking my cheek.

If being a soldier has made me a monster, will there be any mercy left in me when the fighting stops? Will *it ever stop?*

It was gruesome, horrible work, seizing control of the enemy soldiers so we could cut them down. There was no honor in it. But it was survival, and I knew these men and women would show us no mercy.

Rain washed away the gore coating my hands and uniform and boots. It was a false cleansing of blood that I couldn't ever really wash away, of memories and feelings and deaths I would never be able to undo or forget.

My only penance was tasting death with my victims, again and again.

Lo

Mio'e and my sisters gathered around me, a solid wall of defense against the onslaught of enemies who attempted to swarm us from all sides. Just as I'd hoped, we were pulling numbers away from the struggling Forwyn soldiers, dividing our opponents. While the Aerekni soldiers fought from one side, we struck from the other, hemming in our foes.

As I swung and ducked oncoming attacks, every movement felt natural, all ones I was familiar with from endless sparring matches. I knew the footwork to use. I knew the signs to search for to find my opponents' openings and weaknesses. I watched for their tells, signaling when and where they planned to strike. Just as I'd avoid a blow from one of my sisters in a fight, I dodged the swing of their blades.

I used my speed and agility to press in close and take the offense.

When it came to landing a killing blow, I didn't hesitate, not this time.

I couldn't, not ever again. Not when it came to my survival or that of my people. It was kill or be killed. The only way to stop them was to accept the rush of adrenaline in my veins.

My anger cleared my head, pushing aside the haunting images that would normally be dredged from my memories by the new horrors around me. This time, I wasn't overcome with emotions, and I refused to freeze.

My enemies fought for vengeance and destruction, but I fought for peace. I fought so that one day, I wouldn't have to.

Calling on Elhani's magic, I shouted, my voice a ragged cry over the clamor of battle. It was a wordless sound, because words weren't necessary when I knew my god could see our need, could feel my desperation and love for my people, my hope that we could survive beyond this terrible day. Elhani's power filled it, making it echo through the air.

The Alrenians and Teramese around me quaked in fear, their eyes wide as they looked about, as if scanning for another hidden enemy. Some threw down their weapons, fleeing the courtyard. Others froze long enough for my sisters to slay them, never giving them the chance to kill another of our own again.

Stepping forward, I pulled on Elhani's magic again. His song, gentle yet strong, whispered through the air, a warm brush on my cheeks, like a tender caress. Peace and confidence swelled in my soul. Again, I shouted, forcing my enemies to scatter and retreat while they cried out in terror. They were baffled and confused, many not even casting their eyes toward me, but to the heavens, as if they thought it was the cry of a god. Maybe it was Elhani's voice they heard, shouting something deafening and earth-shattering through me. Maybe it was *his* fury they heard, his threat to leave his people alone or suffer for it.

Before I could reach for Elhani's song a third time, arms seized me from behind. A hand slammed against my fingers, forcing me to drop my axe with a clatter. Biting back a startled cry, I kicked my leg back, trying to strike my attackers. I twisted, seeking my sisters in the chaos, but I must have moved further apart from them than I'd realized.

I strained to hear the notes of Elhani's song, determined to use his power to force my enemy to release me.

Something smashed against my head, and the world faded to black.

Kovi

At last, horrified by the magic enveloping them, the Alrenians and Teramese began to flee, forsaking their dead and injured to tear back toward the capital. Surrounded by my surviving brothers and sisters, I only stared after our enemies' fleeing forms.

The rain slowed to a drizzle, leaving us in eerie quiet as the storm quieted and the chaos of battle ended.

I wanted to collapse, to cry out at the horror of all the bodies we had to burn, to mourn. This had been a slaughter—absolute carnage. The academy had once housed nearly a thousand, and though some of our number, like the healers within our infirmary, would still be safe within the academy walls, most had flooded to the courtyard to defend. Others had fallen within the academy as enemies had stormed inside. It was impossible to know our final count now, but a quick scan of the courtyard told me our casualties had been atrociously, gut-wrenchingly high.

But I didn't have anything left inside me but others' emotions. Teramese and Alrenian deaths playing out over and over again, consuming me with their pain and terror. Father, full of bitterness and anger, rotting him from the inside.

And Jalie, always Jalie, overwhelmed by so much suffering I could hardly think.

It was too much to block out, too much to fight against. Weariness consumed me, and I sank to my knees, landing in a puddle of muck. Maybe my ties to Father and Jalie, tangled with the memories of my other severed connections, would drive me slowly mad. Maybe it was what I deserved.

Rhi'il reached out, supporting me with his arms before I collapsed entirely.

"They'll pay for this," he said, his voice fierce and wild with anger. "All of them. Their so-called alliance be damned."

Vaguely, I realized that all hope of a Forwyn-Alrenian allegiance had likely died here, with my sisters and brothers, on this Elhani-forsaken battlefield.

But maybe that mad dream was already gone, if Jalie was fighting for her life, ready to vanish from the world.

Without her, I wasn't sure I could find it within myself to fight for an alliance anymore. I wasn't sure I could see past the evil the Alrenians had committed here today. The blow of grief was too gaping, too raw, to even begin to process yet. It was unreal, like a nightmare I needed to shake myself awake from.

And if I lost Jalie too?

I felt like a soldier with nothing left to fight for. A dreamer left with only ashes in his hands.

My connection with Jalie snapped, her emotions winking out as abruptly as they'd overwhelmed me.

I flinched and tried to reach out, but there was only emptiness.

Elhani, don't let her die. She can't be dead. I can't lose her. Don't take her from me.

Unable to use my shaking limbs to prop myself up anymore, I leaned against Rhi'il and pushed all my thoughts toward her. As if I could still fight for her, even across the miles that separated us.

Hold on, Jalie. Don't let go. Please don't let go.

CHAPTER EIGHT

Kovi

In the wake of the massacre that had occurred, all other feelings gave way to a dull numbness. There was work to do—work that couldn't be delayed. We couldn't collapse with weariness or give way to grief. We couldn't gape in horror at the bodies lying in their own blood, at the unseeing gazes of our friends and fellow soldiers.

And I couldn't lose myself in my fear for Jalie. Not now. I had to trust that somehow, she would be all right. She would survive, as she always had before.

Sidestepping the bodies in my path, I pushed toward the gate, where, based on the groans and cries for help, most of the soldiers still living were sprawled out. I found one of the nuns kneeling beside a dying Alrenian, her hands gentle as she brushed back the sweaty hair matted to his face. Though I knew I shouldn't stop, shouldn't hesitate, I couldn't help but freeze, taking in the moment.

For as much as I wanted to curse the man for the atrocities he'd committed tonight, I couldn't fault the nun for offering him mercy.

"Why not just leave me to rot?" the man choked out, blood bubbling at the corner of his mouth.

Though her amber eyes were soft with kindness, the nun's face was set into a hard line. She'd seen worse things in her short life—of that I was certain.

"Because Elhani created you too, and everyone deserves to have someone hold their hand at the end," she said, her tone confident. I could practically feel Elhani's presence in the air, his song murmuring on the breeze that tugged at her braids. True to her words, she extended her hand, gently taking his calloused, bloodied fingers in her own. "Tell me your name, and let me pray your soul into the next life."

Tears glistened in the Alrenian's grey and gold eyes. Whatever bloodlust, whatever desire for vengeance had led him here tonight, it had all vanished in the wake of his own mortality. In this gentle moment from a woman who had every right to spit in his face and deny him this act of humanity. "R-Roniv," he managed.

"I am Pauni'a," she murmured, and then closed her eyes. She leaned into Elhani's song and began to sing along in Forwyn, her voice mingling with the melody.

Could the Alrenian hear Elhani's song within the nun's? I almost believed it, when I saw the wonder and peace turning his expression gentle. His pain and fear seemed forgotten, all caught up in the awe of Elhani's power.

This time, tears burned my own throat. I wasn't sure anything could fully assuage my anger and grief over what had happened here, over the immeasurable loss we'd sustained. But this…this came close. This reminded me of what Jalie had declared, that there were other Alrenians like her who would be open to peace, if they only took a moment to understand their Forwyn enemies.

As Roniv's hand grew limp in Pauni'a's and his eyes turned

unfocused, she slowly ended her song.

Shoulders sagging, the woman stood and her gaze met mine.

"I didn't think nuns fought," I said. Not the best introduction, but I was at a loss for anything better, the sound of her song still echoing in my head.

"For our people? For Elhani? We will do and be whatever we are called to be." She lifted her chin proudly, strong in the face of the sorrow weighing her down. "My sisters and I are here to help—we have been trained in the art of healing, and our magic is powerful…"

Her voice trailed off as another nun staggered over, blood running from a shallow cut on her forehead.

"Emi! Are you all right?" Pauni'a demanded, darting forward to try to inspect the woman's face.

The woman she called Emi waved her away. "It's nothing.

Pauni'a scanned the courtyard. "Where's Lo?"

Emi's eyes sparked with rage. "I tried to stop them, but they took her."

Alarm darted across Pauni'a's face. "What? The Teramese?" Her eyes searched the courtyard wildly, as if she could still find the soldiers who'd taken her companion. "When?"

"Not long before they retreated," Emi said, her posture rigid.

"We have to go after her! We have to find her before they—"

Emi set a gentle hand on the young woman's arm. "We will, Nia. But our first duty is here, to the injured." Her eyes darted up to meet mine for the first time. "My sisters and I will help in any way we can."

I nodded, once, before turning my gaze to Pauni'a. "Lo is the general's daughter. You can rest assured we'll do all in our power to get her back." As Pauni'a's eyes widened in surprise, I added, "If the Teramese took Lo captive, they want her alive. We have time."

But not much, I added in my head. Without another word, I darted toward the nearest wounded soldier.

The night became a blur. Unfortunately, there were far more dead than living. As the last of the wounded that could be moved were ferried away to the infirmary to be tended by the healers and the most confident of the nuns, we turned to the corpses.

The task of gathering the dead into piles seemed endless. We worked in pairs, shuffling the bodies outside of the walls where they could be burned. Enemy and friend were gathered alike, because there were too many to sort through them all—too many to give individual respects.

And as much as we were loath to give them honor, even our enemies couldn't be left to rot on our doorstep.

Pauni'a's words to the dying Alrenian rang in my ears: *Everyone deserves to have someone hold their hand at the end.*

As the sky lightened to grey to herald the end of this long night, as we gathered outside of the courtyard to set the bodies aflame, and as General Ilowhe murmured a traditional Forwyn blessing—"May Elhani hold your hands and the guidespirits lead you home"—I supposed she was right.

In the midst of this bloody, seemingly unwinnable conflict, we all at least deserved a proper goodbye when we met our ends.

"I'm not sure this is a war we can win." The nun I'd learned was named O'emia stared at her hands. Her palms were caked in dried blood and dirt from helping carry the last of the bodies out to be burned. She and the other nuns had been talking mostly amongst themselves as we soldiers awaited our general's next move.

Despite our exhaustion, General Ilowhe had ordered every able-bodied soldier and nun who wasn't tending to the wounded to gather in the mess hall. A few soldiers had scrounged together a meal of jerky, day-old bread, and cheese. Rhi'il had brought a pot of coffee.

General Ilowhe himself hadn't joined us yet, as he was still with some of the wounded. I imagined he was bidding some faithful soldiers farewell.

"I'm not worried about the war right now," Pauni'a burst out. Her food sat untouched before her. "We need to find Lo."

"General Ilowhe will have a plan," I assured her, keeping my tone measured. I forced myself to take a bite of my jerky, finding it tasteless, but I cradled my coffee mug gratefully. My adrenaline hadn't fully worn off, giving me fuel to somehow keep moving, keep blinking, keep trying to process all that had happened. The coffee couldn't make much of a difference, but it was comforting and familiar, the bitter flavor a jolt to sharpen the senses.

My mind went back to what O'emia had said. *An unwinnable war,* I thought, remembering the countless Teramese I'd seen swarming throughout the capital when I'd been sent with Vander to find Jalie.

Jalie. Just the thought of her name sent a pang through me. After losing my connection to her emotions, I couldn't stop wondering if it was because I was too numb…or if the worst had happened.

A cold sweat threatened to take over. Never had I felt so torn in my loyalties before. I longed to tear out of the academy on my horse Imeo and find Jalie, to ensure she was safe. But to leave would be to abandon my people, injured and suffering. We were desperately outnumbered, and despite the Teramese and Alrenian retreat, it wouldn't be long before our enemies decided to capitalize on our low numbers and finish us off.

Unwinnable.

The Teramese invasion had changed everything. Before, the Alrenians had outnumbered us with their sheer quantity of citizens, but that hadn't been an insurmountable obstacle. Despite their reputation as warriors, not every Alrenian was a trained soldier. And for the past three years, none had been permitted to train or fight alongside the Forwyn.

The Elders may have claimed we were unified, but they'd made it clear from the beginning that the Alrenians would have to earn back our trust before being permitted to hold such power. But now…

General Ilowhe strode into the mess hall and found an empty spot on the bench beside me. With a grateful smile, he accepted a mug of steaming coffee from Rhi'il.

"Yes, of course I'll do everything in my power to find Lo," he said, clearly having overheard my earlier statement. He laid his head in his hands, rubbing his palms across his forehead and sighing. Even with this gesture of exhaustion, he didn't appear weak, only sad and resigned.

There was a long pause as we all sat in silence, our minds sluggish in our weariness and our sorrow.

"But our enemies outnumber us," the general continued, "and they've infiltrated both the city and the palace."

"And they're surrounded by dragons," Rhi'il muttered.

"As much as I'd like to, we can't act rashly." General Ilowhe leaned back, his mouth a solemn line. "And I'm not sure we can linger here, either."

"What?" Mhel, a fellow graduate with Rhi'il and me and one of our good friends, blinked in surprise. His eyes were red-rimmed from sorrow and weariness.

"This is a fortress," Rhi'il said, looking equally shocked. "Where else could we be this secure? Even if they besieged us with dragons, these buildings would hold."

"And with their numbers and resources, it would be easy for them to lay siege for as long as they wanted and starve us out," I argued, before the general could lift his weary head. I could see the dip of his shoulders—a sign of the burden he carried. He'd been the one to order the gates to be opened. He felt responsible for every death among his men and women. And his own daughter was a captive of his enemies. "This fortress would become our grave."

General Ilowhe nodded grimly. "We need a place to hide—and we need reinforcements."

"We should have known long ago that Teramyl could be a threat," I said, shame entering my tone. I sighed. "Anyone living in such a dangerous land has motive to seek territory elsewhere."

Turning to me, the general shook his head. "Firstly, there's no way we could have known. Teramyl had renewed the old treaty they'd established with Alrenor before the barrier had been erected. The Elders had been in amiable contact with the Teramese for the past three years. No official trade had been set up because of our inner conflict and Teramyl's reluctance to become involved, but there had never been any signs of hostility in their letters. No threats."

"You saw their correspondence?" I asked.

"They involved me in some of their correspondence, yes," he affirmed. "They wanted me to be aware of our standings with all foreign governments, in case there was ever a threat our soldiers would need to prepare for." His forehead crinkled. "The Teramese were supposed to eventually send a diplomatic party. Not an army."

"Did the Elders ever show you or mention any letters from the Teramese asking for aid?" I ventured.

My mind darted back to the image of Father standing alongside the Teramese, willing to invade a fortress filled with his own people. The snake. I'd known he was walking into dark territory from the marks I'd seen him leave on Jalie, but turning against the Forwyn was a new low, even for him. I couldn't trust that during his time in power he would have voted to treat the Teramese fairly. And I didn't trust the other Elders anymore, either.

Thinking of my father made shame burn through me, along with a wild desire to claw at my own skin, to throw away my own name. I wanted no part of me to look like him, sound like him, act like him. I didn't even want to bear his name, not anymore.

"It doesn't matter," Rhi'il burst out, who was pulling apart his slice of bread without even bothering to pretend to eat it. "Whatever the

Elders did, right or wrong, most of them are dead now, or they've betrayed us." His gaze turned dark, as if he too were thinking of Father. He tossed a quick, almost apologetic glance toward me, but I didn't so much as blink. Let him hate my father. No one here could possibly hate him more than me.

"Who's to say the Teramese would have stayed peaceful toward us if the Elders reacted differently? It doesn't change that we're facing a war." Rhi'il turned to O'emia. "And it doesn't matter if it's winnable or not, either. We didn't choose it, but here we are." He set his jaw. "We don't have any other option but to fight."

O'emia nodded slowly, her face grave. "I know," she murmured. "It's why my sisters and I chose tonight to fight. Our leader and one of our sisters were murdered by both Alrenians and Teramese. We took a vow to never shed innocent blood, but it seems no one in this conflict is innocent anymore."

"We are grateful for your help," General Ilowhe said, dipping his head toward the young woman. He curled his hands around his mug. "Since we know we must fight, we must decide now where to regroup— and who we can find who will be willing to fight alongside us."

"Who else in the world cares about us?" another of the women asked. She'd come with the nuns, though she wasn't dressed in their colors, and her hair was shorn, as if she'd lived as a slave far longer than the rest of us. Maybe she had. Disgust fired through my veins.

"Wouldn't Forwyth?" another nun asked, her eyes studying General Ilowhe's face.

"Forwyth has kept itself…distanced from Alrenor, ever since the Elders reached out to them about our struggles three years ago," General Ilowhe explained. "We'd hoped they'd be willing allies, but they seem to be uninterested in foreign affairs."

"What did they say?" Rhi'il asked.

General Ilowhe shrugged. "I didn't see those letters, but the Elders were livid."

O'emia sniffed. "We're only foreign to the Forwyth citizens because our ancestors were the ones chosen to be Alrenor's slaves, and not theirs."

"However," the general interjected, "circumstances have since changed. Now that Teramyl is expanding its reaches, Forwyth might find it in their best interest to act, before the Teramese set their sights on their kingdom next."

"What about Misroth?" my friend Huvoki asked. "Didn't they help the Forwyn rise against the Alrenians when Empress Karye was slain?"

General Ilowhe smiled. "That is another kingdom I have considered. Their interest would be in keeping Teramyl contained, away from their kingdom. Especially so soon after the tragedies that already befell them in their recent war." He sat up straighter, as if preparing to stand. "But," he added, "our first step is finding shelter. We will take the time we need—most of our wounded can't be moved yet—but we will leave as soon as we are able. There we can plan." His eyes darted to the nuns. "We'll rescue my daughter and any other Forwyn in Teramese clutches." He sighed. "For now, we rest. We tend to our wounded. And anyone who has any idea of where we can go—any ideas at all—bring them to me. We don't want to stray too far from the capital, and it must be secure and defensible."

I leaned forward, unable to keep silent any longer. Jalie was north. I could check on her during a ride to Misroth. I could find her. My heart pounded in my head, wild desperation threatening to take over every rational thought in my brain. "If you send word to Misroth, who will go?"

Something flickered in the general's eyes, as if he could read my thoughts. "Not you. I have others who can ride fast and hidden. I need you here."

One nod—that's all I gave, but he knew I wouldn't break that silent promise. Every part of my body ached. My chest was a void.

And yet...I'd promised my people would come first.

I swallowed back the threatening panic. *She's capable of defending herself, and she was planning on marching this way anyway. I'll see her again.*

But then, why had her emotions cut off, leaving an awful silence between us? Why couldn't I feel my connection with her anymore?

CHAPTER NINE

Jalie

The nestrae descended like the demons they were, hissing and chanting as they seized me in their claws. Darkness and mist crowded around my vision, but I could see their eyes, black and empty as abysses, and I could see their hulking grey forms, as hard as dragon scales. Their teeth were long and yellow, like rodents', and their smiles were wide and garish.

You made a deal with a demon queen, and you lost, I thought. What would Kovi think? He'd tried to warn me. Terror flooded through me, followed swiftly by regret.

But far worse was the pain—shrieking, all-consuming pain as the nestrae slammed their claws into me and cut, cut, cut. Warmth burst over my chilled skin as they tore through my armor, as easily as slicing through fabric, and carved into me, drawing blood.

I screamed, but Nesrelle towered over them and simply smiled. She met my gaze, and I was lost in the agony she inflicted once again, all without her laying a finger on me this time. It shuddered through me, making every muscle spasm, making it impossible to fight against the demons.

I was sure they'd skin me alive, leave me to bleed out in this dim, misty place. Sure they'd laugh over my agonized body forever until I was nothing but a corpse for them to mangle and burn away to ash. My throat was raw, and still I couldn't stop shrieking against the pain. I couldn't think beyond my sheer terror, my raw desperation for my life. I couldn't see anything other than the cold, horrifying eyes of Nesrelle and her nestrae.

Blackness swept over me, and this time, it wasn't something I dreaded. It was blissful relief.

Please don't let go. The words came from far away, a familiar voice prodding me out of the sweet, gentle darkness, back toward the light. Kovi.

An ache stirred in my chest as I thought of him, his strong arms around me. His lips twitching in a barely-there smile, while the gold flecks in his dark eyes shone. The way he could set aside his duty as a soldier to embrace mercy and kindness more powerful than any I'd ever felt before.

My eyes ached as I opened them. But it wasn't Kovi standing over me—he wasn't there at all. Instead, it was Nesrelle.

The demons were gone, along with the misty grey world in which I'd been trapped. I was back in Aramith, under a velvet-black night sky and surrounded by corpses. Close behind me, Ryke's warmth was a reassuring presence that helped hold off my lingering fear.

Clothed in a flowing green dress that trailed along the ground, the Queen of Death appeared wildly out of place in the aftermath of the battlefield. Her face shone, pale save for her freckles, in the starlight. There wasn't a spot of dirt or blood marring her clothes, not even her bare feet that were planted on the gore-slick street.

I sat up to find every inch of my body aching, but when I glanced at my skin, my armor was intact everywhere except where Daedra had stabbed me. There weren't claw marks or injuries left behind from the nestrae's torture, and I wasn't sure how that could be. I'd *felt* the blood running down my skin.

Nesrelle's grin revealed her perfectly white teeth. "I can still be merciful, you know," she explained, and I realized she must have healed me. Or that the injuries had all been an illusion. Whatever power she'd wielded to spare my life rather than claim a soul for death this year— maybe she had enough to heal me from smaller wounds as well.

When I tried to open my mouth to speak, a sharp burning sensation shot along my right cheek. I clapped my fingers over the spot, finding an upraised, jagged scar rather than a fresh wound.

Nesrelle was still smiling. "But some reminders need to remain. My nestrae marked you with a rune, but not a typical one that connects you to them and their words that draw on your fears. This is one to connect you to *me* and the vows you made. The service you owe me." She stepped closer. "You vowed to take back your throne."

Frowning, I spoke through the pain. "I will." My voice was hoarse, but there was steel in my words, and I was sure Nesrelle could sense that.

"I gave you your curse—and your life—so you would wield the hatred and thirst for revenge you've harbored inside of you." She listed her head. "You claim you grieve for your mother, that you want to make her proud. Don't you want to see justice done?"

I fisted my shaking hands. I closed my eyes, still haunted by the images of all the ways I'd imagined her death. Burning by dragon fire.

Pierced by an arrow. Gutted by a sword. But the painful truth—throat slit into that garish smile—ate me alive inside.

Revenge wouldn't bring my mother back, but maybe it would take those images away. Maybe it would ease the pain, let me breathe and truly live again. Maybe. It was the only way I could honor her.

"Yes," I breathed. *One Forwyn for Mother's life, and then I can build the alliance Kovi and I dreamed of.* Would he hate me for it? Would he understand?

"Then let me show you the one you need to hunt down and slay." Nesrelle extended a hand, but this time, when she clapped it over my arm, there was no pain. Only a vision, like the one my mother's truth-gifted advisor, Vionn, had shared with me during a time that felt like ages ago now.

All Nesrelle gave me was a picture: the face of my mother's killer. A strong jaw with a determined set to it. Full lips in a mouth that looked like it rarely smiled. Dark, deep eyes flecked with swirls of emerald green, swimming with an expression of courage and sadness. There was uncertainty, but not the kind that tormented me. She looked like she knew what she wanted and would never sway in her convictions, not for anyone. Her hair wasn't braided and adorned with ribbons the way most Forwyn women wore it—the way I'd seen her wear it before, on the night of the Autumn Ball…when she'd spared my life in the palace gardens. Now it was loose, the curls as lovely and untamed as she was.

The truth slammed into me, shocking, confusing, infuriating. I opened my eyes to see Nesrelle staring intently at me, watching my reaction. Likely listening to my thoughts.

And even though she knew what I was thinking, I felt compelled to say it aloud. To try to make sense of it and the tangle of emotions growing inside of me.

"The girl who saved my life is the one who killed my mother."

Nesrelle shrugged, as if indifferent. "Lo'laeni Nolanhou is in Inalgoth now, and she is your *amara'rekni*. Kill her."

CHAPTER TEN

Caesiem

As soon as I'd unbound her, Valentra began ranting and raving about our defeat by the Alrenians and our capture.

"I'd rather die than be a prisoner," she fumed, stomping about the small space. Every step echoed dully against stone. "This is humiliating. Inexcusable."

Other than the sounds we made, the silence was as heavy as the earth I was sure was surrounding us. I missed the distant, steady thrum of the sea.

She tried the locked door again and again, all in vain, while I sat in my chair and stared, tracing her movements without truly acknowledging them.

Of course, I'd been a thief and spy long enough to know how to pick locks, but Valentra didn't really know that much about my past. Or even the details of the assignments Revaed had given me when I'd been sent on ahead to Alrenor to gather information. That was confidential, things we'd spoken of in enclosed rooms within the Teramese palace or in messages layered in mysteries and codes while we were apart.

Even though Vander Arros, who had been my fellow spy in Alrenor and one of my few friends in Teramyl, was Valentra's brother, he would have been sworn to secrecy about our mission too. And while I knew her brother well, from our time training extensively as mages together at the palace and our teamwork as spies, Valentra remained an enigma to me. Did she have the warmth of her brother? Could I trust her to be on my side?

Did I even know what side I was on?

It didn't take Valentra long to grow tired of my inaction. "Well?" she demanded, whirling toward me. "Has the great and talented mage of Teramyl run out of ideas? Has Prince Caesiem, Revaed's favorite and heir to our new empire, just *given up*?" Her breaths were ragged, her cheeks ruddy with rage and desperation, and I realized in that moment how much she was counting on me.

I leaned back in my chair, shrugging. There was no urge to fidget. There was no song trapped in my head with a beat that I needed to tap out with my fingertips or foot. Everything in my head was terribly, overwhelmingly silent and still.

"You should address me with respect," I said, but there was no bite to the words. Maybe she wasn't like her brother. He'd never treated me with loathing or disrespect, even if I'd once been a nobody. He didn't seem to begrudge me for the place I'd been given among the imperial family.

Valentra narrowed her eyes, which were still a piercing silver shade, and stalked closer. "Since you're my superior, I'm waiting on your instructions. Sir."

Once more, I shrugged. "You sit down. You shut up. You wait."

Tossing her braid over her shoulder, Valentra scowled at me.

"That's not a plan."

I gritted my teeth, feeling my temper surge. It was almost welcome after the numbness that had started to set in. I didn't know how to process anything right now. The vision about my parents was far too fresh in my mind.

But when I spoke, I kept my voice measured. "Don't pretend you don't have a head on your shoulders, lieutenant. I know there's a reason you hold that rank."

Valentra pursed her lips, duly chastened, and settled into the seat beside me. "Forgive me, prince," she muttered, staring at her boots.

"We wait," I went on after a short pause. "We see what exactly they want with us. We learn more about the place they're holding us inside and how many soldiers are here, watching us. Plans aren't made in mere moments, and definitely not with your emotions." I tossed her a halfhearted grin. "Don't let your anger over being caught dull your senses. After all, I was captured too, so you know it's not lack of skill or training that landed you here."

Valentra sighed loudly, rolling her eyes, but she couldn't fully restrain her smile, making it clear she didn't harbor any true resentment or hostility toward me. "Ah, there it is: the Xalenos arrogance," she said with a laugh.

"Yes," I said, chuckling along with her even if the name *Xalenos* sounded bitter in my ears, like an off-key note spoiling a song. "But you also know it's true," I added, waving my hands in the air as if to remind her of my magic.

"Well, sir, all the plans I ever had to make involved *never* being caught," she huffed, trying to tug the collar of her jacket up higher around her neck, as if she were cold.

Compared to the balmy air aboveground, this space did feel damp and chill. I'd been so caught up in the vision of the past, I'd been convinced the coldness I'd felt had just been from my own feelings of betrayal and shock.

"Which is why you were never the spy," I pointed out.

"Yes, Your Highness. Vander was always better at those sorts of things," she murmured, her eyes growing distant. In that moment, they were warmer than before, her irises a pale shade of gold. She was probably wondering, like me, where her brother was. If he'd succeeded in his mission to retrieve the Alrenian empress. Before the riots had broken out, we'd still had no word from him or the Forwyn soldier, Kovi Ettonou—Elder Ettonou's son.

Quiet settled around us. The images began to rotate through my head again: my mother's frightened face, my father's desperation. Revaed, looking up at his father with far too much humility and respect, agreeing to the decisions that had altered my life forever.

Grief washed over me anew. Everything in me wanted to corner Revaed and demand answers, to see if he would admit to it all. Had he ever cared about me, the orphan he'd chosen and groomed as his heir? I'd always known that as a powerful water mage—and one who had stopped the wild dragon that had tried to destroy Vicidor and kill Revaed, no less—that I was valuable to the Xalenos family.

Had I only ever been a tool to them? A young, impressionable mind to shape and wield however they wished?

Revaed had used me, from the moment he'd taken me in off the streets and fed me with the most luxurious food I'd ever tasted. He'd gained my unwavering affection and loyalty, making me feel more secure and loved than I'd ever had in my entire life, and then he'd forged me into the spy and weapon he needed.

Even, sometimes, a torturer and executioner.

Teramese and Alrenian and Forwyn alike had learned to fear the Xalenos name…and it was, in part, because of *me*. Because I'd let Revaed make me something terrible, fearsome, ruthless.

I squeezed my hand into a fist, trying to distract myself and block out the thoughts. *Can Alrenian visions tell a lie?* I wondered. *Perhaps Meli skewed what I saw somehow, showing me only pieces she wanted me to see, to create the story she wanted me to know. She wants me to doubt, to be weak. She wants me to fail my people. I need to talk to Revaed. He can explain everything. Once I speak to him, I'll know.*

"Was the battle over when they took you?" I blurted out, desperate for even Valentra's morbid tale to turn my thoughts elsewhere.

"Yes, sir. Or near enough," Valentra said solemnly, her eyes turning unfocused, her expression dark. "Most of our forces were dead or dying. A group of Alrenians surrounded me, but didn't even try to go in for the kill. As soon as they disarmed and overpowered me, they bound me and brought me here."

I wanted to ask about Darix, but something stayed my tongue. I wasn't sure I'd be able to conceal my revulsion toward the man, or the fact that I wouldn't miss him if he were dead. But I didn't want to give Valentra any reason to suspect that Teramese officers like Darix disrespected and taunted me all the time. She was one of the few who'd never troubled me, mostly keeping to herself.

Valentra leaned back in her seat, earning a loud creak of protest from the chair. "What was it like, Your Highness?" she asked. "Being a spy, so far from home? Coming to this foreign land all alone?" She sounded genuinely curious.

I leaned back, trying to find words to explain all the emotions, the ways in which I'd softened toward the Forwyn and their plight. I'd entered Alrenor self-assured, feeling justified in my mission to pave the way for an army invasion. In all the stories Revaed had told me of the once-vast empire, he'd concentrated on the cruelty and arrogance of the Alrenians and the fact that they would never help us. We'd known little of the new Forwyn leadership, other than the fact that they had refused our requests for help. I'd assumed that had meant that maybe the Forwyn, despite the generations of oppression they'd faced, had become similarly cruel, perhaps drunk on their new power.

"Coming to Alrenor was...lonely," I said at last. "I had your brother, but...we couldn't be seen together much. We didn't want to draw suspicion and make others wonder what two Teramese were doing in the Alrenian capital together, not when we had little business with Alrenor and their government limited the number of Teramese who could enter their ports."

My mouth twitched, remembering how angry that law had made me. It still burned my chest to think of those arrogant Elders, refusing to accept our starving, dying refugees. I could understand quarantining to avoid permitting a Teramese plague to enter Alrenor—although we hadn't had any major outbreaks since I had been a child—but to turn away the homeless and hungry after wild dragon attacks, when Alrenor had plenty of room and resources for Teramese willing to make their way in a new land *honestly*? It seemed heartless. And so...Vander and I had chosen illegal methods, smuggling ourselves into the harbor, and then immersing ourselves in the underbelly of the capital. He'd worked with thieves and criminals, while I'd stumbled upon well-meaning vigilantes.

"Have you ever had to pretend to make friends and allies, but all along you were lying to them?" I asked Valentra. "Deceiving them to share information with you until you could betray them?"

Valentra glanced away, a frown etched across her brow. She shook her head, as if at a loss for words.

"It was eye-opening though too," I added, gaining courage. Images of the Broken Crown danced through my head: leading the whole pub in merry songs, even if the Forwyn crowd didn't know the Teramese words, playing music that drowned out the tangled thoughts in my brain, and downing drinks with Noa'him after he'd closed up for the night and we both enjoyed the quiet after a busy evening. And then there was Lo, showing the deep love she carried for her people in action as she served the hungry and poor. Her focus as she sparred or trained with her sisters.

The Forwyn were devoted to their religion, powerful in their magic, and tightly knit within their communities. There had been corruption and selfishness among the Court of Elders, just as I'd expected to find, but among the people…there had been beauty. Love. Kindness.

I'd never seen anything like it. The Teramese were all too hungry and afraid to reach out to one another, too terrified of the Xalenoses, the floods, the plague, and the wild dragons to do much more than keep their heads down and work to survive.

"Eye-opening how?" Valentra prompted, pulling me from my memories.

"There's a reason Revaed and I chose to ally with the Forwyn," I said, and proceeded to explain my experiences living among them. Someone else needed to see them as I saw them—as I thought Revaed viewed them. Not as people to be conquered in order to grasp at our own survival, but as people who deserved respect and justice. To live in peace alongside the Teramese in the new world Revaed was building.

Valentra listened quietly, her forehead still furrowed, as if in concentration. When I finished, she finally turned to me, her eyes alight with sadness. "Before we were dispatched to stop the Alrenian riots near the harbor, I heard there was…an issue with the Forwyn. I think the alliance was broken," she said softly. "Other soldiers were talking."

Ice filled my veins. "How?" I asked, imagining Lo as I'd left her back in my room at the palace. Would Revaed deem her an enemy and imprison her? Execute her? My heart thrummed wildly in my throat. "Who broke the alliance? What is Revaed going to do?"

Valentra's mouth was a firm line. "The Forwyn. It was all planned by your betrothed, I believe." She shook her head. "But I don't know what Revaed meant to do in retaliation. We had to leave…"

Her voice trailed off as approaching footsteps sounded outside our door. The lock slid free right before the metal door swung inward. Standing in the entryway, still clothed in her battle leathers with a sword at her hip, Meli surveyed me a quiet moment. In the dim light, the gold sheen to her dark skin was more subtle, the gold flecks in her brown eyes less vibrant. But I knew they were there, marking her as Alrenian as well as Forwyn.

Following my lead, Valentra remained still in her seat, but I could practically feel the malice radiating off her. She only awaited my cue to attack, even if it was with nothing but her fists.

Meli didn't bother to tear her gaze from my own. She studied me as if she could read my thoughts, which, with her truth gift, might haven't been far from reality. I'd heard enough about the Alrenian gift to find it mysterious and powerful, something I refused to underestimate.

"Come," she said. "Let's talk."

CHAPTER ELEVEN

Lo

I opened my eyes to a dark, damp cell. Lying on a scratchy cot, I blinked at flickering torchlight filtering through the bars set in the door, giving me a glimpse of the vague outline of a guard posted in the passage outside. When I shifted, the cot creaked and groaned beneath me, as if threatening to give out at any moment.

The guard turned at the sound, barking out a cruel laugh. "Ah, our prisoner of honor is awake," he taunted.

My head pounded as I sat up, nausea swiftly chasing the pain. I lifted my hand to the braided gold ribbons around my throat, finding them missing. My heart lurched with pain—at some point in the fighting I must have lost them.

Instead, my fingers slid along the leather cord holding Caesiem's pendant. Tucked under my tunic, I'd almost forgotten it was there. Now, the cool feel of the stone was strangely comforting, even if I wasn't sure why Caesiem had given it to me. There was nothing I could do with the power it helped wield.

"Summon the emperor!" the guard called out to an unseen companion. His words bounced off the stone surrounding us.

I repressed a groan and squeezed my eyes shut. Revaed was alive, and the Teramese had taken me captive. And here I was, shut away in the palace dungeons.

Did that mean the Teramese had won the battle for Aerekni Academy? Was my father dead, or a captive too, awaiting execution? And what about my sisters?

I squeezed my hands into fists, shoving aside my growing panic. Instead, I tried to focus my thoughts past the throbbing pain in my head, to formulate some sort of plan. If I wasn't dead yet, maybe Revaed wanted something from me. Maybe I could still find a way to escape and break out any other Forwyn survivors from these cells.

It wasn't long before footsteps reverberated down the corridor and the guard unlocked my cell door, allowing Revaed and the healer who'd nursed me before, after Renni had nearly killed me, to stride in.

"Tend her," Revaed ordered, and the woman settled onto the cot beside me, opening a satchel. She removed a vial, popping out its cork and pressing it to my mouth.

I remembered the strong, foul liquid from before, but I tried to choke it down obediently. This time, my nausea won out and my stomach rebelled. Pulling back, I had just enough time to turn my head before emptying my stomach's contents onto the slimy floor.

Unleashing a stream of curses, Revaed danced back, but some of my sickness splattered onto his perfectly polished boots. I couldn't help myself—despite the pain, as I sat up and wiped my mouth with the back of my sleeve, I grinned. *Serves you right,* I thought.

Voice gruff and violet eyes hard, Revaed called to his guards. One came scurrying in with a bucket and mop, hastily cleaning up the mess.

"Try again," the healer commanded me gently, once again pressing the vial to my lips.

This time, I swallowed the contents successfully.

"Out," Revaed barked.

The guard didn't need further prompting, taking the cleaning equipment with him, but the healer tossed him a worried frown. "But, Your Majesty, I'm not—"

"That's enough for now. Go."

Without another word, she leapt to her feet and retreated from my cell.

I was left alone with Revaed, who towered over me with an inscrutable expression. With his typical flawless appearance, every dark hair in order and his uniform wrinkle-free and fresh, I wouldn't have ever guessed he'd just come through a brutal battle. He looked like he'd spent his days lounging on a throne eating sweets, not murdering my people.

My rage was almost blinding, but I tamped it down. "What more do you want from me?" I demanded, before Revaed could speak.

He seemed distracted, his eyes dropping to my collarbone. I lifted my hand to find Caesiem's pendant had fallen free when I'd leaned over the cot, and now it hung outside my tunic.

"He gave that to you, didn't he?" Revaed murmured, a frown darting across his brow and then vanishing. He lifted his piercing gaze to meet mine.

I clenched the cool stone in a fist, as if it could do anything for me, and nodded. My head throbbed with the movement.

"You've betrayed our alliance at every turn," Revaed went on, "but that doesn't mean you can't still be useful. You don't have to die—and neither do your co-conspirators. We don't need to make your betrayal public knowledge. You can convince your people that the Forwyn at the Aerekni Academy plotted against you, infiltrating the palace with one of their own and trying to sabotage our alliance and your engagement to Caesiem. Or you can admit to everything and express your regrets and desire to change."

"*Boeri*," I spat. "I'll never believe anything you say. You'll tell me to renounce my own people, to marry into your family, and then you'll slaughter the Forwyn anyway."

"They're not dead," Revaed cut in, his tone measured. "The palace servants. Your sisters you foolishly led to the academy." He paused. "Your father."

The breath left my lungs. "I don't believe you," I repeated, even as the wild hope growing in my heart belied my declaration.

"You still have a chance to save them if you cooperate with us. We'll give you time to recover. We'll draw up a speech for you. You and Caesiem will take your vows and we'll put this whole mess behind us. We'll be a united front against any Alrenians who wish to oppose us."

I scoffed. "You want me as your ally, so you put me in a prison?"

Revaed took a step closer, his eyes dark. "If you don't cooperate, our Forwyn prisoners will be executed in lieu of your speech for peace." He paused. "If you agree to not cause trouble, I'll permit you to return to the palace rooms."

I closed my eyes, trying to think through the haze in my brain. Clutching the pendant, my memory flitted back to the last moment I'd seen the man who'd given it to me—his worried eyes. The warmth of his lips as he pressed a kiss to my forehead. Did he know Revaed was holding me in a prison cell? "Fine," I snapped. "So where is Caesiem?" Surely, if he knew what was happening, he'd already have demanded my release.

Right? Doubt creeped in, but I shoved it aside. Out of all the things I wasn't sure I could trust Caesiem about, his loyalty to me was not one of them.

Revaed glanced away.

"He doesn't know I'm here," I breathed. "What would he do, Revaed, if he knew what you've done? What lies are you spinning to him now?"

Revaed ignored me, his bright gaze boring into me. "You care about many people, and that means you have much to lose," he said, his voice low and heavy with a threat. "But I care about few things in this life, which means that now, I stand only to gain. If it comes down to it, I won't hesitate to kill you and everyone you care about. Caesiem need never know if your death looks like an accident.

"It's simple, really: choose peace, choose survival…or die. You could live a happy life with Caesiem. You could bring safety to your people. Or you can watch them all die, because the Forwyn's freedom will not stand in the way of my people's survival."

CHAPTER TWELVE

Emperor Revaed Xalenos

Blood pooled in the streets, splattering on my boots with every step I took. It ran everywhere, defiling everything and adding its own coppery stench to the scents of brine and death.

It made me irritable—even more irritable than I already was.

With careful steps, I trod around the bodies, my gaze lingering without really meaning to on each Teramese face. Dead eyes stared back at me, empty and accusing. It was just another moment in which my failures piled up before me, reminding me of how much farther I still had to go before I could truly feel like I was achieving something for Teramyl. As long as my soldiers were rummaging through bodies, as long as I was staining my clothes in my own people's blood, I wouldn't rest.

I didn't want to look too closely and see the face I was searching for, and yet I couldn't look away. The need to know was greater than anything else.

But I refused to give up hope. I was certain I'd know if I was wrong, and Caesiem really had fallen here. I would be able to sense it if he was gone. There would be some sort of…fatherly intuition about it, making me certain.

Wouldn't there?

Once again, I lifted my gaze to take in the work my soldiers were completing. Men and women alike were sorting bodies, throwing the Alrenian corpses into the hole Darix had created during the fight, a hole he could seal up later with his magic. The earth really would swallow our enemies, devouring every trace of them until even the memory of them had faded. The Teramese bodies were loaded onto carts so they could be borne toward the sea. Usually, we preferred to send our dead off into the Terebrys, but without the ocean nearby, the Great Sea that eventually mingled with our revered waters would have to do instead.

The gods and goddesses would tend to their souls, all the same. Or that's what our priest would say.

Shaking away the morbid thoughts, I turned to General Darix. With far too many high-ranking soldiers dead and both Caesiem and Lieutenant Valentra Arros missing, I'd made some swift promotions among my ranks. And Darix was one of the few powerful mages I had with me in Inalgoth.

"Well?" I demanded. "You said your men and women have been searching for hours. What have you found?"

"Nothing, Your Majesty. No signs of the Alrenians who retreated, no clue as to where they've gone, and no bodies matching the prince's or lieutenant's descriptions." Darix dipped his head respectfully, but unease churned in my gut. There were too many vipers in my army, and I wasn't sure who I could trust to see this job through. Now that I had finished my business with Lo, I was determined not to leave these streets until we'd turned over each body, scoured through each street, and peered into each hidden, dingy hole in the capital within which the Alrenians could have retreated.

I'd burn down every building on this street if it meant I'd find him. Order Darix to split open the earth and consume every last Alrenian who had survived this mess.

Because if Caesiem wasn't alive…

I really did stand to lose almost nothing. There would be little left for me to care about. No more family. No more…

Scowling, I stepped over another body, for once not caring when grime and gore slicked my boots. They were already hopelessly soiled. Fury overtook every other feeling, blocking out my disgust as I ground my heel into an Alrenian corpse's hand, popping tissue and bones.

Narrowing my eyes, I scanned every building on either side of the street—most were businesses, but a few looked like homes.

"Have you searched the buildings yet?"

"We've started, but—"

"Order everyone to evacuate, now. Line them up in the street."

Darix's brow furrowed, a question darting across his face. He knew better than to voice it, though, and it vanished as swiftly as it had appeared. With a dip of his head, he didn't even waste breath on words before he marched toward his soldiers.

"Empty every last building on this street," he demanded. "Get the people out. Line up every single civilian for us to see. Emperor's orders!"

Soldiers straightened from the corpses and marched forward, wasting no time in dividing their efforts and pounding on doors. Any citizen who resisted—Alrenian or Forwyn—was dragged from within without ceremony. Young and old, man and woman, were brought out in a long row. Inevitably, their gazes snagged on me. I tried to ignore the weight of their eyes, all full of fear or hatred.

Instead, I leaned into the desperation and anger burning inside, promising to consume everything else. This work was always tedious—

doling out punishments and threats, watching the lifeblood drain from a body. It was disgusting.

Father had always relished it, finding my aversion yet another reason to hurl his favorite insult at me: *defective*. It made me wonder, sometimes, if he'd considered pulling one of his countless bastards out of obscurity and naming him or her heir instead.

But to serve my people, to find Caesiem…I could shove aside any disgust at the gruesome, filthy tasks that fell on my shoulders.

It wasn't cruelty for the sake of cruelty. It was merely business. Necessity. Survival.

Drawing myself up, I marched up and down the line of citizens, taking careful steps to avoid slipping in the puddles of blood staining the cobblestones. "We are searching for Prince Caesiem Xalenos, as well as the Alrenian rabble who instigated the fighting and senseless slaughter yesterday," I announced, keeping each word crisp and clear. My voice echoed off the walls, steady and calm—the antithesis of everything I was on the inside. "Anyone who has information about the Alrenian criminals or the prince's whereabouts will be handsomely rewarded."

I paused, taking an instant to look some of the citizens in the eyes. I wanted them to see the threat in my gaze when I spoke. I wanted them to know fear, the way I knew it in that instant.

You would know if Caes was dead, I tried to reassure myself, for the hundredth time. *He's more than capable of keeping himself alive.*

"As residents of this street, within sight of some of the most brutal of last night's fighting, you are all considered witnesses. And as witnesses, every single one of you should have something to report. Step forward and speak up, and you live. Stay silent, and you are accomplices of the murderers who ran rampant in our streets last night, and you will die. You have one minute to make your choice."

Rustling. Murmurs. Fear. Rage. I tuned it all out, turning my back to them. Between two buildings, I caught a glimpse of the sea, pure and glistening beneath a cloudless afternoon sky. Each wave lapped gently against the shore, a far cry from the raging beast it had been only hours ago.

I'll find you, Caesiem, I vowed. *We'll survive this.*

I didn't bother to turn as my soldiers carried out my threat for me. Steel sang as swords were unsheathed. Groans and shrieks of pain tore through the air. Bodies thudded to the cobblestones.

I closed my eyes, imagining how long it would take to scrub the streets clean of all the blood. How long it would take when I bathed tonight, scouring the grime and gore off my skin, to feel clean again. But for now, I closed off all other emotions, leaning into the numbness that was taking over.

It's just survival, I thought.

I'd kill every last citizen in this city, if it led me to Caesiem.

CHAPTER THIRTEEN

Caesiem

Nine Years Ago

I was only ten years old when the dragon attacked Vicidor. It came with a roar that seemed to rend the whole world in two, sending fear slamming into me like I'd never experienced before. Immediately, I stopped rummaging through the kitchen cupboards of a condemned home, abandoning a sack of rice—worth more than gold in the eyes of my fellow orphans and me those days—and darted for the nearest boarded window.

My heart pulsed somewhere inside my throat as I peered between a gap in the boards and scanned the grey skies. A form drifted into view, its massive wings and swishing tail instantly giving it away for what it was. In the dim light, its scales were a dull red, the same color painted on the door of this plague home, the color of danger.

The color of the plume of fire it blasted into a row of homes a few blocks down from me, the buildings instantly erupting in a ruthless inferno. Crackling, breaking, roaring—it was as furious as a storm coming in off the ocean, and just as relentless.

Swallowing back my panic, I sprinted for the door. *Get back home,* I thought, my mind whirling. I'd faced death countless times in my decade of life, but this was a new danger, something we'd never expected. Elyxia and Jarex, my fellow orphan and the closest things to caretakers I had, had made vague plans with us before, though we'd never really expected something like this to happen. Dragons were rare, and they didn't usually venture this far south, so close to the damp of the ocean and the thickest of the Teramese jungles.

But here we were, and no amount of damp and rain and ocean brine in the air had stopped that dragon fire from scorching entire buildings in moments. The image of those breaking, flaming buildings seemed seared to my vision, each blink failing to clear away the flash of red and orange that smeared across the world, even now.

The dragon would incinerate my home, my sanctuary, just as easily as those others.

No, not home, you idiot, I thought, pushing my steps toward the jungle on the outskirts of the city. Maelvoc, a rainforest filled with streams and ancient trees dripping with eternal moisture. Its steamy embrace might be enough to keep the flames from burning as readily. I could find shelter near a stream and wait out the attack, let the flames in the city die down.

My chest went hollow when I wondered about my fellow orphans. Where were they? Would they form the same plan? Would they try to find each other? We all knew, deep down, that it was each and every one of us for ourselves. The unforgiving world we knew forced us to be just as unforgiving, to always place our own survival first. Everything else came afterward. It had to be that way.

Everything was chaos in the streets. Men and women and children alike screamed and ran, calling out to one another, searching for safety in a world that had none. They were lost, eyes glazed with terror. I ducked and dodged the mass of bodies, avoiding the miserable fates of others who weren't so quick and were trampled beneath a relentless stampede.

The roar of flames grew ever closer, devouring. Smoke billowed through the air, swirling toward us like a living beast as threatening as the fire chasing it. Ash fell from the sky, drifting on the breeze and coating everything in a layer of dust.

Overhead, the thunder of the dragon's wings beat out like a war drum, calling for destruction and death. The only warning before the creature dipped and sent another plume of fire toward its victims—or dived and seized hapless citizens in its claws. Over and over, the dragon slammed into buildings and plowed down its prey before they could escape. For such a huge animal, I was shocked by how fast it was.

Soon, despite my wild pace, despite the fact that I was nearing the outer district of Vicidor, the dragon was only a few streets away. There seemed no method to its attacks, as if it took delight in watching every street and every building burn and crumble. As if it hoped to taste flesh from people in every portion of the city. As if its mission wasn't only to feed, but to lay waste to the entire capital.

Sweat drenched my back when I turned away, trying to focus on my destination and not on the monster closing in on me. I pushed every ounce of my energy into pumping my legs faster, sucking down air as my burning lungs protested. *Faster, faster.*

Ahead, a small crowd fleeing together caught my eye. The dark imperial uniforms of a guard unit stood out in the sea of dull outfits we citizens wore. And right in the middle of this cluster of guards was a man dressed in the finest clothes I'd ever seen. His jacket of reds and golds blazed like a beacon in the crowd, as bright as the flames chasing us. I wondered if it would work similarly to a target, drawing the eye of the dragon that pursued us.

He didn't appear old enough to be the High Imperator himself, whom I knew was at least the age I assumed my own parents would have been, but he clearly was a member of the imperial family. I wasn't one to heed the gossip I overheard on the streets, not unless it pertained to an abandoned plague home I could ransack, a business throwing out food I could scavenge, or a wealthy target I could steal from. I didn't know how many members of the family there were and I didn't care—not until this moment. Now, I finally had cause to wonder.

Maybe it was the wide eyes of the fearful guards as they glanced over their shoulder at the dragon and the fire licking through the city. Maybe it was the man they were ushering along himself, who looked surprisingly calm despite fleeing from a dragon attack. Or—most likely—it was the compassionate expression on his face as he surveyed the chaos surrounding him, his people shrieking and racing for cover.

"Follow us!" he shouted. "To the forest! To cover!"

Not everyone heard him over the wingbeats of the dragon and its vicious roar. Or their own screams. But some did, hope lighting their faces as they steered their loved ones toward the bodyguards. Some scorned the citizens, fiercely blocking them back so they couldn't press in too close to the imperial man they guarded.

But the man didn't seem afraid, and he didn't let his guards keep the citizens away. "Let them come!" he ordered. "Protect them as you protect me!"

He *cared*.

All this time, I'd never believed the imperial family gave a damn about us. I lived in a world where men and women spat in my face if I begged, or if they even suspected I might be trying to steal from them. Few wanted to spare coin or try to be generous to any of us starving orphans—there were too many of us, and the truth was, most people were starving. There wasn't room for compassion in our world.

When Vicidor wouldn't offer me a scrap of comfort or help to survive, I claimed it myself. I wasn't used to seeing generosity or concern on someone's face like this.

Another blast of flames erupted one street over, and the dragon unleashed a growl that shuddered the very air around me. Tearing myself from my thoughts, I dared to slow my steps just enough to peer at the approaching beast. My heart seemed to double its pace, my pulse hammering so hard against my temples I could feel a headache threatening.

It was too late. The dragon was here. There was nothing…

Something inside my chest stirred, like the echo of a memory I'd blocked out. Adrenaline coursed through my veins and panic threatened to pull me under, but that *something* grounded me, calming my pounding heart. Steadying my heaving lungs.

The scent of the ocean washed over me, a fresh breeze tugging at a wayward curl where my hair had grown long and unruly. I'd always found the briny smell of the Terebrys to have a strange effect on me— simultaneously calming and exciting, filling me with the same thrill I felt when I played or sang songs or the same comfort I felt in our ramshackle home.

Years later, I'd wonder how I'd never realized there was more to my connection and the strange occurrences that happened to me around water than just coincidence. But back then, it was easy to brush aside the way the ocean seemed to rush to me whenever I went for a swim as a trick of the eyes. I didn't know my fellow orphans didn't experience the same thrill I did during a rainstorm, when the drops would bead along my skin and make me feel invincible. I didn't know the way the stream in the forest practically churned in a torrent into my bucket when I went to collect our water wasn't natural—that I was, without intentionally practicing the skill, calling the element to me.

Perhaps a part of me had even repressed my magic by sheer force of will, scoffing at the idea of being a mage. *Could you imagine me, living in luxury in the palace like the other mages?* I'd once scoffed to Elyxia and Jarex. Deep down, the idea of a full belly and security was a tempting daydream. But the thought of being forced to serve an imperial family that had, at least in my perception, never cared for me? I preferred to fight for my own survival on the streets, to care for and serve myself.

I didn't know how obviously powerful my magic had been as an infant. I didn't know my parents had fled to save me from the imperial family. In that moment, all I knew was the call of the ocean, humming through my veins in a way it never had—or I'd never allowed it to—before.

The dragon dove for our street, its roar slamming into me like a physical force. Reacting on nothing but instinct, I leapt before the imperial man and his entourage. Citizens screamed and threw themselves to the ground in a hopeless attempt at dodging the impending flames. Behind me, the guards shouted to one another, shooting arrows that did nothing but enrage the beast.

"Lilaos, spare us!" a woman screamed, a desperate cry to the goddess of protection.

Fire and smoke blasted in our direction, the relentless heat singeing hair long before the tongues of flame could lick at us. I lifted trembling hands, and mentally, I tugged. My mind called to the ocean, to that element that had spent my whole life calling out to me. Power tingled up my spine just as a waterfall surged through the air and crashed into the approaching inferno.

There was a blast of light—glistening silver water meeting furious orange fire—and then a hiss loud enough almost to rival the dragon's earlier roars. Mist sprayed across my face, layering everything with blessedly cool water to temper the heat still lingering from the extinguished flame. Smoke and steam billowed and mingled in a strange dance, blocking my view of the dragon.

But it was clear from the sudden darkness and the cooling air that the fire was gone.

Impossible. It seemed my brain was finally catching up to whatever instinct had took over me, leaving me scrambling to understand what I'd just done.

Lowering my hands, I stared, dumbfounded. As the smoke cleared, even the dragon looked at a loss, its head tilted so one large red eye could stare at me.

The trained guards rallied faster than I could, shouting to one another to stop the threat before the dragon could attack again. Arrows flew over my head, one so close I could feel it dislodge the air near my ear, whirring like an angry insect toward its prey.

One, ten, twenty—a whole volley rained toward the beast. Most of the arrows bounced harmlessly off the dragon's scales, but a handful lodged in its eyes.

Before I could fully recover from my shock, the beast was toppling before my eyes, crashing in a cloud of dust. Buildings rattled with its fall, shaking the ground and nearly knocking me off my feet.

I still couldn't turn, my gaze locked on the dead beast stretched out before me. There was a strange ache in my chest—as if in that moment, before my world was turned irrevocably on its head, I had already realized life would never be the same. That I would never again see my fellow orphans, or my home, or the tiny sliver of secluded beach I'd discovered and frequented, a place that had felt like a secret haven set aside just for me.

It was a hard life, but it was familiar, and the sensation of change creeping upon me overwhelmed me with a feeling of loss.

Voices murmured, but I only caught snatches of their conversation.

Never seen a mage that powerful...

Who is he?

How...

Not enough water mages...

Why...

A hand clapped on my shoulder, jolting me from my thoughts. I glanced back to see the imperial man gazing down, the same compassionate look he'd given the other citizens now trained on me. Except this time, his violet eyes were full of something else too—wonder.

"You saved my life," he murmured. "You saved all of our lives."

I blinked, unsure what to say.

Confusion crinkled his brow. "Who are you? Why aren't you studying with the other mages in the palace?"

"Caesiem," I said, my voice scratchy from disuse. I'd been rummaging through homes for hours on my own, without anyone else to talk to. Not that I'd minded. "I…" My words trailed off, and I shrugged. "I'm an orphan. I didn't know I was a mage."

The start of a smile twitched the young man's lips. "Well, Caesiem, I'm Prince Revaed Xalenos, and I think a water mage of your skill should be living in the palace, where he can train to help save even more lives, like you just did. What do you say?"

Present

Meli led me through a cramped stone hallway, the scents of earth and dampness permeating the air. I wanted to demand answers, but my mind was too abuzz with memories and confusion. As much as I wanted to trust Revaed and everything I thought I'd known, I couldn't deny the power of Meli's truth gift.

And that left me reeling. I needed answers, needed to know what she had to say. Sheer curiosity kept me calm, willing to be led wherever she went to hear whatever she wanted to discuss.

My shoulder ached with every step, but I'd expected a sharper pain. Whatever painkiller I'd been given when I was lost in Meli's vision must have been powerful.

At first, there was nothing but the cramped, dim tunnel, its stone walls lined with spluttering torches. And then I heard the first voices drifting toward us. The tunnel widened and turned, bringing us to an open space where doorways filled either side. Most of the doors were open, and as we passed, I caught glimpses of storage rooms, armories, and training rooms.

Men and women milled about, chatting together, sparring, or watching others line up to spar. Many were Alrenian, but I noticed a few Forwyn among them. Any who had been with Meli must have already bathed and changed out of their leathers. She alone remained clothed in her battle garb—as if she'd been too busy to change.

But as soon as I stepped into view, the easy conversation and movement died. Whispers fluttered through the air, while expressions turned rigid. No one bothered to conceal their hatred.

One of the Forwyn girls dropped the stick she was training with, her eyes sharpening as her gaze caught mine. Her curls were pulled back into a frizzy bun, while her freckles stood out on a face I once would have described as innocent-looking. But now? Now she looked nearly feral with rage.

A'elli, one of my fellow vigilantes from Renni's group.

"You," she spat, already stalking from the room. "You vile, conniving, lying, murderous lowlife. You betrayed us all. You pretended to help Renni and now he's *dead*!" In mere moments, she was in my face, her words rising nearly to a scream. "You disgusting, worthless traitor!"

She threw a punch, wild and sloppy in her fury. I blocked it effortlessly, leaving her glaring at me, chest heaving.

"Stop," Meli ordered, her tone calm yet authoritative. She didn't move from my side, trusting her words to hold enough power that she wouldn't need to physically interfere.

"Why did you bring him here?" A'elli demanded, her voice trembling with emotion. "Why didn't you *kill* him?"

A'elli stepped back, but I didn't trust she wouldn't try to attack me again. I studied her warily.

"Do you trust my gift?" Meli demanded.

Slowly, A'elli tore her gaze from me and glanced at the truth-gifted woman at my side. "Yes," she said slowly.

"Then trust my judgement," Meli continued. "I've seen truths about this young man, and I don't think killing him is in our best interest." A slow smile spread across her lips. "At least, not yet."

Sighing and setting her hands on her hips, A'elli stepped back. She'd always been the quietest in our vigilante group, the most soft-spoken, but now all her fire had risen to the surface. Could I blame her for hating me?

"Fine," A'elli said at last, "but if he does *anything*, he's mine."

Again, that small smile darted across Meli's lips. "Deal."

Without another word, she gestured to me and led me onward, past more doors, more staring eyes, more angry faces. I was stunned by the number of people living underground and the sheer size of this place.

"Take it in," Meli said, slowing her steps to walk at my side and gesture around us. "This is, I trust, only a glimpse of Alrenor's future, where Alrenians and Forwyn live together in peace." She glanced at me out of the corner of her eye. "*Without* Teramese oppression."

My smile was wry. "I assume the only reason you'd let me see this underground hideout of yours is because you're planning to kill me. So then why bother showing me that vision and dragging me all the way down here?"

Meli's laughter was light as she nodded to an older Alrenian man walking in the other direction, his eyes growing wary when they fell on me.

"No, you're not going to die. But showing you these tunnels won't do you much good, if you don't know how to find their entrances. Besides, I think you'll have a strong motive *not* to work against us."

I scowled. "Who are you?"

"I told you. My name is Meli, and I am truth-gifted. Once, I served as an advisor to Empress Karye, curse her name, until she realized that having an advisor who actually shared the truth about how the Life-Giver viewed her treatment of the Forwyn wasn't to her liking. I fled to Hemlaen and served in a sanctuary. And now…now I am here, in the capital, where I've been for two years, using my gift to help both Forwyn and Alrenians prepare for a better future. A peaceful, unified one, without slaves and killing. It's been an exercise in patience, finding recruits, stockpiling weapons and leathers, training, spying, dodging death…"

I quirked an eyebrow as we rounded a bend in the tunnel and approached a flight of stone steps. "You didn't try working with the Council of Elders?"

Meli snorted. "Those arrogant fools? They would have gladly murdered me and the rest of us with Alrenian blood, along with any Forwyn who worked with us. The peace they gave us was a farce. My rebels and me? We've always dreamed of something better."

Though her method of fighting for peace was different, her speech reminded me of what Lo and her sisters believed in. Despite myself, I was intrigued. "Do you think peace is possible?" I asked.

"I think, if more Alrenians and Forwyn accepted the truth about their gods, there could be peace. Or something as close to peace as we mortals can ever attain."

The steps seemed to rise endlessly, until the air's temperature increased, and I detected the rhythm of waves crashing somewhere outside. We stopped before a single metal door. Meli withdrew a key from her pocket and inserted it into the lock before shoving, hard. The door scraped against stone before ushering in a welcome breath of fresh air laced with the tang of the sea.

I inhaled greedily as sunlight pierced through the opening and the sound of gently lapping waves greeted us.

Blinking against the daylight, I followed Meli out to find we were standing on a small rocky outcropping overlooking the Great Sea. It foamed and sparkled beneath a cloudless sky. Based on the sun's height, I guessed it was at least midday by now.

I sucked in a breath. How long had I been out? Was Revaed looking for me?

Revaed.

A sharp pang stabbed my chest, but I wasn't exactly sure what emotion was causing the sensation. Anger? Sorrow? Betrayal? Confusion?

Swiping my hand through the unruly waves of my hair, brushed loose by the breeze, I scanned Meli. She stared out over the water, her eyes distant, searching. Was she drawing on her truth gift, even now?

"Again, A'elli had a point," I said, determined to cut to the chase. What did Meli want with me? "Why heal me?" I nodded out at the water. "Why bring me here, and give away where one of your entrances is?"

"Well," Meli said with a hint of amusement, "for one, this is only an exit. It won't serve you well to return here. And for another, as I already told you, you won't want to betray me."

Meli's gold-flecked eyes were sharp as she scanned my face, as if searching for something. Or learning more truths about me. I shifted uncomfortably on my feet.

"What do you want?" I pressed.

Meli's expression remained hard. "I want freedom for my people. I want to end the suffering and the hate. I want to see Alrenor actually united."

I shrugged. "I'll admit I've put my people first, but I'm not against any of that. I don't want your people to suffer any more than I want mine to—"

"And yet, all you've brought is more suffering." Meli's eyes glinted with suppressed rage.

Guilt simmered somewhere within me, but I stuffed it down,

refusing to let her see.

"I know you've walked in dark places, false prince, and I know how living in a harsh world can make one harsh and selfish."

My tone turned dark. "You fight and kill for your people's benefit, the same as me. I don't see how we are all that different."

Meli lifted her chin. "*You* brought war to us."

For a long moment, silence reigned between us, fraught with tension. I wanted to ignore the guilt raging inside me, but it was persistent. I kept thinking of Lo's face when I'd betrayed her, kept remembering her admission that she couldn't forgive me.

Of course she couldn't. I wasn't even sure if I could forgive myself, but I also didn't see any other way to stop the endless nightmares haunting my people. Images of their hopeless eyes turning to me for help plagued me relentlessly, day and night, forever reminding me of the cost of failure. I thought of other orphans like me, growing up in even worse circumstances than mine had been.

Sucking in a breath, I stared out at the water, letting the rhythm of the waves soothe me. "True, but with the conflict between Alrenians and Forwyn, war would have come to Alrenor all the same."

When I turned to meet her gaze, Meli was glowering at me. "Ah, so that excuses what you did."

I pursed my lips and glanced away. "Again, what do you want? You brought me here for more than just insults, I assume."

Without a beat of hesitation, Meli said, "I want you to join us. To work *against* your emperor."

I scoffed. "You're mad."

Her eyes darted to mine, not a hint of frustration in her expression. "You want to continue to be his pawn? His tool? Can't you see now that all along, the imperial family planned to pluck you from your parents, one way or another, and train you to be their personal weapon?"

Bitterness made my mouth taste sour, but I swallowed both the emotion and the sensation down. "Revaed is my guardian, and the only caretaker I've known who's given me love and protection and a future. A true home. All he's had me do is train in my magic and hone skills that allow me to help my people and be a good ruler someday."

"He's trained you to be his living nightmare, the faithful dog to do his dirty work."

I swallowed thickly. "He loves me. He's like my father. He's my only family."

Meli's smile was knowing and victorious, and it infuriated me. "But you have doubts. Questions."

"Thanks to you," I spat. "I don't know much about the truth gift. Maybe you only showed me specific visions to give me whatever truth you wanted me to believe."

"No." Meli shrugged. "I cannot lie. This gift forbids that."

I reached for my pendant, remembering as my fingers met bare skin that I no longer had it. Lo did. Once again, I thought of her anger, her hurt, and it made me ache.

"Let me put it to you this way, prince: You can agree to gather information from your precious guardian and his soldiers, which in turn will help you understand the truth yourself. Or you and your soldier can be executed. Something about your love of survival tells me you'll pick the former choice."

I scowled at her. A coward's choice.

Or was it?

The truth was what I wanted, wasn't it?

I squeezed my eyes shut. Besides, I could feed partial truths and lies to this underground group of Alrenians and Forwyn. I didn't have to betray Revaed, not unless everything Meli said really was true. Not unless I had no other choice.

"You can't lie to me," Meli cut in, as if reading my thoughts. "Just as the truth-gifted can't lie, no one else around us can lie and expect to get away with it."

"How nice it must be to know everything."

She smiled softly. "Not everything. Just enough to be a blessing and a curse."

"So is your plan to kill me right here if I don't agree to help you?"

"I think you'll agree." Meli withdrew something from her pocket. For an instant, I merely blinked in confusion as it glittered gold in the sunlight. And then, comprehension rushed over me, along with dread as crushing as a tidal wave.

Lo's gold ribbons.

My voice came out raw, trembling with barely suppressed fury. "What did you do to her?"

"I've done nothing. One of my men found these in the street and recognized them from when Miss Nolanhou was presented as your betrothed at your coronation. He also brought news: your dear Revaed discovered Miss Nolanhou has betrayed your alliance."

She held the ribbons out to me. Heart pounding in my temples, I accepted the offering numbly, my eyes scanning the frayed bits and the freshly broken string that had once helped tie the braided ribbons around her neck.

Meli's eyes went unfocused as she gazed out at the water, as if seeing something else entirely. Perhaps a vision. I repressed a shudder at the uncanny way she could draw on truths and know what was happening in the world. "And I've had a vision. Revaed imprisoned the Forwyn at the palace, and he's threatened to kill them all. *If* Lo doesn't publicly condemn her own actions and seal her commitment to the alliance with..." Meli paused, turning to me. "With her marriage to you."

I shook my head, mind reeling. "It won't be that simple. They're a threat if they betrayed the Teramese cause. He'll execute them anyway."

"I know you will help us," Meli went on, ignoring my protest, "because we are going to rescue the Forwyn before he can kill them. And the one person you love more than Revaed is Lo. You won't let him slaughter her people like that and let her blame herself."

"You knew all this when you first captured me? Didn't you just have this vision?"

Meli's smile was bittersweet. "No. I first spared your life—and Valentra's—because I'd had visions about you both, ones that told me you might be more compassionate and interested in our cause than other Teramese would be. And you're their prince. You have influence. I wanted to deal with you first, but I'll be speaking with Valentra soon enough, asking her to join our ranks."

Gritting my teeth and squeezing Lo's ribbons in my fist, I inhaled sharply. "All right. I'll help you. For Lo."

CHAPTER FOURTEEN

Jalie

In the aftermath of the riot of noise and pain I'd endured, everything felt eerily still and lifeless. Ryke nuzzled gently against my shoulder, like a silent greeting welcoming me back from the brink of death. His tail swished back and forth, curling about me protectively as I surveyed the results of the Battle of Aramith.

But it had been less a battle and more a slaughter. Alrenian and Forwyn corpses lay alongside the slain Teramese soldiers, a horrifying reminder of the way I'd lost control of my army. Under Nesrelle's influence, they'd become ravaging monsters, killing anything in their path without discretion. An invincible army.

I swallowed down bile, wondering if any of Aramith's citizens were still alive. And if they were, would they forgive me for leading the army that had destroyed them?

You should have known better than to make a deal with the Queen of Death, I thought, my skin prickling. The warning Kovi had given floated through my head, but I tamped my regret down. There wasn't time for that now.

An empress was only weak if she let her failures consume her.

The thought brought back memories of Mother and her teachings…and the girl who had murdered her. Closing my eyes, I recalled the face of the young woman Nesrelle had shown me. The *amara'rekni* I'd longed to wreak justice on for three miserable years. *Kill her.*

Searching the ground, I found a discarded sword and dagger, strapping both to my belt.

"Lo'laeni Nolanhou," I whispered to myself.

First, I'd search the city for survivors. Then, I'd ride to Inalgoth and hunt down each one of my targets and kill them all.

Revaed, the imposter emperor. Elder Ettonou, my former tormenter. Lo'laeni, my mother's murderer.

As I crept forward, Ryke slunk along beside me, ever my faithful protector. In that place Nesrelle and her nestrae had held me, time hadn't seemed to exist, but here in Aramith, night had come and gone. Now a new one approached, the bloody sun descending swiftly in the west.

I wasn't sure if one day had passed since the battle had ended or more. The only thing that assured me it hadn't been years was the fact that the corpses staring lifelessly at the sky were still fresh, filling the air with the stench of death.

At first, I gagged at the overwhelming scent as I stumbled over the bodies and slipped in blood and gore. Bile laced my tongue with its foul taste. But all too soon, I grew accustomed to the smell. It permeated everything, until it was my whole world.

Death. Destruction.

My vision blurred as I scanned the city. Everything remained quiet.

Maybe everyone was dead. Every soldier who'd pledged themselves to me, every citizen I'd vowed to save. The streets lay still, full of nothing but bodies. Each building I passed sat empty and dark.

Your fault.

I dropped to my knees, ignoring every ache in my body as I choked on a sob. My mind whirled. Ryke pressed his snout against my shoulder, his warmth reassuring as he wrapped his body around mine.

I wanted to lose myself here, to weep until I was spent. To let Ryke cradle me like a child. To cry for everything I'd lost and all the ways I'd failed, to cry for the hopelessness I felt when I wondered how I would save my people now. How could I return to Inalgoth like this?

Don't let it consume you, I reminded myself yet again, forcing myself to my feet. I would search every last inch of Aramith before I gave up and left.

Pain seared my cheek, and I lifted my hand to trace the fresh wound the nestrae had carved into it. The accursed mark of Nesrelle herself.

A noise shattered the stillness of the evening, snapping my gaze to a shadow scurrying from an alley further down the street. In an instant, another was following—and then more. My heart stuttered, wondering if they were Alrenian survivors or Teramese soldiers.

Slipping my dagger from its sheath, I forced my aching body into a jog, clinging to the lengthening shadows cast by the surrounding buildings. Glass crunched beneath my boots as I passed a bakery, its windows shattered. Corpses lay among the shards in the street, and the rows of bread lining the counters within were left for the flies to enjoy. I repressed a shudder when I noticed another puddle of blood inside the shop.

My army had turned vicious, seeking out prey anywhere they could find it. Slaying even the innocent citizens they'd once sworn to protect.

I swallowed, giving into my growing rage rather than tears this time. Once again, the mark on my cheek burned with renewed pain. *I'll kill every last Teramese soldier.*

More noise erupted from ahead as fighting broke out. The figures had already disappeared around a corner, but the shouts and scrape of steel were unmistakable, herding me on faster. At my side, Ryke snarled, smoke twisting from his nostrils as he matched my pace, each one of his steps making the street shudder beneath me.

Perhaps it was Ryke's movement that masked the sound, or maybe it was my focus on the fighting up ahead. Either way, the gust of wind took me unawares, slamming into my back with the force of a punch and sending me sprawling. My dagger skittered out of my grasp, and I couldn't help my moan of pain as my body—still weak and aching from the way the nestrae had tormented me—struck the cobblestones.

Ryke whirled and growled, his tail twitching so violently he nearly struck me as I staggered to my feet. I didn't bother to grope for the dagger, instead drawing my sword and spinning to meet my enemy.

The street lay empty. I scowled at it, my eyes scanning every gap between the nearby buildings, every possible nook and cranny someone could use to hide. Ryke sniffed, more smoke coiling about us as he prepared to unleash dragon fire.

"Don't," I told Ryke, gently. I placed a tender hand on his snout, running my fingertips over his smooth scales, even as I continued to study the space around us. "There might be Alrenian survivors. We can't risk burning the city."

Ryke snorted, as if to protest.

My hand tightened on my sword hilt. "I've survived plenty of attempts to kill me, Ryke," I reassured him. "I'm fairly certain Nesrelle won't *let* me die, not now. Not even if I asked for death."

In answer, my cheek smarted, Nesrelle's mark forever reminding me I was *hers*. My fate wasn't meant to be death. It was supposed to be worse—to bring about the deaths of everyone and everything I loved.

Slinking forward on silent feet, I called out over the din of the fighting, which was already fading. Either the other fighters were moving deeper into the city, or the combatants were all dying off. "Vander, if you've come to kill me, step out and face me."

Rough laughter echoed in answer. I strained my ears, trying to pinpoint where the sound originated, but it seemed to bounce off every wall around me. "You just want me close enough to touch."

Yes, feed our strength, Nesrelle whispered in my mind. *Feed the curse.*

My lips twitched. "Fine, let's agree to fight without magic or curses then. Draw your sword and fight me."

Another gust of wind rushed through the air, swirling around me and whipping my hair into my eyes. I blinked back the stinging tears as dust and pebbles rained down on me. Blood from the street splattered against my armor. I clenched my jaw, using every ounce of strength to keep from being knocked backward.

Ryke snarled and launched himself in front of me, unfurling his wings to block the onslaught. I ducked behind his cover, gasping for breath and blinking furiously against the grit in my eyes.

Vander shouted over the tumult of his own wind magic. "I'm not an idiot, you lying, conniving—"

Something—a fighting instinct I couldn't quite define, or the barest breath of sound that only my subconscious registered—gave away the attack an instant before it occurred. The hairs on the back of my neck rose and I twisted, seizing Tayla's wrist before she could bury her dagger in my spine. She cried out in pain and fury, landing a kick to my side that shuddered through me and shoved me back.

I lost my grip on her, and she stormed forward, leering over me with her dagger. I braced myself, preparing to strike fast and low before she could hurl the weapon at me. Instead, another voice had us both freezing, eyes darting toward the roof of the building on my left.

"Empress Jaliana, come to join the battle again at last. Thought you could hide from us forever?" a taunting female voice rang out. Daedra. She was perched on the rooftop, her form nothing but a silhouette against the dying evening light.

Ryke roared, the sound pummeling against my eardrums, sending earth and walls and sky rumbling. A huge plume of smoke erupted from his mouth, evidence of his restraint as he leapt forward, wings snapping until they blotted out the sky. Cast in his enormous shadow, I gaped as he tore into the building Daedra crouched upon. Bricks crumbled and rained to the street, forcing Tayla and me to dive for cover.

Laughing, Daedra sprang out of Ryke's way with inhuman grace, twirling and drawing a blade. My gut clenched with sudden worry. Nesrelle had promised us the might of dragons, and there was something distinctly not *normal* about the way Daedra moved.

And even if I hadn't told Ryke not to use fire, Daedra was as invincible to its heat as I was. Thanks to Nesrelle and her scheming, wicked deal. I ground my teeth.

But there was no time to lose myself in rage or fear, no time to watch Ryke fight or even to throw myself into the fray with him. As if summoned by Daedra's taunts, my Alrenian soldiers—or whatever they were now that they'd given into this mad bloodlust—flooded all around Tayla and me. It was as if they materialized from the shadows themselves, slipping from between buildings or climbing down from rooftops. Their leathers were still slick with blood, and their eyes were like dark, endless pits, the color all but vanished in the blackness of their enormous pupils.

A female soldier stalked toward me, offering me a feral smile. Her teeth gleamed with sharpened points, and my skin went numb.

My own soldiers reminded me of the nestrae.

With a rabid cry, she threw herself at me, swinging her blade with a wicked glee more reminiscent of the demons I'd been tormented by than my skilled soldiers. She had no fear for her own life, no need to worry about the training drilled into her. She moved with unnatural strength, pommeling her blade against mine with blows that made my bones ache with every block.

I was vaguely aware of Tayla and Vander nearby, each fending off onslaughts by the swiftly growing number of Alrenians. They were clearly capable fighters, moving with the speed and grace of trained soldiers, but the Alrenians were something altogether...*other*. Beneath the leathers they wore, I caught glimpses of what had once been gold-tinted skin, now gleaming and grey. They stared emotionlessly with their cold, bottomless eyes, moving with deadly precision as they struck.

Vander held them off with his magic, throwing his hands up to direct gusts of wind that shoved them backward. But it was clear he was weakening, and he wouldn't be able to repel them forever.

Who cares—he's your enemy, a grim voice reminded me. And yet, some part of me did care, because this wasn't a normal fight. The soldiers we fought were as much my enemies as they were Vander's and Tayla's.

As several Alrenians swarmed me at once, the pain in my cheek flared once more, seeming to pulse in tandem with a desire growing within me, one begging me to feed my curse. To slay my enemies and let it strengthen me. My body shuddered, fear shooting through my veins.

I ducked when one of the soldiers swung for my neck, quickly dodging and then jumping as two more drove their blades lower.

Rise, empress, Nesrelle breathed. *Your mother never would have been so weak. Kill them.*

They're my people, I thought, even as I parried a flurry of strikes, barely stepping out of the way when a soldier tried to sneak up behind me. Soon they'd have me surrounded.

Fight back, a voice snapped in my head, but this time, it wasn't Nesrelle's. It was Mother's.

Sucking down a breath that tasted of salt and steel, I unleashed a cry and gave myself into the power crawling through my veins. It was easy, the way my mind stretched out, seeking until it clamped down on the fears around me. The soldiers might have appeared less than human now, but their fears were still very much those of mortals.

And I drowned them in those terrors, filling their minds with the images of their worst nightmares.

Men and women shrieked and clawed at their own armor or dropped their weapons and fled. I stepped forward and placed my hand on the arm of the nearest soldier. Her eyes were glazed over, but as soon as she sensed my touch, her scream changed into a howl of raw agony. The curse devoured her in mere moments, her thrashing body quickly collapsing and stilling on the street. I stepped around it, too numb to even be shocked by the mangled flesh and unrecognizable face.

I turned on the others, bloodlust taking over. The pain on my cheek felt like a throbbing pulse, but somehow, it also felt like strength. Something red-hot and wild coursed through my veins, tuning me into the way each soldier's breathing hitched. The way their hearts stuttered when they locked eyes with me.

Kill them all.

I was the Queen of Death's executioner. I was fury and bloodlust and vengeance. I was an empress who would make her mother proud, and a monster who was too strong to be held back, too fierce to be withstood.

My blade sang as it swung through the air, cutting through flesh faster than the bodies could move out of the way. Their screams were music in my ears, a beautiful chorus—

Jalie.

I dropped to my knees, gasping, blinking in the starlight. All around me were corpses lying in their own blood. Nearby, Tayla and Vander were somehow, miraculously, still alive, their own swords lifted as if to try to fend me off.

Jalie, the voice said again, and somehow, impossibly, I knew it was Kovi. He wasn't here, but I could hear the deep timbre of his voice as clearly as if he were beside me.

I'm sorry, Kovi. Please help me. The plea seemed nonsensical in my head, and yet also—not. On some level, I believed he could hear me. That even across the miles, he would continue to fight for me, just as he'd promised. *Please don't leave me.*

I shuddered, bile dancing along my tongue. The pain in my cheek sharpened and jolted through my entire body, like a poison radiating outward and chasing through my blood. Nesrelle wasn't pleased that I'd stopped, was she? She'd wanted me to stay locked in whatever trance she'd had me in, to keep killing until there was no one left.

Choking back a cry, I dropped my sword. It clanged against the cobblestones. I stared at my blood-soaked hands, my mind trying to catch up with whatever my body had just done.

They'd been trying to kill me, but once, those men and women had been my soldiers, my people. The ones I'd sworn to protect and lead. Whatever they'd become had been because they'd trusted me, pledged themselves to me and then to Nesrelle when I'd encouraged them to do so.

This is my fault, I thought numbly.

"What are you?" Vander demanded, cutting through the haze in my mind.

I lifted my gaze, studying the fear shining in his silver eyes. He tried to mask it with the firm set of his jaw and the way he lifted his blade, ready to defend Tayla to the death, but he was terrified. The part of me that fed off death, that felt my curse's power growing and Nesrelle's call through the mark on my cheek, longed to capitalize on that terror.

But even if Vander was the enemy, I was terrified of losing myself to Nesrelle's grip again. She would relish Alrenian and Forwyn deaths as much as Teramese deaths.

And what would Kovi think of me? I was the very monster he'd said my mother had been, the type of monster he'd believed we could both avoid becoming...

A sound unlike anything I'd ever heard before tore through the night, wrenching me to my feet. Vander and Tayla staggered back, but my attention was focused on that noise, a noise like an animal crying out for help. My eyes searched frantically, studying the rooftop where Daedra and Ryke were. Now, my dragon was surrounded by even more

Alrenians.

Ryke should have torn Daedra apart. He should have already ripped *all* of the Alrenians to pieces. It should have been effortless for him.

Lungs burning from my labored breaths, I charged toward the building Ryke had smashed into earlier. It was tall, and the climb to the roof would be no easy feat. With a growl of frustration, I threw myself at the bricks before me.

There were narrow crevices in the uneven wall, but some of the bricks were loose or crumbling. My arms trembled from the effort as I scaled the wall, biting back my cry of fear each time loose mortar made me slip and nearly lose my grasp. Higher, higher, every muscle in my body on fire from the effort. I was strong from Nesrelle's unnatural power, but that didn't entirely diminish my weakness and exhaustion from everything my body had undergone. The wound where Daedra had stabbed me was gone, and the nestrae had, somehow, only left the scar on my cheek behind, but each inch of my skin remembered how it had felt to nearly bleed out. To suffer the pain Nesrelle and her demons had inflicted on me.

Arms and legs trembling, sweat stinging my eyes, I glanced up to find the crumbling portion of the wall that Ryke had slammed into. It was loose and treacherous, and I wasn't sure I could make it. When I dared to glance down, I found Tayla and Vander were already small forms beneath me, half-concealed by the growing shadows. It was nearly fully dark, with only the light of the first stars to guide me.

Nausea swirled in my stomach as I forced my gaze back upward. Suddenly, I understood Kovi's fear of heights. The idea of falling helplessly to my death was unnerving, humiliating. Like him, I wanted to face death standing on my feet, on my terms. Being this high was only exhilarating when I was on dragonback.

Another pitiful cry pierced the air. I shoved my fear and doubt aside to reach for the next handhold. *I'm coming, Ryke. I'm coming.*

Picking up my pace, I launched myself upward, clinging to the crumbling bricks until my nails splintered. The loose stones began to pull away with my weight, sending me sliding back down the wall. My heart lurched as I felt myself start to freefall. Using every last ounce of strength, I slammed my hands back toward the wall, grappling for purchase, kicking desperately to find a foothold before I tumbled backward. My hand seized a brick jutting out from the wall and I lurched to a stop, my arm jerking painfully and my knee crashing against the bricks below. But I held fast, biting back a groan of pain.

Slowly, agonizingly, I found a hold for one foot, then the other. I forced myself to glance upward and find the next handhold. And I climbed.

By the time I pulled myself over the rooftop's edge, every muscle in my body was burning and I was soaked in sweat. I heaved a shuddering sigh of relief, but it quickly turned into a gasp of horror and rage.

The roof was flat, affording me an easy view of the scene playing out on it. In the starlight, Ryke's beautiful green scales flashed a dozen different shades, as breathtaking in the dark as he was in the sunlight. His wings were curled against his body, his tail weakly twitching back and forth as he attempted to protect himself. A small wound in his soft underbelly trickled blood, but it shouldn't have been enough to weaken or slow him.

Shadowy forms had surrounded him, their blades burning like silver fire in the night. They struggled to get past his swishing tail and snapping jaws to his weak spots. Ryke could hold out until I reached him—if he needed my help at all. His wound wasn't fatal.

But then I beheld the hint of color on one of the swords. The figure holding it turned, as if sensing my presence, and I saw her flashing eyes, her haughty smile. *Daedra.* She'd smeared her blade with poison, and she must have already wounded my dragon with it.

I swallowed back bitterness. I'd created an army able to withstand the might and fire of dragons, and now that wish was backfiring. They were my own greatest nightmare.

"Ryke!" I screamed. When he tilted his head, his silver eye peered at me pitifully. His wings fluttered, but he was weak, and the figures were moving in closer…

Heart fluttering in my throat, I sprinted for him. Daedra was already stalking toward me, an irritating smirk on her face.

I drew my sword and threw myself at her, a scream tearing at my throat. Behind her, Ryke snarled, taking one of his attackers out with a massive chomp of fangs. But the others didn't fall back, didn't even flinch at the shrieks of their companion.

Steel scraped against steel as Daedra met me blow for blow. She was calm, all but for her bottomless black eyes that gleamed with murderous intent. There wasn't a drop of sweat on her brow, or on her neck, where scales clustered about her throat. I sliced my blade toward them, and it bounced off harmlessly, eliciting a laugh from her.

"You wanted an invincible army," she snapped, plunging her sword toward my chest. "Well, here it is."

I staggered backward. For every movement I made, my muscles screamed in agony. I was spent, the pain from Nesrelle's torment catching up to me. The climb had been more than my body could take, and I couldn't draw a deep enough breath, couldn't stop my knees from shaking simply from the effort of continuing to hold myself up.

With a muttered curse, I collapsed, scaled armor clanking against the rooftop.

Daedra's grin turned feral as she slammed her sword into mine. My grip weakened, sending my blade flying out of my reach. She pressed her weapon to my neck, and I wondered how much of her mind she still possessed. She was looking more and more like the other Alrenian soldiers, lost to Nesrelle's madness. Did she remember her treacherous attempt to murder me? Was she eager to finish the job now? Or was she lost entirely, only seeing another target to slay simply for the joy of the kill?

"You're nothing but a worthless traitor," I spat. "I'm your empress, and you tried to murder me and steal my army." My eyes flicked toward Ryke. He was still fighting fiercely, but like me, his strength was waning. Desperation clawed up my throat. "And poisoning a dragon that is true to our empire? That is the worst sort of crime."

Daedra sneered. "You're not my empress," she hissed. Her sword pressed closer, leaving a smear of the poison she'd plunged into Ryke's bloodstream.

But something made her pause, holding her blade away from my throat. She blinked, her gaze unfocused.

I threw the last of my strength at her, seizing her elbow and shoving it as hard as I could in the wrong direction. The sound of breaking bone was awful, but her cries of pain were worse. She punched me in the jaw with her free hand, felling me in one blow.

Stars exploded behind my eyes as my head cracked against the street. My jaw throbbed furiously, but that was nothing compared to the terror gripping me. I didn't think Nesrelle would let me die, but I didn't want to test that theory—didn't want to taste the poison coating Daedra's blade until Nesrelle deigned to pluck me from the brink of death.

If Nesrelle could do that, a second time.

But when I opened my eyes, screaming at my body to move, to find the ability to fight back just a little longer, Daedra was gone. I forced myself to a sitting position, only to find Daedra, her right arm limp and her left grasping her sword, running toward the other Alrenians, shouting at them to retreat.

"Nesrelle wants us elsewhere!" she commanded, and without a backward glance, not even for the corpses Ryke had left in a circle around him, the soldiers swung over the side of the building and began the climb down. Even Daedra moved with unnatural grace, sheathing her sword and using her one good arm.

Summoning my willpower, I forced myself to my feet and jogged toward my dragon. Ryke whimpered as he shuffled to me, limping from the effort. Tears stung my eyes as I cradled his snout and soaked in his warmth.

"It's going to be all right, Ryke," I choked out. "The antidote grows in Inalgoth. I can save you."

Clumsily, I swung onto his back, and Ryke leapt from the roof, landing with a shudder on the street below.

My mind whirled as I began trying to piece together a plan. Ryke didn't have much strength left, and depending on the amount of poison Daedra had forced into his bloodstream, he could have either days or hours left. I didn't have a moment to waste.

Just as I dismounted, footsteps snapped me back to the present. I whipped around, arm trembling as I held up my sword. I didn't think I had the strength left in me to survive another fight, but I'd die defending Ryke.

Vander and Tayla picked their way around the corpses strewn in the street, their eyes wary.

I lifted my chin, the start of a plan locking into place. "I surrender," I called out, dropping my sword to my feet. Its clang echoed off the buildings around us. "Take me to your emperor."

CHAPTER FIFTEEN

Lo

The scraping of a key in the lock and the whining of the cell door swinging open jolted me from a hazy sleep. I sat up, the world swaying and my head pounding with a dull, insistent throb. I swallowed back a bout of nausea and blinked at the too-bright light of the torch the figure before me held.

"Come with us," the guard snapped as a second one stepped forward and seized my arm.

In my dazed state, I did my best to glare at them as they led me roughly through the cell door and out into the reeking dungeon corridor. The mingling odors of sweat and human filth made my stomach roil, this time with nausea I couldn't resist. I barely had time to lean forward before I vomited bile all over the cobblestones, splattering the guards' boots.

With muttered curses, they tugged me onward, past cells that were clearly occupied. Muffled sounds rose from within: the shuffle of footsteps, the creaks of cots, the whispers of lonely people desperate for conversation—even if it was just the sound of their own voices. I peered through the small, barred windows set within the cell doors as we passed, catching glimpses of Forwyn.

My heart lurched. My people, imprisoned because of *my* failed plan. But I wasn't going to lose myself in guilt, not anymore. I knew better than to blame myself for my people's suffering—this was all Revaed and his cruelty. I squeezed my hand so hard my fingernails bit into my palm, imagining how good it would feel to punch him in his arrogant face.

A sound yanked me from my thoughts, snapping my attention to the nearest cell. As a pair of hands wrapped around the window's bars, I saw a girl's face stare out. The face of the same girl who'd warned me about the Alrenians at the Circle of Serenity when the rioting had started. It felt like that moment had occurred long ago, but if my foggy sense of time was correct, it was likely that only a day or two had passed.

"*Amara'rekni,*" she cried out, her expression twisted with desperation. "Where are they taking you? What is happening? Don't let them—"

"Shut up, you little rat!" one of the guards sneered, slamming his fist against the door so hard it rattled.

Terror flashing in her eyes, the girl bit back a cry and retreated into the shadows of her cell.

I wanted to scream and tug myself free of the guards, but I was weak and disoriented. The corridor shifted unsteadily beneath my feet, making me fear my own eyes would betray me. And my head wouldn't stop pounding, a steady pulse in time with my heartbeat to remind me of the injury I'd sustained on the back of my skull.

Instead, I was helpless as they guided me out of the bowels of the prison and into the palace itself, taking back halls and servant's passages. My emotions teemed all the while, my sluggish mind working at the beginnings of a plan or two.

I was no fool, and I refused to let Revaed outplay me in scheming a second time. As much as he might claim he wanted an alliance and peace between our peoples, as much as he might genuinely want to appease Caesiem, I knew there was no way in all of *goehr* or the Golden After that Revaed wouldn't slaughter the Forwyn he had locked up. He might claim that my cooperation would win their lives, but I knew better. To keep all of them alive would be too great of a risk for a man whose very motto was *survival.*

As soon as the guards approached Caesiem's rooms, depositing me inside without ceremony and locking the door behind me, I did a preemptory scan of his quarters. All his rooms were empty. Both the settee where Caesiem had been sleeping when I'd shared his room with him and the bed itself looked untouched, the covers pulled up neatly on the mattress and the blanket folded over the settee.

Relief spilled over me—a part of my heart had feared a final, deeper betrayal. That all of those stolen moments with Caesiem, every burning look, every kiss, every word, had all been a ruse. Just a way to earn back my trust, if not my forgiveness, and then help Revaed destroy everything I'd worked so hard toward. It was clear that Caesiem wasn't present in the palace at all, which meant that it was likely he knew nothing of Revaed's recent arrests. Or even of his storming of the Aerekni Academy.

But my relief was chased quickly by fear. Even Revaed had seemed concerned when I'd asked him where Caesiem was. Had he never returned from trying to stop the Alrenian riots? Had he been killed?

I pressed my hand to the cool pendant at my throat. His water magic had seemed incredibly powerful, but what if without his pendant it had been weakened too much? What if the Alrenians had overwhelmed him?

Don't let him distract you from your purpose. Not again, I reprimanded myself, thinking of Naina and her words of warning about Caesiem. They seemed so long ago, now.

And how right she'd been—this Teramese man had done nothing but push me off my path from the moment he'd shown up.

Save your people, I thought, sinking onto the settee and laying my aching head in my hands. *That's all that matters.* I wished my heart would listen.

Inhaling deeply, I tried to concentrate despite the pain encroaching my every thought. Naina had always called upon Elhani's healing magic with a sort of musical chant of her own, one that I assumed either matched or harmonized with a strain of Elhani's song somehow. She'd tried to teach me, but back then, my mind had struggled to focus, too preoccupied with haunting guilt and terrors from my past. Memories, like sweet echoes of her voice, rippled through my mind until my chest tightened with unbearable sorrow.

But grief was another distraction, one I couldn't afford. I pushed past it, shoving every aching feeling aside with the expertise and strength of someone who spent every day of her life shouldering impossible burdens. Instead, I leaned into Elhani's music, letting the delicious sensations of his strength and love and comfort waft over me, a balm for my broken soul.

Heal me, Elhani, I prayed, and I began to sing. Softly at first, my voice cracking and wavering, and then louder, until the song grew in strength. I could feel its power—my god's power working within me— crackling in the air. Tingling on my skin. Weaving through me and tugging at the pain, the fogginess, the nausea, the confusion.

I closed my eyes and relished each wave of relief as it came. Even the pain in my heart seemed to ease, as if Elhani had taken a portion of my grief to carry himself.

When I opened my eyes, my body was stronger, and the world felt steadier, my vision clearer. A smile tugged on my lips. *Naina would be proud.* The thought brought a strange mix of sorrow and comfort. A reminder that, in some ways, she was still close, but also not close enough—not anymore.

I stood, grateful that my legs were stable now. Though my healing work hadn't been perfect and my head throbbed dully, it had taken great effort and focus. Mentally, I was exhausted, and I didn't think I'd be able to wield Elhani's magic again any time soon.

But I'd defied an imperial ruler before without magic, and I could do it again. It was time to get to work.

Glancing around, I took stock of my situation. Guards were posted on the balcony outside, a fact that would make escaping out of the rooms unseen difficult, even for me. I'd once crept throughout the palace without invisibility magic, but never directly under the noses of my enemies.

No, I needed a different way out. One that would help me not only get back to the academy to check on Father and the soldiers, but could also prove useful later to smuggle out other Forwyn prisoners.

I paused, recalling my life as a slave. Once, I'd clung to old rumors about secret passages scattered throughout the palace buildings, their entrances tucked behind bookshelves or old picture frames. Some slaves had whispered about a woman using one such passage to escape to freedom, generations ago. But I'd never discovered any hidden entrances, and rarely had time or energy to search for them, much less indulge in fantasies of escape.

Now, I supposed even the most hopeful and fanciful rumors were probably rooted in some truth. If the imperial family ever wished to evacuate a palace under siege or slip out unnoticed for any other reason, it made sense that they'd have ensured passages for just those purposes would exist. Perhaps, because no one in the palace had found a need to escape a place so heavily guarded with its dragons, the passages had been forgotten about over the years, even by the imperial family.

Maybe, just maybe, those rumors had been true all along. I could hope.

And now, in Caesiem's quarters, I had the perfect opportunity to search. After all, these rooms were within the imperial wing, not far from Karye's former rooms themselves. If there had ever been tunnels built for the family's escape, there would be entrances in all of the family quarters.

My search was methodical, starting from one corner of the bedroom and working my way along every inch of the wall, tapping for a hollow spot, feeling for any section that felt different. I pulled every book off every shelf in the room, shifted furniture and opened drawers, removed paintings and drew back rugs.

Hours passed, with nothing but the clocks ticking on the wall and the twitter of birds outside to keep me company.

Shuffling steps at the sitting room door gave me only a few moments' warning to shove the desk back into position and plop down on the settee before several Teramese filed in. Bearing an array of platters full of food and drinks, they began to rearrange the furniture of the sitting room. Interest piqued, I leaned back and watched as they moved plush seats and side tables off to one wall just in time for more servants bearing a table to enter. They set it in the center of the space, unfolding it until a full dinner table rested within the room. Chairs were swiftly brought in, one set on each end, and place settings carefully laid out. On a side table, the men and women artfully set out their food before most left, only a few taking up positions along the wall.

My stomach knotted as Revaed himself entered, dressed in his usual spotless Teramese uniform. But this time, his calm manner had broken down. Jaw set, he moved with rigid posture and a fire blazing in his violet eyes.

"I thought," Revaed announced as a servant shut the door behind him and he settled into one of the chairs, "we should have dinner and discuss your upcoming marriage."

He gestured, and I pulled myself from the settee to slip into the seat opposite his. Blood roared in my ears as servants flitted about, filling our glasses with wine and adorning our plates with glazed salmon and fresh vegetables. They added little dishes of sugared berries and plates of chocolate cake I once would have drooled over. Now, even the tantalizing smell of food and my empty stomach couldn't summon an appetite.

Not with the emperor sitting across from me, his gaze as sharp as a dagger.

"Leave us," Revaed ordered when the servants were finished. Without a word, they bowed and shuffled out.

So you found Teramese willing to be your servants instead of the Forwyn, I wanted to snap, but I kept my mouth shut. I didn't spare a glance at the food waiting in front of me, instead keeping my eyes trained on my enemy.

"What do you *really* want?" I demanded.

Revaed stabbed at a vegetable on his plate, placing it into his mouth delicately and chewing slowly. I sat rigidly in my seat, wondering suddenly if the food was poisoned. If Revaed would forget all his earlier promises of sparing my life and using me to build his so-called alliance, and stage the "accident" that killed me early.

But then he swallowed and leaned forward, his expression intent. His gaze flitted to the pendant around my neck. "You care about Caesiem, right?"

I shifted in my chair, mind whirling. Perhaps, in this case, the truth was better than a lie. Safer. Even if it was complicated. "Yes," I breathed.

Revaed's mouth twitched in a bittersweet smile, there and gone again in an instant. "We have that in common then, at least." He sat back, his eyes going distant for a moment before he returned his attention to his food, spearing another vegetable. "How much do you know of this city?"

I poked listlessly at my salmon, my nerves relaxing just enough for my stomach to remind me how long it'd been since I'd last eaten. It didn't seem like Revaed was ready to kill me just yet, and I needed to keep up my strength, so I forced myself to eat a bite. "What do you mean?" I asked.

Reaching for his wineglass, Revaed took a long swallow. "I mean, how familiar are you with its layout?" He took another sip of his wine, his food seemingly forgotten. Or maybe his appetite was as small as mine. "Of its back corners and hidden hellholes, all its smarmy disgusting places where the worms might crawl away and hide." He sneered. "Of places large enough for Alrenian rioters to sneak away and lick their wounds."

Nerves fluttered through my stomach, as quick and annoying as mosquitos. "Do they have Caesiem?"

Revaed pinned me with an intense stare. "They either have him alive, they stole his corpse, or they threw him into the sea. One I'm certain would never happen, because even if he gave you his pendant, his magic is powerful and he's crafty enough to survive almost anything. And the other I definitely don't believe because I'm confident his tie to the water is so strong that it would toss him back out before it would drown him. Which leaves me with one option."

My mind darted to the rumors of passageways leading out of the palace to unknown locations throughout the capital. Maybe there was an entire underground network where people could take refuge—holes to crawl into, as Revaed had said. Perhaps the Alrenians had stumbled upon them, and that was where they were amassing their leather armor and illegal weapons.

But if I was right and I could help Revaed find an entrance to these tunnels within the palace, I'd be throwing away my chance to escape, to get back to my father and the other soldiers—if they were alive, which was the only option I allowed myself to consider—and save the Forwyn prisoners.

"I know every shadowy alley and dark corner of this city, because

I've been forced to hide in most of them," I said slowly, my tone heavy with bitterness. "But I've never come across anything underground other than the sewer systems." Sewer systems that brilliant Alrenian minds had come up with to direct fresh water into the homes of everyone in the capital, drawing on underground sources.

Revaed scowled, taking another gulp of wine. "Those of course, are already being searched without success."

I smirked. "I suppose even desperate Alrenians are too proud to stoop to living in the sewer system."

"Don't toy with me," Revaed said sharply, dashing my attempt at humor. He studied me carefully, as if he could discern my thoughts with a mere look. "Stelina must be a better healer than even I give her credit for. You're looking much better. Which, I assume, means you are fully capable of coherent thought. Are you sure you're not forgetting something?"

Forcing myself to feign nonchalance, I took another bite of salmon and took my time chewing, pretending to mull something over. Swallowing, I shook my head. "I'm afraid I've never stumbled across anything else in this city. My best guess would be to search the abandoned buildings along the har—"

"Already done!" Revaed snapped, eyes burning as he slammed his palm on the table in an uncharacteristic outburst.

"Then I can't help you anymore," I said firmly.

"I don't think you understand the consequences of not cooperating," Revaed said, setting down his wineglass and rising from his seat. He swung open the door unceremoniously, revealing two guards with a Forwyn girl in their grips. Bound and gagged, she could do nothing but grunt in fear and stare at me with wide eyes.

I knew her. She was the girl who'd warned me about my sisters and called out to me in the dungeons.

Horror clawed up my throat, and I stood from my seat as the Teramese led her in. My brain scrabbled for a way to stop what was happening, even as I could already see it playing out before my eyes. I couldn't erase the memory of Revaed stabbing the Alrenian boy in the chest, couldn't shake the ominous foreboding chilling me now the same way it had then.

"Wait—" I started, but Revaed had already drawn the dagger from his belt. With a careless flick, he plunged the blade into the girl's heart.

I screamed, lunging for her even though I knew it was impossible to stop what was happening. Her eyes darted to mine, terror and disbelief etched across her young face. "May Elhani hold your hand," I choked out between sobs, "and the guidespirits lead you home."

The girl whose name I didn't even know collapsed to the floor, her blood pooling and running across the pristine carpet.

Thud. Thud. Thud. The sound reverberated in my ears, recalling every other body I'd ever watched fall. Edi. Fellow slaves. Naina. Sweat trickled down my back and my chest tightened, but I focused on my anger to clear the sensations. To gather my strength before I lost myself.

"Clean up this mess," Revaed said with a scowl, handing his bloodied weapon to the nearest guard and gesturing at the floor. "And summon the servants to clear the table. I have no appetite."

Trembling with fury, I rose as Revaed turned on me. "You think you're so civilized, so much better than others," I snarled, "but you're just as monstrous, just as barbaric as Karye ever was."

Revaed studied me intently. "I told you. Mercy has no place here, not if it comes at the price of survival for those I love. For my people." He strode toward the door, leaving me kneeling beside the girl's body, the guards already shuffling forward dispassionately to take her away.

"And I told you," I ground out, "I don't know the location of any secret tunnels. Not here, not anywhere."

Revaed shrugged. "I don't believe you. And even if you're telling the truth, the warning was still needed, after your last little rebellion. I know you're still plotting. I know you still hope to defy me and endanger my people. So it doesn't matter if you know about any passages or not. I need you to be amenable to both my requests and our alliance."

His violet eyes were remorseless, his face eerily blank as he surveyed me. "Consider this your warning: cooperate, or more will die."

CHAPTER SIXTEEN

Kovi

The Teramese were lining up Alrenians and Forwyn alike and executing them in the streets. It was brutal, efficient, and made me want to forgo all restraint and command each and every one of those cruel soldiers to fall upon their own swords.

But my magic couldn't control a group that large.

It was just Rhi'il and me on the rooftop, watching the Teramese methodically cut down citizen after citizen in a quiet neighborhood within the Vayelta District.

Sensing my stiffening my shoulders, Rhi'il reached out, his grip gentle yet firm on my arm. "Kovi."

I swallowed back my curse, my mind rapidly formulating plans that I just as swiftly discarded as useless. Rhi'il and I were armed with swords and daggers, for our mission had been to inspect the city for a feasible hiding place, not take on a squadron of the Teramese army. If we'd had bows, perhaps we could have saved a few lives. As it was, to leap out now would be suicide, and Rhi'il and I both knew it.

Still…

"We can't save everyone," Rhi'il muttered, tugging on my arm.

But I refused to look away, my eyes burning as each citizen fell into a heap, their blood filling the street. Aside from the soldiers' footsteps, the slick slice of steel into flesh, and the eerie thudding of corpses, this section of the capital—like all the rest of it—lay unnaturally quiet. No one dared to move outside of their homes, to retaliate against the cruelties committed against their neighbors.

The soldiers' patterns seemed random. They'd choose a street where the rioting had been especially vicious and then select some homes nearby, but never all of them. It was as if they relished the chance to strike fear into Alrenian and Forwyn hearts while citizens observed from their windows and wondered if they'd be next.

It was an effective way to make a proud city cower, randomly slaying both young and old as punishment for the riots. This way, everyone knew that no one was safe. No one was immune.

Who would dare rise again now? Even if they didn't fear losing their own lives in the cause, they would surely worry for their neighbors. In this one hatred, this one cause, the Alrenians and Forwyn were united.

All of Inalgoth reeked of blood and terror.

"Where is the cowardly emperor?" I muttered, half to myself, but Rhi'il answered anyway.

"He probably gave the command and then slunk off to the palace to hide behind his guards and the dragons he can't even tame." I tore my eyes from the slaughter before me in time to catch the bitter smile that twitched on Rhi'il's lips as he lifted his eyes to scan the westering sun. "We should keep going. There's a lot more to search and the soldiers are only going to continue crawling all over this city."

I squeezed my eyes shut. When I'd awoken this morning after a few hours of stolen sleep, all I'd wanted to do was storm General Ilowhe's office and beg him to let me head northward. I'd considered a hundred different excuses—Jalie had a dragon, Jalie was the true empress, Jalie had an army she could command to free the city and leave the Forwyn untouched—but in the end, I knew the general was right. My place was here, with my people. It made my chest ache to acknowledge that, but in my heart, I knew that if the reason Jalie's emotions were lost to me was because she was dead, there was nothing I could do for her. All I could do was trust in her strength and her ability to defend herself, and keep fighting for the people I knew I could still save.

But that didn't stop her from consuming my dreams, from invading every one of my thoughts. One connection might have been severed between us, but that didn't mean the one we'd forged ourselves had vanished. That one seemed more powerful than ever, until there were moments I could almost swear I heard her voice, though it was faint and unclear. Or maybe that was just the product of my frenzied, desperate dreams bleeding into my waking thoughts.

It seemed I wouldn't be able to save anyone. Not Jalie. Not my people.

"Kovi," Rhi'il urged again.

I wrenched myself off the roof, picking my way down the wall right behind my friend. Together, we crouched in the alley, keeping our breathing shallow to stifle the overpowering odor of refuse. Still, I couldn't block out the sounds of the dying only a street over. I couldn't blink away the sight of their blood spraying and their bodies falling.

Muttering a curse, I turned and followed Rhi'il down the alley, toward a silent street cast mostly in shadow from the tall buildings framing it. "There must be something we can do," I insisted.

"I have an idea," Rhi'il said, a wild sort of spark in his eyes. His ideas generally tended to be that way: dangerous and maybe touched with a hint of madness, but never impossible. Not for us. Between the two of us—with my rational, sometimes overly cautious mind and his spontaneous, bold nature—we'd pulled off more than one seemingly crazy and impossible feat in training competitions.

Right now, the only thing that might save some of those innocent citizens wasn't caution, but daring. And perhaps, a bit of madness.

"Tell me," I urged.

"I'll kill you!" Rhi'il shouted, tossing a rock as hard as he could through the pub window overlooking the street we crouched in. Glass splintered and shattered as we sprang back. The pub's interior was empty—everything in the city appeared closed, forced into lockdown after the riots and the Teramese-mandated threats and punishments. In the quiet, the glass raining down on the cobblestoned road was as loud as the explosives we soldiers had trained with at the academy.

I imagined the killings pausing as, one street over, the Teramese began to curse in their language. A woman shouted what sounded like an order, commanding her soldiers to investigate the commotion.

"Now," I muttered to my friend, and he seized me by the jacket collar, making a show of dragging me out toward the street. I flailed and swung punches at the air, slurring protests as Rhi'il continued to yell.

"How dare you lay a finger on her," he raged.

Out in the street, I tried not to let my eyes stray toward the line of citizens, or the bodies already sprawled out next to them.

Rhi'il threw a punch at me, one that I sloppily blocked.

Two soldiers stormed toward us.

"Break it up," the closest man snarled, seizing Rhi'il's shoulder and shoving him away from me. "You two are breaking curfew. No citizens are to leave their homes today. Do we need to throw you in prison?"

I stumbled back, blinking blearily and acting cowed. "No, no," I muttered, dipping my head in false deference.

"Let me go!" Rhi'il screamed, tugging against the soldier. "I'll kill him; I'll—"

The second soldier was at my side in an instant, torn between assisting his companion with Rhi'il and securing me in case I proved troublesome.

Rhi'il and I had our blades drawn and buried in their guts before either of them could even cry out. A third soldier darted forward, but I had him disarmed in moments. In two more moves, he was lying motionless beside the others.

"Stop them!" the woman from before screamed.

The line of citizens was forgotten as half a dozen more soldiers stormed toward us. In one smooth motion, I retrieved my dagger and hurled it into the foremost soldier's neck. He collapsed in a spray of blood, his fellows stumbling over his body as they continued to approach. Rhi'il downed a second with a blade to the eye.

Drawing our swords, we fell into a familiar stance, side by side.

"Good plan," I muttered to my friend, whose mouth twitched in a half-smile.

"I always have good plans, Elha'tonu," he quipped, using the nickname he'd given me at the academy. It meant Elhani-blessed, and he knew it drove me mad when he used it.

Still, I couldn't help my grin. "I suppose you do."

With an enraged cry, the woman drew her own blade and joined her oncoming troops, leaving the line of citizens alone. Giving the survivors a chance to escape at last.

"Run!" I shouted at them, hoping the order would break the haze their panic had thrown them in. With whimpers of mingling fear and relief, mothers and fathers seized children and started to flee down the street. Tears fell as the dead were abandoned.

I prayed they would find safety elsewhere, and not run into another band of soldiers.

Then the Teramese were upon us. Rhi'il tossed me one final look, his eyes glittering with triumph, before we fell upon the soldiers.

Weariness enveloped me as we approached the abandoned boathouse. Not from the fight, which, once we'd taken the Teramese by surprise, ended quickly, but from the bodies of Forwyn we'd passed in the street. From the knowledge that we hadn't saved them all, and that likely, there were many more dead throughout the capital, in other roads that we hadn't even seen.

We'd saved the ones we could, and still, it didn't feel like enough. It would never feel like enough.

Here, everything reeked of mildew and brine, but that was a welcome relief from the stink of death. Boards from a small, rickety bridge leading out to the building creaked beneath our feet, the dying sunlight flashing ruby red in the foamy water swirling below. Set apart from the city along a more secluded part of the coast outside of Inalgoth's walls, this space was ideal to crouch inside and observe.

Waves crashed in a lulling rhythm as Rhi'il and I creaked open the door, swiftly scanning the interior to ensure it really was empty. Nothing but rotting fishermen's boats, a coil of rope, and dust motes dancing in the dim light greeted us. We slipped inside and seated ourselves at one of the grimy windows, searching the Teramese ships docked in this portion of the harbor.

Each crash of the sea seemed to echo in my ears, pounding out the moments that would lead to more lives lost. The only thing that kept me from screaming out in frustration and rage was the reminder that we were fighting to save as many as we could. That this battle might be lost, but we weren't giving up on the war.

Gritting my teeth, I dared to offer up a prayer. *Elhani, let this work.*

Other windows set into the building afforded us glimpses of the street behind us as well. Several torches burned along its sides, perhaps lit by a patrolling Teramese guard, illuminating his way. Otherwise, the city was quiet and empty—no citizens or sailors except the particularly brave or foolish would dare show their faces.

From our position, we could hear snatches of the Teramese sailors' drunken songs and general rowdiness drifting toward us. Though the notes were raucous, their language was rich and musical, lending even the drunken, slurred words some beauty.

From what I could tell at this distance, only the bare minimum of men were aboard each ship to guard the fleet, wiling away the hours when it was clear that no one, for now, was showing any interest in them. The earlier Alrenian rioters, unable to fend off canon fire, must not have attacked the ships. Likely these sailors were merely waiting for a chance to return to Teramese shores with supplies. Or to retrieve more soldiers to bring to Alrenor.

I frowned as my mind whirred through the possibilities.

Rhi'il meanwhile, had already stepped back from the window, his eyes glinting in the waning light. "It's growing dark enough they wouldn't even see us coming."

"We're still outnumbered," I mused aloud. "Are we mad?"

Rhi'il's lips quirked. "All the best ideas are conceived in madness." He winked.

Trailing Rhi'il, I crept out the doorway into the dark, empty street. Keeping to the boathouse's shadow, we approached the water's edge, gazing at the early stars glistening along its silvery surface. We'd spent much of our time in the academy swimming in the sea to build endurance, or even just to cool off on hot summer days in our few moments of free time, so slipping into the harbor now was easy and familiar to us. It was a short distance to each ship anchored in the harbor, but our circuitous route would be a little more taxing.

Despite the balmy night air, the water had already grown chilly. The breeze whispered over my skin, sending a strange prickling sensation down my spine. Each puff of air and swirl of water around me sounded like murmuring to my ears, like something from the deep had been disturbed.

I shook away the ridiculous notion, reminding myself of the numerous times I'd swam these waters without incident. There were tales of water creatures passed around among Alrenians and Forwyn alike, but in every story, those creatures lurked in far deeper waters. Instead, I focused on diving below the surface, trailing after Rhi'il as he clung to each ship's shadow, rising only long enough to swallow a quick gulp of air before ducking beneath the water again.

My muscles burned by the time we reached the furthermost ship on this side of the harbor. Without an instant of hesitation, Rhi'il reached out, water coursing from him in rivulets as he clambered up the side.

I climbed after him, my slick fingers clinging to crevices in the hull until we both paused at one of the gun ports to peer into the shadows. Only the din of laughter and singing on deck carried to our ears, and the interior of the ship rested dim and empty.

Hefting himself over the edge, Rhi'il swung inside and turned toward me just as I dropped in after him. We crouched low, water puddling around us as we took in the swaying rows of hammocks and the scent of mildew.

Rhi'il's hand dropped to his sword hilt, his body tensing. Preparing.

Just as I knew my friend was, I tuned out the distractions around me to heed Elhani's music. It wove through me with a gentle warmth, familiar and thrilling. I could feel it tingle along my skin as I embraced it fully and asked my god to dry the water off my clothes and make me melt into the darkness.

For one breath, Rhi'il was there beside me, water steaming off his clothes as Elhani's magic dried him. The next, he'd vanished.

"Ready to cause some trouble?" Rhi'il breathed.

A smile that I knew my friend couldn't see pulled at my lips. "Absolutely."

We crept up the steps leading to the deck, my only indication Rhi'il was near the subtle warmth of his presence just ahead of me. Each shift of the ship beneath my feet was disorienting, but I'd been forced to train and exercise in all sorts of conditions, until I was nothing if not adaptable. I was always confident in my body's ability to be graceful, strong, and capable. After all, each one of my trainers had pushed me to every limit in order to make it so. I quickly found my footing, becoming steady, assured, and silent.

The breeze kissed my face as we slipped on deck, surveying the sailors sprawled about on crates and barrels or slumped against the railing, all in various states of inebriation. All the sailors left were male, reminding me of some of the Teramese sailing superstitions I'd heard of—that women aboard ships were bad omens. It made me wonder how much they'd been bribed to ship so many female soldiers over to Alrenor.

If the boards creaked a little beneath Rhi'il's and my feet, the sailors were too loud to notice. Some told tales or crude jokes, eliciting hearty laughter from their friends, while others sang and strummed Teramese instruments, their words slurred and ridiculous. One man lay curled up near some netting and coils of rope, snoring loudly.

Playtime, I thought, treading softly behind one of the men seated on a barrel, sloshing his mug of rum as he lifted it in a dramatic arc over his head. "Time for something more serious!" he was saying, belting out his words over the guffaws of his friends. "Now this one I have, this is not a joke, but a true ghost story!"

One of the men narrowed his gold eyes, grinning and swiping his long, greasy black hair back over his shoulder. "Ghosts? I believe in all sorts of wild water creatures, Teros, but even I'm skeptical about ghosts."

Teros's grin stretched wide, his intense green eyes gleaming. He took a loud gulp from his mug and slammed it down on the deck next to his barrel. "Do you want a story, or not?"

All the men interjected with enthusiastic affirmatives.

Teros winked. "Then shut up and listen!" He leaned forward, dropping his voice dramatically.

Holding back the laughter tempting me, I crept up behind Teros and awaited my moment, even as I scanned the deck, wondering where Rhi'il had crept off to.

"Old stories claim that at the beginning of the Alrenians' conquests to build their empire, they actually struck the Teramese Empire first. Perhaps they lusted for more dragons, who can say for sure?"

The sailor who'd interrupted earlier snorted, and Teros shot him a glare.

"Naturally, Teramyl struck back. There was a huge naval battle, right here in this harbor. Countless men and women were killed, Teramese and Alrenian alike. Fine ships were sunk." Teros leaned forward eagerly. "They say water predators fed on the bodies of the dead for days afterward, turning the sea red with blood. After that, it's said that sailors who linger too long in these waters can hear echoes from the cries of the dead, see their bloated faces watching them, smell their decaying flesh lingering in the air…"

A heavyset man sniffed loudly and nudged the man beside him, spilling rum across the deck as he did so. "And here I thought that smell was just Lexo."

Everyone roared with laughter, and I worried I'd lose my chance, that even the suspicious, fearful Teramese would ignore Rhi'il's and my attempts if they lost themselves too much in drinks and japes.

"It's the truth," Teros said in annoyance. "My great-great-grandfather was a merchant to Alrenor, and he passed down the tale of what he saw—"

"How dare you disturb our rest," I interrupted, raising my voice so that its deep timbre thundered over the men.

Every sailor in my vicinity froze, blinking wide, glazed eyes at one another.

Reaching for the nearest crate, currently unoccupied by a man who'd stood to go refill his mug, I lifted it and hurled it against the ship's railing. It cracked and splintered, drawing the eye of every conscious sailor present.

Their bronze faces had gone so pale, it took everything in me to stifle my laughter. Though I couldn't see him, I could tell Rhi'il was up to some mischief elsewhere, sailors across the deck already crying out in fear.

An ominous shout split the air. "We'll drag you to the depths for this!" Rhi'il cried out, his words trembling with mock rage. "We'll bring you to our shadowy tomb and let the sharks feed on your flesh as you drown."

Teros stood, knocking over his mug as he did so. "I told you!" he shouted, but other sailors were already leaping to their feet.

The deck descended into chaos as drunken sailors drew their weapons and teetered across the ship, scanning every shadow for vengeful spirits. Some clutched at charms dangling from leather cords around their necks or wrists. All jumped at the slightest sound, from a breath of wind to a creak of the wooden boards beneath their own feet.

I sprinted across the deck, overturning crates and barrels as I went, sloshing mugs. Somewhere in the middle, I nearly collided with Rhi'il, who heard me coming and seized my arms just in time, dragging me to a stop. I heaved in a breath to suppress my laughter, but the sailors' noise drowned ours out.

"Cheers," Rhi'il said, lifting an abandoned mug. I grasped another and we clanked them together, drinking deeply.

A man paused, blinking his silver eyes at what would have appeared to be two floating mugs, and staggering back.

I threw down my drink, splattering the deck, and drew my sword. It sang as it scraped from its sheath, a clear sound that made every man stiffen and sober up. Even the drowsing sailor was on his feet now, muscles tensed as he readied to fight or flee.

Just like the mug, as soon as I pulled my blade away from my person, it became visible, a gleaming threat in the starlight. It took all my willpower to keep it so and remain invisible myself, but I had practiced feats like this countless times. Beside me, I heard Rhi'il draw his own weapon, growling out his threat.

"Leave this ship, or we'll kill you all."

These Teramese sailors didn't understand Forwyn magic, or perhaps they would have guessed what was really happening. But with their superstitious minds and the Forwyn's tradition of keeping our magic mysterious to the outside world, the Teramese jumped to the only conclusion they understood. Restless spirits, trapped in the place they'd died.

Everything happened swiftly after that, the sailors wasting no time in grumbling about Revaed "leaving them on this godsforsaken ship" and loading up into rowboats to find safety ashore.

When the last of them had rowed out of earshot and far enough into the darkness that they couldn't see Rhi'il or me even without invisibility magic, I released my grip on my power. Slumping against the railing, I wiped a weary hand across my forehead. Despite the entertainment tonight had brought and the hope of having a potential place to hide our soldiers, I couldn't clear the worry and pain from my brain. The images of the dying citizens in Inalgoth's streets. The unending fear that Jalie was lost to me forever.

Darkness clouded over my heart, like an ominous premonition, though I wasn't sure I believed in such a thing. My mind wanted logic and reasoning, something clear-cut I could work through. But magic and the connection it had formed between Jalie and me had followed its own laws, so I couldn't shake this feeling.

She was in danger.

Jalie, I thought, squeezing my eyes shut and seeing her in my memory. The freckles that dusted her cheeks and nose. Her eyes, vivid as the Alrenian summer sky and flecked with gold as bright as flames. Her strength. Her rare moments of vulnerability. The way her face lit up when she realized I cared, realized that whatever was growing between us was powerful and dangerous, but also wonderful and true. A dream worth fighting for.

Jalie. I prayed that somehow, my voice could encourage her across the miles. That wherever she was, she was safe. Despite the dark deal she'd made with Nesrelle, or the dangers of the war she was charging into.

I'm sorry, Kovi.

My blood thrummed in my veins and I held my breath, half-afraid I had imagined the sound of her voice.

Please help me. Please don't leave me.

Was I going mad, or had that really been Jalie, somehow calling out to me across the distance between us?

My friend's voice jerked me from my musings. "Loading all the injured onto this ship unseen is going to be quite the chore," he said, taking another swig of alcohol from an abandoned mug as he plopped down next to me. "But if we hurry, we might be able to start tonight. We can get anyone stable enough aboard and hidden."

"And what about when the sailors come back?" I demanded.

Rhi'il's mouth quirked. "The ghosts will mysteriously steal the ship."

I rolled my eyes. "That's your plan? Don't you think, once we start sailing away in the night, the Teramese will come looking for it?" But my mind snagged on the idea that Rhi'il must have come up with hours ago, when he'd first dragged me into this wild plan. "You mean to lay anchor in Haven's Bay."

It was hardly a bay—more like a sheltered cove off the southern coast of Alrenor. Most residents of Inalgoth knew of it, since it was possible—if difficult—to make the trek to the water and enjoy an afternoon of swimming. But it wasn't marked on maps because jagged rocks made it nearly inaccessible to most ships. But once within, the waters were placid and a ship would be in the perfect hiding place, especially because it was tucked away beneath an overhanging cliff that would conceal it from prying eyes within the capital.

"My maddest plans are usually my most brilliant ones," Rhi'il said, nodding and grinning. "We can sail there tonight and transport some of the injured later, if we must."

He shrugged, his expression taut. We both knew anyone too wounded to be moved was likely not long for this world. Even if they survived their injuries, it was unlikely many days would pass without the Teramese returning to the academy to finish what they'd started.

Rhi'il and I swung over the railing and descended the hull of the ship, splashing back into the silvery water. Once again, a chill swept over me, and I wished we had a rowboat to get back to shore.

You're imagining things, I scolded myself.

But as Rhi'il swam ahead, diving low into the water, something seized my ankle. I kicked, freeing myself from the slimy *thing.* Surging forward, I kept to the surface to avoid whatever had entangled me. *Seaweed,* I told myself.

Something cold and clammy closed over my wrist, its bony grip surprisingly strong. I whirled, water splashing as I met a pair of bright yellow eyes in a face that resembled that of a human woman, but for the silver scales clinging to her cheeks and forehead. White hair spilled past her shoulders, flowing in the water around her.

"Aren't you a fine sight," she murmured, her gaze raking over me as her hand trailed lecherously up my arm, the other still clutching my wrist. She inhaled deeply. "And full of powerful magic." Her eyes gleamed. "But all that magic can't save you from grief, can it? Your heart aches with worry for her."

I blinked, my mind trying to comprehend the being before me. I'd heard tales of water creatures such as nymphs, but I'd never heard of any that could read people like this. The magic rippling around her was strange, making the air feel electric and dangerous.

My voice sounded gravelly. "What do you want?"

She cocked her head, the move more animalistic than human. "The water hides powerful secrets, magic you can't even fathom here on land. Don't you want to see? It could help her, the one you long for."

I scoffed. "You're mad," I said, tugging my arm free of her grip.

The woman's voice turned darker, deeper. "You won't succeed. You can't save both your people and her. You'll have to choose, in the end."

"So you're saying she's alive," I said, my words defiant. Whatever power she possessed, I refused to let her chilling predictions shake me, refused to see anything but the hope they brought.

Jalie is alive.

"Oh, my pretty one. You still think death is the worst fate that can befall the ones you love. Perhaps it is, if it comes at your own hand." She laughed and swam closer, her breath chilly against my face. "I can help you save everyone you care about, or I can show you how to forget the sorrows you carry." She blinked, slowly. Faster than I could react, her hand shot out again, her clutch stronger than ever.

Heart hammering against my chest, I realized the electrifying feeling, the chill crawling down my spine, wasn't just me sensing her power. Somehow, she was leeching my own magic, drawing on Elhani's song. It sounded dimmer in my ears, and I felt weaker. As she opened her lips, her words came out like a lullaby, soothing me even as I knew, deep down, that this was wrong.

Fight it, a voice inside me commanded, but it wasn't nearly as loud as the one telling me to go with the nymph, to see what powers she held that could prevent whatever horrible fate Jalie faced.

The nymph shrieked and her hand tore away from me. I blinked at the blood churning through the water, at the silver flash as Rhi'il drew back his dagger and snarled at the creature before us. Damp white hair clinging to her scaled face, the nymph sank lower in the water, furious yellow eyes trained on Rhi'il.

Her hold on me snapped, and without hesitating, Rhi'il and I swam toward the shore. We didn't stop to catch our breath until we pulled ourselves up onto land. Snatches of other sailors' songs drifted on the chilly night breeze, proving most of the other ships were oblivious to the strange creature in their waters. And also reassuring us that they didn't care about their comrades abandoning their ship for one night.

For now, we had time.

"What was that?" Rhi'il breathed.

I shook my head. "I guess it was a water nymph."

Rhi'il hissed. "Let's get out of here."

But as we crept through narrow back roads and alleys to return to the academy, I couldn't banish the nymph's words from my mind. Couldn't shake the fear that somehow, she'd peered into my future and seen nothing but failure. That she was right, and I couldn't save both the Forwyn and Jalie.

In the end, you'll have to choose.

CHAPTER SEVENTEEN

Emperor Revaed

With a grimace of disgust, I tore the bloodied jacket off and tossed it to my nearest guard.

"Do something with this. Burn it. I don't care," I groused.

Wordlessly, the guard vanished down the hall with the jacket, his boots pounding a staccato beat on the marble floor. Beside me, the remaining guards hefted the Forwyn girl's corpse between them and marched toward the door leading out to the palace grounds. I trailed after them, sucking in the cool air as soon as we stepped into the night, relishing the heavy scent of oranges from a nearby tree. Anything to cover the scent of blood filling my nose, lingering with its revolting reminder of the nasty tasks I was forced to complete.

One orange lay rotting in the path ahead of me, and I kicked it listlessly, watching its juice leave a trail as it rolled beneath a bush.

"Toss her into the sea," I commanded the guards, waving an arm vaguely toward the water.

They continued deeper into the gardens, winding their way toward the cliffside near the Dragon Keep that would offer them the perfect position from which to throw the corpse into the waves. I had no desire to bear witness to them completing their morbid task, so I sank onto a nearby bench. Sighing, I tugged at my undershirt, letting the fresh air waft over my sweaty body.

When I glanced down, my hands were trembling. *I'll do whatever it takes to find you, Caes.*

As distasteful as I found it, I didn't regret what I'd done. Not if it helped put Lo in line, remind her that she couldn't threaten my people and not suffer consequences. I needed her to cooperate, at least long enough to seal the alliance between the Forwyn and us. And then…

I blocked out my wandering thoughts, which kept swinging back to the growing fear that my intuition was wrong, that I'd lost Caesiem forever.

Once, not long after he'd joined us in the palace, he'd contracted a fever that had left him delirious. The finest palace healers had waited on him day and night, shuffling in and out of his quarters in endless rotations. I hadn't been able to rest, hadn't been able to leave his bedside.

"You should rest, Prince Revaed," the healers had scolded me, but I'd refused to leave the chair I'd stationed myself in.

Over and over, I'd placed fresh cloths on his forehead, watching as Caesiem had tossed and turned, only waking occasionally to stare blearily at me.

"Am I dying?" he asked once, his breaths shallow, his skin so pale it was nearly white.

My laughter came out hoarser than I wanted it to. "No, of course not, Caes. You're one of the strongest people I've ever met, and you're not even a grown man yet. A true warrior, a valiant survivor. You're not going to die, not as long as I am here."

That promise lingered in my mind now. *Not as long as I am here*, I thought.

In the distance, I saw the shadowy forms of my guards retreating to one of the palace buildings, likely to clean up. I raked a weary hand across my brow and rose, turning my steps to trace a winding path down to the water. As soon as I cleared the gardens and approached the narrow route descending toward the section of beach set aside for the palace's own use, the tang of the sea drenched the air more thickly than usual. I welcomed the salty smell, familiar and comforting for someone who'd grown up along the Terebrys.

Far below, the waters shifted endlessly, the reflected starlight dappling the velvety darkness in silver. I crept down the path and crunched through the sand to the shore, where I knelt to dip my hands and rinse the blood off my skin. As I drew several fortifying breaths, a sense of peace washed over me.

Other than my fierce love for my people, the only love I'd ever known was my affection for Caesiem. He was the family I'd never had, the one who respected and cared about me like no one else in my life had ever bothered to.

Defective. The word rang in my ears, my father's harsh voice taking me back to every horrifying moment of my childhood.

The way he'd mocked me for my absolute disgust toward the idea of marriage, toward the idea of any sort of romantic attachment to anyone at all. With his endless string of ever-rotating mistresses filing through the palace since my mother had died of illness when I was young, he couldn't fathom the idea that I didn't feel lust, had no desire to feel lust…not toward anyone, ever. He'd tried to beat my lack of romantic interest out of me, anything to avoid the shame of a prince who outright refused to produce an heir. He'd constantly threatened to marry me off, but he couldn't force me into a bed, and that was his greatest source of rage.

At first, I thought finding Caesiem and proclaiming him my heir was a miracle to draw my father's wrath away from me. But Father never stopped looking at me with derision, never stopped reminding me how *defective* and *unworthy* he found me. Instead, finding Caesiem had been a different sort of miracle. A miracle that had brought me the first family I'd ever known.

Resolve settled over me. I withdrew a single gold coin from my pocket and stepped out into the water until it touched my knees. Tossing the gold into the sea, I watched the waves tug it away, down into swirling shadows, and waited.

The nymph's head poked above the surface only a few minutes later, her yellow eyes pinning on me with an intensity that made my skin crawl. Sephrode, the creature Caesiem had commanded to relay messages between himself and me during his days of spying within Alrenor. No matter how many times I'd had to deal with her before, her presence never ceased to put me on edge.

"The pretty one who will never be tempted, not by any beauty or any sweet words," Sephrode murmured, her voice musical as she swept back her long, silky white hair, revealing more of the silver scales adorning her face. "You never want to play games, and you always scowl at me. So what *do* you want?"

I swallowed thickly. "Information. Have you seen Caesiem?"

Sephrode blinked her strange eyes at me. "You expect I'll trade such valuable information so easily, for such a small price?" She lifted a scaled hand to study the glittering gold coin I'd tossed to her.

My glare deepened, and I plucked another coin from my pocket, leaning forward to deposit it into her hand. But her pupils dilated, her lips curving in a victorious smile as she slid her fingers around my wrist. Her pale hand had a bright red cut marring its back, healed and half-scarred. From what Caesiem had told me, the nymphs had powerful healing tonic that helped them recover swiftly from injuries…but I wondered, vaguely, who or what had wounded her. Usually, nymphs liked to trick or seduce their victims into the water, which meant those victims rarely fought back.

"Let go of me," I snarled.

The water nymph ignored my demand. "Shiny coins are pretty additions to my collection, but I'd rather have you." Sephrode tipped her head. "Those lovely violet eyes gleam and shine even brighter than gold." She reached up to trace a cold, wet finger down my cheek, and I wrenched myself free.

Sephrode laughed coldly. "You're no fun. Dull, dull emperor." She sank back into the water. "All I can tell you is that I caught a glimpse of the pretty prince this afternoon. He seemed quite alive to me."

"A prisoner?"

Sephrode listed her head. "Perhaps."

"Where was he? Is he safe?" The questions tumbled out of me, wild and desperate.

"He was near the shore," she said simply, splashing her silver tail. It flashed, like a falling star darting across my vision before dipping back into the dark water. "I could not tell if he was safe. He didn't call to me, and he was up too high for me to call to him." She sighed. "He would be so fun to play with."

"Shut up," I ground out. "Where on shore?"

Laughing, she splashed some water at my face and shook her head. "That's not how this game is played, handsome emperor."

"I paid your price," I said, voice low and measured as I tried to temper my growing anger. My fear.

"You'll have a far greater price to pay soon," the nymph whispered.

Cold seeped through my veins as I stared at the strange creature before me. Caesiem had said something about the nymphs' ability to see into the future, but I wasn't sure that's what she was doing now. Was it?

"What do you mean?" I asked, but Sephrode had already dipped back into the water, pushing away to swim back out into the depths of the sea.

My only answer was the sound of tumbling waves, crashing against the surf.

CHAPTER EIGHTEEN

Caesiem

You'll meet with A'elli and me to give updates here." Meli withdrew a map of the city from her pocket, pointing to a pub located in a corner of the city known for its criminal activity. *The Gilded Fang.* "You've worked together before, and I expect she'll feel more comfortable if she can be the one to keep an eye on you."

I scowled, but nodded.

Hours had passed, in which Meli had questioned me about the Teramese army's current movements—I'd avoided sharing most information, as I could claim ignorance regarding anything that had occurred while I was underground with them, and the recent riots had surely changed plans.

"You'll meet us the day after tomorrow, after twenty-second bell," Meli went on. "Find your excuses to slip away. And tell us everything you know about your emperor's upcoming plans for his Forwyn prisoners."

I shifted in my seat, my frustration growing. "Can't you use your truth gift to obtain all the knowledge you could ever need?" I snapped.

Meli shook her head. "That's not how my gift works. I don't know *everything*. My clearest knowledge always pertains to the past." She paused. "And if you betray us, if you try to lie to me, to withhold information, to try to find and lead your soldiers to this place…" She stared at me, her eyes seeming to pierce into my soul and weigh my intentions as she let her threat hang unspoken between us.

I knew she would be able to detect lies, but withheld information would be trickier. So I kept my gaze neutral, refusing to drop my eyes.

"Valentra will remain here."

Guilt shot through me—likely the reaction Meli wanted. Valentra would face consequences if I flaked, I was sure.

"She's your leverage?" I smirked, feeling a little reckless.

Meli smiled slowly, confidently. "No, I expect she'll side with us willingly, when she sees what we're fighting for—and what your emperor has been doing. Just as you will, soon enough."

I blinked. "You said your gift doesn't show you the future."

"I don't need to see the future to know what you'll be facing."

I leaned back, uneasiness washing over me. Mostly, though, I thought Meli might be a little mad, a little foolish. I'd let her believe whatever she wanted if it helped me get away, back to Revaed and Lo. If Valentra didn't escape on her own—and she was resourceful enough to do so—I was confident Revaed and I could get her out later.

"That should be all," Meli said, folding the map and returning it to her pocket. "I'll see you soon."

I frowned. "And what story do you want me to concoct to tell Revaed where I've been?"

Meli tossed me a grin before glancing back at the water.

Night had already fallen, leaving the sky a deep, rich blue. I scanned the sea, but nothing about the rocky shoreline or churning waters set it apart from any other part of the Alrenian coast.

"You'll tell him you survived because you were knocked unconscious and left for dead with the other Teramese corpses," Meli said. "When you awoke and found more Alrenians prowling the streets, you hid in an abandoned building and tried to nurse your own wounds until you were well enough to return to the palace."

"But your healer already stitched up my shoulder—"

In one smooth motion, Meli drew a dagger and slashed it across my shoulder, ripping my stitches.

I snarled, lifting my hands instinctively and sending water swirling between us.

Meli ignored the threat, wiping her bloody dagger on her leggings. "You tried stitching up the wound with supplies you pulled off one of your dead healers," she went on, "but it was sloppy, and you tore them out when returning to the palace. Now, get going." Without warning, she shoved me, pushing me toward the cliff's edge.

Drawing a breath, I dove for the sea, ignoring the way my shoulder burned and fresh blood spilled over my skin as I lifted my arms. The water seemed to rise up to greet me, the salt burning my open wound as soon as I struck. Water swirled over my head and pulled me down into the shadowy depths, until its weight pressed on me.

But I didn't feel fear, not toward the element that had sustained and protected me all my life. My shoulder throbbed with every movement as I swam back toward the surface, sucking in a deep breath and then pushing toward the rocky shore. I didn't have a single coin or anything else on my person I could use to trade with the nymphs for a healing tonic, which meant I'd have to hurry before I lost enough blood to grow woozy.

When I pulled myself up onto the sand, I spared a glance upward toward the cliff where I thought the tunnel exit had been, but there was no sign of Meli and not a single break I could spot in the rock. No wonder she hadn't been concerned about me leading soldiers back here—even if we found the opening again, it was likely impenetrable from the outside, just as she'd claimed, meant to be an exit only. Meli herself must have used a different route, a hidden entrance back into her tunnels.

My trek back through the city was soggy and miserable, every step full of throbbing pain and a steady trickle of warm blood soaking my shirtsleeve. The streets were eerily silent and empty, full of nothing but shadows and the sharp tang of a city burdened by terror and grief. There were many places that bore marks of the violent riots: shattered windows, crumbling bricks, and stained cobblestones not quite cleaned of all the blood. Our army must have been hard at work in the past day, though, because I didn't see a single corpse left behind.

By the time I found myself peering up at the palace, weariness and dizziness had taken hold. I staggered up the path leading to the gate, where the posted guards widened their eyes and scurried to usher me within the grounds. Before they could even send for help from a healer, pounding footsteps approached, and Revaed, his pants soaked up to the knees, charged forward.

"Caesiem!" he gasped, pulling me into a crushing hug. "You're back. You're alive. You're—you're hurt." Stepping back, his grip still tight on my arm, Revaed spun on the nearest guard. "Why are you dawdling? Get a healer."

"I'll be all right," I murmured, a little unsteady on my feet. I blinked, startled to find that Revaed's violet eyes were glistening with unshed tears, the usual composed mask he wore gone to reveal his relief.

Despite the pain and weariness sweeping through me, warmth filled my chest, a welcome relief after all the doubt and questions that had plagued my mind. Revaed's dedication was sincere and unwavering. I'd always known his father was a monster, but that didn't change the tie between my guardian and me. It couldn't.

Does it matter if Revaed truly loves you, if he used you? a pestering voice asked, but I pushed it away. It was his father that used people, not Revaed. Never Revaed. He was faithful to me, to his people, and the only time he was cruel was when he had to be toward our enemies.

As Revaed threw an arm over my shoulder to help me into the palace, trailed by guards and a flustered male healer, I banished every worry about discovering the truth. About how I'd keep the Alrenian and Forwyn rebels appeased. About Meli's confidence that soon, I'd be crawling back to them, prepared to shatter all ties and loyalty to Revaed.

Never. Revaed was the only father figure I'd ever known, the only family I had. Here I had a calling and a purpose, meaning in an existence that, for the longest time, had revolved only on surviving another day, fighting for nothing more than the sheer stubborn will ingrained in me to keep breathing. This was my home, my place in the world. My safe haven from every insecurity and cruelty.

Nothing could change that.

CHAPTER NINETEEN

Kovi

D arkness lay heavy over Aerekni Academy as Rhi'il and I returned to report our success to General Ilowhe.

"The Teramese might occupy our harbor and possess all of our ships, but now we have one of theirs," Rhi'il boasted. He glanced around the general's office at the faces of those gathered. Along with other high-ranking officials who'd once been our instructors, General Ilowhe had also called for several nuns. For a second, I could have sworn Rhi'il's eyes lingered on the nuns, as if searching for someone.

I cast a sidelong glance at my friend, wondering at his expression, but he turned away.

Standing in the center of the general's office, Rhi'il and I were still dripping puddles of water. We'd been too weary from our use of magic earlier to call on Elhani's power to dry us again, and our news had felt too important to wait even a moment to share.

General Ilowhe raised his eyebrows, clearly impressed. "A ship?"

I launched into an explanation, knowing Rhi'il would be tempted to embellish the story when we needed to hurry. "It should be easy enough to steal some rowboats," I finished, "but perhaps not as simple to do so without being noticed by those aboard the other ships."

"We'll have to leave tonight to work under the cover of dark, and be quick about it." General Ilowhe turned to the nun called O'emia, who seemed to be a sort of leader among the sisters. "Do you and your sisters plan to return to your duties at the abbey?"

O'emia shook her head. "Not now, sir. The Teramese attacked us there, so I doubt we'd be safe, and..." Her voice wobbled, but she swallowed and collected herself. "We've all agreed our place for now is here, tending to the wounded and, if need be, lending our aid in battle. We've all been trained in magic."

General Ilowhe smiled. "So I noticed. Very well. We appreciate your help. Your first priority will be using your magic to tend to our wounded. Help our healers determine who is well enough to be moved to the ship, and who will need to stay behind."

"Sir?" Lieutenant De'oni cut in. He was much younger than the general, only a decade my senior, but a talented swordsman and excellent instructor. Now, his usually confident face betrayed his doubt and exhaustion. "Surely we can't leave any of our wounded here."

"No," the general said, his expression troubled. "My hope is that some of families throughout the city will be willing to take them in." He glanced to O'emia. "Which means that some of our healers, and your sisters, will need to stay in Inalgoth. You'll have to transport the wounded as quickly as you can, once you're able to find nearby homes that aren't occupied by the Teramese."

O'emia nodded. "Yes, sir. Many of the families we helped in the poorer districts were overlooked in the Teramese occupation." Her smile was grim. "Their homes weren't suitable for Teramese soldiers, it seems, but I'm sure those families will welcome *our* soldiers. I'll send one of my sisters to go speak to them now." She darted from the room, the other nuns trailing her.

"Lieutenant," General Ilowhe went on, "give the orders to move tonight." As the lieutenant departed, the general's eyes fell on Rhi'il and me. "I suggest you two change and pack at once. Good work, soldiers."

Rhi'il turned away, but I hesitated. "Could I have a word with you alone, sir?"

General Ilowhe's mouth tightened as he nodded.

"I'll wait for you in the hall," Rhi'il muttered, patting me on the shoulder just once in encouragement before slipping from the office. He didn't know what I wanted to speak with the general about—there hadn't been time to tell him about Jalie at all—but he knew me well enough to detect the somberness in my tone. And he'd seen the way the nymph had taunted me.

As soon as my friend was gone, I stepped closer to General Ilowhe's desk. "I'd like to request a horse and a few days to ride northward, sir."

Sighing, the general leaned forward, dropping all formalities as he shook his head. "I'm sorry, Kovi. I'm grateful for the ship you and Rhi'il found, but I'm still relying on you. I can't spare a single able-bodied man tonight, when we need to get aboard that ship as quickly as possible. If any Teramese spot us, it'll mean another fight. And even if we manage the move undetected, we have too many Forwyn in the palace whose lives are threatened." The lines around his eyes seemed deeper, his eyes dimmer with sadness. "I understand what this costs you. I'm not asking you to prioritize rescuing my daughter over going to the empress. But I *am* asking you to help us rescue the other citizens from the palace. If Revaed has Lo trapped there, I suspect he won't waste any time threatening the other Forwyns' lives."

I kept my face expressionless, forcing my body not to tremble. *Jalie is alive,* I told myself, remembering the water nymph's words. But why couldn't I feel her emotions? Why had my last connection to her been full of feelings of agony, of *death*? What if she needed me? "I understand," I murmured. "I serve my people first."

"As soon as I can spare you, I promise I'll let you go," General Ilowhe said.

I nodded, not trusting my own voice. I knew my place was here. I *knew* it. And yet…

When would my people *not* need me? When could the army possibly spare me when we were on the cusp of all-out war?

"Thank you," the general said, but I dipped my head and left without another word.

Serve your people first. I'd committed to that, made vows to it. I was loyal to the end, and always had been. I'd never imagined a future in which my passion to protect my people would feel like a burden, a curse.

I forced my emotions away, refusing to dwell in pain and bitterness, the way, even now, I could feel my father was. Just as I'd learned to ignore others' feelings, to shove those connections to the back of my mind, I did the same with my own.

Mother's voice echoed in my ears: *Lift your head, Kovi.* I clung to that, hoping that somehow, if I continued to do what was right, what was necessary, Elhani would bless my choice, and Jalie would be safe.

Somehow.

"Are you all right?" Rhi'il murmured, matching my pace as I trudged through the hall, wringing water from my jacket.

I kept my spine rigid, my expression stoic. "Yes."

From the corner of my eye, I saw Rhi'il frown and try to catch my gaze. He opened his mouth as if to protest, but another form approached, striding toward us from the opposite end of the hall.

I recognized her shorn hair and scarred arms. The hard set of her mouth. Mio'e, the woman who'd arrived with the nuns but wasn't one of them. She carried a bundle of bandages in her arms, clearly on her way to take supplies to the infirmary.

She'd moved aside to pass when she paused, frowning at Rhi'il. "It's bad enough you're both trailing water all over the hall," she huffed, "but do you have to drip blood too before you bother going to the infirmary?"

Halting, I spun toward Rhi'il, noticing the spot of blood seeping through his shirtsleeve for the first time. Shame bubbled inside me. How had I not noticed my friend was injured before now?

"It's nothing," Rhi'il said quickly, brushing me off before I could speak. "One of the sailors got a lucky scratch in with a dagger." He shrugged, turning to Mio'e. "I can bandage it up myself when we go to change and pack. Thanks to us, you're heading to safety tonight," he added pointedly, "so a little water or blood is a minor inconvenience."

Mio'e stiffened at his rebuttal, but her glare didn't soften. "There's no such thing as safety in this empire." The hopelessness seeping into her eyes wasn't lost on me. While some of us had enjoyed freedom for the past several years, she'd continued to suffer the horrors of slavery. My eyes lingered on her scars.

Rhi'il grasped her arm, and she started, but didn't pull away. "There will be soon," he vowed.

For a moment, she froze, studying his face. They both seemed to hold their breath, caught in each other's gazes. Then she tore free from his grip. "I hope you're right," she muttered, eyes averted, and hurried down the hall.

I glanced toward my friend. "What was *that*?"

Rhi'il tossed me a cheeky grin. "The ladies love me," he said off-handedly.

But I knew his carefree attitude was forced. I couldn't shake the image of him cradling Ny'ola, our fellow graduate, in his arms at the battle of Wynlaen as she died. I couldn't forget the way they'd flirted and teased one another, the way Rhi'il had spoken when he talked to me about her. Six months had passed, and I knew his heart was still shattered. He wasn't a flirt, and whatever had passed between him and Mio'e just then seemed…different. It hadn't been flirting, but it had looked like something.

"We fought together in the battle," Rhi'il admitted after a long moment. "Mio'e's tough and…" He shook his head. "She doesn't trust anyone and she's brusque toward everyone… But I've been thinking about her ever since. I can't seem to stop. And I *hate* that. Even if she ever spared me a second glance…it's too soon…isn't it?"

I squeezed Rhi'il's shoulder, his damp jacket cool against my palm. "Maybe not."

We were quiet as we returned to our room to change and pack our few belongings, each lost in thought. Each mourning our fallen comrades. Each wondering if we'd ever see a future in which our empire knew peace.

CHAPTER TWENTY

Nesrelle

The worst part of battle was that it always had to end. In the aftermath of the chorus of bloodthirsty cries and screams of agony, silence felt like an endless void. Once the souls tore free of the bodies, leaving corpses with nothing more to give, my delight turned into an endless ache of longing. After the smell of fear faded and only the tang of blood and the sickly-sweet scent of death remained, part of the beauty was gone.

I licked my lips, trying to relish the taste, but it just wasn't the same. The power that had tingled along my skin was already diminishing, and I grew irritable. It was torment, to forever have a desire that could never be sated. To possess a power that could be fueled so fully one instant only to be ripped away the moment my victims left this world completely.

There would never be enough death. Somehow, I knew this—knew that even if I watched the whole world fall, it would end with me standing like this, on an empty battlefield, wishing I could reanimate corpses. Wishing I could watch them die all over again.

But mortals never lasted long, did they?

Scowling, I surveyed the Alrenians crowded before me, the only survivors of Jalie's previous army. As much as I would have loved to see them continue to tear one another apart, I'd forced myself to order that they cease killing. Their numbers were still a hundred strong, vastly diminished from their original strength, but, with their new powers, more than enough for the work ahead.

Daedra stood near the front, cradling her injured arm and licking her lips, as if as impatient to spill blood as I was. In the early morning light, her eyes gleamed all black, matching the scales creeping up her neck and beginning to form along her face. "Anyone left living has fled Aramith," she told me, her eyes scanning the city from where we stood, lined up outside of the gates.

"Forget about them," I said, waving a careless hand as I turned southward. Toward Inalgoth. "We march for the capital. Once it falls, the rest of the empire will follow swiftly."

"And then the glorious days of old will return," Daedra murmured, her dark eyes alight with her lust for power.

Snorting, I turned away, studying the other Alrenians, clothed in leathers and now adorned with dragon scales. They were like my nestrae and yet also a creature all their own. Their vows to me had opened them to be more easily malleable to my will, but they weren't entirely under my control. Some had relished giving into my bloodlust, enjoying the power that consumed them with each kill. Others still had moments where they fought against me, trying to reclaim their minds. Those were the ones who threw me dark glances, defiant yet fearful.

It didn't matter. In the end, my purpose to attack Inalgoth was their purpose. Whether they wanted to follow me or not, they all longed to reclaim the capital from the Teramese and Forwyn.

By the time we reached the city, it would be easy to drag the most stubborn of these soldiers into my will and convince them to kill their fellow Alrenians too. And if not? My other soldiers would dispose of them.

"Should we bury the dead?" a voice asked.

She was a young woman, with dark hair pulled up into braids that encircled her head and eyes that retained some of their original color. If she possessed scales like the others, they were hidden.

"A rebel," I half-sang, striding toward her. My skirt, the hem stained with blood from walking through the gore-slick city streets earlier, whispered across the grass. I tilted my head, studying her. "Breyna, is it?"

Breyna's brow furrowed, her eyes narrowing into defiant slits. I could feel the pulse of her fear, buried deep where she refused to show it. Along with her knowledge that she was facing her end, but with pride. It enraged me. I wanted raw terror. Subservience. Anything more potent to feed on than her insolent courage.

"Yes," Breyna said, lifting her chin. "I am not your pawn. Those were *Alrenians* you ordered our army to kill, not enemies, and they deserved better. Our city—our empire—deserves better."

My mouth twitched in a smile. "Does it? Do you really think you pathetic mortals deserve glory and honor and long lives?" I scoffed. "You're all destined to die, to crumble into ash and nothingness. To be forgotten."

"I refuse the power you gave me. I will no longer bow to you," Breyna went on, stoic. Motionless. She didn't waver as I stared into her eyes. Didn't back down.

Setting a hand on her shoulder, I sent a shock of pain through her, one that rippled throughout every muscle and bone and tendon in her body. She stiffened, biting her lip to avoid crying out. Her agony filled the air around us, a sweet flavor I could taste, an invigorating fuel I could sense filling me, strengthening me.

I leaned forward to whisper in her ear as she choked back a whimper. "Foolish mortal," I breathed. "I'm the Queen of Death. I am your end, the last thing you see before death claims you. Young or old, willing or not, I meet every human at the close of their story, every time. At the very last, you will *always* bow to me."

Stepping back, I gestured to the soldiers clustered around us. "Kill her."

As my army overtook Breyna, I savored her screams, wiping away a tear of joy from the thrill and the power I drew from them.

CHAPTER TWENTY-ONE

Caesiem

One Year Ago

Not long after my eighteenth birthday, Revaed hosted one of his extravagant parties. All evening, I'd laughed and charmed those around me. I'd eaten delicacies and drank alcohol. Lots of alcohol.

Now, a scent that reminded me of citrus and cinnamon filled the air as a young woman about my age leaned forward, bracing me with a gentle hand on my arm. I dragged my eyes up from the mosaic tiled floor, which had started to spin beneath me, and to the glass in my hand, the deep hue of the pomegranate wine within turning it blood-red. How many glasses had I consumed tonight?

I stuffed my hand into my pocket, where I always kept the worn, crinkled paper with my name scrawled across it. Every day, without fail, I took it with me: to training with the other mages residing in the palace or with the finest guards and warriors Teramyl had to offer; to my tutoring where I learned basic lessons like math, reading, writing, and history; and to my sessions with Revaed where I shadowed him and the High Imperator to study politics in action. And even to parties such as these, which Revaed hosted with regular vigor, as if the more he drank and lost himself in social revelry, the more he could ignore his father's cutting remarks or physical punishments.

Deep down, I knew I relished these moments for similar reasons. My parents might not be alive, but I had the same persistent sense of insecurity and grief, the fear that they hadn't ever cared. While Revaed was subject to derision and violent episodes, I was left with unending questions of why I hadn't been enough for the mother and father who'd abandoned me.

"Are you all right?" The woman's voice invaded my brain, shoving aside my muddled thoughts.

I lifted my face to study her, taking in her luminous eyes, a deep shade of midnight blue that reminded me of the ocean. She swept her long, sleek hair over her shoulder, once again filling the air with her intoxicating perfume. It was heady, mingling with the influence of the wine…

"I could be better," I admitted, flashing her a dimpled smile. "With the right company."

Her eyes darkened with her desire as she stepped forward, taking my comment for the invitation it was. She trailed a hand down my chest and grinned, reaching for my wine. I let her drink deeply before setting it aside. "Delicious, but I can think of more fun ways to pass the time when one is at a party, my lord."

I shifted my gaze over her shoulder, to where Revaed was slumped in a chair, downing the final dregs of his own drink. His violet eyes were glazed as he spoke to a woman nearby, someone who definitely wasn't a member of the court. Her red dress was embroidered with fine gold thread and her jewelry spoke of wealth, but she wouldn't be the type of match Revaed's father wanted. But that meant she was just the kind of person Revaed preferred to spend an evening with, deep in conversation, seeking the companionship he longed for. He wasn't yet in his dark stage of drinking, when the woman tried to make a move he rejected, only to move on and leave him as lonely as before, and he sank into depression and self-loathing.

He'll be fine, I thought.

Usually a girl didn't catch my eye. Usually I only lost myself in drinking, wishing it could permanently erase the grief and my sense of…lessness. But tonight—perhaps it was the way her perfume made me feel as drunk as the wine. Perhaps it was the fact that her eyes reminded me of the ocean I loved so much. All I knew was that tonight, I wanted to lose myself in a stranger and try to forget the world.

I woke to that same scent of citrus and cinnamon the next day, but now it was too strong. My head pounded and my stomach turned. I blinked against the late morning light spilling through the half-open drapes in my room, gilding the burnt red walls. For a moment, I studied the stenciled patterns painted along the archway leading from my bedroom to my front room. My entire body was leaden, my mind sluggish.

It took a moment to register the warm arm draped over my bare chest, the gentle rhythm of someone's breathing beside me. Glancing down, I brushed aside the curtain of dark hair attached to the stranger, reaching out to move her arm. I froze, horror curdling in my stomach.

A tattoo of a small fire-breathing dragon stared back at me from the girl's inner wrist. It was the mark the High Imperator demanded each one of his mistresses bear, to signify that they were off-limits to all but him. I'd never expected that one of his mistresses would have dared to attend one of Revaed's parties and approach me. Surely this woman would face consequences as surely as any poor sap of a man foolish enough to touch her would.

Groaning, I gently pushed her arm away and rose from bed, plucking my discarded clothes off the floor. It didn't matter that they were yesterday's outfit, smelling of wine. I had to move. Fast.

Fool, I thought. *What was I thinking?*

That was the problem. I hadn't been thinking. I'd only wanted meaningless escape, and of course, like always, the escape had been temporary. And this time, it came with far graver consequences than a headache and queasiness.

I had to get my thoughts to churn through my haze and come up with a plan, or I was doomed.

But it was too late. Someone must have already tried to summon the mistress from her chambers, only to find her missing. Maybe a servant or guard had seen her leave the party with me last night. Fool that I'd been, I hadn't bothered to ask about the girl and find out who she was. It certainly hadn't ever crossed my mind to be discreet when I'd led her to my rooms.

Heavy footsteps in the hallway were the only warning before the door to my chambers swung open so hard it slammed against the inner wall. The High Imperator himself stormed through the front room and into my bedchamber, trailed not by guards but by Revaed himself.

I blanched, taking in the sneering expression of the High Imperator and then Revaed's wide, terrified eyes. Their gazes swept the bed, where the woman was sitting up, frozen in fear, and then landed on me.

"You," the High Imperator said, his gold eyes full of cold fury. That one word held a hundred unspoken threats, giving me a sensation not unlike melting ice slipping down my spine. "Who do you think you are, an orphaned whelp with nothing but magic to distinguish him from any other homeless, thieving rat, helping yourself to what's mine?"

"Father," Revaed said, stepping between the imperator and me and injecting as much authority into his voice as he could. "It's my fault."

Shock made me speechless.

"What do you mean?" the High Imperator scoffed, turning to Revaed and assessing him like he was a pest who had crawled into his palace.

"I—I encouraged this." Revaed gestured around the room.

Before my guardian could say another word, the High Imperator chuckled, low and deep. "Ah. I almost could have forgiven you, had it been *you* who was finally man enough to lie with the girl." He snorted. "But as usual, you remind us all of how pathetically defective you are."

Despite his attempt at standing tall in his father's presence, I saw Revaed's shoulders slump, the words hitting their mark, like they always did.

"Guards!" the High Imperator snapped, and a group of men and women marched swiftly into the room, their stoic expressions revealing nothing when they saw the imperator's young mistress in my bed. "Take my son away. It seems he needs to learn another lesson."

"No—" I started, but Revaed threw a sharp glance my way. *Don't make my sacrifice for nothing,* his expression seemed to say.

"What?" the High Imperator demanded. "Would you like to join my son?"

I shook my head, forcing myself not to watch as Revaed was dragged from my chambers.

What new horrors would Revaed endure—all for me?

The imperator's eyes landed once again on the girl. "And her…"

Revulsion swept through me when I saw the despair and agony in the young woman's eyes. Maybe her mistake had been a desire to escape, too. I could only imagine the memories that haunted her, knowing the imperator's cruelty.

"Take care of her," the High Imperator finished, turning his back as if he couldn't be bothered with any more of this.

Before I could protest, one of the guards stepped forward. In one motion, he had his sword drawn, slicing it through the woman's neck.

Blood sprayed, and her head rolled, landing with a sickening sound on the floor. Her body crumpled onto my bed, leaving a crimson pool spreading across the ivory sheets.

The wine from last night threatened to come back up as the metallic stench of blood assaulted my nose.

"Caesiem," the High Imperator snapped, and I forced my legs to move, to stand before the odious man. His eyes pierced into me. "Never touch what is mine again. Revaed may think you're his key to earning my affection, he may think you're his perfect heir, but powerful magic or not, you're only ever one misstep away from returning to the streets where you belong."

"Yes, sir," I muttered, bowing my head.

As the guards marched out, bearing the woman's corpse, all I could think about was how much I'd love to draw a blade across the imperator's throat.

CHAPTER TWENTY-TWO

Revaed

One Year Ago

I wasn't sure which was worse: the pain of the lashings or the pain of the words my doting father liked to gift me with. All I knew was that both the pain and the humiliation were familiar acquaintances for me now. Countless scars traced my back from other times I'd disappointed the High Imperator—which was all the time, as my very existence had become a disappointment to him as soon as he'd realized he could never depend on me to produce an heir. That the idea of being romantically involved with anyone disgusted me. That I was, according to him, *defective.*

Another crack of the whip—another slice of pain—and I couldn't stop the scream from tearing at my throat. My bound hands shook against the post the guards had tied me to. Men and women who had sworn to defend me had brought me to the whipping post usually reserved for prisoners, sliced open the back of my shirt without ceremony, and dutifully carried out my father's commands. Twenty lashes.

In my head, I counted each cut of the whip. *Defective.* Snap. *Worthless.* Another jolt of pain. *Disgusting.* Fire searing through my skin. *I only put up with you because you're my blood, my heir…and you can't give me the courtesy of continuing my line?* Hot blood trickling down my back.

Perhaps the only mercy was that, to avoid embarrassment to his name, Father always ensured the lashings took place on the post in the palace dungeons, not in a courtyard out in the open. My humiliation was only for our guards to witness, not for the servants and nobility, or for the public beyond the palace grounds. Mostly, it was his sick way of putting me in my place, as he liked to say, as if he expected regular pain would change me into the man he wanted me to be.

The rancid stench of the dungeons filled my nose, mingling with the tang of my own blood. Another crack of the whip. More tearing flesh. More agony.

Another mercy was that Caesiem wasn't present. Eventually, he would know. He would realize the extent of my father's cruelties and punishments, that even I wasn't immune to his hatred or wrath. Caesiem would know that I'd taken his punishment, and that I'd gladly do so again and again, if it would spare him from what I'd lived with for years. Self-loathing and scars. Loneliness and pain.

But this time, it was bearable, because I was enduring it for him. I gritted my teeth as the whip sliced into me again, trying in vain to keep myself from crying out. The guards didn't speak, didn't taunt or jeer or rejoice in my pitiful state.

I was certain, deep down, they despised this as much as I did. They didn't dare go against my father, but I could tell they pitied me. I wanted to hate them for it, but for many long years, pity was the closest thing to love I'd ever known. And I couldn't hate the ones to feel compassion.

As soon as it was over, one of the men rushed forward with a cup of water, while another unbound my wrists and helped steady me on my feet. I smirked at the guard as he rested my arm over his shoulder to support me. "I appreciate that you used the gentler whip today," I rasped.

The guard didn't respond to my jest. None of them ever did. It was clear they hated this, that they liked to keep a stony silence hovering between us, as if that could erase their guilt. Not that I blamed them. The High Imperator would have ordered them to be brutally executed if they didn't do as he asked.

This was all practically a routine now, the way I forced myself to smile as I teetered forward. The way I slumped as they assisted me into an empty cell, the cleanest one in the dungeons, as they'd prepared it especially for me. The hushed whispers as the already waiting healer tended to my wounds.

And as always, the welcome relief of darkness as I slipped into unconsciousness.

Present

Caesiem was safe, asleep in the ridiculously oversized monstrosity the former empress had called a bed. At some point, he'd half-woken, delirious from pain and the healers' medicines, asking again and again for Lo.

My chest tightened as I thought of the conversation I'd have to endure with Caesiem. Would it break his heart? In my mind's eye, I saw his pendant hanging from Lo's neck. It was a rare gesture for a mage to give up his or her pendant, because few could channel their magic as powerfully as Caesiem without one. And the protection the pendant could offer a person was only effective under the right conditions…

I wondered if Lo knew the significance of her gift, if she understood what it meant. And did she even care, or was she simply using Caesiem?

Bitterness threatened to swallow me whole as I rose from the chair I'd pulled up beside the bed and swiveled away. "Make sure he's resting," I muttered needlessly to the healer half-dozing in the settee on the other side of the room, waiting till he could be useful again. He straightened and stood, bowing low. I ignored him as I swept through the quarters, past Karye's extravagant personal armory and sitting room, and out into the halls. I waved the posted guards away when they tried to trail me.

Lo threw open the doors immediately when I knocked, her eyes blazing with hatred—but also surprise. It's not like I'd bothered with knocking before. I shoved past her into her sitting room, slamming the door behind me.

She backed up warily, surveying me as if hunting for weaknesses. My eyes snagged on the pendant hanging from her neck.

"Caesiem is back," I said, exhaustion making my voice rough. It'd been a long night, and I didn't expect to sleep at all until I was certain Caesiem was all right. "He's hurt."

To her credit, the flash of concern in her eyes didn't appear to be feigned. "Hurt? Where is he?"

I held up a hand when she flung herself toward the door.

"He's resting. I only came here to remind you of the consequences of sharing too much with him when you *do* see him next."

She lifted her chin, looking murderous. "You mean, you don't want him knowing that you killed Naina, or that you broke our fake alliance by storming the academy," she retorted.

My eye twitched as I stepped closer, lowering my tone. "If you tell him anything, I will know, and your people will pay the price."

I didn't wait for her to fling any more insults at me before I left the room and strode back down the hall. If Caesiem found out…but he wouldn't. He couldn't, because this time, it would be harder for him to see that I was only doing this because I was still protecting him, still protecting our people, just like I'd always done. Just like I always would.

CHAPTER TWENTY-THREE

Caesiem

Opening my eyes, I found myself within Revaed's own quarters, stretched out on his enormous bed with Revaed himself half-asleep in a chair at my side. Pain stabbed at my shoulder, freshly bandaged once more, as I sat up against the pillows. At some point, I must have slipped into unconsciousness from the blood loss, but based on the dim grey light trickling through the drawn drapes, it was either still night or very early in the morning.

A heavy blanket of stillness had settled over the palace.

For a moment, I simply stared at my guardian, studying the way he looked younger and more innocent when asleep. Without the weight of the world on his shoulders. The memory of how he'd borne his father's wrath for me collided with Meli's vision. She'd implied Revaed had only ever used me, honing me into a perfect weapon to perform his will. But every moment he'd fought for me or cared for me, naturally stepping into the role of the only father figure I'd ever known, contradicted all of that.

It eased me to see him watching over me, just as he had when I'd been sick or injured as a child.

"Caes?" Revaed's tone was thick with his drowsiness as he stirred. "I'm sorry…I must have fallen asleep." He sat up in the chair, his eyes darting over to a settee across the room, where a healer was curled up, sound asleep. "How do you feel?"

Gingerly, I stretched my arm. "Amazing. How did you…?"

Revaed smirked, gesturing to an empty vial resting on the bedside table. "Our healers are skilled, but as you've taught me, theslynik is positively miraculous."

I scowled. "The nymphs are dangerous, even Sephrode," I said. "You're not a water mage, and she can't be trusted."

"Really, Caes," Revaed said, flicking the vial and shaking his head. "You're starting to sound like the guardian here. *Anyway*, you were losing a lot of blood last night. It was worrisome." His jaw tightened. "I was terrified, honestly."

When he lifted his gaze back to mine, there was no mistaking the concern in his violet eyes.

"What happened?" he asked quietly. "Did the Alrenians take you?"

I shook my head, guilt scrabbling through my chest as I shared the lie Meli had given me, telling a story of hiding, a failed attempt at stitching up my own arm, and barely making it back to the palace. I added a tale about losing Valentra during the battle, letting Revaed assume she was perhaps dead or injured elsewhere in the capital.

"Well, those stitches must have saved your life," Revaed said, running a hand through his hair before catching himself and fixing it. "If you hadn't done anything at all, I don't think you would have made it back to the palace."

My eyes trailed toward the bedroom door, my worry for Lo a constant weight on my chest. "Revaed," I murmured, "I need to see Lo."

Revaed flinched. The sight sent fear snaking along my skin. "I…we need to talk about her," he said at last. "I'm sorry. She betrayed our alliance. All this time, she was working behind our backs with the Forwyn here in the palace. They were exchanging notes, planning to undermine our work here. I had to put all the Forwyn within the palace in the dungeons, to ensure none could threaten our lives, especially after the riots and the losses we sustained."

I swallowed thickly. Meli's news had been true. I wasn't really surprised—had I ever deluded myself into thinking Lo trusted us Teramese to aid the Forwyn?—but I was terrified of what Revaed was planning to do. "What do you mean?" I demanded. "Did you…call off the alliance? Where is she? You didn't imprison Lo, did you?"

The world tilted as I swung my legs over the side of the bed.

Revaed threw up a hand, gently pushing me back. "Wait. She's all right. She's in your rooms, and no, the alliance can be repaired. She's agreed to make a public announcement apologizing for her actions before she marries you. Now that you're back, we'll finalize the wedding plans. We'll appease the Forwyn Elders who've sided with us, and, since they don't know much about taming the dragons, hopefully secure the help of more Forwyn to teach us. Including Lo. She can work with you directly. We'll tame the dragons, send supplies back to Teramyl, share knowledge of how to stop the wild dragons there, overthrow the Alrenians…" He sighed. "And then, we can focus on building a peaceful life here. With the Forwyn. We can still make this work, still achieve everything we hoped for."

The world spun. My mind felt dull as I tried to process it all. Here I was, fearing for Lo's life, and Revaed was talking about wedding plans and dragon taming. I leaned my head in my hands, trying to get the dizzy spell to subside.

Revaed noticed my discomfort immediately. "Drink this," my guardian said, seizing a glass of water from the nightstand and pressing it to my lips.

I gulped it down, thankful for something to do with my hands, for something simple to occupy my mind for a moment. When I finished, my thoughts felt more settled. I knew what I needed to do, what would ground me as questions and uncertainty continued to whirl through my brain.

Sliding my hand into my pocket, I ran my fingers over Lo's ribbons. I had to see her.

"I'm going to talk to Lo," I announced, standing. This time, the world didn't sway, and my body felt stronger.

"You need to rest," Revaed said, but his protest was half-hearted. It was clear he knew arguing with me would do no good.

I shook my head stubbornly, pacing across the room and reaching for the bedroom door. "I can rest later." I needed to see her to reassure myself. To return her ribbons. To hold her in my arms again.

Revaed trailed me as I wound my way through the quiet palace halls, meeting only posted guards who saluted us as we passed. My guardian knew better than to continue protesting, but I could feel his disapproval practically radiating off him.

For an instant, as I stood before the door leading to my quarters, swaying a little on my feet and preparing to knock, I felt like an utter fool. Maybe Lo wouldn't even be awake, and I shouldn't be disturbing her. Maybe she'd had more time to think about the mistakes I'd made, and she'd reiterate the fact that she couldn't ever forgive me. Maybe she'd say she never wanted to see me again.

Drawing her ribbons from my pocket, I clutched them tightly and knocked anyway. Even if she turned me away, I wanted her to have her necklace back.

Each thud of my fist against the door slammed in time with my heart. I waited for a breathless few moments before the door swung inward and Lo's face peeked out at me. The dim torchlight dancing along the walls reflected in her eyes, setting the emerald flecks within on fire.

"Caesiem," she murmured, and she didn't hesitate, didn't sneer at me in disgust. She threw her arms around my neck, pulling me back into the room. She hugged me so tightly I could feel her heart racing against my chest, could smell the scents of coconut and passionfruit lingering in her hair.

There were a hundred things I could have said, but in that moment, the relief of seeing her all right, of finally holding her again, and the thrill of being welcomed so wholly consumed everything else. Cupping her face, I leaned into her, letting my kiss tell her what I couldn't seem to say aloud. She responded immediately, sliding her fingers through my hair as she sighed against my lips.

I forgot everything—the fact that Revaed had followed me here, the pain still flaring in my shoulder, the doubts weighing me down after the truths Meli had shared. It wasn't like losing myself with Lo—it was more like finding myself, like discovering better parts that existed deep within me that I'd believed had vanished long ago. *Home.* The thought burned through me, settling warm and assuring in my chest. Holding her in my arms, tasting her kiss—*this* felt like home.

"Really, Caes," Revaed sighed from the entryway.

Lo pulled away from me, leaving a startling absence of warmth as soon as she left my arms. Ignoring Revaed's snarky comment, she studied my face. "Are you all right?"

"I'm fine," I said when her eyes landed on the bandage that bound my shoulder. "It's nothing serious."

"He needs to rest," Revaed interrupted from where he was leaning against the doorway and scowling.

Lo set her jaw, immediately tensing at the sight of him. "He can rest here."

"As if he'd *rest* here," Revaed scoffed, gesturing between Lo and me.

Lo rolled her eyes and spun toward him, shooting him a fierce glare. Revaed's eyes bored into hers, and for a heavy moment they stared one another down, a silent battle of wills. Something in Revaed's face must have made Lo change her mind.

"I want you back where the healers know to find you right away," Revaed went on, turning to me with an expression on his face that was close to pleading. A strange jolt went through my gut. Was he jealous? Not of what Lo and I shared, exactly, but of our closeness? He swallowed, slowly. "And I want you where I can make sure you're all right," he added, the hint of vulnerability in his eyes unmistakable now. "You—you gave me a scare, Caes. Please."

"Just…give me a moment?" I asked. "I promise I'll go rest after this."

Revaed pursed his lips but offered a single nod and slipped out into the hallway. I listened to his footsteps trailing away before I turned back to Lo.

"Caesiem—" she cut off, her voice breaking, and she shook her head. "I'm just glad you're all right. But what happened?"

"I could ask the same of you," I said, drawing the ribbons from my pocket and placing them in her hand, curling my fingers around hers as I did so.

Lo tossed me a pointed look. "Don't you think you've kept enough secrets?"

"The Alrenians weren't really rioting. It was too organized." I swallowed. "And their gifts—they're coming back somehow. There were men and women fighting like they were possessed, laughing and pulling off inhuman feats with their war and courage gifts." I frowned at the memory of the man who'd nearly slaughtered me before Meli had intervened. "We lost. Horribly." Guilt thundered through me as I thought of my dead men and women, my failure. My magic should have protected them, should have ensured victory. "I couldn't save them."

Tenderness in her eyes, Lo pulled me into another hug, as if she could erase all my failures just with her touch. I leaned into her, thankful she didn't press me for more. I wasn't ready to broach the topic of Meli and her underground Alrenians and Forwyn, or their ridiculous notion that I'd spy for them. That I'd turn against my own guardian.

"I went out into the city," Lo murmured, and I realized she was trembling. I tightened my arms around her, suddenly terrified for her. There was a hollow, broken sound to her words, a heavy grief I hadn't sensed before in our mutual relief to see one another. "One of the Forwyn girls here—she said she'd overheard your soldiers talking about Alrenians at the abbey." There was a long pause. My pulse thundered in my ears as I clung to her, somehow already knowing what she would say. "Naina is dead."

Slowly, she pulled back, blinking up at me with teary lashes. But she didn't crumple, didn't dissolve into weeping. There was a hard set to her jaw and a fire in her green-flecked eyes that reminded me she was no stranger to loss. And she might have been hurting, but she was also angry. A lover turned into a fighter to protect all she cared about.

I brushed away a tear that had escaped down her cheek. "I'm sorry. Are your sisters…?"

She frowned, shaking her head. "I don't know." She clutched her ribbon necklace in a trembling fist. Her eyes were distant as she stared out the window, then turned back to me. For a moment, she looked like she wanted to say more, but stopped herself. "You should get some rest, like Revaed wants." Her eyes dropped to my shoulder, and I realized it was throbbing from my quick movements when I'd hugged her. "It's bleeding again. You probably pulled out a stitch."

I could sense the wall she was putting up between us. "Right." I stepped back. "I…goodnight, Lo." I was out of the room before she could respond, if she'd wanted to respond at all.

Revaed was the one who announced Lo's identity at the coronation, I thought as I joined my guardian, leaning against him wearily as we headed back to his rooms. *Did the Alrenians target the abbey because they connected her to it? Does she blame Revaed and our alliance? Does she blame* me?

I squeezed my eyes shut, pain welling inside. *Does it matter? She already made it clear she'll never forgive you. This is just one more unforgivable mistake she can add to the list. You're a fool, Caesiem, for ever thinking that could change.*

"I'll have the healer look at your shoulder again," Revaed was saying, but I could scarcely focus on him.

You're a fool for thinking you could ever not *be torn in two.*

Half of me loyal to Lo and my desire to be a better man for her. For her people.

Half of me faithful to the guardian who had saved me, again and again, and the Teramese I was duty-bound to protect and serve.

CHAPTER TWENTY-FOUR

Lo

Listening to the sound of Caesiem's and Revaed's footsteps retreating down the hall, I pressed my back against the door, pushing down my anger and grief where it couldn't consume my thoughts. Would Caesiem have listened if I'd told him that Naina had died at *Revaed's* hand? That his guardian had threatened my sisters and used me to attack the Aerekni Academy? That I feared for my father's life because of Revaed?

But I hadn't dared to speak the words, not with Revaed himself within earshot. The memory of the girl he'd murdered in these very rooms was too fresh, too threatening. I'd seen the unspoken words in the false emperor's eyes when he'd looked at me, reminding me of the price I refused to pay if I told Caesiem the truth.

Cruel, manipulative boeri, I thought, stomping back into the bedroom, clutching the ribbons Caesiem had returned to me in my fist.

I had to find a way out of these rooms, but it couldn't be obvious. If Revaed discovered I was escaping, if a single guard saw me…I couldn't risk the chance that he'd kill more of my people in retaliation. I couldn't bear the guilt of being his excuse for punishing more Forwyn.

Even if I knew it wasn't my fault, the weight was breaking me. I couldn't stop seeing the girl staring back at me, the knife plunging into her chest. The images cycled through my head, over and over, threatening to haunt me forever, threatening to paralyze me.

But I wouldn't let them. I couldn't.

Remembering how Naina had helped me banish the memories of the night Karye had nearly murdered me, I sucked in a deep breath and listened for Elhani's song. I concentrated on the way I could feel his magic coursing through me, warm and comforting. Grounding.

A knock sounded on the front door to Caesiem's rooms, tearing me from my thoughts. Before I could wonder if it was Revaed, returned to make more threats, the door creaked open and Elder Ettonou crept through the sitting room to hover in the entryway to the bedroom.

I studied him warily. "What do you want?" I demanded, crossing my arms.

The Elder practically slithered into the room, reminding me of the serpent he truly was. His dark eyes assessed me with barely suppressed anger, burning with silent menace. "To talk with you," he said, stepping into the room and staring at me, like he expected me to bow or offer him some other gesture of respect.

Instead, I turned away, putting my back to him to sink into the nearest armchair. I didn't respect or fear the Elder, and I wanted to make that abundantly clear. "Then talk," I said, folding my hands in my lap and waiting for him to take one of the nearby seats.

He inched forward, leaning against the mantel over the empty fireplace. "I don't think you understand the position we Forwyn are in, *amara'rekni*," he began. "We at last have the powerful allies we need to stop the Alrenian army, to see justice finally doled out upon—"

I rolled my eyes. "No, I don't think *you* understand," I interrupted. "How blind can you be? Revaed and his Teramese army invaded us. They don't care about a true alliance. They want to *use* us, and if we refuse to give up our freedom, our empire, they slaughter us."

Rage flickered through his eyes. The Elder set a trembling hand on the mantel, as if forcibly holding himself back. Tension thickened the air, but I refused to be afraid of a bully. "It's easy to see in black and white, when you're young. And you lived for a few years as a nun, correct?" He shook his head, as if I were terribly naïve. "The world isn't as simple as all of that, unfortunately."

Slowly, I rose from my chair to meet his gaze. "Isn't it?" I demanded. "Isn't it as simple as choosing freedom over slavery, of choosing our people's best interests over our own desire for revenge?"

A muscle feathered in the Elder's jaw. "You have a unique opportunity that you're choosing to throw away," he snapped. "A chance to build an alliance that can change everything for us. That can give us the chance to never have to fear the Alrenians again, that can give us the power of two armies, two peoples. But your selfish desire to—what? try to wrest control of the government yourself?—is going to destroy this opportunity. You've put our alliance in dangerous waters with your little rebellious acts. You need to stop your underhanded scheming and lying now and cooperate with this marriage alliance, before our people's chance at happiness is gone forever."

I scoffed. "You have to be mad. You think that I want power? I want *freedom*." Shaking my head, I choked on a bitter laugh. "If all I wanted was power, I'd gladly marry Caesiem and become their princess."

Elder Ettonou's expression was cold. "So you *are* going to resist the marriage alliance?"

"I'm going to do whatever it takes to keep the Forwyn alive and free," I said. "And it's none of your business, when you're nothing but a traitor and a fool."

The Elder stalked closer, his arms trembling at his sides. "Watch your tongue, girl," he snarled.

I laughed bitterly. "What are you going to do? Kill me and our chance at this alliance you want so badly?"

He lifted his arm as if to punch or slap me, but his movements were clumsy and slow compared to mine. I stepped backward, dodging the strike and seizing his arm at the same moment I slammed my knee into his groin. Groaning, he stumbled, catching himself before he crumpled in pain to the floor.

"You," he spat, but that was all he managed to get out.

I was already calling on Elhani's magic, feeling it buzz through my veins. "Get out," I said, sensing the power living within each word I spoke. "Leave these rooms and leave me alone."

Fear widened the Elder's eyes. With a sharp breath, he drew himself up, whirled on his heels, and stormed out of the rooms. The door slammed behind him, a sound that echoed in my ears.

Furious, I paced the floor, mind whirling. I had to get out of here and find out if my father was alive. I had to find help and form a plan that could save the Forwyn imprisoned in the palace.

I leaned against the mantel and inspiration struck. The one place I hadn't inspected, that might not be checked for a hidden exit, was the fireplace. There were only a few months each year where it was cool enough to actually burn a fire, making it the perfect location to conceal a door.

It took mere moments to run my fingers along the mantel and find the hidden lever. As soon as I depressed it, the rough scrape of stone against stone filled the room, and a portion of the fireplace swung inward, revealing a dark square. Chill air flowed out of the tunnel, making my skin prickle. Glancing over my shoulder, I weighed my options. Did I have enough time to follow the tunnel to wherever it led before one of the Teramese came to my rooms and found I was missing?

But did I have time to wait?

Caesiem was back, and though he was injured, I didn't expect Revaed would waste any time in arranging for our marriage and my public announcement affirming our alliance. And then…then I was sure that despite his promises, Revaed would execute most, if not all, of the Forwyn in captivity.

My escape might also cost lives, but it was a risk I'd have to take. Gathering a lantern and some matches from a nearby shelf, I lit its candle and held it up to inspect the opening of the tunnel. I found nothing but cobwebs and dust coating the stone walls, and steps descending into pure blackness, so deep I could have been staring at nothingness. And then my eyes snagged on a stone that was a different color from the rest. I slid my fingers over it—a lever.

Relief flooded through me. If I hurried, I could leave and return without the Teramese ever knowing. Breathing a quick prayer to Elhani, I stepped within the tunnel, depressed the lever, and listened to the stone scrape, closing me within the shadowy, mildewy space.

Each breath I took echoed as I descended the narrow steps, the candle offering the smallest pool of golden light. As the minutes passed and the steps continued, the muscles in my legs began to burn, letting me know I must have gone far. At last, I reached the bottom, the air heavy with the scents of dirt and mildew and a hint of brine. Here, the walls remained stone, but they were roughly hewn, and the floor itself was nothing but hard-packed earth.

A long stretch led onward, sometimes joining other tunnels that led upward or downward. Deciding I must be somewhere beneath the city now, I chose the level route, pausing now and then to trace marks in the dirt floor to track my path and help lead me back later.

Finally, another set of stone steps led me up to where the air grew warmer and more humid, smelling of the city, and stopped at a door. Heart thundering in my ears, I paused to listen, but either the tunnel blocked out all sound, or whatever awaited me outside was quiet, indicating nothing about where this exit led. Carefully, I extended my hand toward another lever and blew out my candle, leaving the lantern and extra matches within the tunnel. The stone door scraped along the walls, allowing the light of early morning to seep inside. I blinked against the brightness while waiting within the shadows, praying the door wasn't opening near a patrolling Teramese guard.

I found myself in an alcove, set between two huge buildings that overshadowed a towering statue blocking my view. But I recognized this statue—it was a rendering of one of the Alrenian's revered Dragon Keeper captains, his stance proud as he surveyed the marketplace. It was a smaller statue than the one of the empress that had been attached to the central fountain, back before it'd been destroyed by the Forwyn dragon attack.

I was in the marketplace at Akytha District, and something was happening.

A heavy tension permeated the air, filling my body with dread. Something was wrong—very wrong. I could sense it in the uneasy quiet, in the sharp, metallic scent drifting on a breeze that should have tasted of sea brine.

I crept forward, closing the entrance behind me and crouching behind the statue for cover. Peering around its base, my heart lodged in my throat as I took in the scene before me. In the center, near the fountain full of the shattered remnants of Empress Oreva's statue, stood rows upon rows of pikes pounded into cracked cobblestones.

Forwyn and Alrenian corpses were skewered on every single one, their dead eyes staring straight ahead, as disciplined and unwavering as eerie soldiers in an army. The stink of blood and death saturated the air, so thick I choked on bile. My hands shook, sweat collecting on the back of my neck as I tried and failed to tear my gaze from the horrible sight.

Caesiem, I thought, my eyes burning and my chest aching with fury and grief. He wasn't responsible for this, not directly, but I knew who was. Knew the man he served had ordered this slaughter as a warning to the Alrenians for rioting and the Forwyn for plotting against the Teramese.

And Caesiem…did he know what Revaed was doing? Did he know just how brutal his guardian could be? Did he truly think an alliance could *ever* exist when our imposter emperor ruled so ruthlessly?

If Caesiem knew the truth, would he pick Revaed or me? The question persisted, matching the pounding of my breaking heart. I'd known I was a fool from the beginning to let my guard down around Caeisem, but it was too late. I already cared for him, deeply.

Anything between us had been a farce from the beginning. He'd used me, and I'd used him. I would never stop fighting for my people, and I feared he'd never stop fighting for his. Never stop believing Revaed, never stop choosing survival over mercy and peace and freedom.

I'd known all along there was no chance for us. I'd known that we didn't make sense and could never be together, but I'd let myself hope anyway. I'd chosen to be a fool, and now I'd have to pay the price in grief.

Angrily, I swiped a tear from my cheek, my hand shaking as I dropped it to the side.

The idea of pretending to go along with Revaed's alliance to save the imprisoned Forwyn made me want to vomit. I couldn't make the speech he wanted me to, and I certainly couldn't go through with a marriage ceremony. I'd been willing to do it for my people—but to pretend when my heart was crumbling? To wish whatever was between Caesiem and me was sincere and not hopelessly broken? I wasn't sure I could manage it. The very thought made my chest feel empty and hollow, made my bones heavy with sorrow.

It was ridiculous—how could I grieve the loss of someone who had never been mine?

But it didn't matter what my own feelings were. I had to keep up my pretense for Revaed—at least, until I could find a new plan. Until I could find allies who could help me get the Forwyn out of the palace.

Get to Aerekni Academy.

I gazed up at the sky, which was already growing brighter, the sun almost high enough to glare over the tallest rooftops surrounding the marketplace. Had one of the Teramese already gone to my rooms to deliver breakfast? Perhaps I'd already destroyed my chances of secrecy, and Revaed had sent soldiers to hunt for me.

Footsteps tugged me out of my anxious thoughts. A line of Teramese soldiers was marching toward the marketplace's main entrance, like a twisting serpent preparing to strike again. At the forefront of the line, several pairs of soldiers gripped Alrenian and Forwyn citizens between them.

My stomach lurched with renewed horror when I realized the killing hadn't ended. I curled my fingers into fists, my mind racing to form a plan. I had to stop this, but I was unarmed and alone.

Elhani, I prayed, studying the soldiers filing in. There were at least a dozen, with four victims, two Forwyn and two Alrenians. My heart dropped as I scanned their faces and recognized both of the Forwyn: No'ahim, the kindly owner of The Broken Crown, and my sister, Eloiyah. Neither struggled against the guards' grips, as if they knew it was futile and had already made their peace with their impending fate.

My mind coursed through the words Elhani had spoken on the beach, encouraging me to fight for what was right and to make a difference. *This* was what I was meant to do. *This* was the purpose for the warring emotions I carried within my heart: both the fierce love for my people and the burning anger toward the cruelty they faced.

"You sure you want to kill them first?" one of the Teramese soldiers sneered, his eyes like molten silver, heated and bloodthirsty, as he kicked Eloyiah to the cobblestones. "We could skewer them and leave these rats to die slowly."

Sprawled out on the ground, Eloyiah groaned and spat blood. She must have fought hard when the Teramese had taken her—must have only succumbed after they'd injured her. At this angle, I could see her face clearly, could study the trails of blood coursing from her forehead, her nose, and a split lip. But where had they found her? Was she one of the few remaining survivors from the battle at Aerekni Academy? Where were my other sisters? Was anyone else left alive?

Earlier, I'd been too shocked, too horrified, to search the rows of corpses for familiar faces. But now…I turned back, forcing myself to even as my thoughts reeled. I swept my eyes over the garish display, but I didn't recognize anyone. If the bodies of my other sisters or my father were here, they were near the back, hidden by countless other dead.

Another soldier kicked No'ahim to the ground with a dark look in her blue eyes. Sweat glued strands of black hair to her forehead as she wiped a tired arm across it, failing to do anything but smear blood and dirt along her bronze skin. "No, let's get this over with. I'm not here to make them suffer," she muttered. "I'm here to get this bloody job over with, and then I'm getting a drink."

Enraged at the casual way the woman discussed murdering my people, I dug my fingernails into my palms. I trembled with the energy it took to force myself not to leap out and attack them without a plan. Instead, I let my anger wash over me, clearing my mind. Blocking out my whirling thoughts, focusing every intention into one effort. Elhani's song rippled around me, its rich and colorful notes so beautiful and strong I could almost see it as it made my skin tingle, could almost taste it as it flowed inside me.

Eloyiah, I thought. *Noa'him.* Love for my sister washed over me, and love for the man I'd only met a few times, but who was my brother. *Save them.*

Power crackled through me, reminding me of how I'd used Elhani's magic earlier to send Elder Ettonou running away in fear. The magic was growing easier to wield. What had felt so mysterious before now came naturally, as easily as breathing. I savored the words on my tongue, drawing a deep breath as I prepared to stand and speak.

Eloyiah must have sensed Elhani's magic, because she turned her head, her warm brown eyes golden and soft in the pale morning light. Her gaze met mine as the Teramese soldiers shoved their Alrenian captives to their knees beside her and No'ahim, lining them up wearily, methodically, as if they'd been working through the night to dole out punishment upon the people of Inalgoth and leave behind this gruesome message. Likely, they had been.

With the barest movement, Eloyiah shook her head at me. Mouthed a single word: *Elhani.*

Confusion and fear tore through me, shaking my concentration. Elhani's song wavered, the notes fading on the breeze. Desperation thrummed in my heart, in my soul, as I scrambled to seize hold of the music again, as if I could capture each note in my fingers and grip them with sheer willpower.

But instead, Eloyiah spoke inside my head, calm and confident. She'd always had the sweetest singing voice of all my sisters, had always had a way of bringing tears to my eyes when she'd lifted that voice in worship. *That is not Elhani's will, dear sister.* Surprise trickled through me—when had Eloyiah mastered this part of Elhani's magic, to be able to speak within my mind like this? Or was it simply a new level of focus she'd managed to achieve here, with death staring her in the face? *There are too many soldiers for you, even with Elhani's magic,* she continued. *You wouldn't survive, and you* have *to survive.*

No, I protested, and I was startled to hear the word reverberate in my skull. Could Eloyiah hear it? Or perhaps she guessed from the way my eyes watered.

Listen, Lo, and trust me. It's my time.

It couldn't be. I refused to believe it. She was too young, too full of life. Grief made my throat swell and my eyes burn. She was wrong, and I could save her. I could fix this.

Only a few months ago, we'd celebrated her birthday—though she claimed she didn't know the exact date, she believed she was about thirty summers old.

Old enough to have acquired some wisdom, Naina had whispered fondly, eyes crinkling with her smile, *but young enough to have much to learn. It is an honor to reach thirty years, when countless of our enslaved ancestors never saw this many.* She'd adorned one of Eloyiah's braids with a turquoise ribbon, bright and gleaming. *The color of serenity—and of both youth and wisdom,* she'd declared with a wink.

Live to keep fighting. Eloyiah's voice was uncharacteristically firm. Determined. *Save our people. Don't move, Lo—*

The blue-eyed soldier punched one of the Alrenian captives—a young man who'd been trying to fight back. She drew a dagger and plunged it into the base of his skull unceremoniously, leaving him to fall forward, his head slamming against the cobblestones. His arms and legs twitched before he went motionless.

Another soldier beheaded the other Alrenian before she could crawl away. Nausea washed over me as the stench of copper and death filled the air. The woman's head left a bloody trail as it rolled, and I had to tear my eyes away, instead focusing on my kneeling sister.

Lo.

I bit my lip to keep myself from weeping aloud. Why did Eloyiah have to be right? Why did I hear the truth in her words, even when I shook my head, raging against it?

I can save you, I thought.

Another solider snapped Noa'him's neck in one quick motion, leaving his body crumpled and twisted on the ground. I choked back a sob, remembering his kind eyes, his warm smile.

They were coming for Eloyiah next, and she didn't fight. Didn't move. Kneeling calmly on the cobblestones, blood still streaming down her face, she gazed at the corpses lined up before her and began to move her lips, as if in prayer. No, I realized, she was *singing*. Singing as death came for her. Singing a song of the welcoming beauty of the Golden After, of a place without pain or death or grief or fear. Of a place where we were all together again, a family that could never again be torn asunder.

Strong. Poised. Unafraid. At peace. Eloyiah lifted her head and smiled, and let the notes fill this dreadful place with beauty, with hope.

It'll be all right, Lo. Trust.

When I'd first arrived at the abbey, Eloyiah must have seen the darkness in my eyes, the haunting memories tracing every one of my steps. She'd welcomed me with a warm embrace, whispering *You're safe now* into my ear. When I'd woke screaming in the night, fear closing in as I'd opened my eyes to my strange new room, Eloyiah had heard me. She'd been the one to fetch Naina, to join the old woman in praying and singing over me until I'd been lulled into a peaceful sleep.

Lo, tell—

I bit my own hand to cut off my scream as the silver-eyed soldier who'd brought Eloyiah here shoved his sword through her back. It sliced right through her effortlessly, the bloody tip emerging from her chest. A clean strike to her heart.

Her song faltered, blood dribbling from her lips. She lifted her eyes toward the sky, toward the rising sun bathing this scene of nightmares in gold, and then she fell.

Rage and grief and fear kept me rooted in place, kneeling behind the statue of a man who, if he'd lived in my time, would have been my enemy. Weeping silently. Eloyiah's voice echoed in my mind, reminding me over and over to trust her. And if there was anything I was good at, it was trusting my sisters, trusting my family.

But this wasn't a matter of trusting her with my own life. This had been about hers, cut too short. Brutally, callously. Left to be a message to our people and the Alrenians.

My ears rang as I wiped my tears away, as I forced myself to wait in the shadows while the soldiers added the four new bodies to the rows of corpses. They grunted and groaned about how exhausted they were, about how much they hated this tiresome job. Finally, *finally*, they shuffled out of the square, leaving me behind with the dead.

Leaving me behind with my emptiness.

"May Elhani hold your hand," I whispered hoarsely, forcing myself to study Eloyiah's lifeless form, "and the guidespirits lead you home."

I longed to step out of hiding and take down every body and honor them with a better memorial. A proper burning or even a send-off into the sea. Anything better than this—being left as an awful display for animals to ravage.

But I wouldn't waste what my sister had done for me. She'd believed I was meant to live, meant to fight. I wouldn't throw her sacrifice away, no matter how much turning away from the square destroyed me.

World-changer, Elhani had said. I was meant to fight and bleed for my people. Not to sit back and watch them bleed for me.

How many more times could I lose loved ones, before I broke irreparably?

How long before I was entirely alone, with no one left to fight for?

CHAPTER TWENTY-FIVE

Jalie

The temple glistened white against the bruised early morning sky, a beacon that I hoped could promise aid. The vines climbing its stone walls and the garden surrounding the building seemed promising, though from this distance I couldn't tell if it was full of only vegetables and aesthetic flowers, or if it also contained plants that could be used as antidotes.

Ryke hadn't been able to carry us for long that night, every beat of his wings unsteady as his weakened, poison-sick body had struggled to keep going. Instead, I'd been forced to let him land and lead him through the countryside, Tayla and Vander following warily. Now and then, Vander used his magic to send a powerful gust of wind Ryke's way, the force of it enough to hasten the dragon's steps when his strength flagged. We'd stopped briefly for rest, mostly because I knew Ryke needed it. When Vander first suggested it and I'd refused, he'd threatened to tie me up so I couldn't use my curse on them or run away, and I'd laughed in his face. In the end, I'd taken one glance at Ryke, his body slumped miserably as he nuzzled sadly against me, seeking comfort, and I'd relented.

But, when I'd slipped into an uneasy sleep, even my dreams had been restless. Kovi had held me in his arms just like he'd done when we'd said our goodbyes, when we'd made our hopeless promises to one another. Yet any warmth or comfort had vanished when Nesrelle had leaned over my shoulder, her shadows enveloping me as she whispered in my ear. Taunting me. Reminding me that Kovi and I were a dream that could never be. Telling me that he would never grant me my throne. That he would betray me, in the end.

When I'd awoken, I'd found Tayla curled on the ground asleep beside Vander, who'd been studying me warily. His silver eyes were shadowed, and weariness etched lines across his brow. Had he ever slept, or had he spent the entire time watching me, terrified I'd threaten his sweetheart again?

Laughter threatened to burble up, mirthless and bitter, but I'd shoved it down. "I won't kill you," I'd sneered, rolling my eyes as I stood and brushed grass off my smooth dragon scale tunic. I had never been more grateful about how comfortably made the armor was, so soft on the inside I could wear it for days of travel, could sleep in it, and not be in pain.

Vander ground his teeth. "Why would I ever trust your word?"

I smiled sweetly. "Because right now, your wind magic proves useful to help my dragon travel faster, especially when he's too weak to fly. And I know you won't assist me if I kill Tayla. So you needn't worry about her either. Not as long as I need you both."

Even now, hours later, I could sense Vander's wary eyes on me as I paused to take in the sight of the old Alrenian temple. It was the only sign of civilization for miles in any direction, and it appeared peaceful and untouched, perhaps one of the few places the Teramese intruders hadn't bothered to attack or seize. And it didn't appear like one of the abandoned temples scattered across our empire, left for nature to slowly reclaim once the gift the temple dwellers had dedicated themselves to teaching had vanished. Here, the garden was well-tended.

Renewed energy thrummed through my body as I picked up my pace, turning my steps toward the temple.

"What are you doing?" Vander demanded. I didn't bother to glance backward, so I couldn't tell if the way the breeze strengthened and tugged at my hair was from him using his power or not.

"Finding a cure for Ryke," I ground out.

"That's not the plan," Tayla snarled. "We are to head straight for the capital and Emperor Revaed—"

I whirled on them. Beside me, Ryke unleashed a curl of smoke and leaned against me, either in defense or weariness. "You don't make the plan," I said, giving them a smile that was all teeth. "Not unless you want to taste the curse you and your people deserve."

Vander straightened, and for an instant, I could practically see the wheels of his mind turning. He could throw me back with a powerful gust of wind, and if he and Tayla moved quickly enough, incapacitate me by binding me before I could touch them. But he'd seen the other powers Nesrelle had granted me, and as long as Ryke was still able to stand, still drawing breath, it was clear he would defend me to the end. I wasn't their prisoner, not really. They were still mine, at my mercy.

"Trust me," I continued, "we will go before your emperor." With that, I brushed a comforting hand along Ryke's snout. "I'll be back soon," I told him. "Keep an eye on these two for me." I shot the Teramese a warning glare.

Slowly, I crept toward the temple, scanning it for any signs of life. It was possible it was too early for any of its occupants to have risen, or maybe they were kneeling within their sanctuary, lost in silent prayer. The gate opened easily, swinging inward with a small creak and admitting me into the garden.

The heavy perfume of flowers and warm earth filled my nose, reminding me of the palace gardens and filling me with an aching longing for Mother and days gone by. I glanced around, hoping to see the plant that could create the antidote for the nethilys poison in Ryke's system, but it didn't matter. I would need the carefully harvested liquid boiled from its roots, something the temple hopefully stored within their infirmary.

As I approached the door, lifting my hand to knock, sounds trickled from an open window to my left. Someone was humming inside, carefree and content. It made my chest ache and the nestred rune on my cheek pulse with a wave of pain. How could anyone find joy or peace with our empire overrun?

I stepped back, scanning the entryway for some sort of symbol or inscription that would mark which gift this temple was dedicated to, but I saw nothing. Likely, any locals in a nearby town already knew and the dwellers found no need for a sign or inscription. More pain seared across my cheek while I knocked on the heavy wood door, my thoughts trickling toward bloodshed and vengeance.

Nesrelle's voice echoed through my head. *There's no room for joy in this empire, not after all that's happened. The fools. You should kill them for their flippancy when your land is hurting.*

Inhaling deeply, I pushed away her words, doing my best to ignore them.

Footsteps echoed as someone approached, swinging the door outward and peering at me with curious, gold-flecked grey eyes. The young woman's brow scrunched in concern as her gaze swept over me, taking in my wild, windswept hair, my grimy dragon scale armor, and the bright, ugly scar marring my face. She tucked a strand of nearly-black hair behind her ear and stepped forward.

"Do—do you need help?" she inquired.

Though she was taller than me, her fear and doubt made her appear small as I studied her.

Shame prickled through me when I noticed the way her eyes lingered on the knots in my hair and the clear marks from a lost battle covering my body, from the scar on my face to the hole in the side of my armor.

"Empress?" she murmured, her eyes widening and darting over my shoulder, as if searching for my entourage. She dipped into a quick bow, but I gestured for her to rise. "How can I help you?" she continued. "Is everything all right?" She stepped back quickly, ushering me inside.

I strode forward, trying to look regal despite my appearance. "I need the nethilys antidote."

"Were you poisoned?"

I pursed my lips. "My dragon was." Scanning the dim hallway, I took in the plain stone walls and tiled floor. Quiet reigned over the temple, making me think the rest of its residents must have still been asleep.

Regret flashed in the woman's pale eyes. "I'm so sorry, empress," she murmured. "But we don't grow the laevi plant in our garden. We've never had any need for a nethilys antidote here—not in this peaceful place." She fidgeted with the front of her skirt, twisting and untwisting it as she leaned against the wall behind her. "We rarely have need of our infirmary except for illness."

I scraped a weary hand across my brow. "What gift is this temple dedicated to?" I demanded.

"Hope," the woman said, her eyes shining. "If you're in need of help, you could make use of our sanctuary and beseech the Life-Giver."

Hope, a sneering voice in my mind repeated, and this time, I couldn't tell if the thought came from Nesrelle or myself. *There is no hope left in this empire. A useless gift. I could cut these fools down now, leave this temple open for Alrenians with a true,* worthy *gift to make use of.*

Pain flared along my cheek, sending a powerful rush through my veins, a longing that matched the bloodlust I'd felt in battle in Aramith. The curse I bore made my palms tingle, demanding to be used. To strengthen itself and me.

Bile made my mouth turn sour. What was happening to me?

"Fine," I said, gruffly. "I don't have much time to waste, but I'll use your sanctuary."

I stalked past the woman, who didn't move to follow or speak, perhaps too unnerved by my unexpected presence. Instead, I pressed down the hall alone, toward the entryway at its end that offered a glimpse of a bright sanctuary. Early morning sunlight trickled through windows lining every wall, turning the rows of white benches a soft orange the same shade as the fruit that had grown beside my balcony at home. Overhead, a large-scale painting full of vibrant colors covered the entire ceiling, depicting a garden scene in which the Giver of Life posed like a benevolent father, looking on as children played and splashed in a stream. Some sat at his feet, offering him bouquets of flowers and innocent smiles.

I rolled my eyes as I strolled to the front of the sanctuary, pausing at the ornately carved altar. Dust motes danced in the sunlight pouring over the wood, highlighting the flowers and vines decorating its edges. I recalled early childhood memories of priests reading from the Book of Life and speaking from this altar, one that represented the sacrifices the Life-Giver supposedly made for the people he loved so dearly. The work he did unseen to bring us our powerful gifts and the bountiful empire we enjoyed.

But all those blessings I'd accepted as permanent in my childhood years were gone now. Mother was dead. My empire had been stolen. And all I felt was an all-consuming desire to stand there and scream at the Life-Giver, to demand he give an accounting for everything he'd allowed to happen to his Chosen People. To me, his Chosen Empress.

No, the Giver of Life, god of my people, had never been there for me. The only one who'd ever heard my cries for help was Nesrelle, goddess of demons.

Burning with anger, I slammed my fists down on the altar's surface, relishing the ache that lanced through my hands on contact. "You've taken my mother, my throne, my empire, and now you threaten to take my dragon," I whispered, my throat thick with my mounting emotions. "Why? What do you *want* from me?"

I squeezed my eyes shut, forcing the burning threat of tears away. Forcing all weakness to crawl back into the furthest corner of my heart, until all I knew was rage. Nesrelle's cold presence lingered in the air around me, reminding me of my ties to her even when she wasn't physically nearby. She might have demanded a terrible price from my soldiers and me, but at least she'd given us *something* in return. At least she deigned to speak with me.

Opening my eyes, I scanned the sanctuary, watching the shadows cast by the trees outside dance along the walls. What did I expect from the Life-Giver? A vocal answer? An appearance to speak with me face-to-face like Nesrelle had? Turning my back on the altar, I choked out a bitter laugh.

Was that even what I *wanted* anymore? Would answers take away the pain?

My thoughts flickered toward Kovi, remembering the way he'd appealed to his god when I'd nearly been poisoned to death. Recalling how powerful his magic had been, magic that he claimed came directly from his god in a way we Alrenians didn't have access to the gifts that came from our own deity. Kovi's god seemed to listen to him.

"Elhani," I murmured, listening to the way the name flowed off my tongue, sounding harsh in my Alrenian accent.

"You call to me now, after you've struck a deal with the Demon Queen?"

The words rumbled through the air, powerful and menacing. My skin tingled, giving me the same sensation I experienced when a storm was brewing over the sea back home. Spinning around, my eyes met a pair of dark ones set in an ageless face. His brown skin bore a few wrinkles, giving him a sense of wisdom, but other than the aura of strength—of something *other*—crackling between us, there was nothing remarkable about him. He was of average height and appearance, and his clothes were in muted earth tones, travel-stained and smelling of warm dirt and deep forests.

And yet, fear shot through me instantly, making my knees bow and threaten to drop me to the floor.

"I—" My mouth was dry, any excuses I'd been prepared to give melting off my tongue. I couldn't meet his gaze, not directly, not when it seemed to be piercing into my soul, shifting through the shadowy darkness of my rage and grief and growing tally of failures, and finding me lacking. I was nothing—an empress without a crown, a general without an army, a woman with nothing but vengeance driving her.

Shame and confusion writhed through me as I blinked against the stinging in my eyes. The Life-Giver that this sanctuary was dedicated to was supposed to appear in the form of an Alrenian man, with bright golden hair and shimmering skin. This man...he appeared how I imagined the Forwyn might picture Elhani. But why would a Forwyn god be in an Alrenian temple?

Blasphemy, my mind screamed. *Elhani cannot be here.*

"I'm here to save my dragon's life. To save my people." My voice was weak, pathetic. "El—Elhani?"

The man's expression didn't soften. "I'm known by many names. You know me best as the Giver of Life, but little do you know of my true nature."

Horror shuddered through me. *Elhani and the Life-Giver cannot be one and the same.* Everything I'd ever been taught—that the Forwyn were infidels and that the Alrenians were the Chosen People—contradicted what stood before me. My life, my entire understanding of the world, seemed to teeter and crumble, and I was left with doubt. Confusion.

Emptiness.

What if, a voice asked within me, *you're not chosen after all? What if you lost your throne because you were never even meant to be empress?*

My voice was small and pleading as I whispered, "I came to ask…" I swallowed. "For you to spare my dragon's life."

An emotion glinted in the Life-Giver's eyes, and for a moment I thought perhaps the coldness on his face might relent and give in to something more welcoming. But instead, he stepped forward, the air warming like I was standing too close to a blazing sun. Sweat beaded my forehead, but I didn't dare move away. I wasn't sure I was capable of moving at all. "How do you think you can bring life to anyone, when you stand here reeking of death?"

I cringed, even now feeling Nesrelle's influence coursing through me like an invading poison. The nestred rune on my cheek flared again, sharp and demanding. Wrath and bloodlust consumed my brain, and when I peered up, my fear mingled with a growing sense of hatred.

"I pleaded so many times for you to save my mother, to give me something when I was surrounded by ruthless enemies," I said, my throat hoarse. "You let Elder Ettonou prey on me, leaving bruises and broken bones and cuts no one else ever saw. I begged you to help me be the free, strong leader I was born to be. You put me in this position. You let them take *everything* from me." My eyes burned. Despite my growing terror and my conviction this deity might strike me dead on the spot, I couldn't stop the words from pouring out. Were they wholly mine? Or was Nesrelle's influence even here, in the years of pain and resentment that was eating me alive?

"And rather than listen for me, rather than accept what was necessary and be open to hearing what I had planned for your future, you chose to live in the past." The Life-Giver's eyes were pitiless, sharp and hostile. "You chose this path of darkness and pain. Every scar, every regret you bear now—that is yours." He turned away, as if the very sight of me was repulsive to him, and somehow that was the greatest offense of all. I choked on a sob. "You're not fit to be here, bringing your shadowy despair and death to this place of hope and life."

"The dragons are *your* creatures," I cried out. "If not for my sake, then—"

"I have nothing more to say to you, *executioner*," he cut in, using Nesrelle's nickname for me.

The rune pulsed again. *Get off your knees. Fight.*

Blind rage tore through me. With an animalistic snarl, I threw myself toward him, as if I could claw a god to pieces with my sheer willpower. With Nesrelle's dark, desperate strength.

In one smooth motion, the Life-Giver lifted his arms, and my body slammed into the air like I was striking an invisible wall of stone. The force of it hurled me backwards, sending me flying across the sanctuary so hard I slid along the stone floor for several feet when I struck. Pain shot through my bones as the temple began to tremble. Would he bring the whole building down around me?

Eyes widening, I launched to my feet and fled, tearing past the woman in the hallway, who seemed too horrified for words. Tears blurred my vision while I sprinted back through the garden, toward Ryke's slumped form. Shame and hate sizzled through me relentlessly. Nesrelle was screaming in my mind. *Kill them!*

My eyes locked on Vander and Tayla, something like hope and relief flooding me when I realized I could combat the shame and humiliation of fleeing the temple with sating this bloodlust. With strengthening the power growing inside me. What did it matter if my gift was to kill, and not to save?

If this is what it came to, I would watch the whole world fall around me. I would give in to this need to shed blood and feel strong, anything to avoid feeling weak again…

I will always fight for you. The memory of Kovi's voice uttering those words seared across my brain, stopping me dead in my tracks. It stole the breath from my lungs, making my chest ache. For an instant, it was like he was there, speaking those words to me. I could still feel the warmth of his arms, could still taste his mouth on mine. Every promise, every dream he'd shared with me, rang in my head. His hope, despite the impossibility of peace between our two peoples. The impossibility of *us.*

Would he fight for me now, if he saw what I'd been reduced to in only a matter of days?

Hands shaking, I pressed forward until I reached Ryke and could run my fingers along his smooth scales. He shifted his head, one silver eye peering up at me as if he understood. With a soft snort, he leaned in and nuzzled my shoulder.

"No antidote?" Tayla asked gruffly.

I didn't bother to turn to look at her. I was afraid if I lifted my face, Vander and Tayla would be able to see the fear and shame in my eyes, and I couldn't bear that.

"Let's go," I said by way of answering. "We have an emperor to meet."

CHAPTER TWENTY-SIX

Kovi

In my dream, our connection was restored and Jalie's pain was my own. The tangled grief and fury burning within her was all-consuming, almost too big, too powerful for one body to contain. It made my knees shake and my legs nearly buckle as I stood under the same starry sky we'd said our goodbyes beneath.

The air tasted of smoke and ash, the heaviness of the battle in Wynlaen hanging over us. Shadows danced beneath the swaying tree branches, giving me the sensation that eyes were watching. Even the wind seemed to have a voice, whispering warnings in my ears.

Before me, Jalie looked just as she had that night, her gold-flecked eyes bright, reflecting the glittering night sky as she studied me with an expression torn between hope and despair, fear and joy. Even though I knew it was a dream, I pulled her close, relishing how my memory perfectly captured her cinnamon and vanilla scent and the way her body fit against mine. She was warm and surprisingly soft in my arms, and when I kissed her, she tasted just as I remembered.

I pulled back, looking at her in wonder. "You're alive," I said.

"Kovi." Her own voice was full of awe.

It's a dream, the wind whispered.

Jalie's expression changed to one of pain, and in a blink, her face was different. An ugly scar marred one cheek, tracing her skin from her temple to her sharp jawline. It sliced in a strange, ragged pattern, one that tugged at my mind, warning me with a half-forgotten memory. A chill washed down my spine.

Something dark covered the side of her neck beneath those scars, black yet shimmering in the night, before it disappeared under her tunic. They looked like scales. What was happening?

I blinked again, shaking my head, but the strange new image of Jalie didn't disappear.

"What happened?" I asked, reaching up, tracing the scar despite the ice it sent through my veins. "You were hurt."

You know what this is, my mind screamed.

The shadows that had been swirling among the trees were twisting around us now, like a thick, stifling fog.

Jalie trembled in my arms, her eyes shining with unshed tears, but her mouth was a firm line. She stepped back, turning away quickly. "This isn't real," she said, frowning at the ground. "You can't be here. It's just a trick."

I seized her hand, trying to cradle her fingers in my own. Her grasp was cold, blackness writhing around her wrist like a living thing. A serpent waiting to strike—I just wasn't sure if it was poised to hit me…or her.

"What happened?" I demanded, fear making my heart slam against my ribcage. *This is a nightmare,* my brain insisted. Every part of me that had so desperately longed for this dream to be reality now hoped it was purely fiction. "Who did this? Who hurt you?"

Jalie swallowed thickly, agony tracing her features. She shook her head, and I couldn't tell if it was an answer or her way of telling me she didn't know *how* to answer me. "This was a dream. An impossible dream. *We* were a dream." She closed her eyes, tears snaking down her cheeks.

"Jalie…" I whispered, cradling her face in my hands. She was cold, so cold.

"Jalie, are you all right?" a voice taunted, and the shadows coalesced into a form that stepped out from the trees. Nesrelle, Queen of Death, Goddess of Demons. She was dressed in shimmering dragon scales of pure white and gold, a mockery of Alrenor's colors. A black blade was strapped to her side, naked and gleaming in the moonlight.

My gaze sharpened, my fingers instinctively reaching for a sword hilt that wasn't at my side. There was nothing but air.

Everywhere, shadows thickened, swirling around Jalie and me both until I couldn't see her anymore. Couldn't see anything but darkness. Couldn't hear anything but Nesrelle's dark laughter.

"Do you know what's worse than the death you do not fear, soldier?" Nesrelle murmured, her voice suddenly so close it was like she was leaning over, brushing her icy lips against my ear. I repressed a shudder. "Living to watch everything you love be destroyed."

I jerked awake, sweat beading my brow. The sharp tang of brine and the gentle swaying of the ship lulled me, grounding my mind in the present.

It was just a nightmare.

And yet, I couldn't shake the foreboding lying like a weight on my chest, couldn't erase the image of Jalie with the *hilvoku* rune scarring her cheek, the shadows twisting around her as her eyes swam with tears. I'd heard stories of the demons' runes, how they carved them into the flesh of their victims with their claws. Those runes represented haunting words, ones that would plague their victims. But worse was the fact that those scars formed a dark connection between the demons and their prey.

It's not a dream, Jalie, I thought. *Don't give up on us. Keep fighting. Please.*

Sitting up, I scrubbed at my forehead with my shirtsleeve, trying to convince my frantic thoughts that they were nothing but paranoia. There was no way I had actually seen Jalie across the miles, just like it was impossible that I'd been hearing her thoughts. My emotional connection with her had vanished, and I didn't know of any other magical ties that would bind two people in such a way.

My nightmare was only the culmination of my fears for Jalie, my concern about Nesrelle's influence on her, and the nymph's sinister words last night, all playing out in a way that had felt far too real.

Sighing, I swung out of my hammock, noting that most of the other soldiers who'd been sleeping in rows below deck with me had already vacated theirs. I was one of the last ones to wake. Scowling and inwardly berating myself, I made my way up the steps, blinking against the harsh light of midday.

Our ship rested safely in Haven's Bay, under a pleasantly warm autumn sun. Either too caught up in their drunken revelries or convinced our ship had been sent away on official business by the emperor himself, none of the other ships had interfered or pursued us when we'd left the harbor last night. It was possible Revaed could still send ships after us, but we were a small concern. Hopefully, with the recent riots, he would be too distracted to put much effort toward securing one ship just yet.

For now, we rested within a cove the Teramese didn't know about. We were hidden and safe. We had a place to recover and plan, and we had a method of transportation.

It had all been easy. Maybe too easy.

As I stepped on deck, I took in the commotion. Everywhere,

academy students and graduates were attired in the rumpled uniforms they'd arrived in last night, their exhausted faces set into determined, disciplined masks. Anyone not within the ship's cramped infirmary either recovering or tending to the wounded was clustered about the deck, eating a brunch of dried fruit and jerky. There was no sign of the nuns who'd joined the battle with Lo, only Mio'e.

Most of the nuns had remained with the wounded they'd transported to homes within the city, and those who'd come with us had spent nearly every waking moment in the infirmary.

Rhi'il, I noted, sat on a crate near Mio'e, speaking animatedly. I couldn't tell from her expression if she was intrigued or annoyed. But…she *was* listening.

Helping myself to a serving of food, I sat beside Rhi'il, jostling him playfully and cutting him off mid-sentence.

He pretended to glare at me. "If it isn't the Elha'tonu himself, finally awake and deigning to join us regular mortals."

Mio'e nearly choked on her food as she burst into laughter, the sound surprisingly light and carefree. It was so unexpected that even I stopped and stared, though I didn't miss Rhi'il's pleased smile. Now that he'd managed to make her laugh once, I didn't doubt he'd make it his mission to hear the musical sound as much as possible.

"You know I hate it when you call me that, Rhi," I grumbled, popping a piece of fruit into my mouth.

"He's not wrong," Huvoki cut in from his seat on a barrel across from us. His eyes flicked to Mio'e. "Kovi was the star student at the academy. He learns with unnatural speed, and he's especially talented with his magic. Seems Elhani-blessed to me."

At my side, my friend Mhel smirked.

I shook my head, opening my mouth to speak, but Rhi'il, Mhel, and Huvoki were faster, chorusing the words I'd repeated many times to them: "All it takes is focus."

As Rhi'il grinned, I shook my head again and turned away to focus on my food. Pretending, as usual, to be offended. Truthfully, it was like a healing balm to be trading jests with my friends, even if Marukio was no longer with us. A hint of normalcy after the horrors of battle only two nights ago was something we all sorely needed.

"Finish eating quickly, Kovi," Rhi'il said, "because we'll be sparring after this, and you'll need all your strength if you want any hope of beating me."

"Ah yes. Did you tell Mio'e that the only thing more formidable in the academy than my Elhani-blessed skill is your unmatched self-importance?"

This time, it was Rhi'il elbowing me, but when Mio'e and I laughed again, he joined us.

"Could…I spar too?" There was something almost bashful in Mio'e's expression as her dark eyes flicked between Rhi'il and me, before settling on my friend. "I want to be useful and help. I want to be prepared for whatever comes next and…" She hesitated. "Maybe you could help train me?"

"You already hold your own in a fight," Rhi'il said, "but of course. I—*we*—would love to train you."

Exhausted as we were, it was relieving to clear a space aboard deck and join Rhi'il, Mhel, and Huvoki in sparring matches. My other friends and I let Rhi'il demonstrate the best defensive maneuvers and parrying strikes to Mio'e, until she demanded he spar against her. Other soldiers soon gathered around, whooping and cheering as the two faced off against one another. Just as my friend had said, Mio'e could hold her own in a fight. She proved to be scrappy and resourceful, keeping up with Rhi'il for several long minutes before he disarmed her.

Panting, she glared at him. "Again," she demanded.

"Officer Ettonou!" General Ilowhe's voice cut through the laughter and applause on deck, immediately pulling me away from the crowd.

The general had left his quarters to lean against the railing, staring out over the bay. I joined him, studying the glistening waters. Gulls circled and cried overhead, occasionally diving toward the placid sea. Here, everything seemed calm and brilliant in the light of day, but I couldn't look at the foaming waves rolling toward the coast without remembering the nymph and her words of warning.

"It's taking everything within me not to dive off this ship and swim for shore," General Ilowhe murmured, never pulling his gaze from the waters. "To not leave the soldiers I've vowed to lead and protect and run headlong toward the palace, no matter the consequences, just so she knows she's not alone. That I haven't abandoned her." He sighed, shaking his head and scowling.

I gripped the railing so hard a splinter stabbed at my finger.

Finally, the general turned to me, his eyes shadowed, his expression taut with weariness and sorrow. "I know what it is costing you when I ask you to stay. I know because I'm asking the same thing of myself." He pressed his lips into a firm line.

"We'll get your daughter out of there," I reassured him. "I can sketch the palace, and Rhi'il and I can scout around it today. We'll have a rescue plan in no time." I clenched my hand into a fist.

"But do we have the soldiers to implement it?" General Ilowhe sighed. "And then, even if we rescue the Forwyn from within the palace, what about the entire empire? We don't have the forces to expel the Teramese *and* stop the Alrenians."

"That's a little pessimistic for you, sir," I said, a tight smile playing at my lips.

He shook his head again. "You're right. I'm tired." As if to prove it, he wiped a hand across his eyes, squinting up at the sun. "I can't remember the last time I actually slept. And having my daughter alive and in their hands…the worry clouds your mind."

"I know."

The general turned to me, his warm brown eyes intent. I could have sworn there were more wrinkles creasing around them than just two days ago, that there were more streaks of white and grey in his beard than before. "I don't understand what's between you and the Alrenian empress, but I promise as soon—"

"Don't," I said, cutting him off. "Don't make promises right now. I know my responsibilities to my people, and I won't leave them when they're in need. Even after we rescue the Forwyn prisoners, we have the entire empire to worry about."

Sadness pierced the general's eyes as he settled a hand on my shoulder, squeezing it. All formalities dropped entirely between us. "You're a good soldier and a good man, Kovi."

His words warmed my chest, but nothing could melt the ice building there, or the lingering fear and pain that my nightmare had brought.

The air thickened as soon as Rhi'il stepped into the captain's quarters, these moments of peaceful silence bringing all the things I hadn't had time to explain to him to the forefront of my mind. I suspected that he'd spoken to General Ilowhe before coming here, and that meant he was aware of my desire to ally with the Alrenians. With Jalie.

And I also knew that Rhi'il couldn't understand. I wasn't even sure that I could make him understand, even with an explanation. Because…how could I describe what had happened?

Even without glancing up from the desk, where I had a half-finished sketch spread out on the paper before me, I could practically read Rhi'il's churning thoughts. I knew his brow was furrowed, his jaw tense as he fought the frown threatening his face. He hated to frown when he always wanted to laugh.

While others who didn't know him as well thought it was because he thought all of life was a joke, I knew better. I knew it was precisely for the opposite reason—that he was far too intimately acquainted with the pain and darkness drenching life, and he coped with humor and avoidance. I knew it was because he'd do anything to block out the memories of his parents and siblings being murdered in front of him during a failed attempt to escape enslavement. His owners had taken all their rage out on him, only a child at the time, by keeping only him alive and making him suffer all the years he served them. And more recently, he'd lost Ny'ola, the woman he'd cared about, to the Alrenians.

I knew Rhi'il laughed because if he didn't, he would break.

Slowing the pencil's movement across my page, I hesitated, wondering if Rhi'il would speak first. I wasn't exactly sure what he wanted me to say. How could I form words that would help him understand how I'd gone from hating our enemy to caring about her? I didn't even know the exact moment it had happened—somewhere between finding a similar fire burning within her, the same one that lived in me, and holding her when she fought off death's threat from the nethilys poisoning. Somewhere between feeling her fury and determination and courage unleashed on me each time we traded words or blows in a sparring match, and sensing the softness she tried to conceal, her love for her people and her longing for companionship.

Maybe it was because I'd been in such close quarters with her, or because I'd been forced to experience her emotions as if they were my own, but I knew there was mercy and tenderness behind her hardened exterior. But how could I explain that in a way that would convince Rhi'il? How could I tell him that her laughter was like music, her heart was fierce and true, and her life was such an integral part to my every breath, my every thought now, that I couldn't even begin to explain how entangled I was? How desperately I hoped for a dream that might be impossible?

"I thought the nymphs were a myth," Rhi'il said at last, sinking into a chair on the opposite side of the room, close to the door leading to the bedroom.

If it hadn't been for our need to have this space to plan, General Ilowhe would have gladly given it up as additional room for the wounded. But the infirmary was large enough for those we'd brought aboard, since the most grievously injured had remained in the city with nuns and healers. For the past half hour, I'd been given total privacy to clear my thoughts and sketch a map of the palace from memory.

Honestly, I'd been surprised Rhi'il hadn't come sooner.

Slowly, I added the lines to another building on the palace grounds, narrowing my eyes in thought as I pictured it in my head. "I didn't," I responded matter-of-factly. "They're rare in our seas and especially along our coast, because they prefer the Terebrys. There was a book about them in the academy library that I read a while back."

This time, I dared to look up at Rhi'il as he rolled his eyes, his mouth twitching in an almost-smile. "Of course you did."

He waited another beat, letting quiet descend again as he shifted in his chair. "What did she tell you?"

I gripped the pencil more tightly. "Some nonsense about the future."

"*Can* nymphs tell the future?"

Shrugging, I held back a bitter laugh. "I don't know. The book I read mostly expounded on all the things we *don't* know about water nymphs. Most likely she just wanted to invoke fear and drown me." I glanced back at my friend. "Thank you, by the way."

Rhi'il waved it off. "I always have your back," he said softly, "and I always will."

There was another pause.

"What makes you believe…" He stopped himself, as if thinking better of what he'd been about to say. "I spoke with General Ilowhe. He said…" He sighed, fidgeting with the sleeves of his jacket. When he lifted his gaze, his eyes met mine, steady and piercing, demanding the truth from me. "Are you in love with Empress Jaliana?"

I drew in a breath, setting down my pencil and turning to give Rhi'il my full attention. As much as I'd dreaded this conversation, I refused to flinch away or make excuses. "I am."

Even though he wouldn't have asked the question without suspecting it, my straightforward answer seemed to take my friend off guard. He blinked a few times, as if trying to reassure himself he wasn't dreaming. Or maybe he wished he *was* dreaming.

"*How?*"

"She wasn't what I expected. She's not like her mother." I frowned. "Well, she is, but not in the ways I thought she would be."

"She's one of *them*, Kovi. They enslaved us for *generations,* and they thought conquering the world and possessing slaves was their *right.*" Rh'il sprang from his chair, pacing along the floor. "Her mother killed our people for sport! Her mother killed *your* mother!"

Acid burned in my stomach. "I know, but…"

"*But?*" Rhi'il froze mid-step, turning to me with a wild gleam in his eyes. It was as if he were seeing his family's murder or Ny'ola's death playing out all over again, his breath quickening, his face sheening with sweat. I wanted to go to him and pull him into a reassuring embrace, to remind him I was on his side and always would be, but his anger made me hold back.

"She's not her mother, Rhi," I repeated into the building quiet, when I finally realized my friend was still awaiting an answer.

Rhi'il's tone was bitter. "Isn't she, though? She was raised in the palace, being taught all her life she is the *Chosen* empress, a mistress of infidel slaves like us. Does…" He studied me warily, pain in his gaze. "Does she love you too, or is she using you? Have you considered that?"

I swallowed, but my throat continued to feel thick. "I've considered everything. Trust me, I know it all seems foolish and impossible, but…" My words trailed off, every explanation I tried to offer sounding flimsy in my head.

Rhi'il's expression softened. "Tell me the story," he said, returning to his chair. "You already know about…whatever is happening or not happening with Mio'e and me. It's time you shared *your* secrets. Tell me everything."

And so I did, detailing the way a palace celebration meant to commemorate my graduation had transformed into an assignment. I told Rhi'il of my anger and hate and dread as I'd accepted the task. How my emotions had changed to smug amusement when I'd realized how easily I could goad Jalie, how I might be able to find some healing in watching her suffer as a prisoner of the Forwyn. I related my horror as I'd noticed little details about her—the way she loved sweets, the way the morning light made her eyes shine even when she was scowling at me—because she did *not* like to wake early—the way her smile gave her face an innocent, carefree expression when she spoke of the dragons.

"She became human to you," Rhi'il muttered, nodding along to my story.

I explained how similar her grief and anger were to mine. Especially once I connected myself to her with my magic. Then…then all her pain became mine, from her fear of my father to her aching loneliness.

When I finally finished telling him about our alliance and the agreement we'd come to, Rhi'il was studying me thoughtfully. "I think I understand, as well as I can." He shrugged. "I'm not sure I trust her, though. You're my brother, Kovi, and I don't want to see you hurt. And as for the other Alrenians…" He shook his head. "You were there when they attacked the academy. I just don't know if anything can ever change between us."

"Maybe not, but isn't it worth trying? For survival? For winning back the empire that *both* our peoples live in, and reclaiming our freedom?"

"Of course it's worth trying," Rhi'il agreed. "Just…be careful. Empress Karye was always described as cunning and vicious. Jalie might not be exactly like her mother, but she was still raised by her. I mean, who *knows* what Jalie and her army are planning right now?"

I nodded along, trying not to allow Rhi'il's words to remind me of the warning the nymph had given, or the way Nesrelle had gloated.

CHAPTER TWENTY-SEVEN

Lo

Emperor Revaed was waiting in my rooms when I returned, the tunnel door sliding shut with a groan behind me. Silent and motionless, he sat in one of the armchairs on the far side of the bedroom, as calm as if he were simply awaiting a guest.

With a shaking hand, I forced myself to set the lantern down gently before I prowled across the room. The sheer power of my rage made white spots dance in my vision, but I didn't pause, didn't hesitate. Only when I was directly in front of him did I stop, catching my breath. "I'll send you crawling on all fours from this room with my magic," I threatened. "I'll force such fear into you that you'll never dare touch another Forwyn again. You'll never use another death to manipulate me.

You'll never order another massacre in the streets. You'll—"

Revaed lifted a calm hand, and I bit my lip. Not because I had any desire to obey him, but because something about his attitude made me pause. Made me cool my anger and try to think things through.

I'd expected threats, perhaps another prisoner summoned forward and murdered before my eyes as retaliation for my escape—and the fact that I'd obviously lied about my knowledge of secret routes through the capital.

"I'm not here to kill anyone else," Revaed said with a shrug. "Yet." His eyes scanned me coolly.

I refused to let him read my expression and sense my fear, to know that there was ice in my veins.

"First, you're going to lead me down the tunnel you lied to me about, and you will show me where it lets out."

Bile rose in my mouth at the thought of facing those rows of corpses waiting in the marketplace square again. Of having to look at Eloyiah's body, left to bake and rot in the sun. But I could bear it. For my people, I could bear it as I'd borne countless other burdens.

"Then," Revaed continued, his violet gaze cutting into mine, "you're going to return with me to visit the Forwyn in the dungeons, and you will explain to them how you will never be responsible for another of their deaths. How you will ensure their freedom by cooperating with us and renewing our alliance with your public speech and your marriage to Caesiem." His eyes hardened. "And then you will stay here in the palace, in new rooms, or you will break your word to your people."

My body practically vibrated with rage, but I forced myself to nod. Numbly, I led Revaed back toward the fireplace, pressing the lever until stone scraped against stone and the entrance to the tunnel yawned before us. Mind empty of everything but cold fear and burning rage—a conflicting, confusing whirlwind—I lit the candle within the lantern and lifted it to reveal the descending stone staircase leading into darkness.

"How many other tunnels and underground passages are there for the worms to hide and travel through?" Revaed demanded.

When his eyes darted to me, I shook my head, tongue cleaving to the roof of my mouth.

Elhani, I thought, but my prayer died before it began. I couldn't unleash his magic against this man or kill him, not like this. It would be a temporary victory, one that might let me escape to find help, that might buy the Forwyn prisoners some brief time, but that would end in disaster. Revaed had too many loyal to him—Caesiem included—who would continue on his work. And I would be the worst sort of coward to abandon my people to execution.

I'd stay for them, until I could break them out with me, or die at their sides. There was no other choice.

"I don't know," I answered.

"You lied before," Revaed said, a warning in his tone. "Why should I believe you now?"

"I just discovered this tunnel," I told him sharply. "It connects to others, but I haven't followed them yet. I only suspected these tunnels existed when you asked me about them before, and I haven't found any signs of more entrances in the palace yet. Or of the Alrenians. And trust me here, if you don't trust me about anything else: I would love to find those Alrenians and give them justice for attacking and murdering my people, the same as you."

For a quiet moment, Revaed inspected my face, as if weighing my words. But he wasn't a simpleton, and my anger and grief were clearly written in my expression. With a single nod, he turned away and gestured toward the tunnel. "Lead the way."

My mouth twitched as I tried to resist a smile and failed. "You're not afraid of me murdering you in an enclosed space, outside of your guards' earshot?"

Revaed had the audacity to roll his eyes and smirk back at me. "I think you already know the consequences wouldn't make it worth it.

You're no fool."

Without another word, I slipped forward, guiding Revaed down the staircase, our breaths echoing off the walls. When I'd been alone, the darkness had seemed vast and limitless, but with my enemy at my back, the space felt hot and cramped. My skin itched and my eyes burned from exhaustion and the tears I'd shed only an hour or two ago.

Revaed broke the silence without warning. "Caesiem was my family long before he met you, and I'll be here to support and protect and care for him long after you're gone."

Fear crawled up my spine, but I kept walking, refusing to glance back. Was he threatening me, or merely stating what we both knew— that whatever farce of a marriage Caesiem and I agreed to would never last longer than we were forced to pretend?

"But he loves you." Revaed's footsteps echoed as he halted on one of the stairs, and this time, without really meaning to, I paused and looked up at him. Almost unconsciously, my fingers strayed to the pendant hanging from my neck.

My eyes burned. "He's chosen you, Revaed. Doesn't that make you happy? He's chosen you—his family—and he's chosen his people."

Revaed's eyes narrowed, focusing on my pendant. "Has he?" Frowning, he turned away, shaking his head and running a hand through his hair, tousling it until he was a far cry from the usually put-together man he appeared to be. "And all this time, you're using him. He should know better, but…"

Anger churned in my gut, and I wanted to shout at this man and tell him how much I cared. I cared about Caesiem so much it felt like my heart was split in two, bleeding out inside me. I cared so much I'd stayed at the palace and shared countless moments with him I never should have indulged in. I cared so much that every time I closed my eyes, I could see the love in his gaze when he looked at me.

But it wasn't enough to cross the divide between us. Caesiem was steadfastly loyal to this man who he claimed had saved him, and he was dedicated to his people. If I had been in his shoes, I might have even felt the same way. I understood the love that bound him to his guardian and the Teramese people, because it was the same unbreakable tie that tethered me to the Forwyn and my sisters. To my newfound father.

An ache built in my chest, and I turned away, sucking in a ragged breath.

"You'll be what breaks him," Revaed muttered behind me, his voice full of bitter resignation. "And I can only pray to all the gods that I can bind him back together."

Stubbornly, I stalked forward, blinking against the urge to cry.

He was already the one to break me, I thought.

Later, my lungs burned as Revaed led me, our footfalls reverberating in the endless darkness and musty, filthy stench of the dungeons. With every step, the ugly memory of the corpses filling the square filled my head, along with Revaed's warning: *The prisoners in the palace will join them, if you don't cooperate.*

We paused before a small cell, waiting as a guard stepped forward at Revaed's bidding and inserted one of the keys dangling from the chain at his side. As the door groaned inward, I took a step forward and my eyes met a familiar pair, set above a freckled face. My heart lurched in warning.

A'elli.

Spinning toward Revaed, I blurted, "Is this a trick?"

Before Revaed could answer, A'elli unleashed a feral cry and charged, her hands latching around my neck as she slammed me against the damp stone wall of her cell.

CHAPTER TWENTY-EIGHT

Caesiem

With every strike, my shoulder ached and throbbed, my stitches threatening to pull free. If Revaed were here, he'd be scolding me by now, fussing as he led me back to his rooms and demanded I rest. But Revaed wasn't here, only his posse of guards he'd left behind when a servant had arrived with whispered news that had finally drawn my guardian away. As much as I cared for him, his absence had been a relief—finally giving me a break from his worrying and his incessant talk of wedding plans.

Cursing, I took a step back to wipe at the sweat slicking my forehead. I couldn't stop thinking of the vision Meli had shown me, or of the way Lo had looked at me. I'd thought I'd put all my doubts and fears to rest, but this time alone had only reawakened them, forcing my restless body out of Revaed's quarters and to the building housing all of the palace's training rooms.

One of the guards cleared his throat, clearly upset I wasn't obeying Revaed's wishes. "Maybe you should take a break, Your Highness." His eyes landed pointedly on my injured shoulder.

I glanced down at it, noting where blood spotted the bandages, and winced. "I'm fine," I insisted, catching my breath.

The guard clamped his mouth shut, knowing better than to continue voicing his disapproval.

Squaring off against the straw-filled dummy in the center of the training room, I struck it again. Again. Each motion took me back to a time that had felt simpler, when my purpose and my place in life had made sense. When I hadn't been torn in two.

Nine Years Ago

Vander sparred with me as we practiced our hand-to-hand combat, easily blocking my strikes and countering with his own. As a new mage at the palace, I was quick but sloppy in my fighting technique. Vander, meanwhile, had been living and training at the palace since he was six years old. Over and over, he landed strikes I managed to dodge, but each time I moved in close to go on the offensive, I failed terribly. My punches were awkward, easy for Vander to spot and stop before I could land a single one. Each time he'd seize my wrist effortlessly or get in a solid kick that sent me reeling.

I consistently found myself sprawled out on the mat. My muscles ached and my skin was sheened in sweat and stinging with countless bruises already blooming along my arms and legs. Even my face was swollen from a couple strikes to my jaw and eye.

Discouraged, I yanked myself to my feet, blinking at the sweat dripping into my vision as the trainer, a stern-faced man with deep emerald eyes, barked at me in derision. "Little mouse, are you tired yet?"

Swallowing against the dryness in my throat, I shook my head, not trusting my voice.

The trainer towered over me, sneering. "You're too old. I'm not sure what the prince was thinking, bringing you here. I don't care if you're the best water mage he's ever seen, you have no clue how to control your magic, no notion of how to hold your own in a fight, and no idea how to even read or write." He scoffed. "Does he think we're just a charitable cause now, permitting every starving orphan on the streets into the palace? You're a waste of my time."

Gritting my teeth, I refused to respond, tearing my eyes away from him and back to Vander, my opponent. I expected the same derisive gleam in his stare, but instead, I found a pair of sympathetic silver eyes. A friend?

Ever since I'd agreed to follow Revaed to the palace only a few days ago, to take residence in one of the numerous rooms included in the mages' wing, I'd been the object of constant jealousy and anger. Servants hadn't bothered to hide their disgust as they'd drawn me a bath and offered me new, clean clothes. Fellow mages had rolled their eyes or complained about having to spar and learn beside such an embarrassment. No one bothered to keep quiet around me when they gossiped, and those who did know I'd saved Vicidor from further destruction during the dragon attack didn't praise me for it. Instead, they glared and commented about my failure to end the attack before it had started, or to perform my duty as a powerful water mage by studying at the palace from a young age.

"Why didn't your parents send you here when you were young? Now you're just a walking failure," one of the other boys had mocked.

Everywhere, there was anger and mockery, and I knew, ultimately, it was rooted in envy. Revaed had set aside the finest rooms in the mages' wing for me. He'd brought me in personally and checked on me the next morning when I'd been at breakfast to ensure I was comfortable and well.

And today... As soon as Revaed's footsteps charged into the spacious training room, clipping off the tiled floors and echoing along the burgundy walls, the trainer tensed, a half-stifled curse escaping his lips. Vander's eyes widened before I tore my own gaze away.

Across the room, the Teramese prince was dressed in deepest red embroidered with silver flames and dragons. On either side, his guards stood at attention, their expressionless faces staring straight ahead.

"How is your newest student, Byro?" Revaed asked without preamble, stalking toward the trainer.

I hadn't bothered to remember the trainer's name when he'd introduced himself earlier that morning, but now, my eyes darted toward the man, watching as the casual use of his first name irked him. He pursed his lips, refusing to complain, and instead dipped his head as he answered his prince's question. "He is...struggling, Your Highness. He's lost years of training, and it's clear he's gangly and awkward. Too much time starving on the streets hasn't done his body any favors."

Revaed's eyes cut to mine, but his expression was warm and kind. Already, I found comfort and familiarity when I met that violet gaze. Even then, I'd felt a pull toward one of the only people who'd ever bothered to show me compassion, who wanted to see me succeed. "Then he'll dine with me from now on, and eat the same food I eat."

No one dared to speak, but I could see boys and girls of all ages scowling at the proclamation, the obvious favoritism.

"And he'll train with my men and me," Revaed continued, sending a ripple of shock down my spine.

"With all due respect, Your Highness," Byro began, "but you and your men are not mages, nor are you trained in magic—"

Revaed cut him off with a casual wave. "He'll still train with you and the other mages in magic. Just not in combat." His gaze darted back to mine, a smile twitching at the corners of his mouth. "I'll ensure he learns to read and write, too. This *starving orphan* will be my charge and my responsibility." He glanced back to Byros, mirth positively dancing in his eyes as he made it obvious he'd overheard the trainer's earlier mockery. The man blanched with fear. "He'll be *my* charity case."

Present

I stretched my muscles and stared at the straw dummy before me, blinking away the memory. I knew, in my bones, in my soul, that Revaed loved me like his own son. And yet…Meli had planted a seed of doubt in my heart I couldn't shake, and I despised myself for it.

Her words echoed in my mind: *He's trained you to be his living nightmare, the faithful dog to do his dirty work.*

What if Revaed loved me for what I represented? For everything I could do for him? What if he loved me like a prized possession, his chance to appease his father with an heir and his opportunity to gain respect and fear through my magic?

My mind whirled, nausea biting at my gut as an ache opened in my chest. How could I even entertain such thoughts? Revaed had been at my side to tend to my every injury I'd withstood in my training sessions, to comfort me through every childhood illness. He'd been the one to stand against his own father to protect me, the one to listen to me complain about Teramese girls or my demanding tutors.

If he didn't care, who did? If he wasn't my home, who was?

As much as I loved Lo, I knew she couldn't forgive me, couldn't fully trust me. She was as unwaveringly loyal to her people as I was to

Revaed and mine. And as intensely as that hurt, I could understand that.

But what if all my loyalty had been misguided? What if, in the end, neither Lo nor Revaed was on my side?

Again, Meli's words about Revaed darted through my mind, followed by Lo's expression, along with how she'd pulled away from me. Shutting me out.

What if the people I loved most in the world were both lost to me? What if everything I thought I'd understood was a lie?

I punched the dummy over and over, ignoring the agony in my shoulder, the warmth of blood spilling down my arm. Sweat stung my eyes. My wounded muscle protested, but I couldn't stop.

Paranoia had me in its icy grip, and I couldn't seem to shake it. *What if, what if…* it taunted.

"Prince Caesiem!" The guard's sharp words cut through the haze in my brain, like the prow of a ship piercing fog over the ocean. His grasp was warm but insistent as he tugged me away from the dummy. "I'm taking you to the infirmary to see a healer. Emperor Revaed has more theslynik set aside for you as well. But he will kill me if he sees I let you do this to yourself."

A bitter chuckle escaped before I could stop it. Revaed's guard might have been jesting, but it was only half a joke, because we both knew Revaed didn't hesitate to execute anyone he believed posed a threat to my well-being. Another sign I'd always clung to that he cared. He *cared.*

But now, I couldn't get Meli's sneering words out of my head, clawing ugly talons through my heart.

Was Revaed defending his heir, or just protecting his faithful dog?

CHAPTER TWENTY-NINE

Jalie

In my dream, I revisited my memories from the period immediately following Mother's death, though they were distorted and especially nightmarish. Elder Ettonou sneered at me, an angry man discussing the possible death of a fourteen-year-old girl.

Just like they had three years ago, the other newly-elected Elders sat in chairs within the throne room, defiling my mother's place of power with their audacity to rule in her stead. But this time, my nightmare conjured my mother's corpse as I'd seen it in my tent at my army's campsite in the Aramith Mountains: with a bloody slit across her throat and dark, bottomless pits for eyes.

"She'll grow up to be just like her mother," Elder Ettonou said, standing beside me, his grip on my arm bony and painful. But I didn't dare move, didn't dare speak. I couldn't rip my stare from my mother's body, lying in a pool of her own blood. "We should execute her now before she becomes a true threat."

"We're discussing a child, Ettonou," said Elder Mae'ona, an especially wrinkled and grey-haired woman. She leaned forward in her chair, her cool gaze assessing first me, and then the Elder beside me.

"A child?" Elder Ettonou scoffed, his fingers tightening until I felt the stab of his nails drawing blood. I gritted my teeth to hold back my groan of pain. "She's Alrenian, raised and trained by the murderess Karye herself. She's not a child. She's a *threat.*"

"A threat I am proud of." The voice took me by surprise, jolting my gaze back to Mother's body. Despite the gory cut in her neck, despite her dead eyes, her lips moved, curling into a smile.

Fear and grief radiated through me in equal measures.

"I'm proud of you, Jalie," she repeated.

Choking back a cry, I woke to dappled sunlight surrounding me, filtering through a ceiling of swaying leaves. Leaning against Ryke, I felt his warmth and the gentle rise and fall of his chest, reassuring me that he was still holding on against the poison's effects. With his large body, he had more time than I'd had, before the worst symptoms of nethilys poisoning set in. His rhythmic breathing mingled with that of Tayla and Vander, who were curled up together a few yards away, and the soothing murmur of the river somewhere deeper within the trees we'd stopped to rest under.

We'd followed the Brema River along its winding trail all the way from Aramith, its path an easy course to track as we set our grueling pace. Even now, I'd only allowed myself about an hour of rest, based on the height of the sun shimmering through the leaves. Sitting up, I brushed a gentle hand along Ryke's side before rising and pushing my way through the trees. Here they grew more thickly, their ancient, mossy trunks stretching toward the sky like worshippers extending their arms toward their god.

According to the maps I'd studied growing up, the Brema passed near Lorin Forest, a wood full of towering trees older than most of the cities in Alrenor. We had to be getting near to that forest, which also meant we were closer to the capital than I'd dared to hope.

It didn't take me long to reach the river, a vast expanse of glimmering blue beneath a cloudless sky, edged by trees, their giant roots dipping into the water. Moss blanketed the rocks I slipped over to kneel on the bank, dipping my fingers into the river and feeling the liquid course over my fingers. Somewhere in the battle for Aramith, I'd lost my dragon scale gloves, leaving my arms bare and vulnerable. And yet…would I ever be truly vulnerable again, with the curse and Nesrelle's power flowing through me?

I scooped some water into my hands and dipped forward to drink. Catching a glimpse of my reflection, I froze.

The scar marring my cheek was angry and red, a grotesque, ragged collection of cuts. The black scales that had begun near my collarbone now spread even further down my arm, extending all the way to my elbow. I stared at them, at the way they glistened in the sunlight, dark as a midnight sky but sparkling as if they contained hidden stars. Beautiful yet ominous.

"Why have you bothered to even keep those Teramese alive?" Nesrelle's voice cut through my thoughts. I opened my eyes and saw her standing at the river's edge, swirling her toes in the water. Clothed in a blue dress the same icy shade as her gaze, she looked out of place, a court lady in the wild.

I glared at her, phantom pain shooting through my limbs at the sight of the immortal being who had tormented me even as she'd saved my life. "Because Vander can use his wind magic to help Ryke get back to Inalgoth faster."

Nesrelle rolled her eyes. "Then kill the woman. It'll empower you, strengthen the curse you carry."

Temptation prickled down my spine at her words, lust for that rush of power coursing through my veins. But I clenched my fingers, digging my nails into my palms to resist. "If I kill her, Vander will never cooperate. And I want them present to help me gain entrance to the capital, to get me close to their imposter emperor so I can gut him myself."

Nesrelle picked at her nails, sighing softly, almost like a petulant child. "Why are you still resisting me?"

Shadows coiled around her, pressing toward me. There was something both horrifying and mesmerizing by the sight, something that called to the deepest part of my longing for vengeance, yet repelled that corner of my heart that wanted peace.

"Peace," Nesrelle sneered. "Love. You really believe those pretty words that soldier told you?"

Bitterness coiled in my stomach. *I will always fight for you,* Kovi had promised. I could still sense the warmth and safety his arms had given me, even if it had been a temporary refuge. A dream that I wasn't sure could ever come to pass.

"He's using you," Nesrelle continued, prowling closer. Her bare feet trod gracefully over the slick rocks. The hem of her gown rustled along the ground, the smallest whisper mingling with the endless song of the rushing river. "He wants you to give up fighting for your throne so his people can take what is rightfully yours." Her eyes flashed.

"Is it mine, though?" I despised the quaver of doubt in my voice, the lump of fear that had lodged itself in my throat.

"It is if you claim it," Nesrelle whispered. "Just like the gifts I've offered you." She waved a hand toward me, a silent invitation.

In a blink, she was gone, but her words echoed in my ears. When I closed my eyes, I could see Lo'laeni's face. The girl who'd robbed me of my mother and my birthright with one swipe of her blade. Rage quivered through me.

It's not a dream, Jalie. Kovi's words were a deep rumble in my ears, soothing and musical. Determined yet gentle. *Don't give up on us. Keep fighting. Please.*

But Nesrelle's scoffing voice was louder in my head. *Lies.*

I squeezed my eyes shut, shaken by the unknown, by the strange emotions coursing through me. My meeting with the Life-Giver had horrified and enraged me, making me feel equal parts small and powerful. If he despised me, if he claimed I'd damned myself, then so be it. I would be Nesrelle's executioner. If I wasn't meant to be empress, if I wasn't chosen, I would choose myself. I would create my own fate.

My mark flared with pain, igniting renewed bloodlust. I leaned into it, feeling power course through my veins and seep into the water as I immersed my hands in it.

I opened my eyes to eerie stillness. The river continued to burble, but something felt…different. First one and then another silver body floated upward, until there was a whole host of dead fish coursing downstream. With the scent of death tickling my nose, I turned back toward the trees and stood. I approached one, curious. Uncertain. Eager. I set my hand against it, reveling in the pulse of strength I felt. Pushing it into the bark, willing it all into the tree. Overhead, its leaves withered, curling in on themselves as they browned. Cascading to the earth in a sweeping waterfall, some landed in my hair while others crunched beneath my feet.

Once, Nesrelle had claimed some people—those who hadn't shed Alrenian blood—would be immune to my curse, but since then I'd slain fellow Alrenians with it. Maybe no one was immune to it. Clearly, even nature wasn't.

I walked further among the trees, where birds and squirrels, rabbits and mice, bees and butterflies fell dead, collapsing from the trees I touched or the flowers my boots brushed as I moved. Power flared within me, raging, insistent, consuming. My curse—my gift—had wrought all this death in just a few instants.

It was horrifying.

And yet…

The power glowed warm and comforting inside me, promising I'd never be weak, never be out of control again. Promising me vengeance for my mother, glory for my people, and the strength and courage I needed to take back my crown.

And no matter how terrifying my curse might be, no matter how I hated and feared Nesrelle now, her promises were intoxicating.

CHAPTER THIRTY

Lo

Black spots flashed across my vision as A'elli's fingers tightened, tightened. My chest spasmed as I tried and failed to drink in a single breath of air, thrashing against the woman's surprisingly fierce hold. I kicked against her shins and stomped on her feet; I seized her wrists and twisted as hard as I could to pry her away.

Never let an enemy take you by surprise, Pauni'a had always warned me during our sparring sessions, but this time, I had.

Revaed and the guard were shouting. There was the hiss of a weapon being drawn. But everything felt distant, muffled by the pounding of my heart in my ears.

I grasped one of A'elli's fingers, shoving it backward as hard as I could. Something snapped and she screamed. Loosening her grip and rearing back, she moaned. But before she retreated, she dropped her good hand, slipping something into my pocket. With another grunt, she backed up against the far wall, cringing away from the sword the guard was brandishing. Though the bone had snapped in her finger and it was clearly bent the wrong way, though tears glistened on her lashes, A'elli glared at the guard, forcing her groans of pain away.

Inhaling burning breaths of air into my lungs, I leaned back against the cell wall. My throat was raw and swollen, making each swallow painful. I studied A'elli warily.

If my throat hadn't ached so much, I might have laughed bitterly. What a waste, to be fighting my own people when we needed to be united, working to stop the atrocities Revaed's soldiers were committing in this very city, at this very moment.

Revaed's eyes narrowed at Ae'lli as he stepped forward, studying the scene. The guard hesitated, his gold eyes flicking between his emperor and the prisoner, clearly awaiting Revaed's proclamation.

"You would attack your future princess?" Revaed demanded of A'elli, his voice dangerously smooth.

A'elli dipped her head in a false display of reverence. "She's the reason we're imprisoned here," she muttered, tossing me a glare.

And yet…there was something in my pocket. A paper, I guessed. A'elli didn't actually want me dead, which was a shock after our last encounter in the capital streets, where she'd tried to avenge Renni's death. Had the Teramese captured her and brought her here that night?

"I don't remember seeing you in the palace," Revaed continued, tipping his head to the side as he assessed A'elli's freckled face and frizzy curls, dirty and wild from her time in this disgusting cell. "What hole did you crawl out of before my guards arrested you?"

A'elli said nothing, staring at the floor.

My head pounded as Revaed turned to me, his violet eyes devoid of pity. "I'll let you decide if she should live or die."

I gritted my teeth, forcing each word out despite my painful throat. "You brought me here to tell my people I would honor our alliance and ensure they all live."

Revaed shrugged. "Well, this one attacked you, so she doesn't have to be one of the people you choose to save."

"I want her to live."

Lifting his eyebrows, Revaed turned away. "Seems foolish," he muttered. He gestured to the guard. "Stand down."

A'elli rounded on me. "You came to say you'll honor the alliance? Finally? No more scheming and threatening our lives?"

But her eyes flashed with a different message. As soon as the guard turned his back, she relaxed her stance and mouthed, *I'm sorry. I came to help you get the prisoners out. That was for show.*

She *came* here? Had she been captured on purpose? And then she attacked me as a distraction?

She's mad, I thought.

Before I could mouth a message back to her, Revaed called me out of the cell. "Come speak to some of the other prisoners," he ordered.

I tossed a single glance over my shoulder as I exited A'elli's cell, finding a world of hope in the young woman's eyes. *I'm with you,* her gaze seemed to say.

I wasn't alone. But was she the sort of ally I wanted?

Revaed forced me to trail after him throughout the dank dungeons, making promises I didn't intend to keep to captives who made it clear with their glares that they didn't want to hear them. With each vow that I would seal the Forwyn-Teramese alliance through a public speech of apology and a marriage, my heart sank further and further. I knew every word was a disappointment to my people, a way for Revaed to divide us.

At last, we emerged from the dungeons into one of the palace's bright halls, where late afternoon sunshine dappled the marble floors. My palms itched with the desire to reach into my pocket and find the piece of paper A'elli had hidden within it, but Revaed grasped my elbow and guided me firmly down the hallway, toward a large room open on one side to the gardens.

It was like a sitting room or study of sorts, full of plush chairs and shelves lined with old books on battle strategy and proud Alrenian history. Every inch of the room was white, bathed in the golden glow of sunshine entering from the open side. The mingled floral and citrus scents were so strong I had to blink away threatening memories of Karye. A butterfly flitted through the room, giving me the strange sensation that I was entering an enchanted garden, before my eyes fell on one of the walls, where famous Alrenian blades were displayed.

As usual, the palace was a world of excess and beauty gilding a bloody, cruel history.

Stepping within the room, my eyes landed on the four people seated in armchairs, snagging an extra moment on Elder Ettonou, who didn't meet my gaze directly. In the seat beside him was Elder Ilhoa, straight-backed and stern-faced, clothed in shades of steel blue that matched the ribbons adorning her braids. It made me wonder if she entertained the false notion that she still had any authority in Alrenor's new government. Across from them, a shriveled-looking man with grey hair hunched forward, watching me with beady eyes. On his other side, the youngest Elder I'd seen studied me with a calculating expression, the gold flecks in her gaze making me suspect there was Alrenian blood somewhere in her ancestry.

These four were the last of the Elders, the only ones to survive the coup. The ones who had chosen to surrender and side with our enemy rather than fight for our freedom.

Then my eyes landed on another figure, and my gut clenched, as if in dreaded recognition. But there was nothing familiar about the woman, who was not Alrenian, Forwyn, or Teramese. Her flowing red hair and pale skin instead reminded me of descriptions I'd heard of Brevinn natives. Something in the way her icy blue eyes cut into my gaze, scanning me from head to toe, made my skin prickle.

I didn't know her, but everything within my heart and mind screamed at me that she was dangerous. Not to be trusted.

Revaed paused at my side, gesturing for me to take a seat in the nearest armchair. "The Elders requested a meeting with you." He nodded at a guard who had trailed us into the room. "When you're finished, Zalec will escort you to your new quarters."

As Revaed slipped from the room and the guard named Zalec posted himself against one of the walls, I stood stubbornly, staring at the Elders. Perhaps it was the anger of betrayal simmering through me, but I was too restless to sit in their presence.

"Welcome, Miss Nolanhou," said the youngest Elder, her tone anything but warm. "I've been informed that you already know Elders Ilhoa and Ettonou, so let me introduce Elder Hu'ili and myself—Elder Nai'luna. We wanted to discuss how you can best help us in our efforts to solidify our alliance with the Teramese."

Crossing my arms, I pressed my lips into a firm line. "And who is she?" I demanded, cutting a glare in the stranger's direction.

The woman lifted her eyebrows casually, unaffected by my brash attitude.

"Please, sit," Elder Ilhoa interrupted, her tone forceful.

I swallowed back my urge to snap at her, to hurl insults at every single one of them for their two-faced ways. Only the memory of how Revaed had retaliated the last time I'd shown defiance kept my fury under control. For my people's sake, I plopped into the nearest seat.

At that instant, a Teramese servant appeared, bearing a tray full of dishes of fruit. She slipped quietly about the room, depositing the dishes at side tables near each one of us. While the Elders promptly began to eat, as if this were merely an enjoyable social occasion, I ignored my fruit, my eyes boring into the stranger.

Who *was* she?

As soon as the servant left her a dish, the red-haired woman picked up a strawberry and bit into it, chewing thoughtfully. Her mouth twisting in distaste, she tossed the half-eaten berry back into the dish. "Not my preferred fruit," she muttered.

Her eyes lifted to mine and a half-smirk tugged at the corner of her mouth. It was as if she knew the questions whirling through my mind.

Elder Nai'luna turned to me, her voice breaking into my thoughts. "This is Melona, your wedding planner," she said.

I turned to her, blinking in astonishment. "I've never heard of her."

"She's the most renowned planner in Inalgoth," the Elder went on, studying me as if I were shockingly absurd, "and we thought she could offer our people a ceremony that will be the perfect blend of Alrenian and Forwyn customs. Something to show even Alrenians that they can be welcomed into this alliance with Teramyl."

"What the *goehr*?" I burst out, spreading my arms wide as if to encompass the whole mad charade. "Who will fall for this? The Alrenians don't give a single demon tail who I marry. And anyone with half a brain will see it for the political arrangement it is…"

"A political arrangement for the good of all our peoples," Melona said, her voice soft and soothing, almost like a strain of song.

It hit me like a discordant note, filling me with the same emotions I experienced during my nightmares. Something was *off* about this woman. She wasn't even Alrenian, so why would the Alrenians trust her? And she wasn't Forwyn, so why did the Elders think she could assist with Forwyn marriage traditions? My temple throbbed with the start of a headache.

"You use some strong language for a former nun," Elder Hu'ili said, his wrinkled face scrunching at me in distaste as he spoke up for the first time.

I scowled at him. "Considering you're planning my *wedding*, I didn't think you were concerned about me acting like a nun anymore."

Elder Ilhoa shrugged, her tone matter-of-fact. "You agreed to the engagement first, even if it was under false pretenses. It's time for you to follow through on your commitment and serve your people." She reached into her pocket and pulled out several folded sheets of paper. "I spoke to the emperor and requested the honor of writing your speech."

Numb, I took the papers, my eyes scanning over words like *with deepest regret* and *my privilege* and *duty*. My mouth tasted sour.

"It's not a matter of convincing the people you're in love with Prince Caesiem at the ceremony," Elder Ilhoa continued with a wave of her hand. "No one cares about romance right now. We care about hope for our future. About a unified front. About a government that can protect the Forwyn and, perhaps, even convince the Alrenians the most reasonable course of action is to join us too."

Almost unconsciously, I toyed with the pendant dangling from my neck, the earlier ache in my chest spreading. Even imagining this moment, when I would stand across from Caesiem and proclaim false vows, was painful. Not when a part of me wished it could have been real, that in some other world we could have met and fallen in love under better circumstances, where our paths and purposes had aligned. I couldn't picture going through with this without seeing his eyes when he'd last embraced me, without feeling his kiss. Welcome. Like home.

It was all a lie. We could never be anything but a disaster.

Dragging myself from my thoughts, I folded the papers up and shoved them into my pocket. A'elli's note still waited within, hopefully with answers to all my questions surrounding her. And if all went as I hoped, and she was on my side this time, we would be able to break our people free of the dungeons and escape long before Revaed and the Elders could force me to go through with this marriage ceremony.

"We also made a list of customs we expect to be included in the ceremony," Elder Nai'luna added, handing me another paper. "In case you had any ideas of making a mockery of this alliance." Her eyes narrowed. "We expect a true wedding, with all the correct vows."

I took the paper silently.

"The emperor already included Teramese additions, and Melona will help with Alrenian traditions."

I was almost afraid to ask, but I forced the question from my lips. "When is the wedding to take place?"

Elder Ettonou finally met my gaze, his expression a mask, his eyes dark and pitiless. "Tomorrow."

Dread coiled through my stomach. *Tomorrow.* Revaed wasn't wasting any time with preparations now that Caesiem had returned. He wasn't taking any chances I'd have time to smuggle his prisoners out.

That left me with only one option. Showing up for the ceremony after all, and praying that, when Revaed brought all the prisoners out to witness the event, I'd have an opportunity to break them free.

But I couldn't do it alone, and I wasn't sure how many people A'elli might have working with her. I didn't know who'd survived the Aerekni attack. I didn't know anything, and I was out of time.

"Look over your speech closely," Elder Ilhoa said, her eyes shooting daggers at me, as if she could hear my mutinous thoughts. "And be sure you show Melona the customs we need to include in the ceremony. We expect perfection tomorrow." She waved a careless hand. "You and Melona can go stroll through the gardens and set plans. The Teramese created your gown for the coronation, so they already have your measurements. Your wedding outfit will be finished shortly and sent to your rooms."

Stunned, I rose and followed Melona, who had already stood, her tall, graceful form striding casually toward the open side of the room letting out into the gardens. A warm breeze heavy with the scent of sea salt kissed my cheeks as I joined the stranger, pausing beside her as she extended an arm to pluck an orange from a nearby branch.

With a curve of her lips, she began to peel the orange and pull it apart, its juice dribbling like drops of blood across the garden path.

"Now this is a superior fruit," she said. Her eyes were cold as they flitted back to me, and I repressed another shiver and turned to the list Elder Nai'luna had forced upon me instead.

"I'm not sure why they hired a wedding planner when there's not even any time to *plan*," I ground out.

Melona licked the orange juice from her mouth. "Because they're fools, easily tricked," she said, tossing the remaining half of the fruit to the ground and taking a sudden step toward me.

My heart lurched as I glanced up and met her gaze, finding eyes that had once been ice blue now appearing to be pure black, as if they were yawning pits ready to swallow me whole. Her elegant fingernails, dripping with juice, appeared more like claws. When she smiled, her blood-red lips framed teeth as sharp as fangs.

"But you have powerful magic, and you are already starting to see exactly what I've wanted you to know all along," Melona continued.

Yes, I knew she wasn't Melona, a wedding planner. She was something other, something radiating a chilly, overwhelming aura of power and terror. The picture of a nightmare, tainting the beauty of the gardens with her spreading shadows.

"You're the Dark Immortal," I whispered. But I wasn't overcome with fear—I was filled with burning rage.

Every Forwyn story spoke of how the Dark Immortal's job was to carry souls to the Golden After, until she'd betrayed Elhani. Until she'd forsook her important task of comforting humans in their last hours, and had chosen to feed on their despair and fear instead. Her power grew proportionately to people's terror and hopelessness and grief.

She was worshipped by demons and fueled by pain.

The Queen of Death herself.

"The Alrenians like to call me Nesrelle," the Dark Immortal said, blinking. As she did, her eyes returned to the icy blue they'd been before, but I wasn't sure that was any better. Her gaze still pierced into me, assessing me like I was helpless prey. "And I have to say, I've grown rather fond of that name."

I inhaled deeply, trying to calm my racing heart. Launching myself at an Immortal would be immensely foolish, but it took everything in me not to do so. She would have been the one growing stronger in the shadows while my people suffered and died. She would have been the one whispering in Alrenian and Forwyn ears alike, driving hatred and pain and endless war.

Anything to bring chaos and death. Anything to feed *her* and her unquenchable bloodlust.

It was she who would have taken even greater delight than Empress Karye herself when my brother was murdered before my eyes. When my sisters were attacked. When Naina was slain.

With shaking fingers, I crumpled the papers in my hand, letting them fall forgotten to the dirt.

My anger gave me clarity, made the last pieces of my fear flutter away. On the breeze, wrapping itself around me in a living embrace, came Elhani's song. The sweet melody sustained me, until I could sense magic bubbling through my veins. It felt limitless—like I could draw from it and never find its beginning or end.

Like I could stare into death's face right now, and not quake.

"Last I checked," I said, forcing my words to come out slow and measured, "I'm not dying. So why are you here, *Nesrelle?*"

Nesrelle's smirk was vicious. "You're right, you're not dying." She reached out, trailing her fingernails along my arm. I gritted my teeth but refused to flinch away, even when her nails bit into skin, drawing blood. "Not yet, anyway, and it's such a shame I can't take your soul now."

"You're here to taunt me?"

Nesrelle quirked a brow. "To *remind* you. You can't save your people, *amara'rekni.* In the face of what is coming, you are useless." She ran a hand down my cheek. "It's a shame. Such anger and power, but you use it trying to save lives when there are so many who deserve to be taken. You shed blood, but you take no joy in it. You could have been a powerful ally."

I scoffed, stepping back to wrench myself away from her touch. "I'd never ally myself with the Dark Immortal. I'm no fool. I know what sorts of deals you strike."

"Yes," Nesrelle murmured. "So instead of my ally, you have been my prey." Her smile was cruel. "I was there, you know. I fed on his pain."

Her abrupt change of subject didn't throw me off, because it was as if she'd peered into my thoughts to glimpse the constant grief swirling in my brain, pounding against my skull. Once more, the images of Edi's death flashed before my eyes, no matter how hard I tried to command them away. Sweat gathered along my brow, my pulse quickened, and my breathing shallowed. I was going to lose myself, right here, in front of the Queen of Death.

Naina wasn't here to speak into my mind and spare me from the waking nightmares with her peaceful presence. Caesiem wasn't nearby to sing away the darkness with his beautiful voice.

It was just me, facing against everything that haunted me. The blood. The guilt. The failure.

"Yes," Nesrelle whispered, "you failed. You failed Edi when he threw himself in front of you. Your *younger* brother died protecting you, when it was your responsibility to save him."

My entire body shook.

"He loved you, and you repaid him with death. The last thing he saw in this world was Karye, smiling as she cut open his throat."

I was frozen in place, locked in Nesrelle's terrifying gaze as she threw me back into each awful moment, as if I were reliving them all over again. I could smell Edi's blood, could taste my tears as I screamed and cradled him to myself, trying in vain to staunch the flow from his wound. Karye was laughing all over again, mocking me as I spoke frantically to the only family I had left.

"It'll be all right, Edi. It's all right—"

I'd begged and sobbed, promising Karye *anything* if she would command her healers to save him.

And she'd laughed, relishing my pleas as I'd watched the light die in my brother's eyes.

"No, I won't kill you," she'd said. "And I don't want your life in exchange for his. I want you to live. I want you to remember this moment forever, and know that I hold the power here. Never forget that."

Nesrelle towered over me, her very presence pain and despair. Tears streamed down my cheeks, but I couldn't look away from her, couldn't block out the memories. Not this time.

"How do you expect to save your people," Nesrelle asked softly, her brows knitted as if she truly were concerned, "when you couldn't even save your own brother? You are *useless*. A failure to everyone you love."

Naina's death came next—the blood, the helplessness.

Then the attack on Aerekni Academy, all because I'd agreed to lead Revaed and his army there.

And finally, the rows of corpses in Akytha square, all because I'd mistakenly trusted Caesiem rather than uncover his secrets and do something—*anything*—to stop the Teramese invasion.

"I came to remind you that you can't stop what's coming," Nesrelle said, brushing a curl behind my ear with terrifying gentleness. She smoothed a tear off my cheek, smiling softly. "And to relish the pain this knowledge brings you. It fuels me for the future."

And then—she was gone.

I stumbled back into the room where the Elders were gathered, who blinked and studied me in confusion.

"I don't think we dismissed you," Elder Ilhoa said sternly.

Elder Nai'luna sighed, waving an annoyed hand. Maybe the sight of my tears made her think of a fretful child. "You can't avoid this wedding, so don't even try. Go study the speech Elder Ilhoa gave you, and be prepared tomorrow. We will make the final arrangements with the emperor."

It was as if…as if they'd forgotten their wedding planner Melona had ever existed. Nesrelle's power had tricked them entirely.

With a trembling hand, I wiped away my tears and tore out of the room, letting Zalec lead me to my new chambers.

What had Nesrelle meant about what was coming? Was she manipulating the Alrenian army the Elders had once suspected was gathering? Or were more Alrenian uprisings in the works? Or more horrors from Revaed?

Whatever the case, I was running out of time.

Failure. Useless.

The words screamed at me, threatening to shake my nerve and break me. But I couldn't afford that. I had to believe there was something I could do this time, something to atone for my mistakes. I had to believe that Elhani had meant it when he said I couldn't fail my purpose.

But each time I closed my eyes, I saw Edi's dark ones staring back at me, pain and confusion and terror reflected in them as he drowned in his own blood.

CHAPTER THIRTY-ONE

Revaed

Storming down the hallway, away from where the Elders were meeting with Lo, I ordered the first guard I encountered to fetch General Darix. The number of high ranking officers I trusted was dwindling, now that so many were spread out across the empire, or had vanished or been killed during the riots.

Darix wasn't exactly a man I trusted, either, when I knew he had caused Caesiem trouble. But I did trust him as a soldier, as someone who would get a job done.

Stopping in one of the palace's libraries, I sank into an armchair and stared out the window, studying the flowers blooming on one of the vines climbing up a trellis. My entire body was tense, my muscles strained with my apprehension. It wasn't the first time in my life I cursed my family name and longed for a world in which I didn't bear the weight of being a leader.

Darix's first job would be simple. Take a group of soldiers into the secret passage Lo had discovered, and search the tunnels for any sign of the Alrenian insurgents. But his next task…that was more unpleasant.

If Caesiem found out, he would despise me.

But there was no other choice—not when the lives of my people—and potentially even Caesiem's life—were in danger.

I folded my trembling hands in my lap, willing the taut, anxious feeling building a flurry of activity in my chest to halt. If I forced myself to be still, to be collected, maybe I would feel at peace too. I prayed to every god I knew that it would work. I needed to think clearly, to not let sentimentality get in the way of safety. Of the greater good.

Every time I blinked, I could see a younger version of Caesiem before me, that scrawny, wide-eyed orphan who had watched me with such awe after *he'd* been the one to save *my* life. I could see the way he'd wolfed down each meal, the way he'd studied me with lively curiosity as I'd inquired about his past and his magic. He'd been so young and afraid, so grateful to me for extending nothing but simple kindness.

I didn't want to see his heart break, didn't want to risk damaging the trust between us.

I drew a deep breath. His safety had to come before all else.

As soon as Darix shuffled in, dipping into a low bow, I stood, pacing restlessly. "I have a task for you to complete immediately," I said, and proceeded to explain where to find the entrance to the secret passage and what to do. "Take as many soldiers as you need. If any of those tunnels branch off into wherever the Alrenians have been cowering all this time, their numbers are large enough to pose a challenge."

"Of course, Your Majesty," Darix said, with a dip of his head.

"If they are somewhere underground, I doubt they're aware of this or any other entrances into the palace," I mused aloud, "or the rioters would have infiltrated us already. However, whatever you find down there—your next step will be to search throughout the palace for any other hidden entrances or exits. Who knows what forgotten secrets are hiding in these walls."

"It will be done right away, my emperor."

I halted mid-step, hesitating. "One more thing. This task will need to be completed…later. And I need your discretion. No one else is to know about this."

A smug smile twitched at Darix's mouth.

"After the wedding ceremony, I'll need Miss Nolanhou dead. But I need it to appear to be an accident."

CHAPTER THIRTY-TWO

My army marched restlessly toward Inalgoth, stopping only to destroy any civilization we encountered. Wynlaen and its occupants were consumed. An Alrenian temple dedicated to hope was left barren.

My soldiers didn't even pause to eat or rest. They didn't possess such mortal needs, not anymore. Instead, it was bloodlust that sustained them, the powerful need to kill providing them their nourishment and their strength.

The sight of my army cooled my temper after visiting with Lo'laeni Nolanhou. That girl had been a thorn in my side ever since she'd slit Karye's throat. My fingers curled into fists as I imagined watching the light die from her eyes as I squeezed the breath from her lungs and fed my power with her every dying gasp.

But, just as I'd told Jalie before, I had given up my chance of killing anyone. Though mortals called me the Queen of Death, the reality was that I had little control over when they lived or died. Only once a year could I claim a single mortal to send into the afterlife early, and this time, I'd chosen differently. I'd used my power to save Jalie instead, trusting that she would be my executioner. The one to slay not only the Forwyn's precious *amara'rekni,* but to also bring about countless other deaths—Teramese, Forwyn, Alrenian.

Closing my eyes, I drew a deep breath and focused on Jalie—on her churning thoughts, her whirlwind emotions. She was beautifully broken, each one of her ragged pieces so sharp she was like a living weapon ready to cut, to slice, to devour. Her power and conviction were strong—so long as she didn't sway and give into that soldier, Kovi, or any of his ridiculous notions of duty and justice and mercy and peace.

I extended my power, brushing my influence through Jalie's mind. Using my growing connection to her my nestrae had granted me through the rune they'd carved into her cheek, I filled her with thoughts of bloodshed and revenge. Reminding her of her purpose. Reminding her that she was *mine.*

CHAPTER THIRTY-THREE

Jalie

Ryke was growing weaker. Fatigue weighed down his body, making him droop his head and sag his tail until it dragged across the ground behind him. Feeble plumes of smoke curled from his nostrils with each breath, filling the air with its acrid tang.

When I brushed a hand along his scales as I walked alongside him, they felt too cool. My heart seized with worry as I peered into his silver eye.

Already, the evening light was fading, night threatening to descend us into darkness once more. Every step was exhausting, but I couldn't stop. Ryke was running out of time, and I had to reach the capital. Had to find the antidote he so desperately needed before it was too late.

But another need was pressing on my thoughts, growing stronger with each step I took toward Inalgoth. Over and over, I heard Nesrelle's voice hissing in my ear, and saw Lo'laeni's face in my mind's eye. *Kill her. Take your revenge. Fuel your power. Then kill the Teramese and take back your empire.*

A vision flowed through my mind, one of me seated on a throne made of Teramese corpses, blood dripping from my crown.

I repressed a shudder.

Behind us, Vander called upon his wind magic to push a steadying breeze against Ryke, helping his steps along. But I could feel his and Tayla's gaze boring into me, could sense their growing fear. They were right to worry about what would become of them once we reached the capital, once I no longer needed them.

Kill them, Nesrelle prompted. Her voice was starting to sound like my mother's. And sometimes, even like my own.

But Ryke had to come first. I had to save him. He was what mattered, even more than revenge…

Foolish, Nesrelle snarled.

I fought to tune out her words.

"Hold on, Ryke," I whispered, pressing my shoulder into the warmth of my dragon, seeking comfort from him as much as I hoped I was offering some.

If we hurried, we could reach the capital tonight.

"Hold on."

CHAPTER THIRTY-FOUR

Kovi

Under the setting sun, the sea glistened red as blood. Each kiss of the breeze against my face brought a welcome coolness in the gathering evening, soothing the flush of warmth growing from the effort of rowing to shore. This time, uneasiness had tugged at me the instant Rhi'il and I neared the water, settling into the rowboat we'd use to get to the cove's rocky shore and venture back into the capital.

The memory of the nymph's clammy touch made my skin prickle; her strange warnings haunted my every breath. It was as if I could sense her, even now, watching us from somewhere beneath the glistening surface of the waves. Seeing my future and sensing nothing but darkness.

Maybe I would have been better off succumbing to her, letting her drag me into the watery depths.

Repressing a shudder, I lifted my eyes to the beach and found we were already in the shallows. Leaping out, Rhi'il and I seized the boat and splashed ashore, our boots crunching on slick pebbles.

"Kovi."

The word was like another brush of the sea breeze against my cheeks, filling me with longing. It was Jalie's voice saying my name. Jalie's voice coming to life from my dreams and nightmares, my hopes and darkest fears.

Impossible, my mind screamed, even as I turned, the irrepressible need to see her again—to ensure she was safe, to hold her in my arms— taking over every other thought.

I spun toward the sea, catching a glimpse of her golden hair, tinged orange in the dying light, streaming behind her. Her eyes were bright and fierce as ever, cutting into mine. Forever magnetic, drawing me toward her and her aura of confidence and power. This time, there was no sign of the scar I'd seen marring her cheek in my nightmare—only smooth, golden skin and her familiar freckles sprinkled across it.

Clothed in the same simple tunic and leggings she'd worn when we'd said our goodbyes, she let the waves rush and foam over her bare feet.

"Kovi," she said again, but I was already racing toward her, slamming to my knees as if she were—

Pain lanced into my leg as I landed on a sharp rock, the sensation jolting my mind out of the trance-like state I'd found myself in. Scowling, I drew my sword in a single motion. Leaping back to my feet, I pressed my blade against Jalie's neck.

Not Jalie.

The trick fell away, leaving the white-haired nymph instead. She grinned at me, her silver scales flashing red in the bloody light.

I sensed more than heard Rhi'il come up behind me. His own blade hissed as he unsheathed it, ever my faithful friend.

"What do you want?" I ground out, staring into the nymph's wild eyes.

"To make a deal," she said, her luminous gaze scanning my face. "I've already told you the future I see. Division and brokenness and death—for you *and* the one you love. And time is running out to save your people, too. So many will die."

I scoffed, pressing my blade closer, till the edge bit into her flesh. A drop of silvery blood trickled down her neck. "Why would I make a deal with you? What does a creature of the sea have to offer in this war?"

"Water," she whispered, "to quench flame."

I shook my head. "Why would I make any promises to you, when you threaten my life and speak in riddles?"

A wave crashed against the shore, sea spray misting against my face and glistening along her scales. Lifting her arms, she closed her eyes and smiled, as if beckoning to the water. Another wave rolled toward us, larger and more powerful than the first. Foam churned and the sea roared and tumbled, flowing around us until suddenly, we were knee-deep in the rising liquid.

"The power of the Alrenian army is fire," the nymph said, opening her flashing eyes, "but mine has the ability to quench it. All I require is a portion of your magic. It's strong—stronger than what most humans carry within them. Pledge some to me, and your city doesn't have to burn to ash."

My pulse pounded in my ears. "What have you seen?"

With a slow smile, the nymph offered a careless shrug. My blade nicked her again, drawing more inhuman blood. "Death. Destruction. The end."

"Sounds dramatic," Rhi'il said. "And you think we believe that you can see the future? That you can stop what you've seen?"

Chilly foreboding washed over me. I'd seen what the Alrenian army was capable of, and I had no doubt that they were marching for

Inalgoth. But Jalie wouldn't let them harm the Forwyn…would she?

She certainly would never let Ryke or her army set fire to her beloved city.

Despite my nightmare, despite everything within me warning that something was very wrong, that Jalie herself was in trouble, I refused to give in to this water creature. As much as I despised my controlling magic at times, there was no telling when I'd need it again to save the ones I loved. I would take the risk in my own hands, and face whatever the nymph had seen myself.

"Nymphs are tricksters," I muttered, shaking my head. "I don't believe you would truly save us. I refuse."

The nymph snarled, revealing her needle-like teeth. "Have it your way," she said. "They're your fears to face—not mine."

Beside me, Rhi'il shifted uneasily on his feet. "Call back the water," he demanded of the nymph.

The nymph laughed, and the sea rose, surging toward us. A great, unnatural wave for this peaceful cove grew between the ship and the shore, speeding for the beach. With a snarl, I sliced with my blade—and the nymph disappeared.

In her place, a silver fish dove through the air, plunging into the water and swimming swiftly out of sight.

Rhi'il cursed, slamming his blade fruitlessly into the water where the nymph-turned-fish had vanished.

"Run," I said, seizing my friend's arm.

In one breath, we sheathed our blades and turned, the sea roaring behind us. Too close.

We had moments before the wave would overtake us, full of the nymph's fury over her spurned deal. Splashing furiously through the water, we raced toward the rocky face of the cliff overhanging the cove, our only hope to reach a height the sea could not touch.

If we could climb fast enough.

Lungs heaving, legs burning, I sprinted faster than I'd ever run,

Rhi'il matching my speed step for step. Retreating water swirled around our legs, spilling back toward the harbor. The sand sucked at our boots with each step, threatening to trip us and let the receding sea draw us into its tumultuous waters.

Rhi'il stumbled over a rock, catching himself but falling behind. Spinning, I kicked up clods of wet sand as I stretched my hand toward him. "Rhi! Hurry!"

"Don't wait for me," he panted, charging forward. "I'm right behind you, I promise."

We leapt for the nearest rocky outcropping just as the sea hurled toward us, slamming over the beach with breathtaking force. Hand over hand, I grappled for every crevice, every ledge I could find. My boots scrabbled against damp rock, sending sand and pebbles skittering and splashing into the rising water below. Nearby, Rhi'il gasped for breath as he pushed himself harder, wrenching himself up beside me.

Water lapped below us, licking at our boots. Rising, rising.

My muscles groaned in protest as I climbed higher. Sweat trickled down my back. I didn't dare glance at the water and lose speed. With every heft of my shoulders, with every bit of progress forward that I hoped would put space between the sea and me, the sea continued to surge forward.

And then, at last, Rhi'il and I pulled ourselves over the edge, panting for breath as we collapsed on the grass. Below, the water swirled and foamed only a few yards below the top of the cliff face. If we'd been even a moment slower, we would have been lost to the raging wave.

Further out in the harbor, the ship rocked in the disturbed water, but was otherwise untouched. Already the sea was calming, its choppy surface smoothing. Within minutes, the raging water had transformed into the typical peace that Haven's Bay was known for. Glassy and glistening, it sparkled red with the last of the daylight.

"Well," Rhi'il said, running a hand through his damp hair and kicking off his boots to squeeze the water from his soaked pants, "that's a lesson learned. Never anger a water nymph.”

Motionless, I stared out at the sea, trying to catch a glimpse of the creature somewhere in the rolling waves. When I spoke, my voice was quiet, uncertain. “Do you think I made the wrong choice?”

I tore my gaze away to look at my friend, who rolled his eyes. “Absolutely not,” he declared. “The very first thing she did was put you in some kind of trance—it looked like you wanted to bow down and worship her.”

I swallowed, gripped with discomfort at the memory. The nymph’s power had been strange, something I’d never heard of before. And the fact that she’d known how to perfectly capture Jalie’s face…

“And then she spouted nonsense,” Rhi’il continued. “The city burning to ash? Everyone here is fighting for possession of this city— why would anyone, even the Teramese, choose to burn it? And even if that happens…even if this war goes to absolute *goehr*, Elha’tonu, there is *no* way that nymph would use any power you gave her to help us.”

“I think…I fear there could be truth to her words,” I mused. “I saw the Alrenians and their unnatural power, so I know what they’re capable of. And back then, we were surrounded by mountains, nowhere near the sea. How would the nymph know any of this unless she truly can see into the future?”

Rhi’il set his jaw. “Even so, she wanted to manipulate you, not help you.”

Sighing, I stood. “You’re right. I just…” My words trailed off.

What did I wish? That Jalie was here with her army, and I could reassure myself that not only was she alive and well, but also that she was still committed to our alliance? To *us*?

That was out of my hands. There was only one path forward—to keep fighting for my people in Inalgoth.

My eyes flitted back toward the ship. Earlier, when General Ilowhe had bid us goodbye, we’d spoken again of our need to get word to Forwyth. I’d insisted the fastest way would be to secure a dragon and send a message that way, but General Ilowhe had frowned.

"I have a lot of faith in you and Rhi'il, but don't do anything rash tonight. Not that I need to remind *you* of that." His glance darted toward my friend, who had been in earnest conversation with Mio'e.

"Maybe that will be our next mission?" I'd suggested.

"One plan at a time," the general reassured me. "We will find a way."

Now, his words echoed in my mind as I helped Rhi'il up and we turned out faces toward the city walls. *We will find a way.* I prayed that would hold true for Jalie and me, as well as for the Forwyn people.

CHAPTER THIRTY-FIVE

Lo

There was no time to waste feeling sorry for myself, or drowning in my past failures. There wasn't even time for grief. The dead were already gone, long past saving.

If I didn't act fast, this small window of opportunity I had left to rescue the living would vanish, too.

Rising from the bed I'd crumpled upon, when it had seemed like Nesrelle had stolen every ounce of strength and hope from me, I inhaled a fortifying breath and faced the balcony windows. Daylight was dying, tinging the sky a fiery red, like a great dragon had been loosed upon the world and all of Alrenor was burning.

Reaching into my pocket, I drew out the crumpled paper A'elli had slipped to me and scanned its contents. She'd written in a scrawling hand, the ink blotted in several places, as if she'd been in a hurry.

Lo,

I know you probably hate me, and to be honest, I'm not sure how I feel about you. However, saving my people is more important to me right now than avenging Renni and Wilvhe. I might not trust you about many things, but I've seen visions from a truth-gifted friend, and I know your heart is sincere when it comes to helping the Forwyn imprisoned in the palace.

I've found help, people I trust to fight for our freedom from the Teramese. They are the ones who told me about the secret passage leading into the dungeons, and that is when I made this plan to sneak inside, steal a key, and pretend to be locked within my own cell.

But it won't be long before the Teramese guards grow suspicious. I don't have much time, so I'm going to try to share this letter with you and then escape. My first move will be against the so-called emperor and prince. Once they're dead, I think we will have a real hope of defeating the Teramese armies.

Then I'll lead our people to freedom through the passages.

As soon as you can read this letter, come back to the dungeons and escape with us. Keep fighting for your people.

I crumpled the letter into a fist, heart pounding and ears ringing. *Caesiem.*

"A'elli, you idiot," I muttered. "You really *have* gone mad."

The vigilantes had always been brave, if a little foolhardy in their lofty hopes to take down corruption with their small numbers and resources. Perhaps most of it had been desperation. And now, I was convinced A'elli was behaving especially rashly out of grief. She'd lost her friends and now she was under threat of losing her empire to an even worse situation.

To try to assassinate the Teramese leaders alone was madness. She might succeed against one, but both?

Again, my mind darted to Caesiem.

My heart thundered in my ears as I imagined A'elli sneaking out of a hidden exit within the dungeons and ambushing him. He was resourceful and strong and a powerful mage, but he was currently injured, and if she caught him unawares…

Shoving the crumpled paper back into my pocket, I darted to the entrance of my quarters, pounding on the locked door.

"Let me out!" I shouted to the guards posted in the hallway. "Your leaders are in danger!"

A scoffing male voice replied. "You think we're foolish enough to fall for that?"

"Please, I need to speak with your prince," I pled, my tone turning frantic.

The man laughed outright, the sound bouncing off the walls outside my door. "You'll speak with him when he calls for you. You're not the one giving orders around here, even if you are his betrothed. Emperor Revaed made his orders clear. You're to stay inside."

Fury boiled in my veins. I leaned into my anger, letting it disperse my panic and grant clarity to my thoughts.

Invisibility would be no use, but I'd mastered another form of my magic recently, one that would be helpful.

Turning back toward the door, I tuned into Elhani's song and called upon his power to flow through me as I raised my voice. "Your prince is in danger." The air crackled as I spoke. This time, there wasn't a response. Instead, I had a strong sensation that the guards outside were listening breathlessly, while fearfully awaiting the rest of my warning and instructions. "You have to lead me to him. Now."

The door swung open, the two wide-eyed guards gesturing for me to follow them.

CHAPTER THIRTY-SIX

Caesiem

One Year Ago

I've certainly looked better, haven't I?" Revaed jested feebly, his laugh sounding a little strangled. And his voice—his voice was hoarse and weak, a sign he must have eventually succumbed to screaming through his pain. "The theslynik you fetched from the water nymphs has done some good though. What *can't* that stuff do?"

Seated beside the bed in his palace quarters, I scowled, hating that my guardian was trying to make light of the situation. His father had ordered him whipped like a criminal, all because Revaed had stood up for me after I'd made the foolish mistake of touching one of the High Imperator's mistresses.

I swallowed. The girl was dead now, her body disposed of carelessly, my bloodied sheets burnt and replaced as if nothing had happened. If it weren't for Revaed, I might have been dead alongside her, powerful water magic or not. The High Imperator wasn't known for his mercy.

With a quick glance around the room to ensure no servants or guards were lurking half-forgotten in a corner, I muttered, "It's not something to laugh about. How can your father treat you like this?"

Revaed's expression turned bitter. Lying on his stomach with his back heavily bandaged, he looked pale and weary, his hair wild and tousled.

He'd stood up for me many times, redirecting his father's wrath toward himself. Accepting cutting remarks, even public humiliation when the High Imperator chose to make those comments in the presence of the court. But this was the first time he'd been so severely punished in my stead.

"Maybe I'm not worth the trouble," I mumbled, not for the first time.

A muscle twitched in Revaed's jaw as he reached out, seizing my wrist. "Never say that, Caes. Of course you are."

I swallowed a lump in my throat.

"Besides," Revaed went on, "we may have a chance to escape his despotism sooner than we thought." He smirked, though it looked more like a grimace. "Father wants to send spies to Inalgoth to observe the Forwyn Court of Elders and form a plan regarding how we could claim the empire and all its resources for ourselves."

I scowled. "That just means he's expanding his tyranny across borders."

"No," Revaed said earnestly, squeezing my arm. "That's just it. The healers say he's not as physically fit as they'd like for the journey. Apparently surviving the plague doesn't come without its own cost."

"I thought you said he'd gotten sick over a decade ago."

"And it's weakened him, especially now as he ages. Which means…he can't lead the conquest."

I sat back, letting the information sink in. "You will?"

Revaed's smile broadened. "*We* will." He continued, speaking quickly, eagerly. "I think you should be one of the spies to go ahead. You've learned to command the water creatures, right? To call on the nymphs and trade with them? You could give them trinkets in exchange for being your messengers. Father would be foolish not to send you."

Frowning, I shifted in my seat. The nymphs made me uncomfortable with their vicious grins and tricky ways. But he was right. With my history as a thief, I also had talents that few of his other mages or soldiers possessed. My people were starving, suffering, fighting against an increasing number of wild dragon attacks on our cities. Revaed and I had ridden out on far too many occasions lately to hand out food rations and medical supplies, to try to instill hope in a hopeless people.

I could change all of that.

"You could get away from the High Imperator's wrath before he finds something new to try to punish you for," Revaed went on. "And then, when it's time for me to lead our soldiers to Alrenor, you and I can lead together. Away from him."

My mind whirled excitedly with the possibilities. We could build a new sort of empire on Alrenor's shores, away from the cruelty. We would send resources to our people, and we would learn how to tame dragons, a skill that could be used against the wild dragons harming our citizens. Hope ran through my veins, headier than any alcohol.

"I'll go," I vowed.

Present

The sea breeze raked through my hair as I stood along the cliff's edge, staring at the shore far below. Bathed in the sun's last dying rays, it shone warm and golden beside a calm sea, each wave swirling to the sand in a steady, soothing rhythm. The scene was a stark contrast to the one I'd beheld the night I'd called upon the sea creature to take Renni, when the churning waves had been restless under the deep night sky.

But no matter what mood the water was in, it always brought me peace. Each breath of briny air, each kiss of sea spray, felt like coming home. The sea didn't feel quite the same as the ocean—nothing could replace the Terebrys and the wild, unbridled power I felt standing in its shallows, but being here, overlooking the Great Sea, knowing that somewhere past the horizon this very water spilled into the ocean…it was a close second.

It was a strange contradiction, the fact that someone like me, who'd spent a lifetime seeking security, would find comfort in something as wild and unpredictable as the water. Or maybe that's exactly what enthralled me about it. I could taste its power in the air, could feel its ever-changing moods as easily as if they were mine. And I knew, deep in my bones, that the water would protect me, one of its own. Its power was my power. Its anger and joy and freedom—those were all mine too.

Running a hand through my hair, I squeezed my eyes shut, wishing the crashing sound of the waves could drown out the building storm inside of me. After the guards had insisted the healer tend to my injured arm again, I'd demanded a moment of freedom for some fresh air. The guards had glanced at one another uneasily, but when I'd pulled rank, reminding them I was capable of defending myself and I could answer to Revaed for throwing off their protection, they'd relented.

Now, I sank to a seat on the smooth stone, dangling my legs over the cliff's edge. My memories of Revaed only brought pain and uncertainty, along with snatches of the vision Meli had given to me of my parents. The beginnings of pure panic was twisting within my chest, like an angry beast smothering my breath and attempting to claw its way out my throat. I wanted to scream and rage, to call up the sea and hurl it at this cursed empire and watch it all drown—and I wanted to go with it.

I didn't know who to trust anymore. I didn't know where home was, if it wasn't with Revaed—and it certainly wasn't with Lo. If Revaed had spent all this time lying to me… If Lo only hated me and wanted to put distance between us…

With a muttered curse, I lifted a hand and called to the sea. Ever faithful, it answered, sending a shimmering plume of water shooting upward, glistening in shades of red, orange, and gold in the evening light. It coursed in an undulating river toward me, wrapping around and around until I was caught in a small whirlpool, relishing the sea's embrace. Water droplets sprayed against my face and dampened my hair.

Peace enveloped me with its presence, and I plunged all my tangled thoughts into the depths of my mind, losing myself to my magic. It hummed through my veins, as if the water lived in me. It was music to my ears and life to my blood. The knot in my chest loosened, and finally, I took a deep, cleansing breath.

Confront Revaed, I thought. *And then…go to the pub. Speak with Meli.* I dropped my hand, sending the water cascading back toward the sea.

It was time to have the courage to face the truth, even if it rent me in two.

"Caesiem?"

Lo's voice wrenched me from my thoughts.

I glanced over my shoulder to see her approaching, two guards a short distance away, their hands on their sword hilts. Lo's brow was bunched in worry.

"Why are you here?" she asked.

Something was off. I rose swiftly, my mind instinctively stretching toward my magic. "What's wrong?"

CHAPTER THIRTY-SEVEN

Lo

Maybe I should have known before racing through the palace, searching its vast rooms for Caesiem, that I would find him here. Seated on the cliff's edge, water dampening his dark hair, his vivid blue eyes gazed unseeing at the waves crashing and foaming over the beach below. Of course he'd be here, this man who'd told me he was always seeking home, in the place that he appeared the most at peace.

My fingers drifted over the pendant dangling from my neck.

"Caesiem?" I said, approaching on such soundless feet, he didn't hear me until I spoke.

He turned in surprise.

I scanned the area, half-terrified A'elli would spill out of some doorway hidden along the shadowy side of the nearby Keep. "What are you doing here?"

Caesiem, ever attune to my moods, it seemed, stood at once. "What's wrong?"

Mercifully, the guards remained several yards back, out of earshot. I raced forward, swallowing the distance between us and seizing his hands.

Surprise and something else—longing or hope?—darted through Caesiem's bright eyes, there and gone again so quickly I wasn't sure. My heart ached, but there were more important things than trying to mend our brokenness or the ever-expanding gap between us. I couldn't focus on the warmth of his fingers curling around mine, or the way his eyes traced my face, drinking in the sight of me like he was a parched man lost in the desert.

"I'm sorry." The words burst out of him before I could speak.

I blinked. "What?"

Caesiem gently pulled one of his hands from mine and cupped my cheek, his gaze so tender that my heart cracked even more. "I haven't been there for you, and you're grieving after the attack on your sisters. I'm sorry."

"You were hurt."

A muscle in Caesiem's jaw worked. "I didn't need to recover in Revaed's rooms. I—I wasn't sure if you wanted me, but I should have stayed."

My tongue wouldn't move.

"I've made so many mistakes," Caesiem went on, "that I don't expect you to forgive me. I just…I needed to apologize."

Numb, I nodded, clinging to his other hand like a lifeline.

A dark look flashed across Caesiem's face. "What exactly happened at the abbey? How did Naina…didn't the Teramese defend them?"

Tossing a furtive glance over my shoulder to ensure the guards still weren't close enough to overhear, I turned back to Caesiem and lowered my voice. "I'm not sure you'll believe me." I couldn't help the coldness that entered my words, the bitter pang of knowing that Caesiem loved his guardian to the point of blindness and might choose Revaed over me.

His eyes were earnest as he searched mine, as if he could read the truth simply from my expression. "Tell me."

"Revaed brought soldiers and killed the Alrenians," I said slowly, "but then he threatened my sisters." My throat tightened and ached at the memory. "He ordered his soldiers to murder Naina."

Caesiem's gaze continued to darken the more I spoke, and I couldn't tell if it was out of horror or disbelief. All I knew was that I couldn't stop. He had to know the truth, and he had to know it now, when Revaed wasn't around to slay another Forwyn in retaliation.

"He threatened to kill my sisters too if I didn't lead him and his soldiers to Aerekni Academy. He knew the Forwyn would open the gates for me, so he could lead a surprise attack." I blinked, trying to keep the tears from slipping free. "My people...we were overrun. I don't even know if my father survived. Revaed had me dragged back here..."

Caesiem's eyes darted over my shoulder, halting my stream of words. I followed his gaze, my blood freezing in my veins as I saw Revaed step forward, pausing beside the guards.

"What's going on?" he asked, a fearful sort of calm in his stance, in the cool violet of his eyes.

"I wanted to speak with Lo," Caesiem said easily, before I had a chance to fumble for an excuse. "I brought her here."

This wasn't the first time Caesiem had lied to his guardian to defend me, but it still startled me. I tried to read his expression out of the corner of my eye, but his face was a mask.

Revaed nodded slowly. "I think maybe you should come to dinner." Genuine concern shone in his eyes as he studied the bandage on Caesiem's shoulder. "I heard you pulled some stitches earlier and had to see one of the healers again."

"I'm fine," Caesiem interjected. "You know I can't sit still—"

Revaed's expression twisted, as if in pain. "Just, come inside," he interrupted gently. "Food is waiting. You need to regain your strength." His eyes darted to mine, a silent warning. "Lo can eat with us."

Gesturing for us to follow, Revaed turned back toward the palace buildings, the guards falling into step behind him. Caesiem cast me a searching glance before extending a hand.

"We can talk more later," he murmured, and my heart fluttered as if it were a promise. He didn't seem angry, but then again, the mask that had descended over his features remained firmly in place, and I couldn't read him. His eyes seemed stormy and distant, but that could have been because of all he had to process. Maybe he believed me...

I took his hand, twining my fingers with his. For now, I would allow myself to hope.

As we approached the garden path, I scanned the growing shadows gathering beneath citrus trees and among shrubbery. When was A'elli planning to strike? And how? I wanted to reassure myself that she wouldn't try now, with both the emperor and Caesiem in one place, where she'd be outnumbered. But then, I never would have expected her to be so rash as to try to assassinate them on her own at all.

Clearly she was desperate, which meant anything could happen.

"Caesiem," I whispered, "Revaed took me down to the dungeons earlier, and A—"

An arrow whizzed past, slicing so close that it brushed my curls aside. It struck the tree just behind me, but I was already moving, already shoving Caesiem to the dirt path. We slammed to the ground in a heap, my body pressed protectively over his.

If I had a blade...

Swords shrieked around me as the two guards brandished their weapons and seized Revaed, pulling him toward the safety of the nearest building.

"No!" Revaed thrashed angrily against their grips. "Get the prince out of here! Caes!"

Caesiem dragged me to my feet, pulling us back up the path, toward the cliff near the Keep. Toward the water.

Revaed shouted for his guards to release him. He raced toward us, dodging arrows as he went. The guards threw themselves into the garden, racing toward the direction from which the arrows were coming.

Another arrow struck one of the guards in the face, downing him in an instant.

Idiot, get out of here, I thought, wondering what had possessed A'elli to be so careless. She was still sorely outnumbered, and already more guards' footsteps were charging toward us from every direction, hurrying to reinforce their companions.

Just shy of the cliffside, Revaed seized my arms and wrenched me off Caesiem, tugging me against his chest and slamming me into a headlock. "I saw that prisoner slip you a note," he snarled. "I know you two are plotting to kill Caesiem."

"That's not true! I wouldn't ever hurt him."

"And yet you've been plotting against us from the start, undermining our alliance," Revaed went on, his grasp tightening painfully.

Caesiem spun around, his gaze boring into mine, his eyes dark and unreadable. "Don't hurt her, Revaed." His tone was calm. He moved forward slowly, his arms raised, as if trying to avoid spooking a wild animal.

I just wasn't sure if he was wary of Revaed or me. Did he believe me about what had happened at the abbey and the academy? Or did he trust his guardian?

Don't believe Revaed, I thought. *Believe me.*

Revaed pressed a blade to my throat, and a ringing sound filled my ears. My entire body went numb. This was all too similar to the moment Karye had threatened me, one of countless instants that haunted me all the time. Memories I tried to lock away in the recesses of my mind threatened to break through my barriers, to grasp me in their icy claws until they were all I could see, smell, or hear. The sharp tang of blood, the sound of gurgling and corpses collapsing…

No! I screamed the thought in my head. I wouldn't fall prey to that darkness, not again. Gritting my teeth, I forced every ounce of my willpower to conjure something, anything, to distract myself from the force of those waking nightmares.

A new memory gripped me, one of my early days at the Circle of Serenity, when Naina had spoken encouragement to my broken heart. She hadn't known what I'd faced, but she knew that, like most of the other women there, my past was full of horror and loss.

Now, against the darkness, the memory of Naina's words was hope and power and light. *The darkness of your past can no longer hold power over you, because you are stronger now than you were in that moment. What once overcame you is exactly what you are capable of overcoming now.*

Anger swallowed the fear trying to consume me, granting me the clarity I needed. My muscles knew how to fight back. In one smooth motion, I twisted into Revaed, surprising him enough to loosen his grip so I could punch him in the stomach and dart away.

A figure dove from the garden path, dodging Revaed's hunched form and slamming into Caesiem. A dagger glinted in the moonlight.

"Stop the emperor, Lo!" A'elli screamed at me as she raised her blade toward Caesiem's throat.

"A'elli!" I shouted. "Get off him!"

Caesiem shoved her off easily, slamming the dagger from her grasp. It went skittering over the cliff's edge, leaving her gasping and scrambling to get to her feet, to draw another dagger sheathed at her side.

Before Caesiem was on his feet again, she threw the blade, sending it straight for his face. But Caesiem had already called upon the water, and it answered in a fierce torrent. Rippling and roaring, it crashed into the dagger, sending it careening back toward the path. The water rose like a deadly snake, thrashing and wrapping around A'elli—and me.

The whirlpool surged around me, whipping my hair into my face and coating my skin in mist and salt. It didn't quite touch me, but the sheer force of it sent me stumbling back, straight toward the cliff's edge. I tried to cry out, but I couldn't hear anything over the sound of rushing water, and I wasn't sure anyone could hear me, either.

And then it slammed into my body, shoving me over the cliff, plunging me toward the churning sea. My heart lodged in my throat. The water rose to meet me, dragging its wet, cold fingers through my curls, soaking my clothes. Submerged in darkness and the raging currents of water, I kicked upward, fighting to find the surface, but I was thrown and tossed about. Waves pummeled against me, again and again, leaving me swimming hopelessly in a direction I wasn't even sure was up anymore.

Something slimy brushed against my leg, and a new terror flooded me. Had Caesiem called the tentacled creature again? Was he hoping to drown me alongside A'elli? Did he believe Revaed and think I'd found him to try to murder him?

My chest burned as I strained against the force of the water. I would be dashed against the rocky cliffside, or plunged so deep into the sea I'd never see the surface again. Panic seized me as bubbles streamed from my lips, the last of the air caught in my lungs. I was going to die here, all over a misunderstanding. All for a man I'd mistakenly fallen in love with…

And then, hands grasped me, their grip firm but gentle. Someone was swimming through the blackness, each movement strong and graceful and assured. We broke the surface of the water, choppy waves slamming against me in an uneven rhythm. I gasped and choked, spitting up saltwater and blinking tears from my burning eyes.

A single glance back showed me that the water had thrown me far out to harbor, leaving the forms on the cliff mere blots against the starry sky. If A'elli was somewhere in the sea, I found no sign of her. The water was already calming, the waves returning to their peaceful rhythm.

Turning, I found myself staring into a pair of luminous yellow eyes framed by a face dotted with silver scales. Long white hair streamed behind the woman, hanging in wet strands around her shoulders like a curtain. Her grasp remained firm on my arm as she treaded water beside me, studying me as curiously as I watched her.

This was the water nymph Caesiem had summoned before.

A new fear raked through my chest—had the nymph seized me so she could play with her prey like a cat with a mouse? Surely she didn't want to save my life, and was only here to ensure my death.

"What do you want?" I demanded, my voice hoarse.

The nymph's gaze locked on the pendant dangling from my neck. "You wear a water pendant, taken from the Terebrys itself, and the water protects its own."

I frowned in confusion. "You're here to save my life? To help me?"

She set her jaw, narrowing her eyes. "I'm not your friend, human. I'm only obeying the laws of the magic that flows through my veins, the laws I'm bound to. You're not a water mage, but one must care about you. As long as you bear that mage's token, I will protect you, as I must." Her grasp on my arm tightened. "I know where some of your friends are, and I can take you to them."

My mind whirled. Caesiem had flung me out to sea…to save me.

He'd believed me. Not Revaed. *Me.*

CHAPTER THIRTY-EIGHT

Caesiem

Water coursed down my face in tiny rivulets, the aftermath of the whirlpool I'd called upon. The stone beneath my boots was slick, and everything smelled of brine. In the darkness, I couldn't see Lo out in the waves, but I knew she was there. Safe.

A'elli…that was a different story.

I dropped my arms to my sides, trying to catch my breath after the effort it had taken to summon such a powerful rush of water magic. Other than the waves' return to their regular rhythm, the night was eerily quiet.

"Caes," Revaed whispered behind me, breaking the stillness as he stepped forward.

If I tore my eyes from the sea, if I turned to face my guardian, I wasn't sure I could conceal the storm raging within. Every word Lo had said echoed in my mind, along with the rage on Revaed's face as he'd caught her.

"Are you all right?" my guardian asked, his words unnaturally hesitant.

My heart pounded against my temples, making it hard to hear over its thundering beats. He'd used Lo to attack her people—her father. He'd ordered Naina's execution.

That had been his retaliation against Lo and the other Forwyn for breaking our alliance.

Survival above all else.

For so long, that had been my mantra. I'd leaned into it, believing that the world owed me something for leaving me to fend for myself in my youth. Believing my people were entitled to what the Alrenians had, all due to our suffering while Alrenor lived in excess and luxury. Even the Forwyn at least had access to food and shelter, not threatened by wild dragons or floods.

I'd thought every kill, every difficult decision, had been for the welfare of my people. For their security, their happiness, their future.

But what good was all of that, if it came at the cost of others' freedom and safety?

How could I let Revaed destroy the life Lo and her people had fought so hard for, for the scraps of freedom and joy they'd found, all for my own people? How could I build such a future for Teramyl, when its foundation would be bloodied with innocent corpses?

"Is Miss Nolanhou…is she dead?"

Finally, I glanced back at Revaed, who was wiping a hand across his face, trying to brush away the water dampening his brow.

"No," I said, my jaw tight, my entire body tense to keep myself under control. Every inch of me felt ready to snap, to unleash all the ferocity of my rage and betrayal. But it was my desperate loyalty—the final shreds of my hope and love—that kept me clinging to this false calm, praying I could discover something that would redeem Revaed and his choices. Wishing I could open my eyes and find myself in a world in which Revaed hadn't deceived and used me in the worst of ways. A world in which I wasn't questioning my guardian's love. Had this man who had been like the only father, the only family I knew, ever cared about *me* for me at all?

"I'm sorry, Caes…"

I lifted a hand without even turning around, cutting Revaed off sharply with my quick, angry movement. "I don't want to hear it."

My guardian must have misread my emotions, thinking they were guided toward Lo and a sense of betrayal from *her*. But I knew she hadn't schemed with A'elli to attack me. Such a thoughtless plan was unlike her, and as dedicated as she was to her people, I knew she wasn't so callous as to kill me like that in order to protect them.

"Do you know where she is?"

I shook my head. "Only that she is safe."

"I'll send guards to find her," Revaed continued quietly. "I know it hurts, but I don't want to cancel the wedding tomorrow. Our alliance is still important. The Forwyn can help us with the dragons and add to our numbers if the Alrenians choose to rise up again…" His voice trailed off. "We could exile Lo to Forwyth or another land after the wedding, do it quietly so as not to endanger the alliance…"

The wedding. Even now, Revaed's plans swirled through my head, full of the details of the conversation we'd had earlier that day. His talk of bringing the Forwyn prisoners out to attend. His carefully crafted speech, one he had the Elders help prepare and deliver to Lo themselves. He'd acted grateful about the alliance, grateful Lo was willing to cooperate…

And he'd murdered Naina. Attacked Lo's people and her father. He'd kept it secret, all this time. Because he knew…he knew how I felt about Lo and how furious I'd be to know he'd hurt her in such awful ways…

I shifted on my feet, watching the starlight glisten on the distant waves. My emotions were as restless as the churning sea—even when it appeared calm, it was full of endless energy, endless motion. Ignoring everything else my guardian said, I shook my head again and said, "I'll find her myself."

Out of the corner of my eye, I saw Revaed's eyes fly to my shoulder, where I could feel the warmth of blood. I must have torn my stitches again.

This time, I turned my glare toward Revaed. "Or am I prisoner in this palace?"

Revaed tensed visibly, pain etched into every line on his forehead. Shadows swirled in his violet eyes, full of enough grief to almost make me feel remorseful. *Almost.* "A prisoner? Caes, I just want to make sure you're safe…"

"You know I'm capable of defending myself."

He sighed, nodding and blinking his eyes as if in shame. "You're right. Do what you must. I just…you gave me a scare when you didn't return. I trust you and your abilities, but I would never forgive myself if something happened to you."

Scowling, I turned away again, unable to look him in the face. It was too confusing, trying to match this aching sense of betrayal with the look of fatherly love and concern in my guardian's eyes. I needed to get away from Revaed. I'd have to confront him sooner or later, but tonight… Tonight I knew exactly where I needed to go.

The street that the Gilded Fang sat on was more like a dank, cramped alley than an actual road, lined on either side by buildings with

crumbling stonework and dirt-streaked windows. Squatting near the docks leading into the Alrenian Sea, the space stank of human waste and rotting fish, the only open businesses appearing to be gambling houses, brothels, and squalid pubs. Laughter and shouts from fistfights streamed out of the open windows as I followed the limited torchlight toward the very last building on my right.

A creaking, weatherworn sign over the door reassured me the building with grimy windows was indeed the Gilded Fang. When I attempted to glance inside, all I could see was flickering firelight and vague shadows flitting back and forth. Raucous laughter and off-tune music blasted toward me, drunken voices lifted to sing along in harsh Alrenian notes.

My stomach tightened at the sound, the memories of the Alrenian uprising and my lost soldiers far too fresh in my mind. Repressing a grimace, I shoved open the door with my elbow to avoid touching the grungy handle. Just the sight of it conjured an image of Revaed cringing in disgust, a thought that made my chest ache. I forced the picture away and stepped within the dim interior of the pub, inhaling a cloud of tobacco and the mingling scents of stew and alcohol.

As I wound my way around the tables, I found all manner of men and women peering at me with narrowed eyes: Alrenians in expensive attire and others that looked more ragged; people who clung to the shadows in dark clothes to blend in; Forwyn in both simple and fine outfits; and even some people whose skin proved they were a mix between the two races, likely condemned and hated by both sides. Behind the bar, a woman with pale skin and long, gleaming black hair leaned against the counter, chatting with some of her patrons. Her features appeared Toryn, though I'd never met someone from that kingdom. Rumor had it that while their land had been cut off from the rest of the world by the Mirothian-made barrier, monstrous creatures had ravaged their countryside and laid waste to most of their cities. She wore a naked dagger at her waist in a brazen display for an inhabitant of an empire that had long ago made possession of weapons illegal for its citizens. My respect for her grew—in a corner of Inalgoth such as this, she would have to know how to handle herself. Around her neck hung a long, gleaming fang. I wasn't sure what animal it had once belonged to, and I wasn't sure I wanted to ask.

As soon as I stepped near, the barkeep's dark eyes flitted toward me, assessing. "I welcome all kinds as long as they pay," she said, her gravelly voice carrying over the drunken laughter from a table to my right, "but I'm not so sure about a Teramese man right now." Her fingers strayed toward her dagger hilt. "What's your business? Your emperor's mandated curfew isn't for another couple hours."

With a carefree smirk, I shoved toward the counter and placed a single drae before her. "I'm not here to cause trouble. All I want is a drink."

Shifting, the woman sighed before taking the gold coin, inspecting it, and then slipping it into her pocket. "Fine. But any funny business and you're gone. I'll take any sort of criminal before I cater to a Teramese who wants to kill my other patrons." Murder gleamed in her eyes. I didn't blame her.

Nearby, the Forwyn man she'd been talking to snorted as he lifted his mug. "Cheers to that."

"I can vouch for him." Meli's smooth voice came from behind me.

The barkeep nodded slowly, then turned back to me, all business as she took my order. While the barkeep poured an ale, Meli paused beside me. "I have a table back there," she said, nodding to one in a cramped, dark corner over her shoulder.

I couldn't help myself. "No A'elli?"

Meli's brow pinched. "Not tonight, it seems, but Valentra is here."

Nothing in her answer betrayed knowledge that A'elli had tried to murder me. Maybe the vigilante had disobeyed Meli's wishes and gone against her plans. But I'd have to be sure.

Taking my drink from the barkeep, I followed Meli through the crowd, weaving around tables where men and women tossed cards, grumbled about bets, or sang along drunkenly to the tune a scrawny musician strummed. When I tried to peer out the windows, I found the glass to be so dirty that the sea appeared as nothing but a dark smudge. But this close, I could feel its power thrumming through me, warm and eager, a constant comfort even when it wasn't in sight.

I knew without a doubt that the sea had protected Lo, but I wondered where she was. Had Sephrode transported her to shore? Was Lo holed up in a dingy place such as this pub, hiding from bloodthirsty Alrenians and Teramese alike?

I wished she would run away and never look back, that she'd fight to survive and leave her people to do the same on their own. I ached with the need for her to be safe. And yet…she wouldn't be the fierce, stubborn woman I'd fallen for if she turned her back on her people.

As certainly as I knew she was alive, I also knew she'd keep fighting. She'd remain in Inalgoth until she saw every one of the Forwyn safe and free.

As I sank into a rickety chair across from Meli, my eyes met Valentra's, which appeared gold in the dim light. Something in her steady gaze reassured me. She trusted Meli.

"A'elli tried to kill me," I blurted out, setting my mug on the tabletop. I called on one of the droplets of condensation gathering on the outside of my mug, making it float and glisten in shades of yellow and orange as it reflected the firelight dancing in the hearth. It was a small demonstration of my power, something that wouldn't catch anyone else's attention but would remind Meli who she was dealing with.

Both Meli and Valentra straightened, though I kept my eyes trained on Meli. Her gaze widened. "I sent her to spy on the dungeons, to see if we could break the prisoners out through one of our tunnels. I'd worried perhaps the Teramse I saw coming to search some of the passages had caught her. She was supposed to report back tonight, here."

"She won't be," I said darkly.

Sucking in a breath, Meli's gaze went unfocused, likely drawing on her gift. "She was…full of grief. Pain. She was reckless." She shook her head, at a loss for words.

I took a fortifying gulp of my ale. Its quality left much to be desired, but it gave my hands something to do as I considered my next move. With every moment that passed, the hole in my chest expanded, until I feared eventually there would be nothing of me left except darkness and emptiness.

"I believe you," I said after a long moment, once again glancing to Valentra. "If my lieutenant does."

"I do," she said firmly. "I believe we can trust them, sir."

I nodded and turned back to Meli. "Did the Teramese find your rebels in those tunnels you mentioned they were searching?" Another detail Revaed hadn't disclosed to me. Uneasiness crawled along my skin as I wondered how many other secrets he'd kept over the years. Did I even know him at all?

Meli shook her head. "I had a vision warning me, so we retreated to other passages they don't know of yet. But it's only a matter of time before we'll be found." She pressed her lips together. "That's just one more reason that we need to act quickly. One more reason your knowledge could help us. My visions don't show me everything."

"Well, I'm here, as you asked," I said, spreading my arms wide. "What do you want to know?"

Meli tapped the edge of her own glass, tautening her mouth. "You're ready to know the truth?" Nothing in her expression suggested she was gloating. If anything, there was a hint of sorrow reflecting at me in her dark eyes.

Shifting in my seat, I glanced away. My eyes strayed once again toward the windows and the murky view of the sea they presented to me. It was steadying, comforting. The only thing in my life that felt sure and true right now. "Yes," I said at last. "I'm ready for it. Whatever it is."

Lifting her glass, she downed the last of her drink before nodding to mine. "Finish up. We have somewhere to be."

I blinked up at her. "No vision?"

Meli's eyes watched me sadly. "This is one truth that is better seen in person. And even then, I suspect it will be difficult for you to accept."

A few minutes later, Meli tossed some extra coins on the counter in a generous farewell to the barkeep as she and I stood and made for the back exit. Valentra hadn't repressed her shudder when she told us she would wait for us at the pub. The Toryn woman gave a grateful nod to Meli as we ducked out, slipping out into the cool air and slinking through the shadows.

When we exited the cramped, seedy streets on this side of the capital, the breeze turned fresher, filled with the scents of coconut, flowers, and the sea. The city grew quieter, the laughter and chatter and fights of the more raucous crowds melting into the night.

When I recognized the finer shops and businesses surrounding Akytha District's square, a sense of foreboding took hold.

"What do I need to see here?" I asked, avoiding the piercing silver gaze of a guard on patrol, likely a man wondering why his prince was keeping company with a woman such as Meli. The man had no business staring at me with such open disrespect, even if I was questioning my role as heir to Revaed's empire. He didn't know my thoughts.

"The truth of what your people are doing in Alrenor," Meli murmured.

Unease rippled through me as I followed Meli toward the square, the same one where Revaed and I had been coronated, where I'd had to stop angry citizens from attacking us and Lo.

The stench of death and blood washed over me first, making my skin prickle. We paused in the square entrance, and I froze, staring over Meli's shoulder at the nightmarish scene.

"What are you doing?" a Teramese guard snapped, her voice gruff and her green eyes blazing and sharp. Her footsteps clipped rapidly along the cobblestones as she approached, assessing Meli and me suspiciously.

As soon as her stare flicked to me, she blanched and straightened. "Forgive me, Prince Caesiem," she said with a hasty salute. "I didn't recognize you."

With an impatient wave, I dismissed her silently. She returned to her post, standing guard with other Teramese along the walls. Watching and waiting—for what?

There were no living citizens in this space. They were guarding the dead.

Dozens of Alrenian and Forwyn corpses hung from pikes in rows, like a unit of dead soldiers. Nausea swept through me as we stepped nearer, the smell of death and the sound of buzzing flies becoming overwhelming. As much as I wanted to, I couldn't look away.

I'd seen death in all sorts of awful forms before—victims of the plague who'd died alone in the homes my orphan friends and I had scavenged, victims of the High Imperator, and even victims of my own magic. I'd slain in brutal ways to ensure my own and my people's survival. I'd fought bloody battles and summoned a hungry, tentacled beast from the water to consume my enemies.

But this…these were innocent men and women, young and old. Faces of citizens who hadn't deserved to die.

Bile clung to my tongue when I realized these guards were waiting for family members or friends to try to steal the bodies and give them proper burnings or burials. Anything to give their loved ones honor in death, to take away from the horror of this awful spectacle. But the Alrenians and Forwyn wouldn't be permitted that comfort. Our guards would make sure of that.

I forced myself to step forward, forced myself to look at each and every corpse rather than turn away.

"Your emperor ordered his soldiers to send a message to the city—to *all* citizens—in retaliation for the Alrenian uprising and the Forwyn trying to resist his so-called alliance." Meli turned to me, sorrow making her voice waver. "Do you see why I've sought you out, Teramese prince? Do you see why we fight to free ourselves from your rule?"

I stared at my trembling hands, mind whirling.

Survival above all else. I could almost hear Revaed saying it right now, the way he must have repeated it to himself as he'd ordered these deaths. He'd likely been frantic, wondering where I was, wondering if I was dead. He'd fought back in the only way he knew how—the brutal way his father had taught him.

When I blinked, I could see his worried eyes. I could feel his warm embrace. I recalled the safety I'd always experienced in his presence, along with my burning desire to make him proud. I'd served him proudly, passionately. Without question.

"You may be right," Meli whispered, not unkindly. She laid a gentle hand on my shoulder, jerking my gaze back to her. "He might really love you like a son. But is his love worth *this*? Can you justify and support him in this?"

My throat tightened as I studied the blank faces lined up before me, the empty eyes of two peoples Meli fought and bled for. Of a people Lo loved with all her heart, to the point she'd given up everything and risked her own soul.

The void in my chest broke open, a final crack that felt like the end of everything I'd known. I was an orphan boy again, lost on the streets of Vicidor, knowing there was no one truly on his side, no one he could trust implicitly in a dangerous, cruel world. No home where he could feel secure and safe and loved. Nowhere that he belonged.

Meli waited patiently at my side, but I couldn't tear my gaze from the corpses. I had to face the truth.

This was what I'd wanted: to know without a doubt.

Even if this scene didn't answer my questions about whether Revaed really cared about me, of whether he saw me merely as a tool or executioner, it provided another, more important answer.

It told me where I belonged.

"When the world is cruel to you," I whispered, thinking of words I'd once often repeated to myself, "you're either cruel back or you lie down and die."

My eyes flicked to Meli, and something like understanding flitted across her face. Maybe her truth gift was giving her insight into my past, into what those words meant to me. Or maybe she was simply astute enough to see the new meaning they carried for me now.

I couldn't let this revelation break me. I had to fight for something bigger than my own survival, or even just Teramese survival. It would have been easy to give up, to admit defeat and let the cruel world win.

But I'd never let that happen—not before, on the streets in Teramyl, and certainly not now, when it seemed my entire life had been a lie.

I set my jaw. Meli nodded, reaching out her hand, and I clasped it firmly in mine.

"We'll fight back," I vowed.

CHAPTER THIRTY-NINE

Jalie

Hope unfurled in my chest as soon as the walls of Inalgoth rose on the horizon. Beside me, Ryke seemed to understand what the sight meant—or perhaps he sensed my excitement in the way I picked up my pace. Either way, he chuffed out a plume of smoke and leaned toward me, nudging my shoulder.

"Almost there," I murmured gently. "I promise you'll be all right."

"If you're to go before our emperor, you'll have to go bound," Vander announced from behind me.

I whirled, studying his face in the growing darkness. Shadows clung to him, or perhaps they were remnants from whatever seemed to swirl around me. I'd started to notice the gathering darkness recently, making me wonder if others could see it as well.

Vander's silver eyes pierced into me, as if he could assess my soul and sense Nesrelle's influence. Maybe he could tell that even now, the mark on my cheek was burning, urging me to cast off these Teramese irritants and kill them. My fingers trembled at my sides, everything within me eager to reach out and test my curse on Vander and Tayla.

A gust of wind knocked me back. I slammed into Ryke's side, blinking in surprise.

"That wasn't necessary," I growled.

Vander stalked closer, Tayla clutching her sword hilt and bringing up the rear. "I think it was," he replied darkly, sneering in disgust. "You wanted me alive so you could use my magic to bring your dragon to the capital faster. But now that we're here, you're *my* prisoner. I'm not letting you entertain any delusions about who is in control."

My laughter echoed harshly in my ears. "You think you can overpower me? You, a mere mortal without Nesrelle's powers?"

I straightened, calling upon the power singing through my blood. My mind extended invisible, taloned fingers, raking through his brain, sifting his thoughts to find his deepest fears and prey on them.

Tayla drew her blade, the shriek of steel on steel puncturing my thoughts and throwing off my concentration. Vander lifted his arms, launching another gust of wind so powerful it pinned me against Ryke's side, unable to move. It whipped my hair in painful lashes across my face and stung my eyes, making them water until my vision blurred. I growled, trying to fight against it, but Tayla was swift, sheathing her sword and holding up a short coil of rope. She leapt toward me fearlessly, binding my wrists tightly together so that I couldn't retaliate.

Ryke stirred and growled, but he was too weak. He released a pathetic-sounding moan, a heartbreaking noise that reminded me of his helplessness. He was furious for me, but he couldn't save me. Not now.

As soon as Tayla stepped back, Vander released his magic. I drew a deep gulp of air, catching my breath and trying to still the shaking in my limbs.

"It doesn't matter. I wanted you to take me to your emperor," I said, forcing myself to shrug as if I didn't care. Part of me wanted to lash out angrily, to feed them their fears until they were curled on the ground in agony. But that would be a waste of time when I needed them to gain entrance into Inalgoth and the palace.

Behind me, Ryke sighed, his weight against me cooler than it should have been. His body trembled, and yet still, he was trying to turn toward me, his silver eye attentive. It was as if he were asking if I was all right.

"Whatever you do with me, help Ryke," I went on, watching the way Tayla and Vander both gazed at the dragon. They frowned, their bright eyes reflecting a sadness that gave me a sliver of hope. "Don't leave him to suffer and die. He needs the antidote to the nethilys Daedra administered, before he grows weaker." I swallowed, forcing the humiliating word to scrape up my throat: "Please."

Vander nodded, stiffly. "Of course. We aren't monsters, and I have no desire to let such a majestic creature die. We'll save him."

My eyes burned with unshed tears. There was no reason to thank Vander; he was my enemy, and if his people hadn't ever invaded my land to claim it and my dragons for themselves, so many of my problems wouldn't even exist. And yet, at the softness in his expression as he surveyed Ryke, I felt a lightness in my chest, some of the pressure of my fear dissipating.

"We need to hurry," I urged.

Tayla tossed a glance toward Vander before turning to me, her smile tight. "Of course," she said. "The emperor has been waiting for you."

Our arrival at the gate did not go as smoothly as Vander and Tayla had expected. "Halt!" one of the guards on the rampart screamed, glaring down the length of an arrow at us. His wide gold eyes flicked between Ryke and me, and warm pride flooded me with the realization that he deemed me as dangerous as the dragon at my side.

When his gaze lingered on the dark scales growing down my arm, that satisfaction chilled a bit, tainted with uncertainty and fear. I wondered if the shadows that had started to appear for me earlier were visible to him too—dark fingers clawing at my body possessively, like Nesrelle wanted to make it as clear as possible just whose power I bore.

Tayla and Vander paused obediently, lifting their arms to show that their hands were empty. Ryke, however, was clearly on edge. At my side, he tilted his head and peered up with one eye, snorting and pawing at the ground with as much energy as he could muster. Growling low in his throat, smoke trailed from his nostrils as he concentrated on the soldier speaking to us.

"What is your business, soldiers?" the guard demanded, forcing bravado despite the slight tremble in his voice.

A smirk flitted across Vander's lips as he cocked his head, letting a lock of his dark hair fall across his brow. "I should think that was obvious, given the prisoner we've brought for the emperor."

The guard narrowed his eyes. "She may be bound, but what of the dragon? Who is controlling *it*?"

To Vander's clear annoyance, I lifted my chin and cut in. "Ryke is controlled by no one, but he *is* loyal to me. Keep pointing that arrow at me, and maybe you'll see just—"

Muttering a curse, Tayla smacked a hand across my mouth, startling me into silence. I snarled at her, tasting blood from a split lip, but the woman turned back to the guard, ignoring me. "The dragon was poisoned and is very weak. He poses no threat to you, but if we want to ensure he lives another day, as I'm sure would please the emperor, we need to bring him into the city for the antidote before it's too late. And the Alrenian empress would like to meet with Emperor Revaed," she added with amusement.

Slowly, the guard lowered his bow, ordering the men and women surrounding him—all with their own bows at the ready—to stand down.

"Mage Arros. Officer Zyrel. Forgive me for not recognizing you immediately." The guard offered a quick, respectful salute. "To be honest, I thought this was some strange Alrenian trick when I saw the dragon and the former empress bound only with rope." His eyes flicked back to me, lingering distrustfully.

I forced myself to resist the grin twitching at my mouth.

"No trick," Vander growled, "but why don't you help your fellow soldiers out, open the gate, and secure Jaliana before she *does* escape? And send a messenger to notify the emperor of our arrival." He tossed me a warning glance, but I only responded with a demure smile.

I didn't want to escape, not when everything within me wanted to be brought before their emperor.

My entire body hummed with nerves as two guards dragged me along a less-traveled path climbing in a gradual incline toward the palace. When I'd tried to insist that I needed to see the antidote administered to Ryke, or at least bid him goodbye, they'd sneered and yanked me away. Fraught with emotion, my attempts to call on Nesrelle's power and paralyze them with fear failed—and I wasn't strong enough to break the rope binding my wrists.

"Please," I'd begged Tayla, trying to take advantage of the pain simmering in her eyes.

She'd stiffened and turned her back to me, running a cautious hand along Ryke's scales. His head drooped, as if too weak even to lift it high. His eyes were growing glazed; his whole stance was defeated. Only the low rumble in his throat communicated his distress over being parted from me.

"I'll ensure he's cared for, but we're not going to let you remain near a dragon you can command to kill us."

My throat burned, but it seemed pointless to protest that Ryke was too weak to do that. Only a few minutes ago I'd tried to threaten one of the guards with him. Why would they believe me now, even if I assured them neither of us would be a danger to them?

They knew as soon as we both could, we would fight back.

So a pair of guards had dragged me away, tugging me until even Ryke's huge form was only a distant green blot on the street. The palace buildings loomed near, their white columns shimmering silver in the starlight. Familiar scents enveloped me: floral and citrus and coconut, all mixed with the tang of the balmy seaside air. With the arrival of autumn, there was a chill to the breeze coming off the water, enough to make my skin prickle, even when I was wearing my dragon scale armor. It wasn't biting and icy like the cold air near the mountains, but it was cooler than I was accustomed to.

The scent of smoke from both the Dragon Keep and the torches burning throughout the grounds tickled my nose next. As we neared the palace, I increased my pace, eager to go before the emperor. If I couldn't be with Ryke, I had to trust I could do what needed to be done to reclaim both the throne and all the rest of my dragons. Then I could keep him and the others safe.

Sensing that I would no longer put up a struggle, the guards eased their grips, letting me walk freely into the gardens so familiar to me. I was home, garbed in my rightful armor, full of power that buzzed through me even now. Nesrelle's voice called to me, making my cheek burn with her mark and my body tremble with the anticipation of unleashing her strength on my enemies.

"Could you walk a little faster?" the male guard grumbled, but the woman huffed a laugh.

"What are you so impatient about?" she asked him. "Eager to end your shift and go find Celise?"

I ignored their banter, instead focusing on my surroundings, on the mingling emotions I felt with returning home. Mostly, I was overjoyed and eager. Unlike before, I was not powerless.

At last, even with my hands bound, I was a true empress. In this moment, I didn't feel as if I'd make my mother ashamed, or my ancestors turn away or shun me. I was fully prepared to unleash my vengeance and reclaim my birthright.

Kill them all, Teramese and Forwyn. Make them pay. Kill any Alrenians that try to usurp you. Show them what true strength is, what it is meant to be chosen, for you have chosen this path.

I basked in the strength radiating from her words.

You're not alone, Nesrelle promised. *I'm with you.*

And indeed, I could feel her presence nearby, a shadow trailing my every step. A whisper of breath that added to the chill of the breeze, but in a way that filled me with anticipation rather than fear. I would never be lonely or weak again. I'd never be a pawn, or a victim, or a lost and scared little girl.

I'd stare the false emperor in the eyes as I drained the life from him. Then I'd find Elder Ettonou and make him suffer, just like he'd once made me. And last of all, I'd hunt down Lo'laeni Nolanhou, the girl who had stolen everything from me, from my mother to my throne and my very way of life. It didn't matter that Lo had also spared me. She would know my wrath, my pain. Every moment I'd cried myself to sleep in darkness, every bit of agony and fear I'd suffered from Elder Ettonou's fits of rage. She would taste it too.

Jalie.

Pausing just outside the main building of the palace, the one that led to my mother's throne room—*my* throne room—I lifted my head, straining my ears. Behind me, one of the guards sighed and crossed her arms. "You said you wanted to see the emperor. Are you going to go in, or are you going to be difficult again?"

Jalie! It sounded like Kovi's voice, as strong as if he were calling to me from some corner of the garden. But when I glanced over my shoulder to scan the grounds, I only saw flickering torchlight and dancing shadows, swaying palm fronds and a glistening fountain. The sound of a lizard darting up a stone column startled me, and the female guard sighed again and seized my arm.

"Let's go," she muttered.

As two guards posted at the doors swung them open for us, the man on my left grabbed me roughly. Together, my escorts shoved me through the entrance and into the great hall. Skidding across the marble floor, which glimmered orange in the torchlight, I approached the carved doors leading to the throne room with some trepidation. Kovi's voice, whether imagined or somehow—impossibly—real, had thrown me into doubt. My ears buzzed, almost blocking out the sound of Nesrelle's words urging me forward, toward destruction.

When I glanced at the polished floor again, I thought I caught a glimpse of my reflection, but it was all wrong. I didn't see my gold hair and skin—instead, I found myself staring at fiery locks and a milky white face. And that wasn't my mouth; it was a blood-red smirk that filled me with unease.

You're not alone, Nesrelle reminded me, causing my mark to flash with pain. But I wasn't sure that reminder was comforting, not anymore.

If Kovi could see me now…would he hate who I was becoming?

All doubts melted into the back of my mind as the doors opened and I stepped into the all-too-familiar throne room. My eyes fell upon the seat my mother used to rest upon, its decorated sides gleaming in shades of ivory and gold. Before it, resting in a circle among the huge columns decorating the vast room, were the seats the Court of Elders had once occupied regularly, all undisturbed, as if the false emperor didn't care to make the space showy.

In fact, he wasn't even on the throne, but standing against the far wall beside the huge hearth. Beneath the moonlight filtering in from the glass ceiling high above, his dark hair and violet eyes looked especially unearthly. Clad all in black, his fine jacket reflected the style of the ones his soldiers wore, but with beautiful threads of gold and red embroidered throughout, catching every flash of the glowing firelight. Only a few torches were lit, casting huge shadows upon the walls. Most of the light came from the night sky and the fireplace, which drew me forward with its inviting warmth.

The guards fell away, melting into the shadows along the walls rather than guiding me toward their emperor. I wanted to laugh at this man's carelessness, but another part of me felt scorned. He thought so little of my power, of the threat I carried against him, that he dared to keep only two guards present while we met? He had the audacity to stand with his back to me? And he hadn't even deigned to sit in *my* throne, the throne he'd so greedily stolen?

Though my boots echoed with every step I took, Revaed didn't bother to turn and face me. When I was only a few feet away, I paused, my eyes straying toward the firelight. It was tempting to draw on my power and hurl the emperor's worst fears at him right then and there, but something about him piqued my curiosity.

I narrowed my eyes and waited, listening to the crackle of flame and the distant chirr of crickets outside.

"My messenger seemed to be under the impression you came as a willing prisoner," Revaed said at last, glancing at me casually over his shoulder. His expression was calm, but his eyes were piercing. "If I'd known you would have come all on your own, I wouldn't have wasted the effort of sending one of my finest mages to retrieve you."

"I wanted to see the man who seized my throne." I glanced around the room, taking in the dust motes swirling in the silver light cascading through the glass ceiling. "But it appears you have little interest in it.

You send your people to murder mine, you steal my palace, and you don't even bother to appreciate my throne by occupying it?" I quirked an eyebrow, my voice tremulous with my annoyance.

Revaed's smile was joyless. "Maybe I don't crave power the way you do."

I tilted my head. "Not power. Control. Control of my own life. My own circumstances. Enough control to not be a pawn, or a victim. Control of my own future and dreams. Doesn't everyone at least want that?"

"Then maybe we do understand each other." He dipped his chin. "I came to Alrenor for that, and to secure the future of my own people. I guess we are alike after all." His eyes roved over the scales on my right arm, not bothering to conceal his disgust. "At least, in some respects."

For a long moment, we were still, considering one another.

In my mind, I'd built him up to be impressive and terrifying. I'd imagined the man who'd taken my empire would be formidable, would perhaps hold the same awful power over me that Elder Ettonou once had.

But in the end, Revaed was only a man, and, appearing to be somewhere in his thirties, he was younger than I expected. His violet eyes were unusual and beautiful, not openly taunting or vicious. His presence didn't carry the same fearsome aura my mother's had.

I couldn't decide if I was relieved or disappointed.

When I killed him, would all his soldiers prove to be as just as simple to kill? Would my throne really be that easy to reclaim, after all this time?

Revaed shrugged elegantly. Carelessly. "I want you to know that taking your empire and ordering you to be executed…well, none of it was personal. You're just a girl, after all. I don't enjoy killing people. It's just a matter of survival and doing what needs to be done."

I laughed. "Well, I want you to know that *this* is personal."

With Nesrelle's power, I extended my thoughts, seeking out his fears. It wasn't like mind-reading, more like being given fleeting impressions of a person. As I concentrated on Revaed, the bitter taste of defeat and disappointment clung to my mouth, along with a sharper, more acrid terror. Flickering images of people floated through my head. A young man with startlingly blue eyes, calling the sea to him. Destitute-looking Teramese with ash-smeared faces. Crumbling buildings and consuming flames. A whip and a stern, cutting voice.

I flung the terrors back at him, causing Revaed to freeze, his eyes widening. His body trembled visibly, and his bronze complexion paled. Closing his eyes, he squeezed a hand into a fist and grimaced, as if trying to fight off the onslaught. I pressed harder, making him see everything. Making him live it all. I ensured he could smell death, could feel blood staining his fingers. His people, ruined. The young man, dead. And in all of it, he had failed.

Defective…

Revaed's eyes flew open, rage swirling within them. Something inside me quaked at the sight, and my power flew from my grasp. Grinding my teeth in frustration, I took a step forward, but Revaed was faster, towering over me in an instant.

"Unfortunately," he said in a deadly smooth voice, "your power is a little ineffective here." His smile was as sharp as a blade, but it wasn't gloating. It was bitter, resigned. "Whatever abomination that was…well, I've already faced my worst fears and survived. You haven't shown me anything new. I've withstood those terrors all my life, and I can withstand them again."

Suddenly, I was small again. Insignificant. Weak. I wanted to scream, but I was frozen, my mouth refusing to work. Nesrelle's mark was blinding pain, and her voice was shrieking at me to fight, to lash out at this man.

"That's the trouble with someone who has very little left to lose," Revaed went on. "You can't threaten them. I thought you of all people might understand that, but, you still seem…afraid."

Trembling, I flung myself toward the fire, dodging Revaed and plunging my arms into the flames. They lashed eagerly at the rope binding my wrists, filling the room with black smoke that curled like a welcome embrace around me. There was no pain, only warmth and power and strength.

Drawing their swords, the guards shouted and lunged forward, but I was faster. The burning rope broke easily, its shredded pieces tumbling into the fire as I spun toward Revaed. All it would take was one touch, and my curse would kill him.

I wouldn't be afraid. I wouldn't be weak.

But Revaed was already prepared for me, swinging a dagger in one clean, downward arc.

Pain bit into my fingers and shot up my arm before I could register what had happened, pain so sharp and piercing I couldn't hold back my cry. White light flashed across my vision as I staggered back, my heart slamming wildly against my ribcage.

Cradling my left hand, I blinked dully at the sight of it. Blood streamed from three of my fingers, dotting the pristine marble floor with a pool of crimson. He'd severed sections from my index, middle, and ring fingers, nearly to the second knuckle of each.

Bile clung to my tongue when I caught sight of *my* fingertips at Revaed's feet. His cut had been precise, the perfect way to stop me from attacking with my curse. Somewhere past the adrenaline and dull horror rising within me, my brain realized that he could have easily taken my entire hand. That this could have been worse…

But my mind wouldn't grasp that.

Revaed stared at me, his mouth in a grim line. Blood gleamed on the edge of his blade. My blood.

He'd outmaneuvered me.

As he lifted his hand in a silent signal, the charging guards heeded his gesture and halted, their swords still held at the ready. "I learned long ago that even monsters can bleed," Revaed said calmly. "I grew up with one, after all. Became one myself, in some ways.

"Sadly, I haven't yet had the strength to kill my own father. But you—I won't make the mistake of holding back with you." He narrowed his eyes. "It seems you aren't just a girl after all. At least, not anymore." Again, he sneered at the scales on my arm, at the rune scarring my cheek.

With another flick of Revaed's hand, the guards sheathed their weapons. Another pair emerged from the shadows, one of them carrying a heavy set of shackles. My stomach churned at the sight.

"Take her to a healer," Revaed ordered smoothly, "and then put her in the dungeons. Might as well clean her up before her execution tomorrow." His eyes darted to mine. "We may be monsters, but we're not uncivilized ones."

My mind whirled. I'd failed. I had Nesrelle's power coursing through me, I'd been right in front of this imposter emperor—and I hadn't killed him. Instead, I'd miscalculated. Badly.

CHAPTER FORTY

Kovi

Finding a way into the palace garden wasn't particularly difficult for Rhi'il and me, for one thing the Teramese had overlooked was the fact that so many of us Forwyn had once been slaves on these grounds. Or, in my case, I'd been a guard whose business had been to know the ins and outs of the palace, including its weakest points. I was familiar with the back entrance that servants and guards used, a narrow, half-hidden path that led us up toward a quieter part of the grounds.

As soon as we neared the top of the path, our plan to pause and determine how to sneak past any patrolling guards was derailed by the sound of voices drifting toward us.

"Could you walk a little faster?" It was a man's voice, speaking in the merchant tongue, but with a heavy Teramese accent.

Exchanging a glance, Rhi'il and I ducked into some shrubbery along the side of the path and crept forward, pushing as close to the low gate that led into the gardens as we could get. There were no posted guards in sight, but when I leaned forward, I could peer over the gate and make out a pair winding their way down a path. Between them was a prisoner, someone dressed in flashing green dragon scale armor, with arms bound in front.

My heart lurched in recognition. "Jalie," I murmured, even though I knew she couldn't hear me. How did the Teramese have her? Where was her army? Where was Ryke? The questions swarmed me like angry bees, filling me with icy dread.

Rhi'il cast me a sideways glance. "What?" he whispered.

Without truly considering what I was doing, my fingers strayed toward my sword hilt. Everything within me strained with the need to charge forward. "They have Jalie."

Rhi'il pressed a gentle yet firm hand on my arm. It was only then I realized I'd started to step forward without even noticing. "Wait," he said. A wrinkle formed between his brows as he searched my eyes. "Running into a fight without a plan isn't like you."

I swallowed back a laugh. "And hesitating isn't like *you*."

Rhi'il tsked softly, shaking his head. "Elha'tonu, even when I'm in a hurry, I always have a plan. It might be madness, but it's always a plan."

This time, I indulged in a true smile. "You're right." I wiped a hand across my forehead, feeling a layer of sweat already forming despite the coolness of the night. "I'm not thinking clearly."

Rhi'il nodded absentmindedly, his eyes straying back toward the place where the guards and Jalie had been only moments ago. They'd rounded a bend in the path, disappearing behind a cluster of palm trees.

Jalie, I thought frantically, wishing she could hear me. Wishing she could know that I was there, that I would find a way to save her. "They're going to execute her."

Again, Rhi'il set his hand on my arm. "They won't do it *now*. They'll want to make a public statement with her death. We have time."

But I was already moving, slipping through the undergrowth

toward the gate. Two guards had paced toward it since we'd first arrived, their attention only half on surveying their surroundings. They were muttering to each other, gossiping about Jalie's appearance.

I was prepared to command them with my magic when a commotion sounded from several yards to my left, close to the wall. The guards immediately stiffened, hands on their sword hilts as they strode off in the direction of the disruption. Startled, I glanced around to find that Rhi'il had disappeared. My friend was creating a diversion, giving me the opportunity I needed.

Trusting he'd join me when he could, I climbed the wall and swung over the side, landing softly in the dirt. A bird flitted from a branch at my approach, but otherwise, I was quiet, my progress through the thick plantlife all but invisible. With a prayer to Elhani, I let his magic fill me and make me vanish, so that even if someone did notice the way I disturbed the occasional branch or plant, their eyes would convince them it was just a breeze.

I paused when I found the guards and Jalie again, halted in the huge main courtyard, just outside one of the palace buildings. *Jalie,* I thought again, willing her to hear me. Willing her to sense my presence.

The trio vanished within the building as my thoughts raced. Rhi'il and Elhani's magic had gotten me within the palace grounds, but I'd need a clear head for whatever came next. Invisible or not, I couldn't march up to the doors and throw them open without the posted guards retaliating. And though I was confident that I could overtake two guards even without my magic commanding them, I wasn't sure I could do so without them alerting countless other Teramese to my presence.

Leaning back on my heels, I considered the building before me again. A large structure, it housed the throne room, with dungeons below it. If I acted fast, could I force my way in and out—with Jalie in tow—before being incapacitated? If I could move swiftly enough, I might catch her before she was locked in a cell.

"Kovi." Rhi'il's voice jerked me from my thoughts, and I

instinctively glanced to my left, even though my friend was invisible.

"You came up on me silently," I whispered back. "Sound barrier?"

"Sound barrier and invisibility at the same time," Rhi'il boasted. "Did you ever think you'd see this day?"

"Never," I teasted. "You're getting better at your magic."

"But I can't keep this up much longer," he admitted.

I shifted on my feet. "Then you can stay out here while I go in. We can't be seen."

Rhi'il suppressed a groan. "Remember when I said I had your back? That was when I thought you always used that strategic mind of yours in situations like this. I know you care about her, but we're here to scout the palace so we can get our people out of the same prisons they're throwing Jalie into. Don't do something drastic now. We'll rescue her when we break them out."

I gritted my teeth. "I don't think they'll keep Jalie alive as long as they'll hold the Forwyn."

"We don't know when he plans to kill them," Rhi'il pointed out.

"Still. He won't wait with Jalie. Not again."

"What makes you say that?" Rhi'il hissed. This time, when I turned to him, I could see the dim outline of his form. He flickered, flashes of his body and then the garden behind him showing, reminding me of the way a candle sputtered in and out.

"Because she's the former *empress*. The Alrenians were just rioting, and the Teramese want a way to demoralize them as fast as possible. What better way than to execute the person who symbolizes the return of the Alrenian Empire? Besides, Jalie already escaped him once. He won't let it happen again. If I were Revaed, I'd do it tomorrow morning."

Rhi'il was fully visible now, his brow furrowed. "Brutal."

"We've already seen how brutal he is," I said darkly, thinking of the Teramese soldiers lining up citizens in the streets and slaughtering them one by one.

A pair of guards' approaching footsteps on the path stalled our whispered conversation. As the two men neared, snatches of conversation drifted toward us, and we each leaned forward, straining to hear their gossip. At first, their words were in Teramese, and then a third set of steps approached, and the voices switched to the merchant tongue.

Foreboding prickled along my skin as I considered *who* would be here among the Teramese but not know their language.

At first, I didn't catch the words, but the rumble of his voice was familiar enough. Father. I tasted bile, immediately feeling a wave of his emotions—triumph and bloodlust—as the surprise of encountering him shook my ability to block them out.

"Tomorrow?" one of the Teramese men asked. "We weren't informed of this."

"Likely because the emperor has been busy preparing—and now he's with the former empress," another guard said. "Didn't you hear?"

"Jaliana has been found?" my father's words were sharp. "I hope he plans to dispose of her too, first thing tomorrow morning to start off the ceremony." The dark hatred edging his words made my skin crawl.

"I'm sure the emperor will give us his order for tomorrow as soon as he's able," the second guard went on.

"Yes," Father agreed. "It will be a long, grueling day disposing of those vile traitors and that Alrenian monster, but it will usher in the peace we've longed for."

As their footsteps faded further into the garden, my ears rang, my mind full of the horrors Father had proclaimed.

If I'd understood correctly, Revaed intended to hold a ceremony tomorrow that would include not only executing Jalie, but also slaughtering all of the Forwyn prisoners.

Sweat gathered along the back of my neck despite the chill air, and I glanced up at the velvety night sky, suddenly all too aware of the passing moments. The time lost. We didn't have days to stop Revaed or plan a rescue. We only had a matter of *hours*.

"*Goehr's* flames," Revaed breathed, running an anxious hand through his short-cropped curls. He turned to me, eyes wide with fear he was usually much better at concealing. "What do we do?"

A cry of pain pierced the air, loud enough to emanate from the building before us and cause the posted guards to stiffen.

Jalie.

I flew into action, too panicked even to wait for Rhi'il to call upon magic again and stumble after me. Charging over the path, I paused only to scoop up a rock before I leapt up the steps leading to the palace building two at a time. Silent. Fast. The guards narrowed their eyes, perhaps sensing me more than hearing me, but I was already behind the nearest guard. One hit from the rock was all it took to knock the man unconscious.

As soon as he fell, sprawled out before the doors, I glanced up, expecting the other guard to cry out and alarm others. To draw his sword and attempt to attack, even when his foe was invisible. But he was already lying on the ground, a fresh bump on the side of his head.

"Quick," Rhi'il grunted. The guard's arms lifted into the air, as if tugged on by puppet strings, as an invisible Rhi'il dragged the man toward the bushes beside the steps.

Together, my friend and I moved both guards into the shrubbery to conceal them. We probably only had a minute, if not seconds, before a patrolling guard strolled by and noticed that the doors were unmanned. There was a chance whoever noticed the guards' absence might suspect a shift change before he or she thought to search for intruders, but that would only buy us a little time.

Turning back to the entryway, I pushed gently on one of the carved doors. It creaked inward to reveal a dim hallway leading to the next set of double doors marking the entrance to the throne room. Two more guards stood outside those doors, one frowning when she noticed the cracked door.

"Zol?" she asked. "Is everything all right?"

Rhi'il muttered a curse behind me, but I was already flying down the hall.

"Tuiros's blade," the other guard swore, his gold eyes flashing in the shadows. His sword hissed as he drew it. "This may be some Forwyn devilry."

Following his example, his companion scanned the hall rapidly, stepping forward to call out again. "Zol? Are you there?"

I sensed Rhi'il at my back as I moved, dodging the woman and her blade and slamming a solid punch to her temple. She crashed to the floor, her sword ringing as it struck the marble.

The scuffle at my back told me Rhi'il was having a harder time. I whirled to find my friend completely visible as he grappled against the second guard. He'd managed to knock the sword from the man's grip, but now he was struggling, trading vicious blows with his opponent.

I swallowed the distance between the guard and me in two long strides. Another heartbeat, and I had him in a headlock, tugging him off my friend. I waited until the man's kicking and struggling subsided before I released him, letting him drop to the floor beside his companion.

Rhi'il glanced up, almost meeting my eyes as he searched for my form. "Thank you," he muttered, wiping sweat off his brow.

I was already turning, preparing to race toward a side hall that led toward the dungeons.

The creaking of the throne room doors made me whirl, finding myself face to face with a pair of sharp violet eyes.

"It looks like we have an intruder problem," the man announced calmly to the guards flanking him.

Revaed Xalenos, clutching a blade dripping with blood. My heart lurched at the sight, but as the man shoved the doors open further, I didn't see any sign of Jalie within the vast, shadowy space. There were dim corners she could have been confined to, or numerous columns she could have been concealed behind, but something told me she was no longer in the room.

If she wasn't in the dungeons now, then she was already dead.

Guards from the side hall raced out, joining the two pushing past Revaed and encircling Rhi'il and me. As a chill snaked down my back, I realized I no longer felt the warmth of magic flowing through me. I was too distracted, my focus gone in my frantic fear for Jalie. A quick glance toward my hands showed me that I was as visible now as my friend was.

"Take them to the dungeons," Revaed ordered.

They separated Rhi'il and me immediately, one pair of guards dragging him through a passage in the dank dungeons while I was shoved down another.

Regret slithered like a writhing snake in my gut, sickening me with my failure. *Fool,* I thought, cursing my rashness. My desperation. I'd known better. I'd been trained and taught better. But Jalie's scream still echoed in my mind, ragged and raw and soul-piercing. It made me want to rend the world in two, to stop at nothing to find her.

"Let's shove this scum in with *her*," one of the guards said, his laughter grating and cruel. "See if she'll rid us of one of these Forwyn pests before the morning."

My thoughts were too fixated on my anger over my mistake and my concern for Rhi'il and Jalie for the statement to register until they unlocked a cell door and pushed me into its dim interior. As the door swung shut with a clang, I blinked against the darkness, the only light coming from the flickering torch in the passage outside. It streamed through the bars set within the door, illuminating a form seated against the far wall, shoulders hunched.

When I stumbled forward, the figure moved, lifting its head. Torchlight glinted off pale blonde hair and fierce, gold-flecked blue eyes. My heart swelled with the first bit of hope I'd had in far too long.

"Jalie." I charged forward, dropping to my knees to meet her gaze. I scanned her face rapidly, taking in more details about her as I adjusted to the dimness. Weariness painted dark circles beneath her eyes, and a red, angry scar marred her left cheek. "Are you all right?"

A weight settled in my chest when I glanced at the scar again. It wasn't just any scar—it looked like the jagged nestred rune I'd seen marking her in my dream. Unlike my dream, I didn't notice any dark scales tracing her neck, but perhaps there were some hidden under the collar of her tunic, or on her arm, which I couldn't see clearly in the shadows. What had happened to her? What had Nesrelle done?

Jalie was trembling, her expression wary as she studied me. When she shifted, chains from the shackles around her wrists clanked together. "Kovi?" She shook her head. "This is a trick. This isn't real—I'm dreaming."

"Not this time." Extending my hands, I reached out to grasp her fingers, noticing then that her left hand was heavily bandaged. Instead, I clasped her right hand, cradling it gently. I couldn't tell if the blackness around her upper arm was from the shadows in the cell, or the ones I'd noticed gathering around her ever since she'd made her deal with Nesrelle. "What happened?" I asked.

As soon as I touched her, Jalie's eyes widened, her fingers curling around mine. "You're real. You're here. I had so many dreams…heard your voice so many times…I wondered if I was going mad." Her eyes glistened with tears.

"You heard me? I heard you too, but I thought maybe it was just wishful thinking."

Jalie's eyes widened. "Is it the connection? Because of your magic?"

I shook my head. "I've never heard of anything like it and I don't understand it, but I'm thankful you're here now."

Sitting up, Jalie threw her arms around my neck, cold chains biting into my skin as she pulled me to her. Her heart thundered against my chest, but the sound was hopeful, another reassurance that we were no longer apart. That she was *alive*.

I ran my fingers through her tangled hair, breathing in the scent of her, relishing the feel of her in my arms again. She pulled back, only enough to press her lips to mine, her kiss warm and reassuring, but full of desperation.

Desire and something else—that burning, overcoming emotion I refused to name—took over. I slipped my hands around her waist and tugged her into my lap, taking my time kissing her lips before trailing my mouth along her jaw and down her neck. She shivered in my arms.

But my gaze dropped again to her bandaged hand, and my joy plunged back into icy worry. Tenderly, I pressed a kiss to her forehead, and then to the scar standing out starkly against the golden skin on her cheek.

When Jalie opened her eyes to meet my gaze, something regretful lingered in them.

"What did Nesrelle do to you?" I murmured, carefully brushing a strand of hair away from the rune.

She blinked, her gaze darkening, and she pulled herself off me. She stood, her body rigid as she backed up against the wall. It was then I caught my first clear glimpse of her right arm and the dark scales covering it from shoulder to elbow. Foreboding traced a finger down my spine.

"Tell me," I continued, rising and reaching out a hand.

Noticing my eyes on her arm, she flinched away. "You'll hate me."

Pain lanced through my chest, but I stepped forward stubbornly and grasped her chin, lifting her face to mine. "I promised you that I would always fight for you. I meant it then, and I mean it now."

Jalie's eyes widened, fresh tears making them glitter like sapphires, but she blinked them away forcefully.

With a deep breath, she explained everything that had happened since we'd said goodbye. How her attack on Aramith had gone horrifyingly awry, and how Daedra had betrayed her, leaving Nesrelle to rescue her…but at a terrible cost.

My rage was a controlled fire, one that I would let simmer for now until I could unleash it. But it was difficult to still the tremor in my hand as I brushed my thumb delicately over Jalie's scarred cheek, and it was impossible to keep the dark edge from my words as I made her a new vow. "I'll make them both pay for what they've done."

"No," Jalie snapped, pulling back.

I blinked in surprise when something unfamiliar flashed in Jalie's eyes. For a moment, I was sure they were as dark and empty as Nesrelle's were at her most terrifying. For a moment, I could have sworn I was speaking to that fiery haired Immortal, and not the woman I cared about.

"Let—let me take care of Daedra and the army," Jalie went on, but she didn't quite meet my eyes.

Tension thickened the air, and I suspected Jalie could sense my fear, the way I was unnerved by her. My mind recalled how Nesrelle had granted her the power to sense and wield her enemies' greatest fears against them, and my chest ached.

"Jalie, look at me."

She gritted her teeth, sinking back still further and glowering into the shadows.

I won't be afraid of her. This is Jalie. Not Nesrelle. Jalie.

"Don't pull away from me," I whispered.

She jerked her head up, chin tilted confidently as she discarded her uncertainty. A smile twitched the corner of her perfect mouth as she met my stare. The vulnerability and shame had vanished from her face, leaving something confident and almost playful. "Oh. You think you make the orders around here, Kovi?" she teased. "That *you're* in control?"

In a few quick motions, she was behind me, her shackled arms around my neck as she hugged me against her, laughing. Relief flooded me at the musical sound, dispelling my fear and doubt. When I glanced over my shoulder at her smirking face, my grin matched hers. "I don't *think* so. I know I am," I quipped.

Lifting her hands over my head, I spun around and pressed closer, until I'd backed her against the wall. Placing my palms on either side of her, I hemmed her in, letting my breath stir her hair and tickle her cheek. Her laughter vanished, and she inhaled sharply, lips parting.

I dipped closer to devour the last inch between us. She tasted like salt and ash, like remnants of war and pain still coated her, but there was an undercurrent of something sweet and heady. The unmistakable taste and feel of her. Warm, intoxicating.

Though there was an urgency to my kiss, a painful need after our time apart when I'd feared I'd lost her forever, I didn't rush. I took my time, reaching up to cup her face as I brushed my lips against hers gently, almost tauntingly. She groaned and pulled me closer, forcing me to kiss her more deeply, until she went limp in my arms.

Laughter escaped me as I pulled back from the wall, cradling her against my body, prepared to tease her further about how I'd kissed her until she'd gone weak. "See? I..." But when I glanced down, her eyelids were fluttering, and her gaze was slightly glassy and unfocused.

"They treated your injury," I said, comprehension dawning in my mind. "Did they give you painkillers?" The medicine must have begun to set in, making her drowsy. My eyes again darted to her bandaged hand. "Who *did* that to you?" I asked.

"Revaed," she said, and though her head rested sleepily against my chest, her voice was low and fierce with anger. My grasp on her tightened. "He had healers tend to me, because he wants me to be in prime condition for the execution tomorrow morning." Bitterness laced her smile. "I made a mistake." Her words wavered a little. "I thought I could save Ryke and kill Revaed easily with my curse and my new powers. But I was wrong."

"We'll fix this," I told her, my mind already running through the possibilities as I lifted her into my arms.

Jalie giggled, a clear sign the medicine was taking hold. This wasn't like her, but I couldn't help but smile in return. Her shackled arms remained wrapped around my neck as she rested her head against my shoulder, her silky hair tickling my skin. She was shockingly light in my arms, and invitingly warm.

Turning, I shuffled toward the cot in the corner. "You need to rest."

"My beautiful enemy," she whispered, pressing a kiss against my throat.

I froze, my pulse throbbing in my neck, my skin tingling where her lips had been. I couldn't help the discomfort that washed over me at the word. *Enemy.* Why had she chosen to use that one? The water nymph's warnings coursed through me, and I quickly shoved them aside. "Not enemy," I reminded her.

"I was supposed to poison you," Jalie went on, another giggle escaping her. "But I failed."

Her thoughts are just cloudy from the medicine, I reassured myself.

Gently, I lifted her arms so her shackled hands were in front of her again and deposited her onto the cot. "Sleep," I murmured, running a hand through her hair.

She blinked at me, another carefree smile on her face as she reached up, chains clinking. She traced my lips with a finger, until I caught her hand and pressed a kiss to her palm. "My kiss was poison," she said. "But maybe yours was too. Do you think we were always doomed?"

I swallowed. "We're not doomed."

Her gaze softened. "Kovi, I…" Shaking her head, she sighed, leaning back against the cot, forcing me to drop her hand. She curled up on her side. "You're too beautiful to poison."

I laughed outright, stretching out beside her and tucking her against me protectively, as if just by this simple gesture I could ward off her impending execution. My stomach churned when I saw the gaping hole in her armor, near her hip. In the dimness, her gold skin glistened, marked by a scar that should have looked fresher than it did.

I ran my fingers along the mark, where her smooth skin turned rough. My chest tightened with sorrow.

"I'm sorry I wasn't there to help you," I whispered. And I was. I was sorry I hadn't been at Jalie's side during the attacks from Daedra, Nesrelle, and Revaed. I was sorry that even before I'd known Jalie, I hadn't been there to stop Father from harming her. I feared how many other scars were concealed by her armor, and how many more she carried unseen in her grief and loss and fear. "I…I don't know what I would have done if you'd died."

I paused, both ready and not ready to say more. The confession was there, hovering in the air. I drew in a breath, preparing to whisper it into the darkness, to finally name that growing emotion and connection between us.

"I already died once," Jalie murmured, interrupting my thoughts. "When I die again, will you still want me?"

Frown lines pinched my brow. "You *won't* die tomorrow. People have tried to use you, shoot you, poison you, stab you, and imprison you. You've overcome that, every time. Besides," I added, "you have incredible power, and I have magic that can control our enemies. Did you forget how unstoppable we are together?"

Though her back was to me, I could almost feel the hope radiating off Jalie. Maybe a bit of our connection still lingered. It was as if she was at last accepting the fact that I wouldn't abandon her. That I truly meant I would fight not only for myself and my people, but also for her.

"Together," she whispered, laying her head down. Her voice drifted off, her breathing swiftly evening out as she slipped into sleep.

Wrapping my arm around her waist, I cradled her against me.

"Jalie," I murmured, resting my forehead against her hair, breathing in her lingering cinnamon and vanilla scent. "Of course I still want you."

CHAPTER FORTY-ONE

Revaed

As soon as the pair of Forwyn soldiers were dragged away to the dungeons, I turned to the guards who'd remained behind. "Scour the palace and the grounds. Ensure no other Forwyn have snuck in with their unnatural magic."

Saluting, the pair hurried off, leaving me to scowl at the bloody dagger still clutched in my fist. I slammed the door shut and whirled back toward the throne room, the vast space full of shadows and hollow echoes. Chilly, even with the burning fire. Dim. Pretentious. Everything about this place brought to mind eerie memories from the Teramese palace, even if the marble floor, gleaming columns, and hues of ivory and gold were a far cry from the mosaic tiles, terracotta, and vibrant hues one saw in Teramyl.

It must have been the air of arrogance and violence still permeating the atmosphere here, as if the ghosts of the innocents Karye had murdered lingered in this room. As if years of haughty declarations and proud attitudes had tainted the very walls, filling everything with reflections of oppressive regimes.

It was the way my father loved to rule, as if he thought himself worthy of the same fear and reverence the gods were due. The same control over who deserved to live or die, and when their deaths should occur.

You ordered the deaths of citizens too, a dark voice reminded me.

But I shook my head, biting back a cringe as I wiped my bloodied blade on my pants and sheathed it.

I ordered dangerous citizens to be executed to prevent more needless deaths. To protect my people above all else. It was for survival. A necessary choice, to kill a few for the good of the many.

Father never cared about the few or the many.

My eyes strayed toward the gore left behind from my strike against Jalie, and I sneered in disgust, calling for the servants. "Get this mess cleaned up," I said, and without lingering another moment in this accursed place, I stormed out a side door and through a hall adorned in years of Alrenian history gaudily painted upon the walls. Stern statues of past rulers glared at me.

All items Jaliana was likely infinitely proud of, and had once looked upon as hers. Perhaps, if she'd had it her way, she would have erected a statue to her murderous mother and added it to this collection. I repressed a shudder. They were all revolting. From all my years of study, I couldn't recall a single Alrenian emperor or empress in recent history that hadn't been a tyrant, someone who made choices that reminded me far too much of those of my father.

Defective. The word always seemed to chase me, challenging me to be better, stronger, cleverer. I'd raise up an empire with power that father would envy, and safety Caesiem could thrive in.

And I'd ensure it looked nothing like the old Alrenor…*or* Teramyl.

As soon as possible, I'd put men and women to work destroying these relics to the abominable Alrenian heritage. We would burn their books, paint over their art, and tear down their statues.

I'd take great pleasure in bringing this mighty, arrogant empire to its knees.

But first, I would meet with Vander Arros. And then, I had a prisoner to see.

Kovi Ettonou, son of Elder Ettonou and former guard to Empress Jaliana, was the perfect image of soldierly discipline. When I'd beckoned to the armchair before the fire in my personal sitting room, just across from mine, he'd silently ignored me, choosing to stand. He didn't show a hint of curiosity or anger as I dismissed the guards and leaned forward, studying him.

"I'll confess that if I'd known my guards were going to throw you into a cell with the former empress, I would have stopped them. But no matter; even your power can't control this entire palace." I leaned back. "I take it you care for that monster Jaliana?"

"Not everyone who is powerful is a monster," Kovi murmured, "and not everyone who is powerless is innocent."

In the firelight, the gold flecks in his eyes glittered, and I wondered if there was Alrenian blood somewhere in his ancestry. Most likely, more Forwyn than would like to admit to it had mixed with Alrenians over the past two hundred years, whether willingly or not.

I couldn't stop the smile that curled my lips. "You think I'm powerless?" Brushing a bit of lint off my shoulder, I thought of Father, of some of the earliest lessons he'd taught me. "Not all power is rooted in magic or skill on the battlefield. Some involves politics. It's about who holds the most leverage." I tossed the soldier a pointed look. "For instance, I know you won't command me with your magic right now, because I have a whole host of guards outside of this room, prepared to slay you if you threaten me. Even if you ordered me to kill myself, you'd be dead before you ever managed to free your precious empress."

A flicker of irritation—there and gone just as fast—passed across Kovi's face. It wasn't often I was grateful for the High Imperator and his lessons, but in that moment, I was glad he'd hired me the best tutors to learn how to read people. As a ruler, it was crucial to know what was important to others, what they were thinking. What they were willing to do anything for.

"Yes, Vander Arros told me about your magic, and your connection to Jaliana." I smirked. "My guards will have their ears plugged when they fetch you for the execution tomorrow, so don't hold onto any foolish hopes for a last-minute escape. I don't think your magic will do you much good if your would-be victims can't hear your commands." I paused, tilting my head to the side. "But, there is hope. Neither you nor your monster *have* to die. I've heard you are a fine soldier, so I didn't bother with trying to break you through torture. You're better than that. You seem like a logical man, though. If you tell me where the Aerekni Academy soldiers are hiding, I'll spare you both."

At last, there was a crack in Kovi's armor as he smiled, mirthlessly. "If you think I'm so logical, then surely you know I won't be bought with false promises. You'd never let the Alrenian empress live."

"She's troublesome, yes," I admitted, "but there are ways to feign death. I'd let you both go free. To live a new life, under new names, in northern Alrenor. Or across the Great Sea, if you wish."

His muscles tensed; his fingers twitched.

"Imagine it: peace and freedom, away from the horrors of war. Every day, in the arms of your beloved, or whatever it is you romantics enjoy." I sneered at the idea, but I needed Kovi to picture that life. Needed him to cling to it. Needed him to want it more than he wanted anything else. "You could live a long, happy life together."

Kovi's eyes flashed. "Do you think I'm that disloyal to my people?"

"I think you're that loyal to *her*." I leaned forward, resting my elbows on my knees. "Your father told me that you warmed her bed while you were her guard. But Vander seemed to think you felt more than just physical desire." I quirked an eyebrow.

"My father is a liar," Kovi said smoothly. "His words aren't to be trusted."

My patience was wearing thin. "So you are choosing death for her?"

Kovi flinched.

"Tell me where the soldiers are, or she dies." I tapped my fingers on my knee, waiting. "I'll order them to kill her first, so you can watch."

A muscle worked in Kovi's jaw, but he stood motionless, staring me down with undisguised hatred and disgust. He didn't speak. Didn't even open his mouth.

"Death, then?"

Kovi curled one hand into a fist, yet still he didn't answer.

I sighed. "All right. I was afraid you'd make me take the bloody path." Just thinking of all the death and gore that tomorrow would bring made me cringe inwardly. "Death it is."

Calling for my guards, I waited as they plugged their ears and seized Kovi, leading him back to the dungeons. I sank back into my chair and stared into the fire.

I was so, so tired of having to kill.

CHAPTER FORTY-TWO

Caesiem

I told Meli everything. Revaed's plans to hold the ceremony in the main palace courtyard, where all the Forwyn prisoners and their guards could be gathered in one place as witnesses to the wedding. When he'd explained his plan to me, he'd lamented that some of the prisoners might need to be put to death if they opposed Lo's speech calling for unity, but now, I suspected he already planned to kill them all.

Why risk mercy for a few when his mantra was always survival for our people? Of course he would put the execution of countless captives over mercy. And I would have agreed with him once, would have believed him when he told me how sad and burdensome it was to make the hard choices of a leader, but that this was needed to keep our people safe. To keep Lo safe.

I couldn't fall for that now, not when every time I blinked, I could still see rows of empty corpse eyes staring back at me.

Tucked into a private room at the Gilded Fang, Valentra drank coffee and Meli nursed a cup of tea while I sketched a rough map for her on the paper the barkeep had brought to us. "This is where he plans to have the stage for the speech and wedding ceremony to take place. And here is where he'll position the prisoners and their guards." I paused a beat, then added darkly, "Their executioners."

Meli nodded somberly. "I'm sure you're right."

Glancing up at her, I managed a half-hearted smile. "You're sure you can't tell the future?"

"If only," she sighed, shaking her head. "But people change their minds and take different paths all the time. A hundred little moments could shift the outcome of any given situation. I'm not sure knowing the future would even help us here."

Frowning, I stared out the window, watching the smeared, dark outline of the sea. "I know how we could get a glimpse of the future." My chest tightened at the prospect, and I shook my head. "But you're right." I drummed my pencil against the table. "With Lo gone, Revaed may postpone the wedding, and knowing all of this information could be useless. I don't think he'll execute the prisoners until he can find Lo and force her to give that speech. And you said you know of a secret passage into the dungeons?"

Meli nodded.

"We could get them out that way. No wedding needed."

A knock on the door silenced me, causing me to freeze. "Come in," Meli said calmly, shooting me a glance as the barkeep pushed open the door and entered the room. "Laelyth can be trusted."

"She's on our side," Valentra affirmed, her eyes gold in the dim lighting.

Still, I shot the Toryn woman—Laelyth—a skeptical glance.

"It's true," she drawled, her fingers toying with the fang hanging from her neck. "I've seen enough abuse of power in my lifetime to hold no love for your new Teramese emperor and what he's doing." Her dark eyes were sharp as she assessed me. "And I don't fear a monster in human skin any more than I feared the ones that look like monsters and plagued my homeland."

My eyes lingered on her fang, again recalling stories that had drifted as far as Teramyl, telling of creatures that had laid waste to Toryn during its years of isolation due to the Misrothian barrier. A woman who had survived that must be quite formidable indeed.

"As long as you are as determined as Meli and her allies to stop the evils your emperor is committing and fight for *true* Alrenian freedom," Laelyth added, "you are a friend here."

"I am," I said firmly.

"In that case," she said, stepping closer and turning to Meli, "I have news. For all of you." She cast me another look. "There are announcements circulating on the street and papers being hung everywhere. Directed to a Lo'laeni Nolanhou."

My blood ran cold. "What do they say?" I breathed, imagining just how desperate and angry Revaed would be, thinking Lo was plotting to murder me. Perhaps his earlier scheme for a wedding and alliance had been completely abandoned. Maybe I'd already been gone longer than I'd realized, and Revaed thought I was missing again, caught in Forwyn clutches, and this was his latest retaliation.

In answer, Laelyth reached into her pocket and withdrew a folded paper, tossing it onto the table.

Meli nodded for me to take it, so I unfolded it, my pulse thudding dully in my ears as I spread it out over the table for all to see.

Lo'laeni Nolanhou, amara'rekni:
If you do not return to the palace by the seventh hour on tomorrow morning to uphold your end of our agreement, the Forwyn-Teramese alliance will be considered

void, your people will be declared enemies, and executions of the dangerous Forwyn rebels in our custody will begin immediately.
Prove your dedication to your people and the cause of peace and unity, or face the consequences of your violent choices.

Emperor Revaed

"It seems the wedding is on anyway," Meli said flatly. Her eyes had a distant look to them as she stared out the window, and I knew it wasn't the sea she was studying. "He's desperate. Angry. I see…" She shook her head, voice trailing off. "It's not clear. I see images of him ordering guards about to prepare for executions tomorrow."

My hands shook as I plucked them off the table.

"Return to the palace," Meli instructed. "We will carry out our plan to get the Forwyn out during the ceremonies."

"I'll stay with the rebels and help them," Valentra added. "Let Revaed continue to think I'm dead."

"Revaed will ensure his security is tightest during the wedding," I protested. My mind whirled as I tried to imagine saying vows to Lo under such circumstances. In my most unattainable dreams, I'd wished for a future in which someday we could have married…not because we were forced to. But now, I knew I wasn't worthy of Lo. I never had been. The fact that she could even look me in the eyes and not hate me was a miracle—a miracle I didn't deserve. And the only wedding we would ever have would be this farce of a ceremony. A lie to save her people. It sickened me.

"We can sneak our people in," Meli said, leaning forward. "Trust us. This is the plan we were already working on, and it's clear our time is up. We don't have any other options."

I ran a frustrated hand through my hair.

"Will Lo'laeni show?" Laelyth asked, her brow pinched.

"She'll show," I said confidently. "She would never risk her people's lives by hiding. But she won't be fooled by this anymore than I am. Revaed will kill the Forwyn anyway. Maybe not all of them, but he'll definitely kill some, as soon as the marriage ceremony is complete and he can claim an official union between our peoples. He'll slay as a message." I swallowed bitterly.

"And we can count on you, no matter what happens with Revaed, to be on our side during the rescue?" Meli demanded. "I know you're worried for Lo now, but tomorrow, when Revaed is at risk, will you put our people in danger by trying to save him too?"

My eyes burned as I turned once more toward the sea, the one place that felt calming, the one constant balm for my troubled, restless soul. "Lo will be in danger too, if Revaed thinks she's a threat to me. Once we're married and the union is official, she won't need to live anymore. I know he wouldn't want to hurt me, but he'll put my survival over my emotions, every time. And when it's between her and Revaed, I'll choose Lo," I vowed. "*Every* time."

The words felt like poison, like an irreversible moment that I would feel the consequences for, in their fullest, later. But, as much as they hurt, as much as my torn heart bled, I knew they were true. I wouldn't let Revaed touch Lo. I wouldn't let him terrorize her or her people like this, not anymore.

Laelyth cast Meli a doubtful look, but Meli's gaze was steady as she nodded. Her eyes shone, as if she sensed the price I paid with my words and actions tonight. Maybe her gift had granted her more visions of my past, of my bond with Revaed.

"Go back to Revaed and prepare for the wedding. Don't let him suspect anything. And be ready."

CHAPTER FORTY-THREE

Lo

The nymph brought me to a quiet bay, its waters glistening peacefully in the moonlight. Surrounded by high cliffs, it was concealed from peering eyes within the capital. The perfect place for the ship docked there to go undetected. I recognized the location immediately: Haven's Bay.

"There are other Forwyn in these waters," the nymph had explained as she'd grasped my arm in her clammy one, pulling me through the sea. She kept us above the surface, her powerful tail thrusting us swiftly through the calming waves. "Allies."

"Allies on a ship? How can you be sure? Who are they?" I'd demanded.

"I'm sure because I can see many things from the sea," the nymph said slyly, tossing a quick glance over her shoulder, which shimmered with scales and water droplets. "They came from Aerekni Academy."

My heart leapt with hope. There'd been survivors from the academy. Maybe Father was among them.

Movement and shouts from the ship deck signaled those aboard had spotted the nymph and me in the water.

"Can you go on from here alone?" the nymph demanded, releasing my arm and turning to face me.

Here in the calm sea of the harbor, it was easy to tread water. "Yes," I said firmly, trying to avoid looking directly into the nymph's unnatural yellow eyes.

Her gaze darted toward the pendant around my neck, then back to my face. "Good." Her lip curled into a sneer. "Don't try drowning again. I don't particularly want to be forced to help a non-magical human again, all because you wear *his* pendant."

"So anyone could be protected by the sea, if they wore the pendant?" My forehead creased in confusion as I tried to process all the nymph had told me. "I thought Caesiem said the pendants were only useful for mages—"

"They only work for a mage, or someone closely connected to a mage," the nymph cut in impatiently. She tossed her white hair over her shoulder, splashing me in the process. "Whoever the mage loves most in this world."

I blinked, but before I could fully comprehend what she'd said, she dove, her tail flashing in the starlight and then plunging back into darkness, disappearing toward the harbor's mouth.

In moments, I was closing in on the ship. A familiar figure leaned over the railing, calling out to me.

"Lo? Is that you? Hold on!"

A pair of men threw a rope ladder over the side, where it thudded against the hull of the ship only inches above my head. Stretching first one arm and then another, I grasped the lowest rung and yanked myself from the water, my heavy clothes clinging to my body. Cool night air whispered along my skin, making me shiver as rivulets cascaded down the rope, slickening it beneath my fingers and my bare feet.

But as soon as I was near, Father was reaching for me, his grasp warm and secure as he caught both my wrists and helped me on deck.

"Lo," he murmured, wrapping his arms around me in a strong embrace.

Tears burned my eyes, but the word *father* froze on my tongue. I wasn't sure how to respond. As grateful as I was to know he was alive and well, to be here in his arms, to have this chance to finally get to know him, I was also overwhelmed. This was foreign to me.

Even more than that, I was shocked that this man welcomed me at all, after I'd led the Teramese straight through the academy's gates.

"I'm so sorry," I choked out as I pulled back and dared to meet his warm gaze. "I was so afraid you were dead. If I hadn't agreed to bring Revaed to you, he would have killed more of my sisters. But—it was a massacre, and I wish I could have done more to stop—"

But Father was already speaking. "It wasn't your fault," he interrupted firmly. His eyes scanned my body, searching for injuries. "Are you hurt?"

I shook my head.

"Lo!" Pauni'a's voice cut through the night as she tore across the deck. I caught a glimpse of the grey robe she'd wrapped herself in and the curls escaping from her messy bun before she threw her arms around me. "You're safe. You're back. I knew you could take care of yourself, but still…" Her voice trailed off as she fought tears.

Stifling a sob, I squeezed her back, silently thanking Elhani for his goodness. "I'm so glad to see you, Nia." When I finally pulled away, we were both wiping our eyes. Pauni'a was soaked from my dripping clothes, but she didn't seem to notice.

My father slipped a towel around my shoulders, and I tugged it close, once again repressing a shiver. "Are our sisters safe?" I asked, both eager and terrified of the answer. "And…Mio'e?" I wasn't sure how I felt about the vigilante who had chosen to side with us—wasn't sure she wouldn't decide to turn on me and slit my throat in the middle of the night as soon as hostilities between the Teramese, Alrenians, and us were settled—but I still cared. She might have wished me dead, but I didn't wish the same on her.

Maybe that made me crazy.

Pauni'a nodded, but her gaze was sober. She met Father's over my shoulder, and I turned to face him. Despite the tightness in my throat, I forced the words out. "How many made it out alive?"

Father's face was grave. "Let's discuss all of that after you've gotten into some dry clothes." His eyes flitted to Pauni'a. "Both of you." His expression softened just enough that I noticed the ghost of a smile linger on his lips. "I'm sure you'll want your friend close."

Dread settled in my veins.

My mug of coffee felt like my anchor in a chilly, empty world. I huddled on a bench in the ship's galley, mercifully clothed in a dry shirt and leggings, while wrapped in a warm blanket. Each sip of coffee helped reinvigorate me after the long, endless night, sending comfort through my aching muscles. But nothing could take away the guilt and pain of each of my father's words as he explained everything that had happened at the academy.

"It's not your fault," he said gently, resting a calloused hand over mine.

I startled at the gesture. For a moment, hurt flitted across his eyes.

"I'm sorry," I said quickly, reaching out to pat his hand.

Words stuck in my throat as I grappled with what else to say. I wasn't sure *how* to be a daughter. As much as I wanted to get to know my father, as much a I'd longed for family, I wasn't sure how to accept this relationship.

"It's all right," Father said, and though his smile was tense, I thought I detected understanding in his eyes.

It made me realize that just maybe, he wasn't quite sure how to be a father, either.

At my side, Pauni'a shifted. "Tell us what happened to you," she said. On my other side, Mio'e was quiet. She'd welcomed me—not with the same warmth as Pauni'a and my father, of course—but she'd greeted me like a fellow soldier. Like an ally. I appreciated her for that.

I relayed everything about my time in the palace, along with Revaed's wedding plans set for tomorrow and A'elli's attack.

"Now that I'm gone, now that he thinks A'elli and I planned to murder Caesiem together, I'm sure the wedding plans have been changed," I finished. "We probably have more time." I frowned doubtfully. "Although…it's possible Revaed will just claim this as another example of me breaking the alliance. Maybe he'll give up on it and assassinate all of the prisoners early."

Father sighed, pushing his empty mug away. "I sent some scouts to the palace and into the capital to help us make plans for a rescue. My two who went to the palace haven't returned" –he paused, the tightening of his jaw the only giveaway of how worried he was– "but while you were changing, the ones from the city did." Reaching into his jacket pocket, he withdrew a wrinkled paper and unfolded it on the table between us.

The weight to our silence was heavy as Mio'e, Pauni'a, and I scanned it together.

"He's demanding you return in a matter of *hours* for a wedding, or he will murder the Forwyn?" Pauni'a exclaimed, her tone dark with her rage. "But you can't go back there and let him use you."

The world seemed to sway and tilt around me. Of course this was Revaed's next play. He was determined to use me in any way possible, to demoralize my people with my forced union to his heir, to take away the power I had as a symbol of freedom to them. If he let me go, he knew I would continue to fight. If he killed me too soon, I'd become a martyr. But force me to make a public move that looked like I was betraying my people…*this* would weaken the Forwyn in a whole new way. And perhaps he'd finally get the cooperative little allies who'd help him control the dragons, the people he'd always wanted.

I lifted my chin defiantly, already imagining a moment when I could face Revaed again and finally, finally, destroy all his brutal plans. "No, but I can go back and use *him*."

"I don't like this," Father said gruffly, running a hand over his stubbled jaw as he glared at Revaed's message. "You won't be safe returning to the palace, and I don't want you forced into some barbaric marriage with the Teramese. If they even let you live long past the wedding."

Pursing my lips, I met his concerned eyes. Maybe it was the light of the flickering candles in the space and the dim grey of early dawn spilling through the windows, but it struck me suddenly that they were the same rich shade of brown my brother Edi's had been.

"I know Revaed will try to kill me," I murmured. "And the prisoners too. I think it's been his plan all along." My fingers curled into fists. "But this is our chance—our only chance. I wasn't going to run and leave our people before, and now that I've been forced away, that's not going to change. I know we don't have a lot of time to plan, but I have to go. We have to save them."

Sighing, Father ran a hand across his face.

"She's right," Pauni'a said. "And she's fully capable of doing this." Reaching out, she squeezed my hand, grounding me with the sisterly action.

"She is," Mio'e added firmly, and I shot her a grateful smile.

Hesitantly, she returned it.

"I believe in you," Father responded, studying me with a weary gaze. "But what about showing up for a marriage ceremony to one of *them*?" He grimaced. "I hate to see you having to go through with it, even if I know we'll get you out of there right away."

Clutching Caesiem's pendant, I shook my head. "It's all right. Caesiem's different..." I trailed off. "I know it's all Revaed's game, but I'm not afraid to play it." The nymph's words burned through me: *whoever the mage loves most in this world.* In my explanation of what had happened to me in my absence, I hadn't gone into detail about Caesiem's and my relationship, but I could feel Father's curious gaze on the Teramese pendant now. "I think," I went on slowly, "that this is where Elhani wants me to be. Caesiem is on my side."

Mio'e scoffed. "Are you sure you aren't just falling for a pretty face?"

I shot her a look. "Trust me. If he wasn't on my side, I would be dead right now. I think being near him tomorrow will be the safest place I could possibly be." Nesrelle's words threatened to rise up in my mind and taunt me, to tell me any last-minute plans to save my people were doomed. I refused to listen. I clung to the pendant and stubbornly chose to believe.

Father looked skeptical, but he nodded. "I trust you, Lo."

Those words were a lifeline, warming my heart. In some ways, this man was practically a stranger, but in many others, he was so much more. And those were exactly the words I needed from him in this moment.

"We don't have a lot of time," Pauni'a muttered. Her amber eyes scanned my damp, tangled curls and my too-large clothes. "What do we need to do to prepare you?"

I grinned. "Showing up like this is the best way to drive Revaed mad. Don't worry about *preparing* me. Let's make a plan."

CHAPTER FORTY-FOUR

Caesiem

Moonlight painted the water a ghostly shade of white and tinged the wave caps an ethereal silver. Seated on one of the rickety docks just beyond the dingy street housing the Gilded Fang, I gulped down lungful after lungful of the fresh breeze stirring from across the sea. If I focused hard enough, I could have sworn I could pick out a different element in the air, a hint of something richer and wilder. Like I could taste the distant ocean on the wind.

Although my life in Teramyl hadn't been easy, not even within the palace, I consistently missed the ocean. It was always calling me back, the only constant in my life of chaotic revelations and disintegrating loyalties.

Sighing, I stood and slipped my hand into my pocket, withdrawing a drae. The first time I'd summoned a nymph, it'd been unintentional. I'd waded out into the shallows of the ocean, letting it strengthen my magic as I'd practiced, determined to better myself. To no longer be the subject of hatred and derision among the other mages. Back then, I'd only been at the palace for three years, and I'd still struggled to control my power.

The coin falling from my pocket had been an accident. When the nymph had rose from the waves, seizing the gold and blinking at me with piercing, opalescent eyes, I'd been repulsed. Looking back, I now knew the only reason I'd escaped the ocean with my life was because of my magical connection to water. It—and consequently the creatures living within it—always protected its own.

Now, I called Sephrode to me deliberately, tossing my coin into the water and bending every ounce of my will toward my magic. It coursed through me, a heady rush that made me feel like I was immersed in the sea even when I was standing on land. Below, the water responded, the waves that lapped against the dock rising a little higher, rolling forward a little faster.

Sephrode, the white-haired nymph who'd been my faithful messenger throughout my stay in Alrenor, rose to the surface, tipping her head up at me. Water glistened on the silver scales lining her face and droplets clung to her eyelashes. Her yellow eyes were as wide and eerie as ever, seeming to cast their own glow.

"I'd much rather you brought someone for me to play with instead of gold trinkets," Sephrode muttered, flipping the coin between her webbed fingers and watching it catch the light. "What is your request?"

My words caught in my throat. A moment ago, I'd been desperate for answers, hating the fact that I was trapped in heavy suspense. In those moments, it had seemed better to know what was waiting for me in the future, even if it was the worst. But now I wasn't sure I could face the knowing. The thought that I could be doomed to live my greatest fears, that I would be forced to stare them in the face both now and when they happened, was utterly paralyzing.

Muttering a curse, I shoved my hands into my pockets and rocked back on my heels, considering. *Coward. Idiotic. Just ask.*

Instead, I asked the less pressing question, the one I knew the answer to. "Is Lo all right?"

"The girl you threw into the sea?" Sephrode said. "You already know she is." She rolled her eyes. "Next time, couldn't you bring me someone to play with? The tentacled one has stolen most of those my sisters and I would claim."

A chill trickled down my back, but I repressed my instinct to shiver or grimace. "Where is she?" I demanded.

Again, it wasn't the question I really needed to ask. I already knew that wherever Lo was now, she would be back at the palace within a matter of hours. She would never ignore Revaed's message and leave her people to die.

"On a ship," Sephrode said, waving her hand carelessly. Her expression was bored, annoyed. "With friends."

My interest piqued. "A *ship?*"

"Full of Forwyn who escaped," the nymph said with a grin, her teeth like gleaming needles.

Hope blossomed in my chest. Lo was not only safe then, but also reunited with friends. Maybe even her father, if he'd survived…

Please let him have survived. The prayer fluttered through my mind without me knowing which god I was addressing. Truthfully, I believed the gods had abandoned me long ago. But maybe Lo's god hadn't abandoned her and her people after all. Maybe he wouldn't listen to me as a general rule, but if I was praying for Lo? Maybe he would make an exception.

Elhani. If you'll ever listen to me in my lifetime, I ask for just this one thing. Let Lo's father be alive.

One of us deserved to have a father figure.

"None of these questions are the reason you offered me this pretty piece," Sephrode murmured, cradling the coin in her palm.

My breathing was too shallow; my chest was too tight. Even the cool night air became oppressive, feeling too warm, too humid. Swallowing thickly, I forced out the words. "I need to know the future," I rasped.

The nymph blinked, her smile turning coy. "Well, tonight you will return to the palace."

I glowered. "Beyond tonight. Into tomorrow."

Sephrode cocked her head, her eyes predatory. When she licked her lips, flashing her too-sharp teeth, I imagined how gleefully she'd wrap her arms around me and pull me into the murkiest depths of the water, if ever the magical bond forcing her to leave me alone—even to protect me—somehow faded. "Vague questions receive vague answers, pretty one."

"Revaed," I ground out. "Does he—does he die?"

"Not tomorrow."

"Eventually," I muttered.

Her smile deepened. "All mortals die eventually."

The knot in my chest loosened. I didn't dare ask beyond tomorrow—didn't dare *think* beyond tomorrow—but at least I knew I wouldn't be giving his potential killers a helping hand in a few hours.

Despite all the atrocities he'd committed, Revaed still loved me. He was still my guardian. And I didn't want to watch him die.

"What *does* happen tomorrow?" I whispered, even though I knew the nymph's answer would sound more like a riddle than anything.

Sephrode splashed her tail. "A wedding. A battle. Someone important will fall. Someone important will rise." She paused. "And burning, burning. The empire will burn."

Uneasiness wrapped its cold fingers around me, but the nymph had already ducked below the water, leaving nothing but ripples in her wake.

CHAPTER FORTY-FIVE

Revaed

Nine Years Ago

Blinding rage. That was all I felt, so intense it was hard to hear or think beyond the intensity of the emotion overtaking me. Vaguely, I was aware of voices echoing through the training room, but they bounced off me. I couldn't tear my eyes off Caesiem's blackened eye and split lip as he limped through the doorway, his good eye glassy and distant.

Inhaling deeply, I forced myself to calm. It was an unnatural stillness that settled over me, one eerily familiar. The same sort of practiced cool I'd learned to encase myself within when Father degraded or threatened me. It was a mask I'd worn most of my life.

"What happened?" I demanded, my voice cutting the air like a knife.

Caesiem froze, his eye widening as if he thought I was angry with *him*.

He'd been at the palace for two months now, and one of those had been full of training personally with myself and some of my best officers. I'd offered him every kindness and showered him with gifts worthy of a hero—a finely crafted blade forged by our most talented blacksmith, outfits befitting royalty, and renowned tutors who had schooled me when I was a boy.

But maybe that was the problem. Others were noticing the favor and attention I gave Caesiem, and even though he was a hero of the capital, mages and other nobility alike were growing jealous. They saw him as a gangly orphan off the street, a nobody without noble blood or any control over his powerful magic. It irked them that a child who couldn't even read had ascended to a favored position so quickly.

Maybe it was because of Caesiem's vulnerability, of the way he didn't fit in, that made me care. I could see my younger self in him, and that filled me with a determination to protect him.

I saw, for the first time, my chance at having a family in a way I'd never dared to believe I could have one before. Perhaps Father would allow me to become Caesiem's guardian and claim him as my heir...

After a few moments' hesitation, Caesiem dipped his head respectfully and answered my question. "It was nothing, Prince Revaed. Just a...misunderstanding."

My fist curled at my side. "A misunderstanding? Who did this?"

Caesiem swallowed. "Some of the other mages." He bit back a grimace of shame. "They're stronger than me. Better with magic. Better at fighting."

Because they've been doing this for years. Because they aren't recovering from a lifetime of malnourishment and fighting for their lives. "What are their names?"

Perhaps all the meals I'd shared with Caesiem had earned more of his trust and brushed away some of his fear of me. He, like so many citizens, had learned to dread the Xalenos name because of my father's ruthlessness. But now, he met my eyes, and seemed to understand I wasn't accusing him of any weakness or fault in this matter.

Standing straighter, he rattled off a list of names, his voice firm.

Turning to Pados, I ordered, "Send for a healer for Caesiem. Afterward, if he's cleared for training, continue to work with him as usual." I glanced back at the boy, who'd stepped further into the training room, his stance already more confident. "I have business to tend to this morning."

Pados dipped his head as I strode from the room, pulse thrumming with purpose.

Steam from my plate of roasted duck, figs, and seasoned potatoes rose pleasantly in the air. Adding a scoop of buttered rice and vegetables, I set the dish in front of Caesiem and offered him a warm smile. His black eye was more swollen than before, and his shoulders were hunched with weariness.

If only he knew just how much I empathized with that exhausted feeling.

As always, he ate ravenously, not one to waste time on small talk. I had the distinct impression he wasn't quite sure what to make of me yet. He hadn't decided if he could fully trust me, if my kindness was truly borne of generosity.

"I always wished I had a little brother," I said thoughtfully as I pierced a potato with my fork.

Caesiem stilled, swallowing and setting down his utensils. This time, when he met my eyes, his face was full of shock…and hope. "Truly?"

Nodding, I added, "I've even thought having a son would be nice." I laughed. "You're too old to be my son, but…what would you think, if I were to become your guardian?"

Caesiem fidgeted with his fork. Even exhausted and hurt, he was restless, full of an endless energy I envied. "You want to be…*my* guardian?"

I smiled, hoping it was reassuring. "You're smart, brave, and kind. Not at all like my father. Not to mention, the High Imperator longs for me to produce an heir, and he is starting to worry I never will. This would appease him—but also drive him a little mad. It's the perfect solution for me. And…" I added, lowering my voice, "I've always seen a bit of myself in you. I'll admit, I've already hoped to at least be your friend. But I'd prefer if we were family."

This time, Caesiem couldn't stop his fingers from drumming on the table. "An heir," he repeated. "You're saying *I'd* be your heir?"

I nodded.

Caesiem sank back into his chair, considering. Studying me thoughtfully. "That would mean I'd someday be the High Imperator."

"Hopefully a day that is far off from now, considering it would require my death," I responded with a wry smile.

"Sorry," Caesiem blurted out, cringing. "I didn't mean…"

I waved his embarrassment away. "No, you're right to think about the future. Accepting this position would require responsibilities on your part, far greater than the ones we've placed upon you as a mage. You don't have to give me an answer just yet. Take your time considering."

Caesiem nodded, ducking his head to push at the food on his plate with his fork. But not soon enough to conceal the glistening tears swimming in his eyes.

I swallowed back a lump in my own throat. "By the way," I added gently, "those mages won't ever bother you again."

"Never?" Caesiem's voice wobbled a bit, and he still hadn't dared to lift his head again.

"They've been dismissed from the palace in shame. Never to serve our army again." I lifted my wineglass, taking a long gulp, as if the act could erase the images that flashed through my head on an endless cycle: pools of blood. Glassy, dead eyes watching me.

Father had been right about leaders needing to make difficult decisions. I just hadn't ever imagined that such a weighty choice would ever be made…not *easy* exactly, but simpler…all because I'd acted to protect someone I cared about. Someone I felt responsible for. Other than the citizenry, I'd never experienced such an urge to defend another before.

What Caesiem didn't know—and didn't need to know—was that the law was unshakeable. Mages were meant to serve the crown, or they would be put to death. When I'd demanded Father make an exception, he'd refused and told me I had only two options: let the mages continue to harm Caesiem, to corner him and threaten his life, or end them.

It was disgusting, but I didn't regret my decision. I was prepared to do anything to ensure Caesiem never faced the truest horrors of this world, never had to bear its deepest cruelties in the ways my father had made me. He would never be mistreated or abused again. He'd want for nothing. I'd make sure of it.

"Thank you," Caesiem breathed, finally meeting my eyes. Such relief washed over his features that, even with those bloody images haunting me, I couldn't help but smile.

No, I didn't regret my choice at all.

Present

Seated in an armchair in former Empress Karye's rooms, I stared into the hearth, where a crackling fire roared. It did little to warm the chilly air, which seemed to have less to do with the autumn night and more with the vast, austere quarters I was residing within. I'd claimed them to make a necessary impression, not because I liked them. They were too pretentious, too full of Alrenian arrogance with their war paintings and statues. Every room was twice the size of my rooms in Teramyl, and I'd already thought those had been excessive. No torchlight, firelight, or candlelight could quite reach far enough to brighten these rooms' shadowy corners or high ceilings.

Instead of feeling opulent, the rooms felt oppressive.

They brought memories of Father and his criticism to the forefront of my mind. The whip lashings. The public mockery. The searing anger.

Familiar footsteps broke into my thoughts as Caesiem slunk inside, pausing in the doorway to the sitting room I lounged within.

I didn't move at first, a heavy weight settling on my chest. Did he hate me? Or was he full of grief that I'd tried to shield him from, all because he'd lost his heart to a deceitful enemy? Did he understand why I'd made the choices I had? Would he ever?

"Did you find her?" I murmured, my gaze resolutely turned toward the fire.

"No."

I couldn't read his tone from that single word, but I could sense the weight he bore. It was in his earlier trudging footsteps, in the way, when I finally dared turn to look, I noticed he slumped against the doorframe. It was in the way he didn't quite meet my eyes.

"But she'll see your message," Caesiem went on. "She'll come."

"I'm sorry, Caes." My words were barely above a whisper, but he stiffened and glanced up at me, eyes searching. "I can't call off the wedding now. I can't...I can't risk more uprisings like the one the Alrenians just put us through. And I can't let any chance to control the dragons slip through my fingers. Our people are counting on me. On *us*."

A muscle jumped in his jaw.

"Rulers have to make hard decisions, to help their people survive."

Caesiem stared at the floor. "Do you think," he asked quietly, "those hard decisions have made us lead like your father did?"

The question made my blood freeze. "I don't take joy in executing criminals." *Unlike my father,* I didn't need to add. "I don't fight for power. I fight for survival."

Caesiem closed his eyes. "I know. But…do you think everyone we've killed…were they *all* criminals?"

I hesitated, staring into the fire. Images of dying citizens swirled in my head. Were they innocent? Perhaps. But had their deaths been an obstacle on the path toward Teramyl's welfare, a necessary sacrifice for the good of my people? Absolutely. "Maybe not all of them, but I'd consider anyone willing to stand in the way of peace, of the safety and livelihood of our people, to be a danger. There were plenty of rioters—and citizens who did nothing to help us in stopping them—who murdered our people." I sighed. "Executions are never easy. But they are part of the burden of being a leader. We must put the good of many over that of a few. Someday, when we have peace in Alrenor, between Forwyn and Teramese—it will all be worth it."

"Right." He was quiet for a long moment, before taking a step back. "I'm going to get some rest. Before the morning." His eyes flitted toward the windows at the far side of the room, at the black sky slowly melting to grey. His wedding was mere hours away, and I hated that I'd let the Elders convince me into the arrangement, that they'd insisted upon it as part of their cooperation in my new government. I hated that I believed them when they claimed the Forwyn who knew the dragons best would never assist us, never give up their secrets for taming the creatures, if there wasn't a wedding. But I feared it would break Caesiem, in the end.

As Caesiem turned to leave, I spoke again. "Don't let her break your heart, Caes. I know her betrayal must sting. The world has always been cruel to us. But you still have me. You'll always have me."

Caesiem glanced over his shoulder, his expression wistful. Most often our relationship felt brotherly, but in moments like this, when he appeared so young, he really did seem like the son I'd never had. The son I'd do anything to protect, to spare from the cruelties of the world, when he'd already endured so many.

"I know," he repeated, and then he was gone.

CHAPTER FORTY-SIX

Jalie

I woke with Kovi's arm wrapped securely around my waist, holding me close. Curled against him, his heart beating steadily beneath my ear, I couldn't recall the last time I'd had such a full, restful night of sleep.

For a moment, I let myself forget where we were. In the dark stillness of our cell, I could imagine other surroundings. We could have been in my bed, enveloped in luxury. I let myself pretend this was another morning in the palace, with pastries and coffee and tea awaiting us. With the promise of listening to Kovi's laughter, of spending the day with him. I imagined a world in which a future with him was not only possible but easy, one where I could fall asleep in his arms every night. Warm. Safe. Wanted.

Squeezing my eyes shut, I drew a deep breath, relishing the beat of his pulse, reminding me this wasn't a dream. He was here. He had come to help me. He'd proven that his words were true. He really would fight for me. He cared…

My heart warmed, the walls I'd carefully fashioned around it cracking just a little more at these thoughts. Once, I would have refused to believe this man could ever be anything but my enemy. Once, I would have cringed at the mere idea of his embrace. Now, it seemed natural to…*feel* something when I looked at him. To trust him and dream with him. I marveled at how much had changed in so short a time, all because Kovi and I had opened ourselves up to finding all the things that bound us together, rather than the ones that drove us apart.

A twinge of grief pierced my chest. Even if we survived what was to come, could this fragile thing between us last?

Chains jingling, I lifted my arms, brushing my fingers along the stubble dotting Kovi's jaw, relishing this moment in which I could see him a little disheveled, a little vulnerable. In sleep, his stern mask had melted away, leaving behind a peaceful expression that made him look almost carefree.

As I stirred, Kovi opened his eyes, a grin flitting across his face. The flickering torchlight from the hall fell just right to illuminate the golden flecks in his gaze. "Good morning," he murmured, his voice husky.

My jaw tightened as he sat up, pulling me with him. My fanciful dreams fell away as I took in the cell we were in. "This is the morning I'm to be executed," I said bitterly. My wrists were chafed from my shackles, and beneath my bandages, my mutilated fingers ached with renewed pain.

"And I told you," he said, pressing a kiss to my forehead, "that won't happen. We have more than enough magic and skill between us to stop that from happening." He explained to me the threats Revaed had made to him last night, while I'd been in my medicine-induced sleep. "It doesn't matter if his guards plug their ears to my voice, not when your power can affect them without sound, and I have other ways Elhani's magic can help us. Wait for my signal once we're outside, and we will show them that we're unstoppable."

I'll always fight for you.

I let his earlier vow wrap around me like an embrace, steeling my courage and reigniting my confidence. Somewhere in the back of my mind, Nesrelle hissed, sparking the desire to use the curse she'd granted me. "You're right," I murmured, flashing him a smirk. "I came back to reclaim my palace. Today is the day we teach these arrogant Teramese a lesson."

Kovi's grin was fierce. "There she is. My empress is back."

Hope stronger than anything I'd dared to cling to yet bloomed in my heart. "Empress," I murmured. "You're going to help me take back my palace?"

His smile faltered, but only a little. Tracing the scales on my arm with a finger, he breathed a sigh. "I don't like your deal with Nesrelle," he confessed, "but I meant what I said about an alliance. If you fight for peace with my people, who am I to stop you from claiming your birthright? I want the future we dreamed about."

I swallowed thickly. "I do too," I whispered. "I want it with you."

"Then the first step is to survive today," Kovi said firmly. Cupping my face, he kissed me, long and hard. "For luck," he said when he pulled away, leaving me breathless. "Not that we need it."

Echoing footsteps were already sounding in the corridor, approaching our cell.

An anxious part of me, the part of me that remembered being a scared little girl hearing her mother was dead and she was alone in the world of her enemies—that part of me feared Kovi's kiss had been a goodbye.

Of course not, I reprimanded myself.

As a group of guards halted outside the cell door, peering through the barred window, Kovi and I stood and waited for them to take us away. Although I wished we could incapacitate the guards right here with my ability to instill fear and Kovi's commanding magic, I knew it was unlikely even we could escape the entire host of Teramese in the palace. Neither his magic nor my power would allow us to control an entire host.

Besides, a part of me relished the idea of going before Revaed and defying him when he ordered my execution. If I couldn't force him to crumple in fear, I could incapacitate the soldiers he ordered to kill me. We could defy Revaed publicly, and then—maybe then—I'd finally have the chance to kill him myself.

Now, Kovi reached out, taking my good hand in his and threading his fingers through mine. The gesture bolstered me, reminding me that I wasn't alone this time.

You weren't alone before, Nesrelle muttered in my ear, making my scar ache. *I'm here, giving you power to execute your vengeance. What more could you need?*

I swallowed, trying to repress the wave of bloodlust she launched at me. I feared losing control again with Kovi so close. What if she demanded I murder *him?*

I can take my throne back without you, I thought at Nesrelle.

Her only response was a chuckle, low and dark. Full of the promise of violence.

The door groaned as the foremost guard threw it open, tossing me a toothy, gloating grin. Behind him, at least half a dozen Teramese men and women, all dripping with blades, stood on full alert.

It was flattering that they recognized the threat Kovi and I posed to them, especially when they had my hands restrained.

"Time for your execution, empress," the first guard sneered, his silver eyes alight with undisguised hate.

Instead of fear, eagerness washed over me. Lifting my chin, I shot him a wicked grin and hoped he could read my lips. "I'm ready."

CHAPTER FORTY-SEVEN

Lo

The palace loomed over me, the site of my deepest failures and greatest victories. The one location I'd spent three years running from, trying to block out the memories. It was ironic that the only way I could put this place and its horrors behind me was by facing it, again and again.

Today, no matter what happened, I was ready.

Pauni'a had spent the early morning hours tending to my hair, reviving my curls and letting them spill to my shoulders in ringlets. "You deserve to wear your ribbon colors, you know," she'd said, her amber eyes solemn. "I know you were upset when you left the abbey."

My voice was broken. "They reminded me of Naina. Each time

she'd added one to my hair, each time she'd comforted me over my losses or commended me for my accomplishments. I hated that I'd betrayed her."

Pauni'a blinked, trying to hold back her tears and failing. When she lifted a carefully braided set of ribbons—each color I'd been bestowed throughout my years with Naina, minus the nun grey—I'd found my own eyes burning. Carefully, Pauni'a wrapped the ribbons over my hair like a headband, securing my hair out of my eyes.

"You didn't betray her, or us," Pauni'a declared as she worked. "You were just finding your true calling in life. Wear them with pride, Lo, and know Naina would be smiling down on you now. I'm sure of it."

When she finished tying the ribbons, I turned and threw my arms around her, choking back a sob. "Thank you, Nia."

I'd bid Pauni'a and my other sisters goodbye on deck before joining Father in the rowboat that he'd use to take me ashore. As soon as we stepped onto the sand, he pulled me in for a hug. "Keep to the plan. We'll be right behind you," he murmured. When he stepped back, his eyes were misty. "You look like your mother," he added with a half-smile. I hadn't been able to hold back my tears at his proclamation.

Now, those words echoed in my head, buoying my spirit as I approached the front gates.

The guards stiffened as I approached. One with piercing green eyes stepped forward, his impassive face giving way to the smallest twitch of his lips, the barest trace of a taunting smile. "Miss Nolanhou," he said. His eyes flicked toward the city, where bells tolling the seventh hour had begun to ring. "Just in time."

The guards opened the gates, well-oiled hinges swinging them open soundlessly. I stepped into the familiar grounds, inhaling the scents of flowers and coconuts. The garden was still bright and vibrant in the golden light of an early autumn morning, the air not yet cool enough to kill off any of the plants. Birds fluttered among branches overhead as I wound my way along the path, listening past the tolling of the bells, the steady chirr of insects, and the distant rhythm of waves to the rising murmurs of people.

My heart thrummed in my ears as I made the final turn and approached the palace's main courtyard, leading to the building that housed the throne room itself. The courtyard was large enough to fit twice the stalls and people that the Akytha District's marketplace could, created so that Alrenian Dragon Keepers could land their mounts here to swiftly report to the empress, as they had in Karye's days. Or, in years long before my time, the perfect size to welcome numerous foreign dignitaries and their extensive retinues.

Now, it was filled to brimming with chained and guarded dragons and people, all facing a wooden dais that had been erected against one of the stone walls encircling the space. The dragons rustled and moved restlessly, some making their annoyance known with their low growls.

My stomach churned at the sight. Not only was it appalling to see the beautiful creatures chained up like that, but also…this fact would change our carefully crafted plans. I swallowed thickly, trying to calm my rage and concern. We could free the dragons and the Forwyn. We had Elhani and his magic on our side. We *would not* fail.

Ahead, the dais itself was empty, still awaiting the start of the ceremony. Teramese muttered to one another in their language, shifting on their feet in eager anticipation. Other than those clearly assigned to guard the creatures, they gave the dragons a wide berth.

I picked out the four surviving Elders standing to the right of the dais, dressed in their finest array as if this truly were an occasion worth celebrating. There were even some Alrenians and Forwyn in one corner, their wary eyes watching the Teramese guarding them more than the dais where the ceremony was to take place. Unshackled as they were, they were likely just citizens Revaed hoped to intimidate, ones he wanted to use to spread the word about how far he'd go to enforce obedience and peace under his new reign.

At the very front, pressed closest to the dais, the Teramese had clustered the Forwyn prisoners, each shackled at the wrists and ankles and flanked by two guards.

Cold fury hardened in my chest. I'd lost my interest in vengeance long ago—back when I'd discovered it did nothing to fill the void grief had left in my heart. But justice? Freedom? Safety? I would gladly fight for all those things, both for myself and my people.

You're not alone, I thought, wishing I could say the words aloud to my people. *I'm not here to betray you. I'm here to fight for you.*

Sucking in a deep breath, I placed a hand over Caesiem's pendant. *Elhani, are you with me?* I strained my ears, and somewhere beneath the rumble of Teramese chatter and the clanging bells, I caught the low hum of Elhani's song. Soft and soothing, yet somehow powerful and encouraging too.

"What if Revaed kills you as soon as the ceremony is over?" Pauni'a had asked last night when we'd planned, her eyes wide and terrified at the thought. "There has to be a different way."

"No," I'd replied, unable to keep from smiling. This time, there was no doubt in my mind that I was on the path Elhani had set for me, and that knowledge filled me with peace. "I'm the distraction. I need to be up there. And I'm not afraid."

I repeated the words now, letting them ground me. "I'm not afraid," I murmured.

The final bell announced the hour, and the carved doors of the palace building swung outward, revealing a cluster of people. Revaed was at their forefront. Quiet settled over the crowd, their brimming anticipation almost palpable.

Stepping to the courtyard's entrance, I raised my voice to a shout. "Emperor Revaed!"

His violet eyes swept over the crowd and found mine, a soft smile darting across his face. "Miss Nolanhou. And here I was afraid you were going to be late to your own wedding." Gesturing to the posse of guards surrounding him, he ordered, "Lead her away to prepare. Quickly. We have no time to waste."

CHAPTER FORTY-EIGHT

The guards led us to the palace sanctuary, two pulling away to shove open the doors that opened into it.

Unexpected emotion welled in me at the sight of the once-familiar space, where years ago I'd attended dutifully with Mother, sitting in one of the ornately carved benches facing the altar and the towering statue of the Giver of Life. Etched from marble, his face was that of a stern, benevolent father. It had always reminded me of the similar statues of our previous emperors and empresses, as if he were just another older, wiser, more powerful ruler in our ancient ancestry. Maybe it was a subtle way to connect us, the Chosen People of Alrenor, even more to the god we worshipped, the one who had bestowed so much luxury and strength upon us. Marble columns lined the walls, stretching to a high ceiling that depicted glorious paintings of the Life-Giver's time on earth, when he'd visited mortals regularly. When he'd first granted the Alrenians our coveted gifts. Windows on two of the four walls allowed plenty of golden light to spill into the space, transforming a room that would otherwise be cold with so much marble into something almost inviting.

As a child, I'd been in awe of our time in the sanctuary. Once I'd lost Mother, the Forwyn had never forbade me outright to go to the sanctuary, but I knew our Alrenian priest was long gone—either sent away or dead in the takeover. And more than that, I'd been angry at the Life-Giver for stealing Mother away from me and leaving me, one of his supposedly Chosen people, to suffer at the hands of those who worshipped another god.

Now, I was surprised to find I wasn't appalled at the mere idea of the sanctuary. As I crossed the threshold, I was overwhelmed instead with a sense of nostalgia, something akin to comfort as memories of attending services with Mother swept over me. The candles. The voices lifted in song. The crackle of paper as the priest had paged through his enormous copy of the holy text.

But instead of the beautiful, familiar sight I'd expected, the sanctuary was in ruins. The statue of the Life-Giver was toppled over, its marble arm severed from its body, and its head splintered, the cracks running from its temple to its nose. The benches looked as if soldiers had tossed them, leaving them lying broken and forlorn. Dust motes danced in the morning light, but rather than making it warm, the light just emphasized its destruction and emptiness.

My heart dropped to my stomach as I met Revaed's gaze. He was, predictably, standing near the fallen Life-Giver statue, and the only other occupant in the sanctuary. The chains attached to my shackled wrists clanked as I tugged, trying to pull away from my guards and launch myself at the imposter emperor.

"What have you done?" I snarled. "Even a barbarian like you should recognize that demolishing a holy place is sacrilege."

"This is not my god," Revaed said, staring at the broken statue. "And I suspect he's not really yours either." He lifted his eyes to meet mine. "Vander Arros told me of the deal you made with the one you call Nesrelle, turning your back on your god." He kicked a small chunk of marble away with his foot, brow scrunched in confusion. "Which surprised me, since I thought you Alrenians took pride in being chosen by your Life-Giver." He scowled at the sanctuary, as if every adornment within it was a personal affront to him.

Gazing at the ruined sanctuary, I felt numb. Lost. It was as if some of the last warm memories of my mother were being ripped away from me and ruined by enemy hands. No matter how conflicted I felt about my recent encounter with the Life-Giver, no matter how angry I was at him, seeing something so revered and important to my people desecrated was heart-wrenching.

"Monster," I hissed. "Isn't it enough that you slay our people, that you stole my empire? How dare you destroy a sacred place." My shaking fingers curled into fists, the wounded ones on my left hand smarting with fresh pain.

Revaed shrugged. "Would a monster give you one last chance to bid your place of importance goodbye? To pray to your god and make whatever final atonements or confessions you wanted?" He gestured toward the marble altar, the one untouched place in the sanctuary.

They'll pay for dishonoring you, Nesrelle murmured in my ear. *We'll make them bow before us both.*

I gritted my teeth. "I have no need of that. Take me out of here." I could sense Kovi's gaze on me, the heaviness of it. Was he surprised at my refusal? Saddened? Was he as horrified at the Teramese destruction as I was? I didn't want to look, didn't want to meet his expression and possibly let him see the darkness in my eyes.

I didn't want him to know that Nesrelle's mark was burning on my cheek, bloodlust and an overwhelming desire to slay anyone in my path taking over. I wanted to taste that power again, to feed the constant ache in my chest. To unleash my fury and hurt on the world until I had none left to feel. To let the entire world drown in those emotions instead of me.

Somewhere, a quieter thought tried to remind me of Kovi's gentleness and mercy, of how it had felt only minutes earlier to wake up in his embrace. But Nesrelle's voice was louder, more insistent. And I was overcome with grief and rage, too raw, too blinding, to resist her.

Revaed swept past, his face impassive, neither relishing my suffering nor taunting it. He was all business. All method. As the guards tugged on my arms, following Revaed's path, they led me through a series of buildings and courtyards, past rooms where more statues were being torn down, paintings were being destroyed, books were being ripped apart or tossed into fires—all symbols of my Alrenian heritage, all being desecrated. Each step made the pounding in my ears grow louder, drowning out Kovi's low voice as he tried to get my attention, tried in vain to soothe me. Each sight made sparks dance across my eyes as I relived moments with Mother and her court: walking through *that* hallway, studying *this* statue and learning the story of the empress it represented, or sitting in *that* armchair and reading one of the countless history books penned about our empire.

Tears burned my eyes, but I refused to cry. I wanted to scream in rage, to break off my shackles and slam my palms against all these wretched imposters who were destroying my lineage, my history, my *home.*

But I was helpless, for now. The guards guided us to the doors leading to the palace's main courtyard, and another set of guards pulled them open. Every adult dragon from the Keep, even Ryke, was chained up and guarded by Teramese, while Alrenians, Forwyn, and Teramese alike were gathered in rows closer to a wooden dais. My eyes lingered on

Ryke, relief rushing through me at the sight of him standing upright, head held high, every sign of sickness gone. At least the Teramese had made good on their word to administer the antidote to my dragon. He was chained, but he was alive.

Despite the large crowd and the trapped dragons, the courtyard was eerily quiet, ringing with the echoes of the bells in the city, the ones that had just finished proclaiming the seventh hour. Forwyn, Teramese, and Alrenian faces all turned and stared at Revaed. Some eyes fell on me.

"Emperor Revaed!"

The voice came from a young woman shouting in the merchant tongue, her accent slight but undoubtedly Forwyn. Sweeping my gaze past the crowd, I found her at the courtyard's entrance, a familiar figure with her stance tall and proud, her jaw set. She was dressed in a plain tunic and leggings, her curls spilling loosely to her shoulders. Her Forwyn ribbons were in almost every color, bound together in a beautiful braid she wore like a headband, while around her neck were more ribbons in gold, wrapping around her throat like a choker. Even at this distance, I could see the determination and courage sparkling in her eyes.

Shock washed over me. It was the girl who'd both ruined and saved my life. The cause of my greatest suffering and losses.

Lo'laeni Nolanhou.

CHAPTER FORTY-NINE

Lo

As soon as the guards brought me to the rooms I'd once shared with Caesiem, several Teramese women set to work draping me in layers of red silk, from a pair of trousers to a long, elaborate tunic and belt, all extravagantly beaded and embroidered in flashes of gold. Matching slippers adorned my feet, plush and comfortable, yet impractical for fighting in. Inwardly, I cursed, wishing I could forego the part of the wedding ceremony that involved them dressing me like a fine sacrifice they were preparing to offer to their gods.

But I held still and let them dab my neck and wrists with perfumes, and tame my already frizzing curls with coconut oil. They lined my eyes with kohl and brushed color over my cheeks and lips. They clasped bracelets and bands on my bare arms, added a gold necklace set with fiery rubies and pearls around my neck, and clipped long gold and red earrings to my ears. As if they'd been instructed or they instinctively knew better, they didn't touch Caesiem's pendant or the gold ribbons around my neck.

They must not have been told about the ribbons in my hair, though, because after she finished pulling my curls half up and leaving the rest to frame my face, one of the women reached for the headband to remove it. It was the first time I'd bothered to make a single protest. "Those stay," I said firmly, gazing into the mirror and locking eyes with the woman.

Pursing her lips, she abandoned my ribbons and, with the help of another woman, draped a sheer gold veil over my head. I blinked at the foreign sight in the mirror. There I was, clothed in the colors of my enemy, arrayed like one of them.

It only took a matter of minutes for them to finish dressing me and lead me out of the quarters, where the guards who had brought me here joined them in ushering me back toward the courtyard. Each woman was arrayed almost as finely as I was, all in various gem-bright colors that flashed in the early morning sunlight.

As we made a turn in the hallway, we nearly collided with another small crowd: Caesiem, dressed in fine pants and a shirt in colors similar to mine, surrounded by guards. He halted, glancing over his shoulder to meet my eyes. He looked…exhausted. No amount of gaudy clothes could conceal the tiredness around his eyes. But when his gaze locked onto mine, it was as intense as ever.

"Lo," he breathed, shoving one of the guards aside and darting to me.

The women parted for him, one of them practically swooning when Caesiem seized my hands, cradling them in his.

"Your Highness," one of his guards said, his blue eyes unsympathetic, his mustache quivering with annoyance. "It's time. The emperor…"

"Give us a moment," Caesiem snapped, not tearing his gaze from mine. I couldn't look away from him either, couldn't seem to catch my breath. "Leave us."

The nymph's words kept running through my mind.

Everyone scurried from the hall, guards and my posse of attendants alike, and a hush fell between Caesiem and me. Everything in his expression washed the doubts and pain and fear away. When I met his eyes, I saw the man who'd called upon the sea to save my life, who'd shown himself to be loyal to a fault to any he cared for. The man who'd sung me to sleep to chase away my nightmares and tended to my injuries. The man who'd proclaimed *I* was his home.

The pendant protects the one the mage loves most in this world, the nymph had said.

I pressed my fingers to Caesiem's pendant and stared straight back at him, my anchor in this churning sea. I didn't want him to bear the burden of choosing between his guardian and me, but Revaed had given us no choice. And in this moment, I had no doubt who Caesiem would choose.

"I knew you would come," Caesiem admitted at last, "but I won't lie and say I wish you hadn't." A dark lock of hair fell across his forehead as he dipped his head toward mine, so close I could feel his breath.

I squeezed his fingers. "It's all right," I whispered. "We have a plan."

Someone pounded on the door at the end of the hall—the one leading to the courtyard. A guard, likely ordered by Revaed to hurry us along. My heart jolted.

Caesiem nodded, once. "Lo, I…" His eyes were dark, swimming with sorrow and regret. "I'm sorry. I should have—" Another knock sounded, cutting him off. He cursed and shook his head. "Do you trust me?" he asked quickly.

"I know you're on my side."

His mouth tightened. "Always." He looked like he wanted to say more, but the door flew open.

"Your Highness!" a guard shouted.

"We're coming," Caesiem responded, dropping my hands and sweeping forward. The guards and attendants heard him and rushed out from an adjoining room, immediately falling back into place.

"Wait a moment," one of the women urged, seizing my hand in her cold one.

My stomach fluttered in anticipation as Caesiem was escorted outside first. Were Father and his soldiers in position? We hadn't expected the dragons to be in the courtyard too, chained as they were. Could we free them along with our people? Use them to fight against the Teramese, now that I had Forwyn who'd trained with the dragons?

Mind whirling, I followed as the women ushered me forward. It was time, and all I could do was pray we were ready.

We emerged out a side door that trailed beneath swaying palms and wound past fragrant flowers in all sorts of colors, from blue embyth to pure white sythrel.

The murmuring of the crowd was soft now, more like the gentle rhythm of the waves washing over the shore on a peaceful night than the tumultuous sound they'd created earlier. Even the dragons had stilled, as if sensing the change in the people around them. After all, they *were* perceptive creatures. I clenched my jaw as my entourage fanned out around me, separating me from the crowd as we pushed toward the dais. My palms grew clammy when I heard the hissing whispers as I passed.

Traitor.

An embarrassment to our people.

She's selling herself and her people to the Teramese like a whore.

Each scathing word spoken in Forwyn lanced through me like the sharpest dagger. To my shame, I didn't meet their eyes, didn't want to see the hatred and betrayal in their gazes. They didn't know why I was here. They didn't know what Father, his soldiers, and I had planned.

There was a small cluster of people waiting on the dais, including more guards, but as soon as my eyes caught Caesiem's, everyone else fell away.

I trust you, I mouthed, and though there was still pain in his eyes, the softest smile played about Caesiem's lips.

"At last," Revaed murmured as he stepped forward to take my arm and guide me up the final stair leading to the dais. "Before I make my announcement or you begin your speech, I have a question for you." He gestured toward the far corner, where half a dozen heavily armed guards hovered near two shackled prisoners.

They were Empress Jaliana and her Forwyn guard from the Autumn Ball: Kovi Ettonou, my father's prized solider. Kovi had been one of the men who hadn't returned from scouting the palace last night, and now I knew why. My heart slammed into my chest, my mind torn between worry and relief.

"Did you want the former empress executed to open the proceedings, or as a wedding gift after the ceremony is over?" Revaed went on, in a tone that sounded more like he was asking if I preferred to have red or white wine served at the after party.

As clearly as if it had just happened moments ago, I could still see Jaliana's shocked face from the night I'd stopped Wilvhe from killing her. Now, she wore a haughty expression, her golden skin shimmering in the early morning light as she pulled herself to her full height, which was considerably shorter than her mother's had been. But despite her smaller stature, she emanated power and strength and confidence. Her eyes glittered with something *other* that was utterly chilling, and I could have sworn I detected shadows coiling around her form, as if the darkness itself was drawn to her. Maybe it was my imagination, or maybe there was something else, something supernatural, at work here. Maybe it was tied to the horrifying curse she bore. All I knew was in that moment, there was no hint of the fear or vulnerability I'd witnessed in the garden.

Perhaps she deserved to die. Perhaps her death was necessary to help my people, the one service Revaed could offer me today that I would gladly accept.

And yet…

My eyes flitted to Kovi, who'd somehow, despite his shackles and the guards holding him back, positioned himself slightly in front of Jaliana. Protectively. As if even now, he was dedicated to guarding her. Memories of the way they'd danced together at the ball twirled through my mind, the way their eyes had fastened on one another as if no one else existed. There was a deep connection there, one I might never understand.

If Kovi trusted the empress, and Father trusted Kovi…

I couldn't forget the way Elhani's voice had urged me to rescue Jaliana, either. There was a reason he'd wanted me to spare her that night, and maybe that reason still existed now.

You are a fighter. Elhani's words rang out as clearly in my mind as if he were standing right beside me. *But you also carry great love and compassion in your heart. The time for fighting and justice will come later.*

"Not now. Later," I told Revaed firmly.

His mouth twitched. "Very well."

Leading me to Caesiem, who stood at the center of the dais, Revaed turned us both to face the waiting crowd. My eyes landed on the countless chained Forwyn lined up before me, surrounded by heavily armed guards. My stomach churned, and it took everything within me to keep my expression impassive.

Passing me papers covered in beautiful script—the blasted speech they Elders had written for me—and a speaking trumpet, Revaed's violet eyes met mine for one too-long moment. The threat in them was clear. *Do what is expected of you, or watch your people die.*

Lifting my veil, Revaed scowled and plucked the ribbons from my hair. My stomach lurched, but rather than try to take them back or let him see my discomfort, I flashed him a cool smile. Facing the crowd, I cleared my throat and began without delay. "My esteemed fellow citizens…"

It took every ounce of discipline I'd learned in my training as a nun to keep myself from rolling my eyes, from letting sarcasm seep into my tone. I was constantly tempted to lift my head and scan the crowd, searching for familiar faces, searching for my father, but I had to act naturally. Just as the soldiers were trusting me, I had to trust them. They knew the plan, and the chained dragons were a setback, but not an impossible one.

At my side, Caesiem remained poised, his face a mask, but I could sense the tension emanating from him. I longed to reach out and take his hand, wished we could steal one more moment of privacy.

Every word from the speech made me want to cringe.

Unified front…

A new, peaceful empire is dawning…

This beautiful alliance…

My heart is full of remorse for my earlier mistakes…

Please join me…

Strength…

Peace…

Lies. All lies. But I forced each word out, my voice unwavering and strong, echoing through the still crowd with thunderous power. Every eye was on me, just as Father, his soldiers, and I had hoped would happen.

I was the beautiful distraction. I was the blade we'd thrust into Revaed's back. I was the fire that would burn this new empire to the ground.

Nothing but silence reigned as I finished my speech. Countless Forwyn faces stared back at me, their expressions hardened in defiance and anger. Even the Teramese seemed to believe this was too solemn of an affair for applause or cheers.

Someone approached, gently plucking the speaking trumpet and paper from my hands. I glanced over my shoulder to see one of the women who'd accompanied me slipping back across the dais to stand in a row with the rest of the Teramese. Their shimmering gowns were almost too bright to look at directly. Then Caesiem was threading his fingers through mine, the feel of his calloused palm against my skin reassuring me. He brushed his thumb over my knuckles and, as we turned to face a waiting Forwyn officiant, leaned in close.

"Whatever comes, I'm on your side," he whispered, his breath tickling my ear. A reminder I didn't need, but welcomed all the same.

I turned to meet his eyes and flashed him a small smile.

The proceedings passed in a blur. I wasn't familiar with Forwyn wedding traditions, as I hadn't exactly grown up seeing many conducted. Slaves often exchanged vows secretly, if they managed to at all, and it wasn't as if I'd been invited to weddings when I'd served as a nun. But my mind was elsewhere, constantly wondering if Father and his soldiers had arrived. Wondering if Karos would hearken to me again, or if his unpredictable nature would flare in this crowd.

"Step forward," the officiant intoned, and I blinked as Elder Ettonou and Revaed each grasped one of the torches burning along the perimeter of the dais. Together, they approached a stone altar piled high with wood, lowered their torches, and set it aflame. Handing Caesiem and I each a scarf, the officiant gestured toward the licking flames. "This act represents Teramese and Forwyn unity. As each of you toss your scarves into the fire, you will be demonstrating that you are both willing to compromise, to give up selfish desires for yourselves and your people in a joint cause to do what is best for *both* peoples."

A chill ran through my body, but I stepped forward numbly, tossing my scarf—embroidered with the Forwyn sigil of the rising sun— into the fire and watching the flames devour it. Beside me, Caesiem followed suit and dropped his, which bore the Teramese symbol.

"Emperor Revaed and Elder Ettonou, please come forward to

show your acceptance of this alliance and your burning away of your old focuses for the new by placing your own scarves in the fire." The officiant handed two new ones to Revaed and Elder Ettonou, both of whom approached the altar on either side of Caesiem and me to make the symbolic gesture.

The roaring of the fire filled my ears, and I was barely aware of the words the officiant spoke next.

Next thing I knew, he was grasping my wrist and leading me away to place my hand in Caesiem's. There was a gentle look in the officiant's dark eyes, a warmth I hadn't detected earlier because I'd barely spared him a glance. He didn't appear to hate me, but I didn't think he pitied me either. Maybe he understood what I was doing, my loyalty to the Forwyn cause. Maybe he recognized I was no victim, no pawn. Not anymore.

When I turned to Caesiem, his eyes were intent and focused. He squeezed his fingers gently over mine as the officiant lifted a braided pair of ribbons formed into a necklace. "Orange for loyalty," he declared, "and green for the new life you begin in service to two unified peoples."

I gritted my teeth as the officiant draped the ribbons over my head, letting them join Caesiem's pendant and my gold ribbons. Caesiem swallowed as the man repeated the declaration for him, adding the same braided ribbons around his neck.

The officiant proceeded, urging us to repeat our identical vows, first binding us to one another and then to both the Teramese and Forwyn people. *I vow to serve and protect Caesiem. To put his needs above my own. To be loyal and true to the end of my days, or may Elhani and the gods see my faithlessness and condemn my wavering heart.*

I vow to serve and protect our people. To put their needs above my own. To be loyal and true…

I meant the words…for my people, at least. Even for Caesiem, whom I'd gladly fight to protect. But for Revaed and the Teramese?

They'd proven how untrustworthy they were.

Elhani, you know why I am here, I thought.

"Kneel and pray to Elhani with me, as is Forwyn custom," the officiant murmured, and there was a comforting tone in his voice. I looked to him, seeing the focus in his eyes. *Pray with me.*

I twined my fingers tightly with Caesiem's. We kneeled together, bowing our heads as the officiant raised his voice, holding a benevolent hand above us both.

"Elhani, we ask your blessing on this union and this new alliance forged here today. We seek your approval, a sign that you will guide our future rulers in your wisdom and power…"

As he finished, the officiant removed the ribbons from both our necks and tossed them into the altar as an offering to Elhani. Then he bid Caesiem and me to rise and turn to the crowd. "Kneel before your Crown Prince and your new princess, heirs to a glorious new empire."

My chest tightened at his words, at the way the Teramese shoved the Forwyn prisoners forcefully to their knees. Shackles clanked. Behind me, Jaliana and Kovi grunted as their knees slammed to the dais, more chains clinking.

"Thank you," I said, letting my words echo over the still square, which was quiet enough I didn't need a speaking trumpet this time to project my voice. Before gesturing for everyone to stand, my eyes flicked through the crowd, wondering where my father was. Wondering where his soldiers were. Not all were adept in using Elhani's magic, which meant not all would be invisible. Some would be hiding in plain sight. Prepared for the words I'd planned the night before, the words that had a perfect double meaning for this moment. "You may rise."

Caesiem gave me a sidelong glance, perhaps noticing the way I straightened. Tensing. Preparing.

The Teramese surrounding Karos cried out in surprise as men and women—some concealed by cloaks and others appearing as if from thin air as they dropped their invisibility—began their attack. I sensed

Revaed and his guards stirring behind me, but I didn't give them the honor of even turning around to look. Water roared, and I heard more than saw Caesiem call upon the element, creating an impenetrable wall between us and everyone else on the dais. I could trust him to keep us safe long enough for me to help my people.

And this time, I knew exactly what I needed to do.

I kept my gaze trained on the Forwyn prisoners, lifting my voice and launching into the same song Eloiyah had sung before her death. It mingled with the tune of Elhani's music swirling through the air, until the notes blended so seamlessly, I couldn't tell where my song ended and his began. Each word was in a language I didn't know, and yet somehow, was as familiar as my own heartbeat, speaking of love and peace, of freedom and a home I'd never known yet missed all the same. The song grew in power, the magic stirred in my blood, and my thoughts cried out to my god like they never had before.

Lights flared amidst the rows of shackled prisoners, bright and warm and pure. Tears stung my eyes from their sheer power, but I couldn't stop staring, taking in the wonderous sight. The lights were coalescing, taking shape. Dozens of Immortals in the forms of men and women clothed in battle armor appeared at the prisoners' sides. My knees went weak as I realized they were singing with me, joining in the notes until they echoed forcefully off the courtyard's walls, until the very ground seemed to quake beneath us. They extended their arms and took the prisoners' hands, another flash of light flooding the crowd.

Shackles sprang free, chains clanging as they slammed against the cobblestones.

Blinking, I glanced to my left, away from Caesiem, where a blindingly bright form stood at *my* side. Edi, his smile encouraging and sweet as he finished the final note of his song. Quiet descended, and for an instant, it seemed like nothing else existed in the world but him and me.

"We're always near, Lo," he whispered, his eyes shimmering, and then he was gone.

Mind whirling, I turned back to where the Forwyn soldiers had freed Karos. The dragon's scales—black and fiery red—flashed in the sunlight as they undid the chains. He bucked and snarled, showing fangs. When he extended his wings, the force rippled the air and caused the Forwyn to stagger on their feet.

Karos was furious. Unpredictable. Smoke curled from his nostrils, from his mouth, and I could practically feel the anger and intent radiating off him. His black eye gleamed as he cocked his head and trained his gaze on the Teramese corpses and the Forwyn soldiers encircling him. In his mind, even the soldiers who had freed him might be enemies. They were all strangers, and he was surrounded, his brothers and sisters all still in chains.

My blood was like fire in my veins, and every word I spoke was pure power. Elhani's magic thrummed inside me, wild and yet…mine to command. His Immortals may have vanished from my sight, but I knew in my bones they were still there, just as Elhani himself was, fighting for my people. Fighting for me.

"Karos!" I cried out, and the dragon stilled at the sound of my voice, dipping his head when he found me.

He would heed me—and only me.

My lips curled in a smile as I stretched out my hand, beckoning him forward. The Teramese within the crowd were too horrified to move, too shocked by the freed Forwyn and now the wildest, most feared dragon of them all. I knew their paralysis wouldn't last, but it sent a surge of pride and satisfaction through me to see them realizing just how formidable my people could be.

We'd brought a tyrannical empress to her knees. We'd claimed her empire as our own. We'd tamed her dragons.

Of course we wouldn't let Teramyl overcome us now.

We were survivors, warriors, victors. We'd faced slavery and loss and horrors unnamable and innumerable. We could face anything and overcome it.

"Wait." The voice rang out in the quiet, musical yet firm. It was hauntingly familiar, causing a chill to run down my back.

As if compelled by a force greater than myself, I froze. Even Karos stilled. Caesiem's water crashed to the dais, splattering across our clothes and faces and misting the air.

No one moved except a single figure, who stepped through the crowd, tugging back her hood to reveal her fiery red hair.

Nesrelle.

CHAPTER FIFTY

Kovi

Earlier

Rhi'il was chained and flanked by two guards, lined up with the other Forwyn prisoners at the front of the crowd. While guards escorted me through the courtyard and toward the dais at the front, he met my gaze with his usual strength, his eyes shining with determination. Though he had every reason to blame me for our predicament, for my incompetence, his expression didn't reveal a hint of anger or resentment.

As always, my best friend—my brother in arms—had my back, like he'd promised.

But the sight of him still sent a fresh wave of pain through me, reminding me just how greatly I'd failed him and my fellow soldiers. How deeply I'd failed every one of the Forwyn prisoners now likely awaiting their execution. Unease filled my chest as I scanned each face, most weary and hopeless, resigned to whatever terrible fate awaited them. They were the expressions of those who'd fought and lost, who knew they were out of time. Those looks made my blood run cold.

Then the guards turned me toward the dais, and my eyes locked on the Elders standing in a solemn row, their clothing extravagant, their faces careful masks. My fingers curled into fists, clinking my chains. Father must have sensed my burning stare, for he turned, his dark eyes focusing on me. Though his expression remained inscrutable, a muscle twitched near his eye. Fury? Shame? Concern?

Did he care at all that his son had been captured? Had he even known before this moment?

"Snake," I murmured, my voice so low it sounded more like a growl rumbling through my chest. "Traitor."

If Father heard or read my lips, he showed no sign. Turning away, he again scanned the crowds, refusing to give me another moment of attention.

So that was how it would be, then. He was only proud of me when I accomplished something *he* thought was noteworthy. He was only interested in a relationship with me when he thought I was mindlessly serving his cause, whatever twisted one that was.

Bile filled my mouth as I scanned the four surviving Elders. I was full of anger and shame. I'd trusted them to lead and protect us Forwyn, and they'd sold out to Teramyl. They were willingly subjecting their people to tyranny, imprisonment, and even death…all to save their own lives and sate their lust for revenge against the Alrenians. They wanted the power the Teramese had, and rather than fight for freedom, for justice, they had chosen to ally themselves with a powerful enemy to remain in influential positions within this new empire.

As Jalie and I were lined up on the dais, I jostled against the guards, not enough to escape—there would be no overpowering the number that had surrounded us even if their ears weren't plugged—but enough to place myself just slightly in front of Jalie. My eyes took note of everyone's position, scanning each weapon, both visible and hidden.

Surely General Ilowhe and the remaining soldiers would strike today. Everything was happening faster than we'd anticipated, but I knew the general. Knew my brothers and sisters in arms. And, though I'd barely met her, I had a strong feeling that Lo, daughter of the general, wouldn't go through with this ceremony without a plan to rescue the imprisoned Forwyn.

As if summoned by my thoughts, Lo was led forward by a cluster of Teramese women. While I took note of the way they'd draped Lo in extravagant red and gold and plentiful jewelry in the Teramese style, I caught the creeping movements of Forwyn soldiers in the distance. They melted from the shadows at the edge of the garden, like they were stepping out of nothing. Some, I knew, had mastered Elhani's magic well enough to conceal themselves, but others drew on skills honed at the academy or from years of enslavement. My sketches of the palace had served my brothers and sisters well, even if I'd failed in my latest mission to scout out the area and return to report to them.

My chest tightened—I should have been there. I should be free and unchained, able to rescue both my people and Jalie. Instead, I would have to trust that together, she and I would be the unstoppable force we'd been before in battle.

"Ready to strike at my signal?" I murmured, leaning as closely to Jalie as I dared.

But Jalie kept her eyes trained ahead, an eerie darkness in them, reminding me of that instant last night when I'd thought I'd seen Nesrelle rather than her. Uneasiness crawled along my skin as I noticed shadows swirling more thickly than before. I wasn't sure if this observation was a consequence of me being more in tune with Elhani's magic, or if it had to do with how much Jalie was letting Nesrelle's power influence her, but something had changed.

Jalie, I thought, praying our mysterious connection would let me speak into her mind, to tear her from her bloodthirsty focus. When I turned, I found it wasn't Revaed Jalie was staring at with revenge in her eyes.

It was Lo. Somehow, Jalie must have found out that Lo was the *amara'rekni*. My heart hammered in my throat.

You allied with me, I pled, wondering if Jalie even heard me…or if she was ignoring me. *With my people. You promised to spare them. Revaed is the one who wants to execute you, who took your empire and injured you. We can stop him…*

But whether she heard me or not, Jalie's wholehearted focus seemed to be on revenge. My eyes scanned the marking carved into her cheek, one that she'd admitted connected her on an even deeper level than before with the Dark Immortal. What if Jalie was slipping away, to truly be lost to me forever?

What if she really couldn't be saved?

The words I'd once said to her—at a time that now felt like a lifetime ago—came to mind, making my chest ache with their futility. *We have a choice. Maybe we don't have to be monsters.*

What if, with power and circumstances like ours, there was no choice? What if the only way to protect our people was at the cost of our own souls, and the last vestiges of whatever innocence we still clung to?

The wedding ceremony must have been at its close, for next thing I knew, the guards were shoving Jalie and me to our knees and the officiant was praying to Elhani. The words slammed into my chest forcefully, a mockery of everything I'd strived for as a soldier of my people. This Forwyn man asking Elhani to *bless* this union and alliance of Teramese and Forwyn, to recognize this horrible farce of a marriage, was laughable.

As Lo turned with Prince Xalenos to face the crowd, crying out for them to rise up, I recognized the same frustration and anger written across countless Forwyn faces. Men and women stood and shifted on their feet, chains clanking. Though their shoulders were slumped, their eyes downcast, I caught a spark of rebellion in their expressions still. They hadn't fully given up. Their forced subservience to the Teramese could still bring their fire back to the surface, and that gave me hope.

If Empress Karye couldn't break us, Emperor Revaed couldn't either.

Forwyn leapt from the crowd, some shrouded in cloaks to conceal themselves while others materialized that very moment, throwing off Elhani's power of invisibility. They surrounded the Teramese guarding the largest dragon present, a magnificent, well-muscled beast with scales of black and red and umber. He snorted and thrashed against the chains clamped around his neck and legs. Though the Forwyn were working to free him, I feared this dragon wouldn't be able to distinguish friend from foe in his enraged state, so desperate was he to be free.

And then Lo began to sing, her voice ringing out melodic and strong, bouncing off the walls and resounding with such power that I was sure every person in the courtyard could hear her as clearly as if she were standing right next to them. Magic flowed through the words, hitting the same notes Elhani's song did. I could feel his power radiating off her, lending her such command that for a moment, the whole world seemed to still and listen. Even our enemies were rapt, entranced by Elhani's magic coursing through her.

At least, until shouts pierced the air again as the Teramese guarding the dragon began to fall. Revaed called out to his guards to seize Lo, but the Teramese prince threw up his hands and called on…water magic. I gaped as the sea itself answered his silent command, rushing in a torrent to create a wall that blocked all of us—Revaed, guards, Elders, and Jalie and me—from reaching him and Lo.

Caesiem Xalenos was a powerful water mage…and he had chosen to *protect* Lo.

Shaking my head, I stood to my full height, trying to gaze over the water, but I couldn't see the Forwyn prisoners or Lo. I could, however, find the dragon, who was free and snorting smoke as he turned on the Forwyn soldiers. I gritted my teeth, longing to pry the shackles off my wrists. Longing for a sword. I should have been down there, protecting my brothers and sisters. Then a new thought struck me: *Does compelling magic work on dragons?*

"Karos!" It was Lo. The dragon paused, cocking its head. Watching Lo with one intelligent black eye. He lowered his head in deference, and my heart swelled with hope and awe. This dragon was loyal to Lo, as fiercely as Ryke had bound himself to Jalie.

"Wait."

A new voice echoed throughout the courtyard, its power slamming through me with such intense force that at first, I was too aware of my overwhelming dread to recognize it. Caesiem's water wall collapsed, splashing and soaking everyone on the dais as it poured off its edges. Blinking against the sting of saltwater in my eyes, I scanned the crowd until I saw the only form moving, one draped in a cloak. She pushed back her hood.

The Dark Immortal, Nesrelle herself.

Rage clawed up my throat, and for an instant, I didn't care that she was immortal and couldn't be killed. I longed to wrap my hands around her neck for all the suffering she'd caused my people and Jalie. I ached to use my magic on her and force her to slit her own neck, to fall upon her own sword.

But instead, I watched, as frozen as everyone else in the crowd, as she stalked forward, ascending the steps to the dais with as much grace as an empress entering a throne room. Though her hair cascaded in perfect waves and her smile was serene, she wasn't clothed in a flowing gown like when I'd encountered her before. This time, she was dressed for war. Black and ivory dragon scales gleamed in the morning light, and a belt lined with rows of naked daggers was settled about her slim waist. Before, she'd often gone barefoot, but today, she wore supple leather boots. She looked like an Alrenian warrior, except that her piercing blue eyes were cold, without a hint of the warmth of gold flecks, and her skin was almost translucently pale, without any shimmer.

"My congratulations on the new union…and your alliance," Nesrelle said as she reached the top of the dais, flashing Revaed a wicked smile. When she turned toward Caesiem and Lo, undisguised hatred marred her expression, twisting her beautiful lips into a sneer. I realized with a start that the pair still had their hands clasped, fingers entwined. Water dripped off their fine wedding clothes. I couldn't see their faces, but their stances were tall, proud. Not quaking in fear of Nesrelle at all.

As swiftly as Nesrelle had shot them a glare, she turned away and shrugged, her smile sliding back into place.

"What do you want?" Lo demanded, her words shockingly loud in the silence that had fallen over the courtyard.

"I wanted to recognize the new alliance as well," Nesrelle answered, reaching into a bag tied to her belt, almost concealed by her cloak. "With a gift."

Her bag was…dark and dripping.

Foreboding thundered through me as Nesrelle reached inside and drew out a heart, congealed blood staining her creamy white fingers. She tossed it into the still-burning fire on the wedding altar and laughed.

Beside me, Jalie made her first sound—a choked sort of whimper. Instinctively, I extended a hand to comfort her, but my shackles bit into my wrists and prevented me from reaching her.

"I considered waiting for the executions to begin," Nesrelle murmured, listing her head as she considered Revaed, who hadn't moved a muscle. "But it seems your plans for today are going awry, and I grew bored."

With a flourish, she gestured toward the gate. It was then I heard it—distant screams, carried on the breeze, along with the scent of smoke. Not dragon smoke, which had its own unique tang to it, but normal smoke. Somewhere, there was a fire burning.

Nesrelle's eyes flicked to Jalie for the first time. "Your army is here, little empress. But," she added, her mouth sliding downward into a false frown, "I'm afraid your city is burning."

CHAPTER FIFTY-ONE

Jalie

Nesrelle's voice had whispered through my mind as she'd tossed the heart into the fire, sending a shockwave of pain radiating outward from my cheek through my entire body. It was almost as jolting as when she touched me, sending tendrils of agony through every inch of my being. I hadn't been able to hold back the sound that escaped me in a gasp, a pathetic moment of weakness overtaking me.

Poor Breyna, Nesrelle had taunted. *She wasn't as willing to serve as the rest of your soldiers.*

Now, a new kind of pain tore through me as her spoken words echoed in my head, repeating on an endless, horrible cycle.

I'm afraid your city is burning.

It was true. Already the distant scent of smoke permeated the air, while the sky over the city was rapidly being consumed by a billowing cloud. Blackness swallowed the morning light, and though the city was concealed by the vast courtyard walls hemming us in, I could imagine the way the beautiful white buildings would be flashing in shades of orange and red as flames licked their way through the city. Though there was plenty of water and stone in Inalgoth, there were also beautiful palms and gardens, homes and shops built of wood, and countless citizens who were all in danger.

My earlier bloodlust melted into despair and horror. My people were under attack by the very army I'd rallied to save them. My city was being destroyed by the one who'd promised me my throne. Everything I'd done to reclaim Alrenor was crumbling into destruction—a horrible, nightmarish failure.

Chaos erupted as Nesrelle vanished with a mocking laugh, just in time for Alrenian warriors in leathers, all splattered in blood and in various states of eerie transformation, to climb the gate and leap into the courtyard. My breath caught in my throat at the sight. The warriors moved as if the effort cost them nothing at all, their actions swift and far too strong to be natural. Nesrelle's power within them was growing— but so was the rest of her influence. As each soldier landed, I caught sight of black scales flashing on patches of their exposed skin, of wild eyes that were more pupil than anything else, as wide and horrible as pits leading to hell. They screamed and slashed their blades with vicious fury, without care of who they attacked, who they killed. Each was hopelessly lost in Nesrelle's grip. Each only wanted to slaughter, to spill blood, to serve their mistress and revel in their power.

Unlike during the battle of Aramith, they didn't attack one another. Nesrelle must have given them new orders. Now they worked as a team, cutting down Teramese, Forwyn, and Alrenian alike. Thankfully, there were few Alrenians in attendance, but the blood these soldiers wore had likely come from citizens in the streets…

Remember Lo'laeni, Nesrelle urged. *Kill her first.*

Bloodlust burned through me, consuming and irresistible.

Releasing a guttural cry, I launched every ounce of my focus and strength into seeking out and exploiting the fears of the Teramese guards hemming me in. In mere moments, they crumpled to their knees, shrieking, or had hurled themselves off the dais, drawing their blades and swinging at invisible foes.

I was about to leap off the dais when a Forwyn man darted toward the edge. "Kovi!" he cried, holding up something that glinted in the last of the sunlight. A chain of keys.

"What took you so long?" Kovi asked, but his tone was teasing.

"No appreciation for my talents," said the young man, rolling his eyes in mock annoyance. With a grin, he hefted himself onto the dais and unlocked Kovi's shackles. There were two daggers stuffed in the young man's belt, one of which he handed to Kovi.

Grasping it, Kovi's eyes darted to me, but his friend's expression turned wary when he met my gaze.

"Rhi'il. Please free her," Kovi urged.

Jaw tensing, the man named Rhi'il stepped forward, inserting the key into the lock and, with a click, snapping my shackles loose. With a snarl, I tossed them to the dais and scanned the area for Lo'laeni. I caught a glimpse of her charging forward, racing down the steps with Caesiem on her heels.

Caesiem

The building clouds sent a pang through my chest. This city wasn't the city I'd grown up in, but in many ways, it had become home all the same. It had given me the woman I loved, the only person left in this world I trusted.

And now, no amount of water I could call on my own would be able to quench a fire large enough to create clouds like those. The scent of smoke and ash swirled on the air, climbing up toward the palace in a painful reminder that even if the battle was won here, the capital was lost.

Tearing her soaked veil off her head, Lo tugged her hand from mine and turned to me. Her wet curls clung to her face. "You said you're with me?"

"No matter what," I vowed.

Lo spun toward two of the nearest Teramese soldiers. "Get back!" she shouted at them. "Drop your weapons."

The men cried out in alarm and dropped their swords before turning and fleeing into the fray. Lo seized one blade as I retrieved the other, blinking at her in awe.

"What was that?" I demanded.

Her smile was grim. "I'll explain later."

And then she was racing off the dais.

Jalie

The courtyard was filled with the blood and chaos of battle. Shrieks from the injured and the dying reverberated through the air, along with the clang of steel on steel. Blood and sweat and smoke tainted a space that had only moments ago smelled of the sweet perfume from the gardens.

Ryke and Karos, either by Forwyn design or their own willpower, had broken free of their chains, snarling and snapping at figures who drew too near to them. Forwyn prisoners who must have seized weapons in the fray fought alongside Aerekni Academy soldiers and…even some forms that appeared to be Alrenian. But the leather-clad, wild-looking army Nesrelle had brought was fiercest of all, leaving piles of corpses in their wake as they clove through Teramese, Alrenian, and Forwyn without remorse.

My body shook as another flash of pain shot through me. Nesrelle's voice echoed in my head, urging me toward Lo'laeni. Maybe I hated Nesrelle, maybe I feared for my city…but the power of the battle frenzy she fed me, the desire for the revenge I'd waited *years* for…that blocked out all other emotions. All other goals. I couldn't tear my eyes from the Forwyn woman, her bright red Teramese outfit like a beacon in the crowd.

"Jalie—" Kovi started, but I ignored him, charging after my enemy.

I'd spent too many lonely nights weeping for my mother, longing to know who'd stolen her from me. I'd made too many passionate vows to honor her memory and slay her killer, if I ever had the chance.

Kovi seized my wrist, halting me mid-flight.

"Let go of me!" I snapped, my hair whipping across my cheeks as I spun to meet his eyes.

Pain flashed across his face, there and gone again in an instant. Even when his plans fell apart, even in the midst of battle, he was ever the disciplined soldier, reining in his emotions and concealing weaknesses an enemy could exploit.

"Incoming!" Rhi'il shouted, just in time for Kovi and I to spin toward the Alrenian woman launching toward us, her bloody sword lifted over her head.

Her cry was feral as she slashed for Kovi's neck, but I was faster. I leapt forward, slamming my palms against the torso she'd left exposed during her jump. My hands met hardened battle leather, but that was no match for my curse. My power flowed through me greedily.

The woman was dead—a mangled, unrecognizable corpse—before her body hit the ground.

Kovi

"You need this more than we do," I said, seizing the blade from beside the dead woman and tossing it to Rhi'il.

For a moment, his face was blank, his eyes studying Jalie with renewed uncertainty. Assessing an enemy.

"Rhi," I repeated, and he shook his head, rushing to my opposite side, letting me be the barrier between Jalie and him.

Together, we spun as the Teramese guards Jalie had filled with terror recovered, charging toward us as one. This time, either because she was weary or distracted or because she wanted to finish them off, Jalie didn't use that power of fear. Instead, she thrust herself into the fight fearlessly, dodging swings and blows and ducking low to touch her hands to our enemies and end them. She fought without a weapon, using her curse alone.

With my training, I could hold my own with just a dagger against swords. Rhi'il fought fiercely, each step, each thrust, each parry an elegant move as graceful as I'd ever seen.

The three of us made short work of the Teramese guards and the others—Teramese and Alrenians alike—who hurled themselves toward us.

In only minutes, I found myself scanning the dais and realizing there were only bodies with us. At some point in the chaos, Revaed, the Forwyn officiant, and the Elders had vanished. Maybe they'd dove into the fighting or had already been killed. Or maybe they'd fled.

My eyes narrowed as I searched the courtyard for them, my gaze flitting over far too many Forwyn corpses. Some of my people had claimed weapons and were fighting back, but too many were defenseless.

Something struck Jalie's temple, dropping her to the floorboards, which groaned as she struck. She lay motionless, blood trickling from the wound.

Triumph that wasn't my own slammed into me, giving away my father even before I whirled around and watched him appear. Sneering, he pulled back his fist.

Rage turned my vision hazy. The *coward*, striking out at his enemy when he was invisible. Apparently, he was more experienced in Elhani's magic than I'd realized.

"Why fight alongside that Alrenian abomination?" he demanded, his eyes darting between Rhi'il and myself. "You took a vow to serve your people. Do it now and fight alongside the Forwyn and the Teramese who just bound themselves to us." His eyes bored into mine. "This is your last chance, son, before I declare you a traitor and let the emperor execute you."

Lo

Caesiem and I fought our way through the fray, ducking and swinging and slicing at feral-looking Alrenians who threw themselves with terrifying skill at their foes. Their eyes were nearly entirely black and eerily emotionless, their bodies already red with their victims' blood. Black, scale-like growths marred portions of their skin, looking a lot like whatever was on Jalie's arm.

Over and over, Caesiem called upon the sea, its foaming waves surrounding us in a vicious whirlpool that kept our enemies back. Anyone who stepped too near got caught up in its pull, finding themselves tugged too far in and gasping for breath. I didn't let my gaze linger as they kicked and fought, drowning on land.

I had one focus, one mission.

Relief flooded me as Karos stepped forward, knocking the last of the Alrenians between us out of the way with a sweep of his powerful head.

"We have to get these Forwyn out of here," I told Caesiem, shouting to be heard over the din of battle, even though he was right next to me. "Too many of them are children. Follow me."

I lifted my arms to climb onto Karos when the ground rumbled, a crack forming that was just wide enough to tip me off balance.

Behind me, Darix chuckled darkly. "I don't think so, princess. You're not stealing away on one of *our* dragons."

Kovi

My laughter was mirthless. At my side, Rhi'il was tense, staring daggers at the man who was supposed to be my father.

"That is your choice, *Father?*" I managed, nearly choking on the title as I knelt next to Jalie, cradling her in my arms and checking her pulse. It beat steadily against my fingers. Her eyes fluttered, filling me with relief.

Elder Ettonou cast another glance at Jalie and scowled. His bitterness was so strong, I couldn't push it aside. It was an all-encompassing poison shuddering through me. "If you've chosen to side with her, you're no son of mine."

Rhi'il cast me a look, one burning with indignation, but I refused to let my hurt show. "I once was proud of our Elders," my friend bit out, taking a step closer to my father, "but if all that's left of them are other men and women just like you, I'm ashamed. I've fought and bled alongside Kovi, and he's nothing but honorable and kind and dedicated.

The opposite of *you*. If he says the empress is worth protecting, I believe him. I'm honored to call him my brother."

The Elder drew his sword. His expression was eerily blank, as if he had shoved aside all emotions but his undying quest for revenge and power. As much as his feelings had overwhelmed me before, now they were muted. Dulled. It was almost as disorienting as their earlier strength had been.

"I'll execute you both myself for your treasonous actions, and then kill the monster you defend before she wakes."

His sword slammed into Rhi'il's as the two clashed furiously, Elder Ettonou proving to be shockingly adept. It was clear I'd inherited my tall, muscular frame from him, and perhaps even my natural agility in battle. His steps were assured, his every motion graceful and confident and strong. Maybe he'd practiced daily in the palace training rooms. Maybe he'd unleashed his pent-up anger there, when he hadn't been taking it out on Jalie…

A pair of Alrenians tore up the steps toward Jalie and me, their dark eyes fanatical. Leaping to my feet, I flung my dagger at the first man's face, imbedding it in his eye. He collapsed in a heap as the woman charged. I ducked beneath her blade and dove, coming up in one smooth motion with the dead man's sword.

She spun and growled at me, an animalistic sound that sent a chill down my spine. These soldiers had given their allegiance—their very souls—to the Dark Immortal, and it was changing them. They hardly seemed human anymore. Instead, it was as if they were Nesrelle's puppets, mindless pawns only bent on killing.

A cry dragged my attention away from my foe. Rhi'il had been drawn away from Elder Ettonou, instead surrounded by two of the remaining Elders and Revaed. Though he was outnumbered, he was holding his own.

But he wasn't the one who'd cried out.

Jalie was awake, pinned beneath Elder Ettonou. One of his knees dug into her chest as he pressed his sword against her neck.

Lo

One of the palm trees at the edge of the courtyard tipped and swayed, crashing straight toward Karos and me.

With a snarl, Karos launched forward, extending his wings to envelope me—right before the tree collapsed. I felt it slam into him, its impact shuddering through his body and rocking the earth. Beneath my dragon, the world was dark, the growing stench of smoke and even the screams from the fighting dulled.

Panic seized me. "Karos?" I asked, brushing a hand against his warm scales. "Are you all right?"

Karos snorted gently, lifting a wing and turning his head to peer at me. With a mighty shake, he knocked the tree off him, sending it rolling to the ground, where fighters jumped and dodged to avoid its path.

"Thank Elhani," I breathed, throwing my arms around Karos.

Karos huffed, the most embarrassed sound I'd ever heard a dragon emit.

"I know," I said, grinning as I pulled back and met Karos's eye. "I like you too."

Turning, I found Darix and Caesiem squaring off. Darix's eyes gleamed, his expression taunting and eager. I had the impression he'd been waiting for a chance like this for years, longing to prove he was better than the orphan-turned-heir. Longing to overcome Caesiem's revered water magic with his earth magic and prove that he was worthy of a higher station of honor among his people.

"Caesiem!" I called out.

Caesiem's soaked clothes clung to him, highlighting his every muscle. His dark hair was plastered to his forehead and curled near his ears, dripping into his eyes and forcing him to blink against the salt. But there was no fear on his face, only concentration. Resolve hardened his jaw as he lifted his hands, pulling on both water and the blood that puddled in the courtyard. It swirled in a murky, pink wave that was both horrifying and mesmerizing.

"Go on, Lo," he said without turning back to me. "Get as many as you can out of here. I'll take care of Darix."

There was a threat in his tone, and I didn't argue. I leapt atop Karos, urging him forward, even while the earth quaked and rumbled again as the two mages clashed.

Caesiem

"Filthy traitor," Darix spat at the same instant one of the decorative boulders from the gardens vaulted through the air—straight for me.

Throwing up a wall of water, I pushed it back toward the soldier, forcing him to dodge.

"Emperor Revaed gave you everything. A home, a future, an *empire?*" Darix sneered, as if the very sight of me disgusted him to the core. "When you became his heir, you pledged yourself to Teramyl, and yet you're throwing your lot in with your little Forywn whore?"

Fury crackled within me, as powerful as any of the flames raging in the city below. I sent another wave of water crashing toward Darix, so vicious it roared in my ears as it churned forward. He responded with a stomp that rent the earth at my feet in two, cracking cobblestones and throwing me to the ground.

Nearby, men and women locked in the fray cried out, toppling over or sliding on stones slick with blood and sea water.

"You wouldn't even be anything or anyone if it weren't for charity and luck," Darix shouted.

I leapt to my feet and spun to meet him as he stalked forward. Two could play this game.

"Was it luck that slew the dragon that day?" I asked. An Alrenian screamed an animalistic battle cry and lunged, splattering me with gore dripping from his blade. I flicked my wrist at him, a single thought slamming bloody water into his face, swirling and raging, following him even when he tried to flee it. Drowning him. He collapsed somewhere near my feet, but I was already moving forward, my gaze locked onto Darix.

Darix scoffed, opening his mouth as if to speak. His eyes, though…they lingered on the corpse.

Deep down, he was afraid of me.

I cut him off before he could gather his words. "Was it luck that helped the Teramese armies overthrow Alrenor?"

He gritted his teeth, eyes flashing with rage as he turned back to me.

Darix was a powerful mage, but shifting the earth and uprooting trees took an enormous amount of focus and energy, even with the pendant hanging from his neck.

But my magic?

Even without a pendant to magnify my power, the sea was a part of me, like a natural extension of my body, a piece of my soul. It was home. Each time I called to it, it called back to me. It was as easy as breathing.

And the water always took care of its own.

I stopped right in front of Darix, who couldn't quite conceal the trembling in his body. "Was it luck that slew our enemies, time and again, without even lifting a blade?"

Darix curled his shaking hands into fists. "Then put aside your magic and fight me like a man, on equal footing." His sword hissed as he unsheathed it.

I grinned, drawing my own weapon. "All right. No magic. No cheating."

Darix pointed his sword at me, matching my smile with a nasty one of his own. "And when I've finished killing you, I'll take my time dealing with that unnatural Forwyn witch of yours."

Kovi

The words were out of my mouth before I could consider the consequences, Elhani's magic heeding my summons immediately.

"Get off her," I commanded.

His movements jerky, eyes wide with horror, Elder Ettonou staggered to his feet, blinking at Jalie's prone form. She stirred, a thin line of blood trickling down her neck.

"Drop your weapon."

His sword clanged to the dais, and he turned to me, mouth silently pleading. His fear and rage and desire for vengeance once again became my own, but I could endure them. To protect Jalie, I would endure anything.

Elder Ettonou had made it clear that he would gladly slay both me and those I cared about for his own gain. Thoughts of mercy had disintegrated in the fury consuming me. This snake of a man was not my leader *or* my father.

The memory of him seizing Jalie and dislocating her finger came back to me with vivid clarity. I could still see the bruises he'd left on her. The way Jalie had spoken of Elder Ettonou, it sounded as if those were only two of countless occurrences when he'd abused his power and taken out his wrath on her in dishonorable ways, making her life miserable. Relishing every chance he had to torment her.

My words came out sharp and clipped. I'd make him suffer. "Break your finger."

Elder Ettonou's nostrils flared, but his hand did my bidding, snapping the index finger of his right hand. He groaned in agony. Fear lanced through me, chilly enough to cool my bitterness.

As quickly as his rage had seized me, I regained control. I shook my head, forcing Elder Ettonou's feelings to crawl to the back of my mind. I couldn't let his hatred and vengeance become mine. Already, remorse flooded me when I studied Elder Ettonou's broken finger. As much as he deserved the pain, he was still my father. And I had more important things to do than waste my time on him.

"I should have Jalie give me an account of every injury you inflicted on her, and have you dole them out on yourself," I said, fisting my hands as I stared into his wild, fearful eyes. "But I don't want revenge, only justice." My eyes flicked to the sword at his feet, considering. "The way I see it, *you* are the traitor to your people. *You* aided in the attack on Aerekni Academy, and because of that, countless of my brothers and sisters lost their *lives*. My cousin Marukio—Mother's nephew—is dead because of *you*. Tell me, *Elder*, what would be the just punishment for such crimes?"

He trembled, cradling his broken finger and studying me warily. He knew exactly what the punishment for treason would be, both under Alrenian and Forwyn rule. "Son," Elder Ettonou said, his voice cracked. Broken. But there was only fear and hurt for himself in his emotions. Not remorse for what he'd done to me or anyone else.

I ground my teeth. "You made it clear how you feel about me. *Never* call me that again."

"Your mother always believed in mercy," he went on.

This time, all my years of discipline could barely contain my roiling anger. How dare this man bring up my mother? "You want to speak of mother and what she believed in *now?*" I stalked closer to the Elder, glaring at him. "You never cared to consider her when Jalie was the one in need of mercy, but you want to use Mother as leverage against me when you're the one wanting compassion?"

"Kovi," Elder Ettonou barked, "as a soldier, I know you seek to do the honorable thing."

"What is the honorable choice here, Father?" I demanded, not quite able to stop the pain from slipping into my words. It hurt, staring into his eyes and knowing he cared about power and greed and his own desires more than he'd ever cared about Mother or me. It hurt to see that the man I'd longed to build a relationship with was nothing but a worm. It hurt to know that, after all, I really was an orphan.

"Kovi," he said again, his tone weakening, once again turning pleading.

I stepped back, disgusted with his cowardice. It tasted sour on my tongue, and I hated that I had to feel it with him. "I'm not going to kill you. By blood, you *are* still my father."

"Thank you," he whispered.

Glancing back at Jalie, who was sitting up now, wiping blood off her temple and blinking dazedly at me, I drew a deep breath. Considering my next words. Determining what the right thing to do would be. Could I really let Elder Ettonou go free?

A scream of agony ripped my attention away, back to Rhi'il fending off his attackers.

One of the Elders lay dead, sprawled across the floorboards in a pool of blood with her eyes staring emptily at the clouds of smoke creeping across the sky, up toward the palace. The other Elder had vanished, perhaps pulled back into the rest of the fighting.

But Revaed...

Revaed had gained the advantage, somehow pinning Rhi'il to the wooden boards with a dagger shoved straight through his arm. Raising his sword, he loomed over my friend, a strange expression of disgust and determination sharpening the lines of his jaw.

"Rhi'il!" I shouted, leaping forward, my mind scrambling to refocus my thoughts, to hear Elhani's song, to scream a command that would stop Revaed.

The emperor shoved the blade into Rhi'il's heart.

CHAPTER FIFTY-TWO

Lo

The ground quaked from Darix's attacks as I hurtled toward the edge of the courtyard. Although I knew Father had hoped to free all the dragons, both the Alrenians and Teramese had overwhelmed our soldiers, cutting them off from the creatures. I didn't know where the keys to unchain the others were, didn't know if there was any way we could get to them when the Alrenians had so quickly rushed in, fearlessly pressing Forwyn and Teramese alike back from the dragons.

Earlier, in the shadows at the garden's edge, I'd caught a glimpse of fleeing Forwyn. But now the fighting had spilled into the area. Some men and women crouched behind trees or decorative boulders, trying to hide, while others clashed against Alrenians in the open, dodging shrubbery and trampling the once-stunning flowers lining the path.

It was easy to plow my way through the battle atop Karos. Our biggest challenge was to avoid trampling allies as I spurred him forward. He snarled at a cluster of Alrenians still near the gates who'd drawn bows. Arrows sang through the air, whooshing over the fighting as the soldiers aimed for Karos. He snapped at the projectiles easily, his powerful jaws crunching them in half before they could find their mark. Only one made it through, bouncing harmlessly off his scaled side.

As soon as we reached the garden's edge, where palm trees crowded the narrow path, I dismounted, flinging myself to the ground with one hand still clutching the sword I'd stolen. "*Werik*," I called to Karos, commanding him to wait in Alrenian, the language all dragons had been taught since they were hatchlings.

A group of Forwyn boys and girls, the oldest appearing to be fifteen and the youngest only twelve, were hiding among a small grove of palms trees. They were still close to the fighting, and not well hidden. Clearly they'd all been too young when we'd gained our freedom to become as talented as I had at sneaking around as a slave—a trait that had been all too necessary for my survival.

Glancing over my shoulder, my eyes scanned Karos. He was a large dragon, but without a saddle that could strap riders in securely, I wasn't sure more than three at a time would be able to ride safely. And there were at least ten children hiding. I turned back to the boys and girls, the foremost of whom—a girl of about fourteen—met my eyes, her own expression pleading. Her gaze flicked to two Alrenians prowling through the gardens, the blood of the Forwyn they'd just murdered dripping off their blades.

Whirling toward them, I set myself on the path between them and the hiding children.

My hands were steady and my breathing even as I secured my grip on my sword and settled into a fighting stance. Once again, my anger cleared my mind, helping me focus on Elhani's song and my purpose. *Protect these innocent boys and girls. Get them out of here.*

The soldiers' gazes locked onto me, and they launched forward, weaving around trees and plants to meet me on the path.

"Maybe you'll put up a better fight than the others," the woman said, her dark hair coiled atop her head, one side of her gold-toned neck and face marred by black scales climbing from her collarbone to her temple. When her eyes met mine, all I saw were pits of emptiness. A chill raced down my spine.

The man, his entire throat covered in scales, chuckled in response as his eyes scanned me from head to toe. "Doubtful," he said, lifting his sword.

The world seemed to shudder and alter, shadows shifting through the garden around us like living beings. I blinked, scanning the movements warily, wondering if other soldiers were creeping up, trying to ambush me.

A scream rent the air and my blood went cold. *Thud. Gurgle.*

They were the sounds of a throat being slit, of a body hitting the earth as someone left their victim to choke in their own blood as their life spilled out of them.

My head whipped to the side just as Empress Karye stormed out of the shadows, marching down the path straight toward me. There was murder in her eyes as she drew her dagger, glinting gold in the dim light. Torchlight flickered on her face, casting her in an orange glow, adding to the wicked, bloodthirsty gleam in her eyes…

As if from nowhere, Edi leapt out between us.

All it took was one swipe of Karye's blade.

A strangled cry echoed through the air, and it took me a moment to realize it was my own.

Not real, I thought, even as my hands shook and my body seemed to freeze, turning to ice.

This was in the past.

You failed me, Edi said, suddenly on his feet again, glaring at me. His neck was a bloodied ruin. At his side stood Naina and Eloiyah and

Jo'elli, all scowling. *You failed us,* they whispered.

Somewhere, as if from far away, there was laughter. Taunting. The Alrenians were jeering at me, enjoying this moment as I quaked with fear and despair, reliving my darkest nightmares, my deepest failures.

But I'd walked with these terrors as my constant companions for years, and that meant, time and again, I'd faced and defeated them. They hadn't overcome me yet, and they wouldn't overcome me now.

Not. Real.

With a cry, I turned back toward the Alrenians, straining my ears for the faint notes of Elhani's song. *Come back to me.* It did, filling the air until I could no longer hear Edi's accusing voice, until I could no longer detect Karye's footsteps stalking me like I was her prey.

Magic swirled within me, a powerful, uncontainable whirlwind. When I opened my mouth to speak, the air turned electric, crackling around me with a presence far mightier than my own. "Leave," I demanded. "Drop your swords and flee."

The soldiers' expressions turned from gloating to terrified in an instant. Their swords slammed to the earth as they turned, racing down the path as if their lives depended on it. They charged straight into Karos, whose waiting jaws rent them both in moments.

Heart pounding, I spun back toward the hiding Forwyn.

"We'll have to do this over several trips," I explained, meeting the eyes of the girl I'd noticed before. She nodded gravely. "Karos can fly three of you at a time to safety."

Several of the boys and girls glanced warily at the dragon, whose snout was darkened with his victims' blood.

"Don't be afraid," I said. "He knows you are friends. He'll keep you safe. But we need to hurry."

Caesiem

Years ago, when I'd first been taken into the palace and my skill in both magic and fighting had been questionable, a group of mages around my age had cornered me, beating me. They'd made it clear they thought I was worthless, that my defeat of the attacking dragon had been mere luck and I'd never have control of my power. They'd thought I was undeserving of Revaed's attention, that I was nothing but a charity case. They envied and hated me, and they wanted me to fear them.

But rather than instill fear, they'd awoken my desperate side, the side of me that had kept me fighting when I was half-starved and stealing for food. The side of me that strove for security, for survival, for a place in this world that I could call home, above all else.

When Revaed had asked me their names, I'd trusted him. He'd banished them from the palace, and I'd known then I never needed to let another fellow mage intimidate me. But I didn't want to always depend on Revaed to survive, so I threw myself into my training, vowing I would never be cornered and bested like that again, without a clue how to defend myself.

To live, I would master the powerful magic thriving within me, and I would learn to wield a blade with enough ability to inspire fear in others.

And all that time, whether because he'd seen other mages disappear at Revaed's bidding or because he'd seen me master my skills, Darix had kept his hatred reined in. He hadn't ever tried to attack me as the other mages had, not outright. Instead, he'd limited himself to cutting remarks, backhanded compliments, and threats that were just small enough to be overlooked or brushed aside.

Now, as our swords slammed against one another with such force my bones vibrated, it was clear that Darix was releasing years' worth of pent-up rage. I ducked and dodged his strikes, keeping my focus on my goal. Stop him. Survive. End him.

Though Darix had brute strength on his side, his fury made him sloppy. He swung fast and wide, making it easy for me to sidestep, and opening his body up for a counterattack.

I met him blow for blow, biding my time, watching his weak spots and letting him unleash his energy. With how swiftly he was expending it, I knew I could outlast him easily, the same way I could continue calling on magic far longer than he was able to.

Sweat beaded his face as he narrowed his eyes and leapt forward again and again, trying to push me back toward the wall. Trying to hem me in. As he lunged high, aiming for my neck, I swung low, my blade biting into his thigh before he could jump back. He moved before my sword could cut deeply, but it was enough.

I'd drawn first blood.

Biting back a grunt of pain as blood spilled down his leg, darkening his pants, he came for me again. We clashed together, swords blinding in the sunlight. As more smoke clouds roiled overhead, most of the daylight winked out, washing the courtyard in twilight dimness. Making it easier to focus on my opponent. Blood trailed him while he moved, each of us circling and lunging like we were partners in a strange, deadly dance.

Countless times, Darix had been squared off against me in sparring sessions. We'd exchanged blows as often as we exchanged barbed words. But that had been with the understanding that, like it or not, we were on the same side.

Not anymore.

I struck again, another shallow wound to Darix's side.

With a snarl, he stepped back, and the earth shuddered. At first I thought it was the chained dragons behind us, still fighting to free themselves and either join the fight or flee.

But then I felt the dip as the earth fell out from beneath my feet, shoving me off balance. I swallowed back a cry when I found myself teetering on the edge of a crack in the earth leading to a yawning pit. My heart slammed against my chest, anger and panic comingling within me.

All around, fighters cried out, some screaming as they toppled into the crack while others leapt away, circling around to rejoin the battle.

I'd thought Darix had worn himself out, but I'd underestimated him.

"Cheat," I shouted, but Darix just laughed, stepping forward to seize me by my shirt collar. Probably in the hope to rip the leather cord that held my pendant from my neck. His eyes widened when he found only bare skin, no water pendant.

"No matter," he muttered, shoving me before I could retaliate.

I flailed, my blade falling from my hand and clattering to the ground as I dropped into the pit.

Jalie

For a moment, the world swayed, pain pounding in my head as I reached up and found warm blood on my temple. The cut on my neck was inconsequential, but the blow to my head had made me lose consciousness for an instant, and I knew that was an injury that could seriously disorient me in a fight.

But no sooner had I had the thought than Nesrelle's voice echoed in my head, filling me with her power. *Kill.* The pain vanished, a frenzy for the battle taking its place, strengthening me with a burning fire.

I leapt to my feet, rounding on Elder Ettonou, who was trying to slip away, sneaking toward the steps leading off the dais and into the courtyard where the battle raged.

A part of my heart cracked a little as I glanced over my shoulder toward Kovi, who was lunging for Revaed. Too late. Revaed slammed his blade into Kovi's friend, and I knew it was a death blow.

Focus, Nesrelle snapped.

Twisting back, I caught sight of Elder Ettonou racing through the crowd in the courtyard below, sliding on bloodied cobblestones and ducking beneath swinging blades. Heart pounding in my ears, I launched down the steps after him, slamming my palms against anyone who jumped in my way. Screams rang out as I toppled soldiers with a single touch. They collapsed in pain, shrieking until my curse consumed them.

Daedra herself leapt out at me, swinging her blade, half her face gleaming with scales. But I barely noticed. My vengeance against her would come later. I dodged and kept running.

My entire focus was on Elder Ettonou, the man who'd made my life for the last three years a living hell.

Now it was his turn.

Yes, Nesrelle breathed. *Make him taste the pain you felt.*

I caught up to him as he creaked open one of the doors to the palace, scrambling into the main hall. Hearing my footsteps, he spun around, eyes widening. He cradled his broken finger against his chest as he stopped, his face twisting in a sneer. But his hatred and disgust couldn't conceal his terror. He knew I had him cornered.

"I told you someday you wouldn't have your Council or the dragons to help you," I said, stalking forward, each one of my words precise. "I told you I'd make you suffer."

Elder Ettonou's throat bobbed as he swallowed, eyes darting about the hall as if seeking an escape. There was no one else around, no one here who could aid him. And his own son had commanded him to drop his weapon, leaving him defenseless.

He was finally stripped bare of everything that had made him horrible and powerful, and now he was nothing but a small, writhing worm.

I laughed. Or maybe it was Nesrelle, laughing through me, relishing the pain and fear radiating off our victim.

"Please," he whispered, voice tremulous. "Your people—they

didn't see any honor in striking down an unarmed enemy. Face me honorably. Like your warriors of old."

"Like you faced me, leaving bruises and breaking bones when I was a mere child?"

Elder Ettonou flinched and stumbled back. "Please, I'll do anything," he whimpered.

"There's only one thing I want you to do."

His back struck the wall and his pleas turned to hysterical shrieks. I ignored them, hoping he listened to my words through his shouts.

"I want you to know," I murmured as the space between us dissolved, "that I've thought of this moment for years, when you slaughtered my people in brutal ways. When you tormented me. But you never broke me. You only made me stronger."

When I extended my hand, placing it on his arm, my gesture was gentle, almost tender.

After all, this man had also granted me my greatest gift. He'd helped me embrace the power Nesrelle had given me. He truly had made me stronger.

Now, his terror and agony made *us* stronger.

And his screams were music to our ears.

Lo

Karos landed after his first trip of flying the children to safety when the ground rumbled and shook again, nearly jostling me to the earth. Snorting, Karos shuffled as I rushed forward, watching cobblestones split in two—right where Caesiem and Darix were locked in battle. My heart lurched to my throat as Caesiem teetered on the brink.

I leapt on Karos's back, and he launched into the air before I could even shout the word to fly. It was as if he sensed my urgency. He knew Caesiem was a friend and ally, knew we had to save him.

The air tugged at my curls and pulled them free as Karos spread his wings and launched forward. We soared over the battlefield, screams of friends and foes clamoring in my ears. My eyes landed on Father and other academy soldiers fending off a small horde of rabid Alrenians. My chest tightened. I longed to be everywhere, aiding everyone.

As we dipped lower, my eyes snagged desperately on Caesiem. *Hold on,* I thought. *For just one more moment, hold on.*

Darix shoved and Caesiem collapsed into the pit. A scream tore from my throat. We wouldn't be fast enough. It was too late.

With a snarl, Karos dove and lunged for Darix, who was gloating, staring into the pit at his falling enemy. He didn't turn until the last moment. There was just enough time for him to shout in horror before Karos's wide mouth engulfed him. I turned as the dragon bit down, silencing Darix's scream.

And then we were dropping, the darkness rushing up to meet us as Karos tucked his wings against his body. He dipped until I started to slide forward, and for an instant, I was sure I'd lose my grip and free fall off him. I squeezed, every muscle in my legs and arms aching. I clutched one of his spikes in my fingers so tightly my hands went numb. My breath caught in my lungs, and I couldn't have screamed even if I'd wanted to. I couldn't think beyond my desperate need to hold on, to survive, to rescue Caesiem and make it back to the surface.

Then, as abruptly as we'd dropped, Karos's wings snapped open wide, the tips rustling and scraping against stone. Air churned and rushed around us as his muscles strained, flapping his wings with every ounce of power in his body. My hair slapped my cheeks and stung my eyes. I blinked back tears, daring to peer over Karos's side now that we were rising slowly upward, angled horizontally enough I could lean without falling off.

A rush of relief surged through me at the sight of a figure caught in

Karos's claws. I nearly sobbed aloud as my dragon rose back to the surface, depositing Caesiem onto the cobblestones.

"Caesiem!" I leapt off Karos's back, throwing my arms around him.

He drew me close, burying his face in my hair. "I love it when a beautiful woman worries about me," he breathed, his warm breath tickling my ear. The same words he'd once said when we'd first met and I'd demanded to walk him home.

I laughed aloud and pulled back, scanning him for injuries before my gaze settled again on his face. There wasn't time to waste, but just for a moment, I let myself relish being in his arms. Having him safe.

Caesiem grinned, relief bringing a joy to his face and sparkle to his eyes I hadn't seen in too long. For an instant, the burdens he carried seemed to fall away, his shoulders no longer slumped. The darkness in his gaze retreated.

A shout pierced the air as more Alrenians and Teramese surged forward, rounding the crack Darix had created. Most of the Teramese held back, fear widening their eyes when they realized Karos was free and encircling me protectively, but the Alrenians hurtled themselves forward recklessly. Their minds were locked on one thing only: slaughter.

My eyes shifted uneasily from them to the gardens. They were far too close to the remaining children.

Caesiem tensed, his body preparing for another fight, his gaze tracking mine.

"I have to get the children to safety," I said, reluctantly tugging myself from his arms, my smile fading.

He kissed me, once, the softest brush of his lips. "Go," he urged. "I'll hold them off."

I charged back toward the garden, Karos on my heels. A stray Alrenian leapt from the shadows where he'd been crouching behind a bush near the palace doors, perhaps awaiting a moment such as this to ambush an unsuspecting victim. My sword was on the garden path, abandoned when I'd mounted Karos to save Caesiem.

Ducking the Alrenian's swing, I kicked him in the shin, distracting him more than hurting him. It was enough to make him pause, enough for me to press in close and land another kick to his groin, a punch to his throat. He reared back, and I ducked to seize one of the cracked cobblestones Darix had dislodged, hurling it at the man's head.

He collapsed, and I didn't wait to see if I'd knocked him unconscious. I didn't need to. Karos was right behind me, snarling viciously. I heard a scream and the snap of bones, enough to know that my dragon had ensured the man would never threaten me again.

Caesiem

Even my magic could weaken with this much use. The water churned and foamed around me, as much a protective barrier as a deadly weapon to drown my foes. But even as the bodies of the attacking Alrenians piled up, I could feel my concentration slipping. My mind was tired, and my body was growing weak in response.

Sheer exhaustion was setting in. I dropped the water, letting it splash against the cobblestones and mist my face. The relief of releasing my magic was short-lived, because another cluster of Alrenians, at least half a dozen, was waiting for me as soon as my wall of water descended. They fought not only with weapons, but also with fire, throwing it toward me the way I could command water. The elements clashed in the air, steaming around us.

Seeming to grow tired of failing to burn me, the Alrenians raised their swords and pressed in closer. I drew my blade, meeting my first enemy, then the next, swirling and dodging as I fended off their strikes. A third edged closer, a fourth not far behind. They were spreading out, preparing to surround me, and I wasn't going to be able to keep holding them off forever. Sweat trickled down my brow, stinging my eyes.

A fifth Alrenian circled around, officially hemming me in. Together, the soldiers stepped closer, pressing forward, their blades swinging. I sent a weak spray of water toward one, but my focus faltered.

So tired.

A gust of wind slammed into the group, knocking over two of the soldiers and leaving them sprawled across the cobblestones. Another blast of air struck, sending a third off balance and giving me an opening to plunge my sword into his gut.

And then Vander was there, his silver eyes meeting mine as he rushed to my side.

For a moment, our enemies were disoriented, giving me a chance to catch my breath.

"Vander?" I asked, all astonishment. I hadn't seen him since Revaed and I had sent him on his mission to capture Jaliana. Had he seen me aiding Lo? Fighting Darix and some of the other Teramese who'd attacked me? Did he think I was a traitor?

"I'm with *you*," he said firmly.

I wasn't sure if that meant he knew the extent of my treachery against Revaed or not, but relief poured over me to have my friend at my side. The only mage and one of the few Teramese I'd ever trusted. It was good to know that my trust hadn't been ill-founded.

With a grin, I lifted my blade to meet the next surge of Alrenians.

Kovi

My world narrowed to a single point, a single focus. Revaed and his furrowed brow as he drew back his blade. Revaed as he tossed it with a clatter to the dais, sneering in disgust. Revaed as some of his soldiers, breaking free from engaging the Alrenians in the courtyard below, surged to the dais, surrounding him. Their blades glinted as they pointed them toward me.

Desperation and disbelief overtook me, followed by an overwhelming sense of numbness. Rh'il. My best friend. My brother.

How could I have been so distracted by my anger as to leave him to fight alone when he needed me most?

I'd been single-mindedly focused on protecting Jalie, on ensuring Elder Ettonou never laid a finger on her again. I'd allowed my sense of betrayal and grief and anger to blind me to everything else. I'd lost my focus.

First, I'd rushed thoughtlessly into the palace to save Jalie, bringing Rhi'il into this mess. And now…now I'd made another mistake.

The worst mistake.

Somewhere, vaguely, I was aware of emotions that weren't my own. Terror and desperation and pain. All-consuming and awful. But in my own shock, they were easy to ignore.

Instead, I felt nothing as I fended off soldier after soldier. Sweat trickled down my back. Blood splattered my face, grime and gore coating my hands, my clothes.

I felt nothing.

Nothing.

And while I fought the Teramese who charged me, others surrounded Revaed, ushering him off the dais and away, toward safety. The others held me off, preventing me from attacking their emperor or reaching my friend.

It must have only been moments later when I plunged my blade into the last soldier, but it felt like years had passed. I didn't care about more attackers as I dropped my sword and kneeled beside my friend. I was sick of battle. Sick of death. Sick of watching my brothers and sisters slip into the Golden After.

"Rhi'il," I breathed, grasping his shoulder.

Rhi'il was clinging to life by some final scrap of willpower, blood dribbling out of his mouth as he choked on air. Blinking up at me, he offered me a pained smile. "Do you think there's ale in the afterlife? I was really hoping for a celebratory drink after we won this."

My vision swam. "Yes, Rhi. For you? Of course there will be."

His breathing turned ragged, and he coughed weakly, more blood flowing from his lips. I wiped it away with my shirtsleeve, squeezing his shoulder.

"I wish I could have told Mio'e…how strong and brave she is." He coughed again. "Kovi? I'll…I'll…save a drink for you."

Rhi'il's eyes unfocused, his last strangled gasp leaving his body. His chest stilled. My hand trembled as I brushed my friend's eyes closed.

It felt like the blood coating my hands wasn't from my enemies, but Rhi'il. It felt like I'd been the one to drive the blade into his heart. It had been my mistakes that led to this.

I forced myself to rise to my feet, to stuff down the emotion threatening to seize me in its relentless grip. I was a soldier, disciplined into putting battle strategy and victory first, and grieving later.

Striding back across the dais, I lifted my sword and scanned the battlefield below, the dwindling number of people still left living to fight. Smoke was swirling up from the city in thicker clouds now, raining ash upon the blood-slick cobblestones. Dragons roared, tugging at their chains furiously, their eyes wide and gleaming, their nostrils flaring. They knew better than to breathe fire in this enclosed space when they were trapped, but their rage was palpable. They wanted to fight, to strike back at the people who'd chained them up.

A free dragon soared overhead, a flash of black and red before it vanished into the smoke. My eyes locked onto Ryke, also unchained and diving toward an enemy, scooping the soldier up in his claws and rising upward to drop him from a deadly height.

Jalie and Elder Ettonou were nowhere to be found. Fear raked talons down my back until my eyes snagged on a figure racing toward the steps. Her hands were coated in blood, the once-white bandages on her injured one stained with gore.

Climbing the last step, Jalie spun to survey the battle, as if she hadn't even noticed me. Her jaw was clenched with determination, her body poised and ready to fight. I noticed where her eyes lingered, all the way across the courtyard to where a form stood at the edge of the gardens.

Lo.

Jalie

I sensed Kovi approaching, but I didn't rip my eyes away from Lo'laeni.

Avenge your mother, Nesrelle whispered in my ears. *Feed your power even more. Kill her.*

I leapt forward, prepared to launch myself back down the stairs and through the battle, toward my target.

Kovi seized my wrist, holding me back, just as he had before.

"Please," he said, the slightest hint of a pleading edge creeping into his tone. "Don't do this. We're allies. You and me. You promised—"

"She *murdered* my mother," I said, tugging my arm with all my strength. Kovi's grip was vice-like, as strong as the shackles that had held me only moments ago. I didn't add that Lo had also been the one to save my life, the night of the Autumn Ball. I didn't want to think about that for fear it would dredge up guilt. I refused to feel guilty when revenge was within my grasp.

Honorable Alrenians didn't let the killers of their loved ones go free. They respected their loved ones' memories by avenging their deaths. It was justice.

It was the last act of love I could give my mother.

And with that thought, I deflated, letting my arm fall limp in Kovi's grasp. Tears swam in my vision, but I could see well enough to catch the concern scrunching his brow.

"Jalie," he whispered, his voice turning gentle, his grip going slack.

"*Empress,*" I retorted, yanking back my arm and fleeing.

It was time Lo'laeni accounted for what she'd done three years ago.

CHAPTER FIFTY-THREE

Karos had just launched himself into the air, the last of the Forwyn boys and girls on his back, when movement pulled my attention back to the courtyard.

Karye was charging toward me, her pale hair streaming behind her, her hands dripping blood as she dodged fighters and leapt onto the garden path.

I shook my head, clearing my thoughts. Not Karye. Jaliana.

Where her mother had stood tall and proud, Jaliana was unusually short for an Alrenian, matching me in height. Her gold-flecked blue eyes blazed with hatred, not yet consumed with darkness the way Nesrelle's soldiers' gazes were, but just as bloodthirsty. An angry red scar marred one cheek, looking like jagged cuts from a blade…or claws. Black scales traced her arm from her elbow to her shoulder. Her left hand was wrapped in a bandage coated in blood and gore.

My stomach roiled at the sight, at the visible proof of the nasty curse she carried and the horrific deaths she must have doled out in this fight.

Somewhere amidst the battle, she must have stolen a blade from a corpse. It appeared to be Teramese from the black hilt they favored, the steel smeared with gore. But she held it loosely at her side, probably more interested in using her hand to attack me with her curse than fighting with a sword.

"Lo'laeni Nolanhou," she said, stalking forward with her chin held high, her eyes flashing with her hatred. It was then I noticed the hole in one side of her armor. She'd clearly suffered much since she'd fled the palace, but there was no sign of the fear or vulnerability I'd seen darting across her face the night of the Autumn Ball.

I inclined my head, shifting my grasp on my blade. "Empress Jaliana," I said, smiling pleasantly, as if we were exchanging words at a party. "Yes, I am Lo'laeni."

She smirked. "I prefer Jalie."

I forced my smile to widen. "And *I* prefer Lo."

Eyes narrowing, she moved in closer, the fingers of her right hand twitching, as if she could hardly wait to slam her palm against my skin and watch her curse destroy me. "I figured you would prefer the title *amara'rekni*. It is the only thing that makes you significant, isn't it? The one thing that elevated your meaningless life to something of importance?" She sneered. "I want to hear you say it. Admit who you are, what you did."

Maybe I should have been afraid, but I was only angry. When I saw the blood dripping from this arrogant girl's hands, I saw a young woman following in her mother's path. I saw rows of fearful slaves. I saw a flashing dagger and bodies collapsing in their own blood. I saw Edi, stolen from the world too soon.

And when the anger flowed through me, it cleared my head. There was peace and calm inside me as my muscles tensed and my feet shuffled, prepared to fight. Elhani's song rippled around me, powerful and comforting. I knew what to do, just as I had when I'd come to face Revaed and all he'd planned for his prisoners and me.

Once, I'd quaked in terror of Empress Karye, but I wasn't that girl fighting for her life anymore.

Now I was a warrior, a daughter, a sister, a friend. And I was fighting for my people.

I wasn't afraid.

"My name is Lo Nolanhou," I said, voice strong and fierce, "daughter of Lai'ell. Your mother was a slave master to my entire family. She sent my father away before I could meet him, and my mother when I was young. She murdered my brother. And when she tried to murder me, I struck back and bought my freedom—my people's freedom—with her blood." I set my jaw. "I am the *amara'rekni*, and if I had to kill your mother all over again to protect my people, I would."

With a fierce cry, Jalie hurled herself at me, swinging her blade straight toward my throat. Steel shrieked as I brought my sword up to parry and shoved, pushing her back. We wove around trees and shrubbery and flowers as we clashed, each of us matching the other strike for strike.

Beneath the warm layers of fine clothes I wore, sweat trickled down my back. As we pushed back toward the courtyard, closer to the gate, I found its doors were broken, twisted like a giant had forced them open. But the true cause became apparent as a shadow fell over Jalie and me.

Ryke and Karos roared as they slammed into one another, all talons and fangs and flapping wings. Black and emerald scales flashed while they twisted, colliding and snapping at each other in midair. Jalie's and my battle had become theirs.

Each time I thought I was pressing an advantage, Jalie proved her expertise by moving in an unexpected way, dipping when I thought she would charge, sidestepping when I expected her to lunge. She'd probably been trained since birth, raised with a sword in her hand from the moment she could walk.

But I had years of hard training too, days of pushing myself to run until I couldn't take another step, to do pull-ups and square off in sparring matches until my skin glistened with sweat. I had experience from deadly altercations in the street, not just from trainers that I knew would never hurt me. Jalie's recent injuries spoke of true battles as well…but had she struggled to survive all her life? Did she know what it was to fight every moment, to walk with fear as a constant companion?

Most important of all, though, was the fact that I felt no fear now, whereas Jalie was a wild tangle of conflicting emotions. Rage and grief, terror and pain—she was like an uncontrollable fire that could just as quickly burn out as it could destroy me. She fought for revenge, but I fought for my people.

We drew closer and closer to the mangled gates, until we were locked in our fight right within their entrance, the walls hemming us in ahead and behind while the battle raged to my right and the city stretched out below. Its streets were flooded with men, women, and children all fleeing for their lives, corpses strewn across the ground, and wild Alrenians fighting Teramese soldiers and attacking citizens. For a moment, even Jalie staggered back from me, blinking at the terrible sight. Buildings and homes were burning, the flames turning the beautiful water channels ominous shades of red and orange. Deadly black smoke plumes coiled through the air, turning everything hazy until I had to squint my stinging eyes to see clearly.

A hole yawned in my chest. My people were down there too. Though I might have hated it as much as I loved it, this was *my* city, full of as many good memories as bad.

Jalie blinked back tears, whether from the thickening smoke or her own heartbreak, I wasn't sure.

"You weakened my empire!" she shouted, slamming her blade against mine with such force, I staggered. She struck again and again. "This never would have happened if Alrenians had the throne. We would have been strong. We would have seen the Teramese coming; we would have stopped them!"

Maybe I'd been wrong earlier, and her emotions were her strength, not her weakness. Her eyes sparked with determination, with conviction. She wasn't going to lose this chance at vengeance, not even if it cost her everything.

"I think it was already crumbling from your mother's poor choices," I snapped, landing a kick to her leg.

She grunted, rearing back and sneering through the pain.

"Your people lost their gifts," I continued. "And they'd spent years making cruel choices like the ones your mother made, until all the other peoples of the Great Kingdoms hated them. It wasn't just me or the Forwyn. The Misrothians joined with us. All because we'd had enough of Alrenian cruelty."

Jalie stared at me, her eyes darkening, eerily similar to the gaping blackness of the Alrenian soldiers' pit-like eyes. For a second, I thought I saw a flash of red hair and milky white skin, like *Nesrelle* was the one peering at me.

Just like with the soldiers before, past terrors assaulted me. Naina's body crumpled nearby, her neck gaping open, blood pooling from the wound. Her eyes blinked up at me. "You failed," she choked out. "You failed me."

Useless. Nesrelle's voice hissed in my ears, making horror snake through my heart. My knees locked; my breathing hitched.

Eloiyah was being murdered by Teramese again, right before my eyes. I could smell the blood, could feel it as it splattered across my face.

You've failed them all! Nesrelle's voice rose in pitch.

"No," I breathed, forcing my gaze upward, back to Jalie. She grinned as my legs buckled, as I struggled to keep myself upright.

Numbness shot through all my limbs and my grip slipped on my sword hilt. The world tilted and swayed, like everything was abruptly off-kilter.

Breathe. I remembered Naina's words, each time she'd talked me through one of these moments, when I'd been trapped in an endless cycle of nightmarish memories. *Listen to Elhani's song. Hear the notes. Feel his strength.*

I sucked in one breath, then another, focusing on how it felt to draw in air. Concentrating on how the smoke tasted on my tongue. How the ground felt, stable and unshifting, beneath my feet.

I caught a note of Elhani's song. Another. The more I strained to hear, the more I shoved all other terrors and thoughts aside, the louder and clearer the notes became.

My breaths evened out. My muscles strengthened, and my grip on my hilt tightened. I lifted my chin, straightening my spine…

But Jalie was already moving, taking advantage of my distraction. She slammed her good hand against my shoulder, her fingers digging into the fabric of my shirt, nails biting.

The instant seemed to stretch into an eternity as I gaped at her hand. Her curse seeped into me, a strange chill consuming my body, trailing icy fingers along my skin. My eyes met Jalie's—wide, triumphant—and raw horror cracked open inside me as I realized Nesrelle's words were coming to pass. I was useless. Again. I would die without seeing my people rescued, without helping my father win this battle, without wresting the empire from Revaed's greedy hands.

It was over.

I'd failed.

Caesiem

The Alrenians fought fiercely, recklessly, as if they didn't care what happened to them as long as they took out everyone around them. Though their numbers couldn't have been greater than fifty, they fought like a regiment ten times as large. Their strength was unnatural, and everywhere they went, they crippled their foes, tormenting us with our greatest fears until we were frozen on the battlefield. Some Teramese and Forwyn dropped to the ground, screaming, while others fled.

But my fears—my fears inspired me to fight harder. *Survival above all else.* Sometimes there was blood dripping from my hands, blood that could never be washed away. Other times Lo was crumpled at my feet, dead. And still others, I was driving a blade into Revaed's heart, meeting his violet eyes as they widened with disbelief and betrayal.

These fears, though, were ones I battled all the time now, without the help of the Alrenians' unnatural power. They were the fears that pushed me to lift my blade and keep swinging, to call on the water when I wasn't sure I had an ounce of strength left and keep sending it toward my enemies. They were the fears that inspired me to not only fight for my survival, but to also fight for Lo, to fight for justice, to fight for something better when this world was cruel and dark.

And then, across the courtyard, movement jolted my attention away from the Alrenian I'd just cut down. I wrenched my blade free from his chest and spun in time to see Lo and Jaliana locked in a swordfight, Lo's every movement strong and confident, matching the empress blow for blow. Still, uneasiness churned in my stomach at the sight. Lo could hold her own, but all it would take was one touch from Jaliana…

My eyes scanned the tumultuous fray between them and me. Bodies were piling up, Teramese soldiers and Forwyn—some who hadn't even managed to grab a weapon to defend themselves—along with the rare Alrenian. More Teramese were charging out from the palace, reinforcements rushing to provide help, but it was clear we were losing. And the smoke was curling closer, the air growing thick and cloying from the city burning below.

The capital was falling.

Countless more soldiers were still up and fighting, locked in a furious battle for their lives and clogging my path to Lo.

"Go!" It was Meli, charging up beside me to join Vander in pushing back another onslaught of Alrenians. Her leathers were smeared with blood, and the gold flecks in her dark eyes burned with determination. "Help her."

At her side was Valentra, whose expression was hard as she surveyed the damage the Alrenians were causing, shifting her bloodied blade from one hand to the other, since she was equally skilled with both.

Together, the women and Vander charged, opening a path for me. I raced forward, ducking strikes and dodging kicks, lifting my blade to block swings aimed for my neck, my chest, my legs. Leaping, I skidded across the slippery stones, bounding over bodies and circling around the crack in the earth Darix had opened up.

Overhead, Karos and an emerald green dragon slammed into each other, all claws and fangs and snarls as they grappled in the air.

"Jalie!" a Forwyn man clothed in an Aerekni uniform shouted. He was racing toward the women from the center of the courtyard, fighting his way forward just as I was.

And then, just ahead of me, Lo stopped, staggering, her expression terrified, her sword starting to slip from her hands…

"Lo!" My cry was ragged with desperation, tearing at my throat.

Sweat beaded on my forehead as I ground my teeth, fending off another strike and stretching my mind toward the sea. *Just this one more time. Please…*

Jalie launched herself at Lo, seizing her by the shoulder.

Revaed

The courtyard was burning, flames leaping from corpse to corpse to devour bodies, permeating the air with the stench of burning flesh. At some point, the Alrenians, who charged unharmed through the fire, had brought their torches up from the city, as if determined to burn us all alive. Fire licked at the plants and tree trunks edging the gardens, swiftly devouring. Black smoke filled the air, making it hard to see. The roar of flames was everywhere.

Even if the stone buildings of the palace couldn't burn—unless this fire was somehow as hot as dragon fire—there were plenty of living things around it that could, and the smoke was deadly enough. Ash descended from the skies, coating my hair as I turned to the guards hemming me in protectively.

"We can get you to safety, Your Majesty," one of them was shouting, but I shook my head.

"It's over! Order the retreat." I swallowed thickly, scanning for Caesiem. Failing to find him. I suspected he was at Lo's side, feared he was lost to me. But I wasn't sure, and seeing the biting flames with no sign of water fending them off—that terrified me most of all. "We must find Caesiem."

My gaze snapped to the thrashing dragons on the far side of the courtyard, all chained to the walls. They wouldn't burn. When they'd driven us all out, the Alrenians would unchain them. They would know how to tame the beasts, if not as the Forwyn had, then with vylae and brute strength as their ancestors had. And then they would burn us all, laying waste to everything. My people would be lost all over again, the land meant to be our sanctuary only turning into another tomb.

"And kill the dragons," I added.

My nearest soldier—Zalec—snapped wide green eyes toward me. "What?"

"Kill the dragons!" I shouted. "Now!"

As the others shoved me away, toward the back entrance of the nearest palace building, Teramese archers hastened to obey. My orders were repeated, sent across the perimeter. Any archers not engaged in a fight for their lives lifted their bows and shot. Arrows rained toward the beasts, smoke writhing around the missiles as they hit their marks. Some struck the creatures' scales and fell, but others pierced eyes or their open maws. Countless arrows landed and the dragons groaned and snarled, snapped and writhed, trying in vain to escape.

One by one, they fell. Dead.

A shame, I thought. But a necessary shame. Another hard choice to save my people. *For survival,* I reminded myself.

"Retreat!" the word was screamed in Teramese across the courtyard, echoing over death cries and the hair-raising, animalistic shrieks of the Alrenians. "Retreat!" It was the cry of defeat, a battering ram to my chest. It reverberated endlessly in my ears.

I'd failed. We would fight another day, but so many of my men and women had been lost, and more would be lost still in the coming battles. I wasn't sure where we could go, or what we could do against the terrifying power this army wielded. Unnatural. Horrible.

I scrabbled toward the courtyard, prepared to hurl myself around flames and over bodies to find Caesiem.

Two of my soldiers seized my arms, wrenching me back. Holding me. "I order you to—" I snarled.

"Stop!" Zalec shouted, cutting me off. "We can't run the risk of losing both our leaders. We have to get you out. We'll find him."

Lya stepped forward, saluting, her blue eyes fierce. "I promise," she said, her lithe form darting into the crowd, several more soldiers at her heels.

"Out! Now!" Zalec cried.

More Alrenians charged for our group, but my soldiers fought them back, a protective barrier between me and my enemies. They were in survival mode—choosing to defend me at all costs. It was no longer about my pride or my desire to serve my people in war. It was about living to see another day, about leading them forward through this disaster. And they would give anything to ensure I could fulfill that purpose.

Lifting my jacket collar over my mouth and nose, I slammed open the doors to the building housing the imperial living quarters. I led my soldiers down halls full of cracked statues and torn paintings, leaping and dodging over the debris toward the rooms that had once been Caesiem's and Lo's. Toward the secret entrance she'd shown me.

It was likely the market square it led to was just as overrun as the palace was, but it was our best hope at escape.

"You first," Zalec commanded as I pried open the door and peered into the darkness.

"You have to get the others out!" I snapped. "You have to find Caesiem!"

He nodded sharply. "And we will. But you are our leader. We also need to get you to safety, so you can lead us to victory another day." His eyes were fierce, unyielding.

My heart slammed against my ribcage, but my mind understood the wisdom in his words. After all, I'd just been thinking the same thing. The army was looking to me. My people needed me.

Gritting my teeth, I glanced back over my shoulder. "Zalec, I'm trusting you on this. All of you."

"I'm sending two soldiers with you," Zalec said, gesturing to a man and woman flanking him. "The rest of us will go back. We'll lead our soldiers to safety. We'll find Prince Caesiem. You have my word."

And with that, I led the retreat, my hands shaking as I descended the steps, promising myself this wasn't the end. Promising myself Caesiem would be all right. Promising myself my people would make it, no matter the cost.

Lo

A long moment passed as Jalie and I stared at one another, motionless. As I waited for death to claim me, for the horror of Jalie's power to overcome my skin.

But nothing happened. My heart continued to pound against my sternum, my blood rushing in my ears. My lungs continued to drag in breaths of smoky air, filling my mouth with its acrid tang.

I was alive.

Jalie reared back, shock and horror flaring in her eyes as she scanned me, seeking evidence the curse she bore was claiming me. She stared at her palm, her eyes flicking back to me.

I started to laugh.

"No!" she shouted, her voice cracking. She slammed both hands against my shoulders, again and again, while I kept on laughing.

"You *murdered* her! You shed Alrenian blood. It should claim you. It should take you!" Furious tears gleamed in her eyes. "It should kill *everyone* I touch. No one is immune, and especially not the guilty. Especially not *you*!"

I caught my breath, swallowing back my laughter just as Caesiem ran to my side. "Lo," he breathed, wrapping his arms around me and tugging me back, as if to yank me from Jalie's presence. "Are you all right?"

My gaze snapped back to Jalie, who was ghostly pale, looking as lost as I imagined I must have appeared only moments ago when she'd plagued me with my worst fears. "I'm fine," I said, my lips curving in another smile.

Caesiem was trembling with exhaustion, but still he managed to summon another wave of water, surrounding Jalie in a rushing whirlpool. It splashed and roared around her in an endlessly flowing circle, misting her face and plastering her golden hair to her cheeks. She cried out, trying to push through it, to no avail.

"Jalie!" Kovi charged forward, his expression taut, eyes darting between Jalie and Caesiem and me.

"I'll kill her," Caesiem snarled, releasing me to lift his blade and turn on Kovi, who'd thrown himself in front of Jalie, his own weapon raised to defend the empress. "And I'll kill you too if I have to. Step back."

"Caesiem," I interrupted sharply. "He's on our side."

Caesiem tensed, his body positioned between Kovi and me.

"He's my father's soldier," I continued. "You can trust him."

Kovi slowly lowered his blade. "Don't hurt her. Please." There was a pleading edge to his tone. Against all reason, somehow he truly did care for Jalie.

I gaped.

Caesiem's expression was grim, his blue eyes glowing with a feral light as he studied Kovi warily. "Give me one reason why she should live right now when she just tried to murder Lo."

Kovi's brow knotted as he glanced back to Jalie. "I..." His voice trailed off. "I'm not saying you shouldn't take her as a prisoner. Just don't hurt her."

Opening ber mouth, Jalie's eyes shot daggers at him, but whatever she'd considered saying, she thought better of it and clamped her lips shut. She seemed to realize that in this moment, fighting was useless, though her gaze threatened murder if we let down our guard.

Commotion interrupted us, drawing my eyes back to the courtyard. More Alrenians had flooded the battlefield, pouring in through a back entrance to the garden, the same way I'd arrived earlier. Though they weren't the first ones to come brandishing torches, they were the first to start turning the entire battle into an inferno. They set fire to the gardens, the corpses in the courtyard... They danced through the flames without being harmed, and they used their nightmarish powers to manipulate the fire to leap up tree trunks, swirl through the air, and burn flesh.

The scent was appalling, a sickly-sweet odor. Choking, I pulled my shirt up, trying to cover my mouth and nose. And then the Teramese began shouting in their language, words that I couldn't understand but that made Caesiem stand at attention, concern darting across his face.

Arrows surged from every direction...straight toward the chained dragons. The beasts roared and strained against their shackles, snapping at the projectiles launched toward them. Arrows snapped in half, devoured by the powerful creatures. But the volleys didn't stop, and the dragons had nowhere to go. They flapped their wings in vain, snarling their rage and fear and hurt.

More arrows hissed through the air, piercing dragon eyes and soft underbellies. Eliciting ear-splitting growls and groans. Felling the beautiful beasts, until one by one, they collapsed. The ground shuddered; the world tilted. The dragons writhed and struggled, some turning their heads up and unleashing a final mournful call to the unreachable sky. And then they seized. Still. Motionless.

Playful Torla, with her crimson scales. Quiet, loyal Ivez, his silver and blue colors a sharp contrast to the fire and smoke churning throughout the courtyard. Lithe, silver Ziltha, the first dragon I'd ever managed to draw near enough to touch. The first one I'd grown to trust when I'd tended to them as a slave. And the others... Every last dragon that had been chained within the courtyard lay dead.

All those proud, lovely, glorious animals—slain callously by the Teramese.

It took me a moment to realize I wasn't the only one screaming. Jalie's cries mingled with mine, full of horror and sorrow. She beat fruitlessly against the wall of water enveloping her, tears mingling with the sea splattering her face.

Overhead, Ryke and Karos stopped abruptly, dropping to the

courtyard to unleash a terrible sound I'd never heard dragons make before. It was like a keening wail, their heads lifted to the swirling black smoke as they mourned their fallen brothers and sisters.

"We have to get out of here," Kovi said, wrenching me from my grief and dragging my attention back to him.

"Where's Father? Our soldiers?" I choked out, frantically scanning the courtyard.

But as if my words had summoned him, Father was there, ash-streaked face drawn with weariness and sadness. A small host of soldiers were behind him, even some Teramese and Alrenians, fighting back foes.

"Retreat!" Father shouted. His eyes landed on me, relief filling his gaze. "Lo, take your dragon. Get out of here."

Caesiem turned back to Jalie, his complexion paler than usual, his shoulders slumped. "I can't hold her much longer. If we're not killing her, we need to secure her as our prisoner."

Kovi's voice was quiet, his eyes full of regret. "I will do it," he said, and as Caesiem dropped his wall of water, the soldier turned to Jalie. Powerful magic electrified the air, making the hairs on the back of my neck stand up.

Kovi's tone rang with Elhani's power when he spoke again. *Compelling magic.* I recognized it instantly from stories Naina had shared about it, but I'd never seen someone wield it before. "Jalie, you will *not* harm Lo or any other Forwyn. You'll come with us without a fight."

Jalie's eyes widened, her body trembling. "You…you promised," she stammered. There wasn't anger in her eyes anymore, only a terrible sorrow. The look of someone betrayed. "You promised to never command me like that again."

"And you made a promise to me too," he muttered bitterly, glancing at me. "A promise to not harm one of my people. Let's go."

Jalie glowered, pulling back, but Kovi's tone was firm, unrelenting. "Follow me."

Fists curled at her sides, the empress trailed after us stiffly, her movements clearly forced by Kovi's magic. Her eyes burned with defiance and pain. I forced myself to look away, surprised to empathize with the agony of betrayal I detected in Jalie's expression.

She'd just tried to kill me. I had no reason to pity her.

We ran to the dragons. Kovi approached Ryke warily, until the green dragon tilted his head in recognition and then dipped down low, inviting him to climb on. He lifted Jalie into his arms, who flailed and spat but couldn't truly resist—not while under his magic's influence. He deposited her effortlessly onto Ryke's back and swung up behind her. His expression was as hard and unreadable as stone as he slid his arms around her. Jalie stiffened, but a murmur from Kovi that I couldn't hear stilled her.

Meanwhile, Karos soared through the plumes of smoke rising off the battlefield, his gold eyes searching until they landed on me. He dropped before Caesiem and me, allowing us to leap onto his back. Caesiem clung to me tightly, his arms a welcome refuge in a world where everything felt horribly wrong.

As our dragons launched into the air, Father led survivors from the courtyard, fending off enemies as they went. Others carried the wounded, as many as they could rescue from the devouring flames. Even with the rush of wind in my ears, the screams of battle and the roar of fire still carried on the breeze.

I glanced back, only once, to see the capital—a city that had once been all ivory buildings, lush greenery, and shimmering water—now nothing but flame and smoke and ash.

CHAPTER FIFTY-FOUR

Nesrelle

All those lovely orange trees were burning, their trunks blackening, their leaves curling in on themselves and disintegrating into ash, and the delicious fruits they bore withering beneath the licking flame. Sighing, I swept through the wall of fire, waving my hand at the pesky smoke wreathing about me, and marched toward the nearest palace building.

The one that housed the throne room.

Everything else burned, but I'd ordered my army to leave the palace untouched. Well, mostly untouched. The location didn't hold any nostalgia for me—that was a mortal emotion I'd discarded long ago anyway—but it did seem a shame to let it all crumble to ash.

I'd want someone to rule from this palace eventually, after all.

The door groaned as I shoved it open and slipped inside, sneering at the painted scenes covering the high ceiling, full of inaccurate portrayals of the Life-Giver and myself. My bootsteps echoed on the marble floor as I stepped over the remains of Elder Ettonou.

His death had been especially potent, full of delicious pain and terror. So much terror.

In the end, he'd always been afraid of Jalie, even when she'd been nothing but a scared, motherless girl.

Shoving the last set of doors open, I strolled into the throne room, scanning the marble columns and the glass ceiling. Immaculate and pretentious, just like so many mortals liked their buildings.

Daedra and a handful of other soldiers already awaited me, standing at attention on either side of the black and ivory throne.

I flicked my fingers and my grimy battle armor vanished, replaced with a flowing gown in shades to match the imperial seat before me. When Daedra bowed and lifted her hands, the crown she offered no longer resembled the gaudy headdress of past Alrenian rulers, but the crown I'd crafted in my own imagination. Wrought of black metal and sharp edges, it was both lethal and elegant.

"Thank you," I crooned, plucking the crown from Daedra and plopping it on my head.

I paused, studying the throne for a moment. So many had died over this. And many more would still.

Turning, I sank back into the uncomfortable seat and rolled my eyes. For an empire known for its luxury, it seemed a pity they hadn't bothered to craft a plusher throne.

Daedra remained kneeling at my feet. "It is my pleasure to serve you, Your Imperial Majesty, Empress of Death."

They'd shoved Jalie into the ship's brig, where she sat slumped against the wall, her gold-flecked eyes staring at nothing, her pale hair a wet, limp curtain around her face. Her storm of emotions had been snuffed out as swiftly as a candle flame, but I knew it would return. This numb state was a minor setback, a way for her to reckon with her temporary loss.

"You did well," I said, striding across the slick floorboards and leaning against the wall. It was dim and dank down here, the endless motion of the ship and the stench of sea and fish considerably irritating. Another reason Jalie was so forlorn, perhaps.

She lifted her eyes to study me, the smallest hint of her hatred and anger smoldering in her gaze. "You burned my home." Her voice was raspy from weeping over the lost dragons, over the destruction of her city. She glared at her hands. "And when the time came for revenge, the gift you gave me *failed*."

I tsked. "I don't make the rules. Your Life-Giver did that. I suppose that means he doesn't think Lo'laeni was worthy of death yet." I shrugged. "Maybe he considered what she did to your mother to be self-defense." I sniffed.

"It was still a kill," Jalie snarled.

I grinned widely. "Oh, I agree. All that fear your mother felt as she slipped away into the afterlife…it was as powerfully intoxicating as the emotions I've fed on from any other death."

Jalie's eyes flashed, more of her fire returning. "Mother didn't fear death."

Listing my head to the side, I shrugged again. "Believe what you want."

"I hate you," she continued. "I want you to…" Her voice cut off as I slammed a wave of pain into her and spoke into her mind.

I don't care how you feel about me, you're mine. I stalked forward. "And," I continued aloud, "I know that as much as you hate me, you still hate

Miss Nolanhou more." I leaned forward, my lips twitching with a victorious smile. "I suspect you also hate that Forwyn soldier of yours too, for what he did to you. Using his magic to control you again?"

She cringed, reeling backward as if physically struck.

"You might as well give in to the bloodlust and power I've given you," I hummed, stroking her cheek. She grimaced but didn't pull back. She didn't have anywhere to go but into the wall. "I gave you more than a curse to use against him."

Jalie blinked up at me, considering. She was so naïve still, so young. If she'd seen the endless years I had, the fickleness of mortals…she would give up this wild notion of love. She'd give in to the desire to watch the world crumble at her feet, to unleash the pain within her onto the rest of humanity, until she never had to hurt again. She could let their despair and fear fuel her own power and strength, rather than succumbing to the weakness that love and grief and her own terror brought.

"You can still fight for your throne, little empress," I continued. "Think of me as…keeping it ready for you. Just like I cleared the way for you with fire. Haven't you considered that a burning city expels all the vermin? A new capital can be rebuilt from the ashes. And your palace still stands." I leaned forward, lowering my voice to a whisper as I gestured upward, indicating all aboard the ship. All Jalie's enemies, old and new, who'd subjected her to another prison.

Her breath caught, a flash of hope igniting in her gaze.

"Take it back," I urged. "Kill them all."

TO BE CONTINUED

NOTE FROM THE AUTHOR

Thank you for reading *Empire of Monsters*! If you have a moment, please leave an HONEST review on Amazon.

In a war of empires and hearts, there are no winners. Only survivors.

Defeated…
With the capital in ruins, the Forwyn and their allies are forced to flee. Lo will risk anything to protect the ones she has left, but her people's numbers and hope are dwindling.

Broken…
Promises have been broken and loyalties severed. Jalie determines to slay her new captors…even the one she loves. And Kovi finds he must make his final choice between his duty as a soldier and his duty to his heart.

Lost…
Meanwhile, Caesiem grapples with the fact that he was merely a weapon forged to do Teramyl's bidding. He and Lo must navigate through both the ties that bind them and the obstacles that push them apart.

Desperate…
As the four fight for their people, their hearts, and their lives, they'll face the Queen of Death's conniving power and their own failures.

Save the empire…or die trying.

EMPIRE OF RUINS

Book Four of the *Cursed Empire* Series

ACKNOWLEDGEMENTS

Getting to the end of this book feels very similar to reaching the end of that marathon I ran. I'm deliriously happy and exhausted, and maybe a little battered. And I kind of just want to nap on the couch and eat snacks in celebration…but sadly, book writing doesn't burn calories the way running does.

I'm not sure if it's the fact that I didn't realize this series would go from my expected 3 to 4 until I was drafting this one, or simply because life threw a lot of curveballs at me throughout the process, but this book has (so far) been the most challenging in this series. And yet, here I am, happy to say I can be proud of what it's finally become.

Of course, that wouldn't have happened without some amazing people who always have my back. My alphas, Sheree Whitelock and Julienne Calhoun, who are there for every step of the way for every single book. Malcolm Carter, who is going to keep being mentioned in these books until someday, maybe, you read them. (But if you don't, your support and encouragement still keeps them happening.) My husband, who might also never read this series, but who kept asking me, "How much more do you have left in your book?" and also asked a much more welcome question: "What will we do to celebrate when you finish it?"

And of course, many thanks to my beta team: T.M. Ghent, Maura Klotz, Rai Larson (AKA Team K-Yum), Maren Bivar Letemple, and Sara Smith.

Also my street team: K.B. Benson, Amanda Chaperon, Erin,

Megan Ellis, T.M. Ghent, Tralyn Hughes, Maura Klotz, Taylor Lust, Leah Salinsky, Sara Smith, Hannah Stansel, Meaghan Swanson, and Merrit Townsend.

And thank you to all the authors I've been able to befriend along the way. Whether it's joining in with me on writing sprints, discussing the woes of navigating this sometimes-lonely path (or marathon track, sheesh), or sharing helpful writing or publishing or marketing tips you've learned…you have all done so much for me. I'm pretty nervous about leaving someone out, but…you know who you are. <3

The following is a sneak peek at the first chapter of *Empire of Ruins*, book four in the *Cursed Empire* series.

This chapter is unproofed and not finalized. Details are subject to change.

RACHEL L. SCHADE

EMPIRE OF RUINS

CURSED EMPIRE 4

CHAPTER ONE

Nesrelle, Empress of Death

The city reeked of death and ash, and I relished every breath. As I strode through the streets, I waded through puddles of blood and stepped over piles of corpses, many charred beyond recognition. Blackened husks of stone buildings and shattered glass and channels of water tinted pink with gore—that was the sum of the dazzling white capital Inalgoth now.

It was perfection.

Smoke curled in the air, a constant haze that hovered over the city like a warning. *These streets belong to the Empress of Death now. See it and despair. Enter and suffer.*

Once, thousands had walked these streets, caught up in the division and hatred mortals always seemed to preoccupy themselves with. Now, all had either perished or fled. No one living lingered here but my faithful army.

And already, just like me, they were growing restless.

I found Daedra beside a statue of the Life-Giver, his chiseled face gazing with cold disapproval upon the ashes drifting through the street. Her own eyes were nearly as dead as those of the marble effigy, her irises completely swallowed up by her pupils. Scales devoured a full half of her face, glistening in the dim, perpetual twilight of a city wreathed in smoke.

"When do we march on the rest of the empire?" she asked, bloodlust simmering in her gaze.

"Patience," I murmured, laying a hand on the Life-Giver's marble shoulder, injecting my power into the touch. Splinters spiderwebbed upward toward his face, crumbling it into pebbles that rained down at my feet. A smile pulled at my lips. "Success requires planning."

Daedra shifted impatiently, tossing her gaze toward the sky.

"Besides," I continued, "quick deaths aren't nearly as satisfying as slow torture. We want them to know the end is coming. To see and dread it."

Satisfaction settled upon Daedra's face. "To soak up their fear and pain."

"Exactly." I stalked toward the nearby bridge, setting my hands upon its charred stone railing and leaning over to watch a bloated corpse drift by. "And in the meantime, I have a visit to make."

I was gone before Daedra could comment, the air tugging as I envisioned my destination. Already, the Teramese emperor's thoughts called to me, a siren song beckoning me toward his suffering. Calling me to replenish my power in the presence of his despair.

Tucked away in a darkened room within an abandoned Alrenian sanctuary within Hemlaen, Revaed was sprawled out upon a settee, staring into the embers dying within the hearth. His bloodshot eyes were glazed, studying nothing as he clutched a half-empty wineglass in one hand. His dark jacket had been cast aside, leaving him in nothing but an undershirt. Contrary to his usual polished appearance, he was a wreck, his touseled hair wild, his shoulders slumped.

Though on the outside, he appeared dejected and lost, rage boiled inside him. His thoughts were a tangled mass, full of loss and grief and the same pain of inadequacy and loneliness that had haunted him since he was a child. It was beautiful, poetic…almost enough to make tears swim in my eyes. But it wasn't enough, not yet.

Revaed didn't tug his eyes away from the fire as he spoke, his voice deadpan. "You're not like any goddess I've ever heard about."

I shuffled forward, my bare feet leaving a trail of blood in my wake. My black dress, embroidered with gold, fire-breathing dragons mimicking Teramyl's sigil, whispered along the polished stone floor. "Ah yes," I said, "Tuiros, your god of death who looks like a hunched old man." I snorted in disgust. "Or Xeli, goddess of pain, who has the gnarled face of a hag." I stretched my arms wide, drawing his violet eyes toward me as I grinned. "Did your people never consider that death could be beautiful?"

Revaed huffed out a humorless laugh. "Is that why you're here? To take me away to some underworld now that you've slaughtered my people?"

"Unfortunately for you, you still have more time left to live."

Sipping his drink, Revaed gestured about the empty bedroom. His guards shifted outside, but they couldn't hear us. I'd made sure of that. Not that there was anything they could have done to stop me. "Then what does some goddess of death want with me? Did you bring me another heart?" His lips twisted in a mirthless smile.

"Every heart left in Inalgoth has been burnt to ashes, I'm afraid," I murmured. "No, I'm here to discuss what's troubling you."

Revaed's brow pinched. "That would take a lifetime."

"*One* of the things that is troubling you," I clarified. "Your beloved heir, Caesiem."

Revaed's throat worked as he set his glass down on the table beside him, the embers of his fury stirring into something hotter. Life sparked in his eyes again. "Is he dead? Did you kill him?"

"That's not what I do. I merely usher the dead to—"

His voice pitched low and threatening, but he was unable to conceal the way his words trembled. "What did you do?"

I rolled my eyes. "He's not dead. He left you for the girl."

"He wouldn't turn his back on Teramyl," Revaed bit out, but doubt darkened his expression. His thought echoed clearly in my head: *He gave her his pendant.* His grief was all-consuming. After all these years, the one living person in his family who didn't hate him had abandoned him.

I cocked my head to the side. "You feared all along this could happen, once you saw he loved her."

Revaed turned back toward the fire, his back rigid. Motionless, with his hands clutching his knees so tightly his knuckles blanched white.

Striding closer, I leaned in close and whispered. "How will he aid her people, when you are the one who stands in his way?"

Repressing a shudder, he turned to me, eyes glistening with unshed tears full of loathing. I drank in the sight, breathing deeply as I inhaled the misery permeating the air. "He loves me. He wouldn't threaten me."

"You've used him, and he's dangerous. Whom do you love more? To whom do you owe the deepest loyalty? Caesiem, or your people?"

He leaned back, seizing his glass to take another swig. A few droplets spilled, dripping down his shirt, staining it like blood. He didn't seem to notice. "You're more twisted than the gnarled old hag we call the goddess of pain," he muttered. "Aren't you?"

I picked at my nails. "Call me what you want, but you know I speak the truth. This is why you sit here, cowering in Hemlaen, unable to think clearly. To plan. I thought leaders made the difficult choices. Survival above all else, correct?" I grinned.

Revaed's gaze was hard. "What does the goddess of death know of survival?"

"More than you would imagine," I breathed. "I don't wish everyone to die."

He blinked, his churning thoughts turning skeptical.

I smiled, dipping my tone into something heartbreakingly gentle. "If everyone died, who would be left to suffer?"

ABOUT THE AUTHOR

Rachel L. Schade was born on the first day of summer in a small town in Michigan. She attended The Ohio State University to learn how to write obnoxiously long papers, cite people who use big words, and discuss her passion: books. She has a great love for the color blue, sunshine, chocolate, and not folding her laundry. Currently she lives with her husband and fur babies, and surrounds herself with books and coffee on a regular basis.

You can email Rachel at **rachelschade@gmail.com**, or find her on Facebook and Goodreads: Rachel L. Schade, and on Instagram: @rachelschadeauthor.

www.rachelschadeauthor.com